THE SEVEN SINS OF FITZWILLIAM DARCY

JULIE COOPER

Quills & Quartos
PUBLISHING

Edited by Polaris Editing and Regina McCaughey-Silvia

Cover by Josephine Blake, Covers & Cupcakes

To Dennis, whose wife has never required blancmange

April 28, 1812

Elizabeth Bennet glanced up at the ornately painted ceiling of Netherfield's music room, trying to distract herself from the tears attempting to escape her control. The chamber sat between a large drawing room and the library—it could be opened up from either side to enlarge the seating available, should the family choose to hold a musical evening. But the dining parlours downstairs were the rooms required for today's celebrations, and it was here they had come to say their farewells in privacy. Jane, surely the most beautiful bride in the world, beamed a smile of radiant happiness.

In a few minutes, Jane would be donning one of her new carriage dresses and leaving behind their sisterhood forever—although Elizabeth knew she was surely being maudlin and foolish to consider it so. But the lump in her throat would not shrink, no matter her joy in the occasion.

"Oh, Lizzy, you must not be sad. We will only be away for a month or two at most, and I will write often. We will first visit Mr Bingley's maternal relations, and then—"

Elizabeth had, of course, listened to the wedding trip itinerary many times, and but for Jane's pleasure in repeating it, she would have interrupted immediately. As it was, Jane had barely finished describing the Scarborough leg of the journey before Elizabeth reminded her sister of the time. "We had best go to your chambers now. I cannot wait to see the look on Mr Bingley's face when he sees how fetching you appear in the blue merino."

Jane impulsively reached for Elizabeth. "Oh, Lizzy, why am I so happy? I do not deserve it, but I promise, everything will be wonderful, wonderful for our whole lives."

Elizabeth embraced her sister tightly, heedless of wrinkles to her own new gown. It was at this very moment that sounds from the adjoining drawing room reached them.

"Oh, Mr Darcy!" came a voice that could only be Louisa Hurst's. "This is an occasion which defies explanation."

"If only you had not departed so hastily and stayed away so long!" Caroline Bingley enjoined.

"It could not be helped," said the low, cold, formal voice of Bingley's friend.

"This wedding is a tragedy and nothing less," Miss Bingley continued. "I should be dressed in mourning crape."

"Bingley suffered a rejection from the woman he loved," Mr Darcy opined. "I suppose it made him vulnerable to the affections of another, encouraging him to pursue the first female who looked amiably upon him, without giving himself time to heal from his disappointment. It is certainly an unfortunate match, in comparison."

"I never saw him so happy as when he was courting Miss Newell-Stickney." Caroline sighed. "I know her father's refusal to consider his suit was a very great disappointment to her—the man is beyond proud, and him only a baronet's son. I have heard she regrets her father's opinions very much. They say she wept buckets of tears attempting to change his mind."

"I saw Mr Newell-Stickney at my club recently," Mr Darcy disclosed. "And it is possible he has come to believe his rejection an unsuitably hasty one. It should be said that he did not admit it outright—nor did he mention Miss Newell-Stickney's, er, buckets. But I should think he has regrets, as it might have been a good match for her. Of course, it would have been a superlative one for Bingley."

Elizabeth listened to this conversation in open-mouthed astonishment, hardly believing what she heard. Unfortunately, Jane, it was obvious, believed completely. A look of horror appeared on her pretty face gone suddenly white, and without another word, she turned on her heel and quit the room, quietly slipping out the door.

For a moment, Elizabeth was torn between going after her sister and giving the mannerless complainers in Jane's new family circle a piece of her mind. But as tempting as the idea was, her first consideration must be Jane's crushed feelings. For her sweet, gentle sister to be assaulted by such information on her wedding day, no less, and from the rude and arrogant Mr Darcy! The entire neighbourhood had been happy to see the back of him. Why did Bingley wish him to be here? Why, why had he even come?

With mounting wrath in her heart, she turned to follow Jane, making no effort to be quiet, taking some satisfaction in the harsh sound the door forcefully closing behind her. Let them wonder exactly *who* had overheard their unkind and unwelcome opinions.

⚜

Unfortunately, Jane had, evidently, taken the gossip even worse than Elizabeth had feared. She could not find her anywhere, not in the mistress's chambers nor even the dressing room, where her new maid, Harper, was packing a few final possessions; Mrs Bingley had not been there, she said. Elizabeth searched the house, growing more and more frantic. It was not until Aunt Gardiner found *her*, that she discovered just how desperate the situation had become.

"Lizzy," her aunt whispered. "Please, come with me."

Elizabeth followed Mrs Gardiner to the chambers that had been assigned to her aunt and uncle, conscious of a sense of foreboding. She expected to find a weeping Jane in the room, but she was nowhere to be seen.

"Your uncle was making arrangements for our departure when he discovered a problem," Mrs Gardiner explained, once within the privacy of the chambers. "Jane is waiting in our carriage, refusing to move, insisting that she leave with *us* when we go. Neither your uncle nor I can gain any coherent answers from her. I hesitate to go to your parents, for they have, perhaps, been making merry for some hours now, and I am uncertain of being able to depend upon discreet, sensible conduct from either. I am hoping you can help me with some idea of what has gone so wrong. I had never seen a happier bride, and now...oh, I cannot believe Mr Bingley would behave so poorly as to cause such a dispute!"

A tear escaped Mrs Gardiner's eye; to see such distress and consternation upon the brow of her normally placid aunt was shocking in the extreme. "I assure you Mr Bingley has done nothing!" Elizabeth cried. "Allow me to speak with her. I am aware of the cause of her dismay, but let me try to help her see reason before I explain anything else."

Jane was the most forgiving creature alive, and surely she would not allow a few nincompoops to destroy her wedding day—nay, her entire life!

Unhappily, it appeared she was, indeed, open to such destruction. Jane, her face turned into the velvet squabs, only wept copiously and would not even look at Elizabeth, no matter what she said. "Jane, this is most unlike you," Elizabeth pled finally, nearly in tears herself. "If you love Mr Bingley, you must uphold the vows you have made to him."

At last, Jane met her gaze. "You have never been in love, Lizzy. If you had, you would not consider grieving and offending the love of your life by holding him hostage to a marriage he cannot want."

"He has a strange way of showing you he does not want you—by *marrying* you."

"He did not know that Miss Newell-Stickney regretted his loss, as anyone would. He must have the opportunity to set his life to rights."

"Jane, even if this is true—your conclusions with

which I heartily disagree—it is *too late* for all that. Your marriage was witnessed before God and man. It cannot be undone. The *only* thing to do is move forward."

But at this sage advice, Jane grew even less sensible. "Had you ever been in love, you would never say this," she sobbed. "I will not inflict myself upon him, a rash second choice, no matter the law. No, never!"

"If you continue this course, dear sister, you will be exposed to the contempt of the world for caprice and instability, he to its derision, and both of you to misery of the acutest kind!"

"I am already in misery, and expect to be so for the rest of my days. He, at least, will have a chance for happiness if I am not hanging about him like a noose around his neck. I will remove to my uncle's house instead of his."

"What of me? What of all your younger sisters?" Elizabeth cried, at her wit's end as to how her sensible, even-tempered sister could have adopted such an incredible attitude. "Care you not for how we will all be looked upon and scorned? This is madness! Almost, I believe I am speaking with Lydia or Kitty! You cannot behave so ill!"

But it was all useless. For once in her life, Jane stubbornly refused to concede, and Elizabeth could think of nothing better than to return to her concerned aunt and uncle and explain what she could.

"Jane overheard some awful gossip regarding Mr Bingley's feelings about a prior connexion, which she unfortunately believes—and which has brought her to despair. I will share more if it becomes necessary, but please, it is *all* nonsense, and we must stall for time! Can you put it about that she is...um...indisposed? You must not depart yet, I beg you! Tell Jane you will stay for a day or so, put her to bed, and I will work to change her mind. Please!"

"Perhaps it would be best if I go to Mr Bingley and ask *him* to speak with her," her uncle suggested.

But Elizabeth firmly objected. "She is not rational, and she *will* say something regrettable, at least while she is in her current state. Please, you must do your best to prevent her from speaking to *anyone* until she is calmer and can recognise reason."

Sighing, her uncle departed, prepared to deal sternly with his niece and remove her from his carriage, whilst Aunt Gardiner shook her head. "Lizzy, you must do something quickly. If your mother gets word of this, I can only wonder what the outcome will be."

"I will do my best," Elizabeth promised.

"Do better than your best!" Mrs Gardiner cried as Elizabeth hurried away.

৩৯৫

Elizabeth felt as though she were living in a terrible dream, praying that any moment she would waken. What could she do? Would Miss Bingley retract her words in the face of a potential scandal? Would Jane believe it if she did? It was unlikely. Her uncle was probably correct that only Mr Bingley could resolve the issue, but to have Jane begin her marriage with such a mortifying situation! Worse, what if there was some small, inconsequential grain of truth in it? She feared Jane would never recover. Feeling helpless and uncertain, she faced the crowd gathered in the largest dining parlour and spilling out onto the terrace, merrily enjoying the views of Netherfield's vast park and back gardens, all still laughing and talking in the early spring sunshine of a perfect day—all of them believing Jane was merely changing into her travelling clothes and suspecting nothing of the potential for scandal. Mr Bingley appeared as cheerful as she had ever seen him—looking for all the world as if he were the most fortunate groom in England; in no way did he resemble a man pining for a lost love. *Should* she approach him? But Jane, whom she was so accustomed to thinking of as a sensible being, had suddenly *lost* all reason. Her sister *had* been up since dawn after going to bed at midnight—and they both had missed quite a lot of sleep the previous several nights as well. *Could fatigue account for any of this insensible freak? If only!*

What should I do? What can I do?

It was all Mr Darcy's fault. Instead of quelling those two ill-mannered Bingley sisters as a gentleman might, he had *encouraged* them with his vulgar, gossipy judgment and interference. She remembered the assembly, when he had made his opinion of herself known, and his offensive treatment of the pitiable Mr Wickham. Everyone had rejoiced when he had taken himself off to London—the day before the ball at Netherfield—and never returned. Mr Bingley had begun calling even more often as soon as Mr Darcy was out of sight, followed by his hosting a house party of several weeks' duration—inviting a number of amiable guests—then a series of teas, dances, hunts, and musical evenings, with enough invitations to please the most sociable. They all had felt themselves vastly entertained. Mrs Bennet had even refused to allow Elizabeth a visit to Mrs Collins in Kent, so anxious she was that all her daughters be available to meet Netherfield's parade of single gentlemen—who surely *must* be in need of wives of their own.

The necessity had been only in Mrs Bennet's mind, although at least Jane and Mr Bingley's romance had continued to flourish. Elizabeth felt, however, that she had been on tenterhooks for months, devoting nearly every hour of every day to keeping an eye on her younger sisters, and spending far too much time either scolding Lydia and Kitty into good behaviour or reminding her lackadaisical parents to address it. It was vital they not give the Bingley sisters real cause for complaint—more so than they already had, anyway. When Mr Bingley had finally declared himself on Easter Sunday, Elizabeth had cried tears of relief—relief that her family had not laid bare their worst selves to Jane's detriment. The banns had been called over the next three weeks, and the wedding was the event of the year for the little community; and now, at the very moment when Jane's happiness was nearly achieved, Mr Darcy had ruined it all with a few thoughtless remarks.

As if to mock her pain, the arrogant Mr Darcy appeared on the east side of the terrace, arms folded, staring out at the company with a pinched expression, as if he were smelling something unpleasant. The recently introduced shy and serious Miss Darcy was nowhere in sight. How could a man so handsome be so boorish? Watching him standing there—remote, condemning—something within her snapped.

He had been the fount of this trouble; *he* ought to be the one to fix it.

With an impetuosity born of desperation, of fatigue, and of fear, she marched directly to him.

"Miss Bennet," he said, beginning a bow.

"Stop!" she hissed through a haze of red fury. "Do not bow to me as if you were a gentleman!"

Mr Darcy's astonishment appeared beyond expression—he straightened, staring at her, a tinge of colour appearing on his cheekbones. It was not at all what she had meant to say—but she found, once begun, the flow of temper and distress could not be easily checked.

"Be thankful *I* am not, either, else I would even now be ordering you to name your seconds, you-you..." She could not think of an appellation low enough to describe him, to make him *taste* the ruination accosting every hope and dream she had ever had—but she called him the worst one she had ever heard. "You bottle-headed buffoon!"

If she had expected he would be affected by her unmannerly display, she was to be disappointed. At her defiance, his brows rose, and his initial astonishment was replaced with an expression of smug humour. "Perhaps, Miss Bennet, we should walk a little away from the gathering, before your, er, forthrightness is overheard."

She knew she ought to apologise, to curtsey and walk away before debasing herself further. Yet, that smirk upon his face all but shouted her inability to retaliate; the only thing she had managed was to display her own flaws while disturbing him not at all.

He offered his arm, which she ignored, instead turning towards a path to the gardens. Her stride was an angry, quick one—she was too furious to pace sedately, too near tears to apologise. Hopefully, he would not follow, for his supercilious, smug self-importance had already caused a loss of dignity so severe, she might never find it again.

Charlotte Collins watched something very strange: Elizabeth, tearing away across the park, while Mr Darcy practically chased behind her!

Now, this is something!

Then Mrs Collins sighed. Knowing her friend, she would spend this rather fortuitous conversational opportunity doing something spectacularly stupid, such as taking Mr Darcy to task over the insignificant misfortunes of Mr Wickham, even though he had not a tenth of Mr Darcy's prospects!

However, there *might* be a positive outcome to be had, or at least the *beginning* of a positive outcome. Close at hand, Charlotte's father was laughing and drinking with Mr Bennet and Mr Goulding. Had not Papa done more for Jane's romance with Mr Bingley than Jane herself? Heavens, had it been left up to Jane Bennet, the man would *never* have known she was interested! It had been Papa who ensured he *did* know, who not only encouraged *him* at every turn but encouraged *the neighbourhood* to consider it practically an accomplished fact. Once the expectation had been formed, why, the two had very little to do except call the banns! Determinedly, she approached her father to whisper in his ear. It was for Eliza's own good; once she had secured a husband, there would be as much time for falling in love as she could wish.

Darcy took a sideways glance at the fiery eyes of the passionate, furious Elizabeth Bennet and sighed to himself. He had lived eight-and-twenty years without feeling any particular urge to make a woman his own. He had been shocked by the one woman—*her*—who had finally freed those desires. It was not simply the urge to mate, which he was accustomed to bridling, but the urge to have and to hold, to love and to cherish, by reason, by reflection, by unqualified, unalloyed inclination—by everything.

What a load of drivel, Darcy. You want her. That will not change. You have certainly done your duty to common sense and dignity. You may as well finally admit defeat.

She looked over at him at last, as if surprised he had followed. He was not surprised, not any longer.

"How could you?" she asked. "I do not understand! How *could* you?"

It was difficult to understand, he agreed. *She is the next thing to impoverished, at least once her father dies. Replacing Georgiana's portion would not be the work of a moment. Of course, it is due to Georgiana that I am here at all.*

"I *expect* ill-mannered behaviour from *them*," she continued. "I have been subjected to nothing but their criticisms, their disparagement, their unkind opinions, ever so subtly expressed, for a six-month. Did it never occur to you that perhaps, after spending a few evenings with Mr Bingley's relations, Miss Newell-Stickney determined that all the money in the world could not compensate for such a family?"

Family, he sighed again to himself. *Her family is, for the most part, a mortification. Those two younger sisters of hers ought to be sent to a nunnery for a few years to learn some discipline. I am unsure what could be done to keep the mother from embarrassing her eldest daughters. A house in Cornwall?*

"Are you even *listening* to me?" she cried. "Of course you are not. Why would you?"

The path she had chosen had come to a dead end at Netherfield's summerhouse, a charming, stone-walled building perfectly positioned to take advantage of a small escarpment, with views of the morning sunrise and afternoon shadows—Darcy thought it a lovelier jewel than the mighty, impressive country house that reigned over the park. Miss Bennet, he realised, had a new choice now; she could turn around and walk the other way, a tacit acknowledgement that she had poorly chosen the direction of her headlong march, or she could stubbornly stomp up the summerhouse steps as if she had meant to arrive here. He was betting on the latter. This was a female, he judged, who did not often give way to unreasoning fury—he had watched her enough to know that laughter and cheerfulness were her common temperament. But when she did, she was *magnificently* unreasonable.

Whirling, she stormed up the summerhouse steps as if chased by demons.

Darcy looked around. It was as if the sun had suddenly broken free from an overcast sky; his day had abruptly gone from drab and dull to vivid and exciting. His mood transformed from concern and guilt to enthusiastic glee. *This* was what it was to be *anywhere* in the vicinity of Elizabeth Bennet. He had missed her so.

He raced up the steps behind her.

Darcy supposed that it was up to him to take the lead on the conversation, seeing as how Elizabeth was staring out the summerhouse window, plainly uninterested in speech.

"I take it we are speaking of your discovery of Charles Bingley's previous, er, romantic disappointments?" He and the Bingley sisters had all heard the slamming of the door in the adjoining music room when they had been speaking of the unfortunate Newell-Stickney episode. He supposed it was slightly better than Mrs Bennet hearing them, but it *was* regrettable that it should have been his Elizabeth.

As he had hoped, she spun to face him. "I do not understand! That you would not only encourage such tales but add to them with your own ill-advised conjecture shows an unforgivable lack of conduct! What is *wrong* with you?"

In retrospect, he could see her point. "But of course, we had no idea anyone was eavesdropping upon our private conversation," he explained patiently. Her pretty eyes narrowed, and she moved to within a handsbreadth of him. He could smell the scent of her hair—lavender and something else. He discreetly tried to take a deeper sniff. Helpfully, she moved even closer to him, her fine eyes blazing.

"*Eavesdropping?* We had been in that parlour for ten minutes before your vulgar conversation began. Did you think to, oh, let me see, *shut the doors* before you began conversing about the forlorn *hopes* of my sister's new *husband* for *another woman?*"

She was breathing rapidly, her chest rising and falling with her displeasure; it was very distracting.

"Well, you *were* being rather quiet about it. Obviously, we would never have spoken had we known you were there. It does seem a bit unfair to blame us as if we purposely did. Clearing one's throat is a useful hint, or a polite cough." He saw that she was growing a bit red in the face—not that he particularly minded her temper. By gads, she was beautiful in a snit; he could listen to her rail at him all day. Nonetheless, whilst he appreciated a rosy complexion as much as the next man, he did not wish her to overexert herself.

"Perhaps you ought to calm down."

Unfortunately, she did not seem to understand his concern.

"Calm...*down*. You think I ought to *calm down?*"

"Is your hearing a bit off today? Are you truly uncertain of what I said? We are standing quite near to one another."

"I knew you were selfish. I knew the feelings of others make no difference to you. But are you *stupid?*" she shrieked. She whirled, as if to beat a hasty retreat, but the hem of her dress or the heel of her boot caught upon a low table, and she stumbled, pitching forward. He lunged, trying to catch her, to prevent her from a hard fall—but his own footing was precarious. When he understood they were both going down, he rolled them to avoid various and sundry pieces of furniture he did not wish her to land upon. It was not easy keeping her from hurting herself, either, for the little minx's instinct clearly was to attack first, ask questions later. While she did not seem to realise the proximity of a particular part of his anatomy highly susceptible to pain, she was a tigress nevertheless—no hair on his head, no bit of exposed skin was safe from her. He was forced to subdue her with his large frame so that he could preserve his eyesight. He only hoped she was innocent enough to remain ignorant of the effect of her struggles upon his lower regions, which, being oblivious, did not realise they were not allowed to participate in the fun.

So busy was he protecting all the vulnerable parts of his body, he did not realise a new danger had entered the room.

"Mr Darcy!" came the shocked, high-pitched protests of Sir William Lucas.

"I will second you, Bennet," Mr Goulding solemnly offered.

"Lizzy! Have you lost your...your..." Mr Bennet seemed to need a moment to search for the word he meant. "Your mind?"

Darcy sighed, looking down upon her with some regret. "If I remove myself from your person, will you allow me to retain the use of my eyesight? Might I preserve what hair I have remaining?"

She only stared at him in furious indignation. It was probably as much answer as he could expect. Carefully, he lifted himself away from her and rose. He offered his hand to her, but she ignored it and lithely got to her feet without any assistance.

The three gentlemen were in varying degrees of drunkenness and wholly enraged at what they supposed they had witnessed. "I have a new set of duelling pistols," Goulding proposed. "Happy to lend them to you, Bennet."

"I am more shocked at what has happened," cried Sir William, "from that knowledge of what the manners of the great really are, which my situation in life has allowed me to acquire. About the Court, such instances of flagrant breeding are *not* common!"

"Shows just how little time he has spent at Court," Darcy muttered under his breath, but Elizabeth heard him and narrowed her eyes.

Thomas Bennet swayed on his feet. "Darcy! Same your neconds! We...will shettle this as mental-gems. As gentlemens. Now!" He emitted a loud belch.

"Papa!" Elizabeth cried, startling from her silence. "You must not speak in this unreasoning manner! It was not what you think!"

"I shall send young Reggie to fetch m' pistol case." William Goulding nodded, his head bobbing like a duck in a pond. "Fine pair. Made by Manton. Light and trim as you'll find."

"Mr Darcy, you *must* apologise!" Sir William shrilled.

"Quite a sensible suggest—" Darcy began, but Sir William interrupted him.

"From the town square! Every man, woman, and child in our fair community is owed an apology for such a brazen breach of decorum!"

"*And* the Ship of Common Sense sails for ports unknown," Darcy drawled.

"Get cher pistols, Goulding!" Mr Bennet ordered, clutching a chairback to remain upright. Mr Goulding hastily made for the door.

Elizabeth glared at Darcy, her message clear. *Fix this!*

Thus, he did.

"Stop!" he ordered, and such was the authority in his voice, that Mr Goulding did, indeed, halt in his tracks.

"Gentlemen, you have vastly misinterpreted what you interrupted," he said, his voice calm and matter of fact, but nevertheless commanding—a particular talent of his, he knew. "I admire and love Miss Bennet, and she has fortunately agreed to become my bride."

"What?" cried Elizabeth. "I would rather be dea—"

"She would rather have waited until after Mr and Mrs Bingley's celebration was complete to announce our happy news," he interrupted loudly, placing an arm about her and none too gently tugging her into his side. "But of course, she would never wish for her *betrothed* to be forced to meet her *beloved father* on the field of *honour*. Would she?"

She frowned up at him. He gave her his best 'what else could I do?' look.

"No," she finally answered, sullenly. "I would not."

"It is settled then." He beamed at the gentlemen. "I do hope and *insist* you will wait to speak of our engagement to *anyone* until Miss Bennet has the opportunity to share the happy news with her mother and sisters."

Mr Bennet slowly looked up at him, plainly trying to force his faltering vision into focus, his drunken mind lurching after each word. "You are...rich, t'be sure...can give her more...fine clothes, fine carriages...than

Leebing. Bingle. *Bingley*. But...can you make her happy?"

"Without a doubt," he assured.

Within the shelter of his arm, he heard his newly betrothed snort in apparent disbelief.

Mr Bennet shook his head in a matching scepticism; the action apparently severed his last remaining tie with gravity, and he toppled to the floor.

The two other gentlemen were obliged—Darcy did *not* offer to assist—to aid an only partially revived Mr Bennet back to the house. As soon as they were out the door, Elizabeth jerked herself away. It was a great pity; she felt perfect in his arms, as he had always suspected she would.

"Well, this is a fine mess. An engagement? How do you propose to extract us from it?"

He rather liked hearing the word 'us' from her lips. "I suppose you object to allowing things to remain as they stand?"

"This is *not* a joke! The greatest gossip in Hertfordshire believes we are *engaged*, not to mention my own father! And that Mr Goulding, of all people, should have witnessed what he thought—"

"All the more reason to simply go with it, to my way of thinking," he offered.

"I cannot *believe* you just *said* that! From almost the first moment we met, your manners impressed me with the fullest belief of your arrogance and your conceit." She went on a bit longer in this vein, but he did not pay particular attention. Something she had said before the disruption of father and gossips had just struck him as possibly pertinent to her current mood of disgust with him.

"You mentioned a 'we'," he said, interrupting her diatribe.

"So dislikeable a man as I have never…what?"

"We," he repeated. "I have a very good memory. You said, '*We* had been in that parlour for ten minutes before your vulgar conversation began.' Who else heard?"

She blinked up at him. For a moment, he thought she might not answer. But then, and to his very great dismay, her eyes filled with tears. "My sister, Jane. She is inconsolable, convinced that she has done wrong in marrying him. She will leave here with my aunt and uncle, she says, so that Mr Bingley may have his freedom to pursue…others."

"This is a rather astonishing report," he said, with massive understatement. It explained a good deal of Elizabeth's pique.

"As if you cared," she said bitterly.

But it did not explain all; he had not had any idea she was so prejudiced against him. Most of it could be laid at Wickham's door, he was certain. Still, he had to accept that her initial ill impression had been his own doing. It was possible he ought to account for at least some of his previous poor performance.

"I am certain you have retained a misimpression of me from the first. You see, it is a great nuisance when I go anywhere new," he explained. "Relentless deference, officious attention, every parent parading their marriageable misses before me in an endless display of awkward exhibition. At the assembly…I mean, at our initial, um, interaction. That Bingley should try to raise the hopes of the general populace that I might be there to, um…"

"To *dance?*" she interrupted. "Oh, bad form, Bingley. Heaven forbid you go to an *assembly* and *dance.*"

"That was sarcasm, right?"

"Argh!" She stalked to the large window overlooking the valley, giving him her back. He hoped she was too angry to cry again. He hated to think of her in tears.

He had some choices to make, it seemed. If he were a true gentleman—as defined by his family, at least—he would make things right with Bingley and his new wife, pay a great deal of money to Mr Bennet, Sir William, and Mr Goulding to smooth over Elizabeth's reputation, take his sister away, and never think of this place or the people in it again. But as Georgiana had gently noticed, he had fallen flat in *that* field already. If the last five months had taught him nothing else, it was that society's most rigid rules counted for nothing compared to the happiness of those he loved; life must be lived with passion as well as honour, and pride must be booted from the picture. It was rather humiliating to understand how little Elizabeth wanted him, but she did not *know* him, not really, and it was his own fault. Still, he could use that.

He approached her quietly, standing as close to her as he dared. Other than a slight stiffening of her spine, she did not acknowledge his presence in any way, standing frozen like a statue. He much preferred her temper.

"Six sins—of varying degrees of magnitude—you have laid to my charge," he began.

"Only six? I could swear there were a dozen," she said.

He smiled, glad she was still spiritedly challenging him.

"You may tell me whether or not I have recalled their number correctly," he agreed. "The first, that I, at our first meeting, insulted you most cruelly."

She spun on her heel to face him, forcing him to adopt a more sombre mien. "I accused you of nothing!"

He rubbed his chin, as if in deep thought. "Perhaps not explicitly. But can you deny that my thoughtless remark formed a ground-work of disapprobation, as it were, upon which succeeding events and opinions have built your dislike?"

She pursed her lips, but then gestured as if she were a queen allowing a courtier to make a point. "Very well. I will allow it as your first 'sin'," she replied haughtily. "It makes no difference to me."

"The second, that I have materially injured Mr Wickham. Thirdly, that I indulged in gossip and scandalmongering regarding Mr Bingley's romantic past. These are my actual offences; the other three are more in the nature of defects or flaws in my character." He ticked them off on his fingers. "Fourth, a selfish disdain for the feelings of others. Fifth, arrogance and conceit—which failings I will count as one, since they are so interrelated —and sixth, a general inability to behave in a gentlemanly manner. Have I got it all?"

A look appeared on her face that could only be called triumph. "You have forgotten the one in which *I* was not your accuser. Do you not recall that *you* once confessed to possessing a resentful temper as well?"

It was all he could do to hide his smile. "There you have it then," he agreed, nodding. "The seven sins of Fitzwilliam Darcy. I propose a bargain, Miss Bennet.

Meet seven challenges which I shall offer you. I give you my word that these challenges shall in no way suggest any sort of insult to your honour or feelings. Agree to this, and I will move heaven and earth to ensure that your choice of husband remains forever and always your very own."

"You cannot be serious! And if I do *not* agree?"

"I would ask you to be reasonable," he said, knowing he was playing with fire at the way her large, dark eyes narrowed at him. "No matter what you decide, it will take some days to bring the matter to a conclusion. Those days can be spent in worry, as seconds are chosen and an appropriate field of honour determined—"

"Surely, you would not, *could not*, duel with my father!" she cut in.

"I would, of course, discharge my weapon into the air," Darcy promised gravely. "Unfortunately, your father, I judge, will do his best to kill me no matter what I say or do. Equally unfortunate, my uncle, the earl, is rather fond of me. I do not suppose he would take kindly to my death, however deserved." He added a melancholy sigh for effect.

"You could simply *refuse* the stupid duel!"

He raised a purposely incredulous brow at her.

She looked as though she wished to tear her hair out. Or his.

"There *must* be a way to avoid a duel—you *know* there is because you have promised to find one if I meet your seven ridiculous challenges," she argued.

"Yes, to be sure. Alas, it will be *extremely* costly and involve a great deal of rather humiliating bowing and scraping," he explained. "As well, I might point out that *you* are the one who fell upon *me*, whilst *I* only sought to prevent you from harm via toppling upon unforgiving furniture. Thus, little as I wish to remind you, one must hold you responsible for initiating the misunderstanding motivating your father's ire in the first place. It seemed a consequence of your temper, which I would otherwise never mention. Requesting a few non-lethal, innocuous challenges of my own seems very little to ask in recompense."

"Is life—*my* life—just a game to you?" she cried, giving him her back once again.

He waited a few moments, wanting nothing more than to place his hands upon her neat little waist and draw her back against him. But of course, he also wanted to live to see another day, so sensibly kept his distance. When he judged she had enough time to see the only rational solution was to accept his terms, he offered his *coup de grace*.

"As 'earnest payment', so to speak, and by way of the apology you are owed, I vow to heal the breach between your sister and Bingley today. Immediately. If I cannot, we shall dispense with any challenges and skip straight to the grovelling and theft of my personal fortune."

It would not hurt his cause to make the offer, as he considered, since he meant to settle her sister's affair without delay, regardless. Bingley and his new wife were two of the softest people in England, and if he could not effect a reconciliation between *them*, why, he would never have a chance with the sister. To be sure, Bingley would *not* be pleased with the source of his wife's distress. It might even take him an hour or two to forgive Darcy for it.

She turned back around to face him again, her expression resolute.

"Very well, Mr Darcy," she replied. "You have my word. Seven challenges only, and *I* shall be the arbiter of what constitutes an insult to my honour." To his surprise, she held out a hand.

He took hers in his much larger one, marvelling at its softness. Her grip was as firm as a man's when she shook. She dropped his hand immediately thereafter, marching from the room as rapidly as she had once entered it.

For a moment, he only watched her go—slim back straight, stride swift and purposeful. His smile could not be repressed. *Now there goes a woman worth fighting for,* he thought. And with a lift in his steps that had been absent for months, he followed where she led.

❧ 3 ❧

After warning her aunt and uncle that help was on the way, Elizabeth returned to the party in progress on the terrace. To her amazement, everyone was still in much the same positions as they had been when she left them...had it been, even, thirty minutes? An hour? The sun had moved, and that seemed to be the extent of any motion. Mr Bingley was still chortling with his neighbours, Mrs Long and Mrs Hurst were trading criticisms, her mother was laughing —too loudly—with Lady Lucas; Lydia giggled with Kitty and Harriet Forster, whereas Colonel Forster—the only officer invited to the breakfast—looked benignly on, probably not listening to a word. Various other neighbours stood about the terrace, chatting amicably, whilst servants moved through the company carrying trays of drinks and delicacies.

They need fewer drinks and more delicacies, she thought, recalling her father's unreasoning response which had created the mess in which she now found herself. She spotted Mr Darcy pulling aside Mr Bingley. She could not help but trail them at a distance, just to try and obtain a hint of possible reparations to her sister's new marriage. They quickly disappeared into the house, however, making it impossible to follow them in without appearing obvious.

"Eliza!"

Mr and Mrs Collins approached her, Charlotte beaming in a most excessive manner—the exact opposite of Elizabeth's mood. To her surprise, her friend opened her arms to embrace her.

"It was a beautiful ceremony," Elizabeth said with a little dread, for they had shared these sentiments when they had arrived for the breakfast. Had they already heard what her father had witnessed?

Any hope that this might not be the case was crushed, however, with Charlotte's next words.

"With another wedding to come!" Charlotte enthused. "We are so excited to hear of your news! Oh, Eliza, I am so happy! I wonder how elderly is the man who holds the living for your betrothed's estate... Pemberley, I believe it is called? I hope you will not be offended that I delight in any possibility of being near neighbours again!"

"Charlotte! I am not...it is not..." she stumbled in her speech, coming to an abrupt impasse in her thoughts. For the news to spread so quickly was horrible! "You...you have been speaking with...your father?" she asked tentatively, and with a good deal of dismay.

"Sir William was in every way thrilled by witnessing the proposal," Charlotte enthused. "And of course, Derbyshire must be so lovely..."

Charlotte finally noticed what Elizabeth already had —the stiffness in her husband's posture; his usual voluble manner was cloaked in absolute silence. "Are you not eager to congratulate Cousin Elizabeth?" she urged.

"As to that, I am certain no greater honour could touch any person, and except for a delicacy of comportment, I would not hesitate to express my joy. I cannot help but wonder, however, if there has not been some mistake made, or error of confusion. Mr Darcy is engaged to his cousin, Miss Anne de Bourgh."

Elizabeth stifled an involuntary protest. It ought to have been most welcome news, and had it come from any other mouth, Elizabeth would have heralded it as glad tidings of great joy. Some contrary, prideful part of her nature, however, could not allow his assertion to go completely unchallenged.

"Their engagement must be of a peculiar nature indeed, if he is free to offer for other women during the course of it."

Collins's paunchy face looked troubled.

Charlotte, who had blushed at his announcement, simply pretended not to hear it. "We must make plans, my friend. I cannot wait to discuss them with you!" she said.

Mr Collins cleared his throat to interrupt, giving his wife a frigid stare of disapproval. "From their infancy, Miss de Bourgh and Mr Darcy have been intended for one another—it was the favourite wish of his mother, as well as my esteemed patroness, his mother's sister, Lady Catherine de Bourgh. She has often related the particulars, assuring that the union only wants a bit more nourishment before coming to fruition. I know you would not like to insert yourself between two branches of such a venerable family tree, a disruption to any budding romance."

"I cannot know the age of Miss de Bourgh, but I understand that Mr Darcy is not far from his fourth decade. If they have been betrothed from the cradle, surely decomposition is a likelier outcome than any blossoming, with or without my *insertion*."

Charlotte, evidently, could see that only distraction would avert her husband from his sycophantic course. "Oh, Mr Collins, I see the servants are bringing out marchpane cakes. How pretty they are!"

His head shot up, nose quivering, as though he were a bloodhound on the scent, and soon thereafter was dragging his wife in the direction of his prey.

❦

"You said *what*?"

Bingley's question had ended in a high treble key, his astonishment and disbelief obvious.

Darcy scratched his chin, biting his tongue against the temptation to blame Bingley's sisters, who had all but pushed him into that drawing room to express their grievances.

"We did not realise anyone else was nearby. It was unforgivable, and I apologise. But you must put it right —you are the only one who can." In as few words as possible, Darcy explained the course of separation Mrs Bingley had threatened to pursue.

"She said *what*?"

If anything, Bingley's voice had risen to an even higher octave.

On the walk back to Netherfield, Darcy had discovered the whereabouts of the new Mrs Bingley from Elizabeth, and he had warned her to prepare Mr and Mrs Gardiner for a visitor. Doubtless, she had immediately done so. There remained only his own part to play, but Bingley was being rather slow to grasp the situation.

"You have to reassure your new wife of your love and affection. She might put up some resistance, but you must be persistent."

With some frustration, he saw the muddled expression appear on his friend's face. If left to himself, Bingley would dither and vacillate and talk himself out of confronting anyone or anything. *If Elizabeth wants to count character flaws, she would find plenty to tally here.* It was one of the reasons why Darcy had believed Theodosia Newell-Stickney to be an ideal match for him; she had the fortune to replace Caroline's future settlement and a backbone to share with Bingley. A stab of guilt that he had failed to persevere with the Newell-Stickneys had penetrated at the precise moment before Caroline and Louisa dragged him into that drawing room.

He bore with Bingley's dithering as long as he could —which was not long. If this marriage was not put back on course, and quickly, his own prospects would suffer appreciably.

"You must *go* to her, and at once. She is in the blue chamber, with her aunt and uncle Gardiner."

"But I have no idea what to say!" Bingley's pitch had risen to an actual screech.

"Listen to me." Darcy clapped his hands upon his friend's shoulders to force him to meet his gaze. "Life is not some piece of foolish romantic fiction, where for the lack of one sensible conversation, the plot extends thirty chapters. You are a *married man.* You have a means of convincing your *wife* of your *affections* that you had no *access* to a few hours ago. Unless you are a blithering idiot, you can mend your fences without much *talking* at all."

He saw the moment when Bingley realised what he meant; he had recently given Bingley quite a long lecture, explaining a few home truths he doubted the fellow had learnt in his previous limited experience. *You are welcome, Mrs Bingley.*

"Oh...um...where did you say Jane is?"

Bingley's voice had returned to a more normal timbre.

"Come," he said, determined to walk Bingley to the very door and ensure *he* entered, and the *Gardiners* exited. No distractions were to be allowed.

At the door of the Gardiners' chamber, he rapped firmly. Mr Gardiner answered his knock. The pair required very little convincing to make themselves scarce, practically fleeing before them.

Bingley turned back to Darcy at the door. "Since when do you read 'foolish romantic fiction'?"

"It was a very dull time of year for Bath," Darcy explained.

"Ah. Wish me luck."

"You do not need luck. You are already beyond fortunate. You are married to a woman who would rather endure misery for the rest of her days than see *you* miserable for one."

Bingley smiled. "Right you are," he said, shutting the door behind him.

I was not wrong, he thought reasonably. *Miss Newell-Stickney* will *make some lucky man a dependable bride. But Bingley did not make much of a mistake either, I suppose. His home will be a happy one. He is loved.* With a sigh, Darcy turned away from the Bingleys and went to work on his own happy ending.

It was over two hours before the company mercifully departed—including the Longbourn and Lucas contingents, all of them having so overindulged in food or drink or both that they had not even noticed Elizabeth did not accompany her parents. Well, Charlotte had noticed—but only smiled slyly at her as Elizabeth slipped into the library to hide until everyone was off. Elizabeth had determined to walk home—the excitement of her feelings demanded it, as well as the tranquillity such an exercise would provide, even if her hems suffered.

Her anger at Mr Darcy renewed in the quiet of wondering. *Miss de Bourgh could* have *him and his blossoms!*

It was beyond embarrassing that Mr Goulding, of all people, should have witnessed... what he thought he had witnessed, after her history with his son, Reginald. The senior Mr Goulding, at least, was a gentleman who was unlikely to say anything to anyone of what had occurred with Mr Darcy. Sir William Lucas had, evidently, limited his revelations to his daughter, for no one else had said a word. But for how long? Sir William was a notorious gossip. Mrs Bennet had, once or twice, given her long looks, but it seemed impossible that she had learnt *anything* of the supposed engagement, for she remained uncharacteristically silent. Surely Papa had been too much in his cups to confide one sensible sentence to her?

Somehow, word had got out that Mr and Mrs Bingley would not be leaving for some time while the carriage transom was repaired—she was certain it was a ruse invented by Mr Darcy, and she would have been grateful to him, had he not been the cause of the excuse's necessity. Fortunately, no one had remarked upon the absence of the couple amongst their company, but of course, everyone would believe them preparing for their journey to London.

At least Jane could no longer leave with the Gardiners, who had been in one of the first carriages to set out.

Lizzy dearly hoped the newlyweds were having a productive conversation. Still, the longer the delay to their departure, the greater her anxiety. Could they not resolve their issues? Was Jane persisting with the detestable idea of separation? Would Mr Bingley grow impatient? Would he eventually agree with her, if she persisted in the notion?

When all was perfectly quiet and none of the home's occupants were about, she removed to the gold drawing room because it was nearest the front entry where, hopefully, she would hear the Bingley carriage being brought up the drive. She was unable to settle or peruse the magazine she had taken from the library, too restless and worried. The house was silent as a tomb. Her slippers made no noise on the thick carpets as she peered out the window overlooking the drive, willing the carriage to appear.

Nothing! Not any sign of a carriage or of servants

bustling around, loading trunks. Turning away from the view in frustration, she abruptly crashed into a chest so broad, it could only belong to one man of her acquaintance—Mr Darcy. Unfortunately, his unexpected appearance startled her enough that she cried out—and not delicately or daintily, but a full-bodied screech of surprise. He caught her arms to steady her, but then he spoilt the gentlemanly action by tugging on his earlobe and shaking his head, as if she had ruined his hearing.

"Why do you sneak about so silently?" she snapped. "A man so large should be unable to manage it. You really ought to warn a person, rather than slink about like a...like a housebreaker."

He opened his mouth to say something, seemed to think better of it, and closed it again.

"Have you heard anything from Mr Bingley?" she asked, before he could remark upon her own incivility. "It has been so long! It seems to me he ought to have had time to resolve things with her by now, if he were able to do so. Perhaps you ought to interrupt with your own efforts?"

"Absolutely not!" Mr Darcy disagreed, with a quite unnecessary vehemence, in her opinion.

"You do not understand," she implored. "Jane is very soft at her core, but when agitated, she is likely to be a tiny bit inflexible, especially when borne down upon."

Rudely, and completely inexplicably, he began to laugh. She had seen him smile for the first time today, and a part of her mind had reluctantly acknowledged the beauty of his face when he did so—but that he should *laugh* at her worries now! It was a complete reinforcement of all her earliest, most negative impressions of his character.

"You are a beast!" she accused, feeling helpless against the arrayed forces opposed to the happiness of her sister, and perhaps selfishly, the happiness of herself —since Jane was determined to make a laughingstock of them all. A tear fell, and then another—and it was even worse than that he should have watched her lose her temper or screech like a banshee.

Argh! That this brute should see her cry, for the *second* time that day, was unacceptable. She tried to stalk from the room—but he was excessively quick on his feet for such a big man, and she found him blocking the only exit before she could reach it.

How she wished she was a man, able to stand up to such physicality! Why were females not taught the art of boxing instead of useless skills like netting purses? How many decorated purses did a woman need, anyway? How many gifts could she make of them, when everyone she knew had already netted one of their own?

He laughed at her still. Oh, he effected a sober countenance now, but the laughter was there, in his eyes. How could she have failed to notice the devil in him, when she had once thought him so stuffy? Another tear escaped her control. She hated him!

"Do not cry, my love," he said gently, his big hands cupping her face.

"I am not your love!" she hissed.

His brow furrowed. "Well, you are," he said. "It is only, I am not yours."

"You are mocking me, sir!" she accused.

"No, no, no," he protested. "Or if I did, it was only because you are so adorably innocent. I promise you, Mr Bingley has made everything right with your sister. I expect the carriage to be called any moment now, because they will want to reach London before dusk."

She bit her lip, unable to discern a tease in his words. *Oh, if only I could be certain whether he is speaking the truth!*

"I apologise for what I said about Bingley regretting the loss of Miss Newell-Stickney. He is most fortunate to have won a wife so loyal as Mrs Bingley, and he knows it. There is no question but that Mrs Bingley is the better choice of bride, once the Newell-Stickney fortune is disregarded. You and I shall *not* remain thirty chapters apart on this misdemeanour."

"Thirty...what?" Truly, he was quite unfairly handsome, especially when he was trying to be kind—even if rather nonsensical. Kindness likely did not come easily to him.

But he ignored her question. "Listen, do you hear that?"

Releasing her, he went to the window. As soon as she followed him, she saw the reason for his optimism.

Busy servants were carrying trunks out the front door. The Bingley brougham was pulled up the drive, along with another carriage for servants and luggage. Harper and Mr Bingley's man were already waiting beside it. Quickly, she hurried out to watch the loading, followed by Mr Darcy—and not five minutes later, Jane and Bingley, both immaculate in their travelling clothes, appeared on the doorstep.

The next several minutes were a blur of hugs and farewells and good wishes. There seemed absolutely no remnant of Jane's earlier upset; she was blushing and pretty and looked at Mr Bingley as though he had personally arranged the beauty of the day for her viewing pleasure. Mr Bingley seemed tranquil and jovial and extremely happy with his lovely bride. Elizabeth wondered how the situation—so dire and dreadful only a few hours earlier—had been resolved, but of course, there was no time for meaningful explanations.

Mr Bingley helped Jane into the carriage and followed her in. The obviously contented pair waved at them as the door was closed, the step raised, and before Elizabeth could comprehend it, the vehicle was growing ever smaller in her sight, the horses kicking up little puffs of dust upon the long drive.

"As long as I live, I shall never understand it," Elizabeth murmured softly.

Beside her, Mr Darcy glanced her way. "If I have anything to say about it, you certainly shall, and sooner rather than later."

Incomprehensible, like everything else he utters. She could not help but take his measure, alone as they were upon the portico. He was such a *big* man, Elizabeth again realised. He dressed and moved with an ineffable grace, one almost did not realise it—and of course, he was also lean and sinewy, the very opposite of Mr Collins.

And she was—temporarily, at least—engaged to him.

The idea made her almost inexpressibly wary, and being far too tired to spar with him, she decided it best to begin her long walk home. All she wished was to be *gone.* "I shall bid you a good day," she said formally, giving him a small curtsey. Turning away, she had reached the first step before he said anything.

"You cannot walk all the way to Longbourn, especially alone."

"I most certainly can," she said, without stopping.

"Well, you *can*, of course, but you will not," he said, falling into step beside her. "I do not suppose you ride?"

"In this dress?"

He examined the pale pink and white satin concoction, appearing to consider. "Perhaps my sister has a riding dress that might work for you. Does not a good gallop to shake out the cobwebs sound ideal, after such a day?"

She sighed, stopping her retreat to face him. "Firstly, your sister and I are built upon entirely different lines. Secondly, I do not ride. Not now, not ever. Thirdly, I have walked this distance many times and do not find it a hardship, nor am I in any danger. I appreciate your concerns, but all I want to do is return home and fall into bed, and I have neither the will nor the patience to argue about it."

He was smiling again. "*Firstly*, I would never argue with that ambition, I promise you. *Secondly*, why do you not ride? I think I have heard that your sister does."

She sighed again, not in any mood to be teased about the number of times they had tallied their thoughts and opinions today, nor to explain her fears of riding. "I never learnt," she blatantly lied. "If you will excuse me?"

"I brought the curricle from London," he said, instead of politely withdrawing. "Have you ever ridden in one?"

"I...no," she admitted.

"Will you allow me to bring you home in it?"

Reggie Goulding was fond of racing about the local byways on his high-perch phaeton, although such a vehicle was ill designed for country roads, and her father said he would break his neck one of these days. Still, she had seen Mr Darcy's vehicle; it was larger and heavier and quite in the first stare of fashionable modes of transport. Besides, she had already claimed an ignorance of riding, and her pride could not tolerate revealing another fear, although why she should care about his opinions was beyond her at the moment. She was just so very weary.

"Yes," she replied simply, sighing once more.

4

Darcy stared at the dog. The dog stared back. Darcy was certain his own expression was indicative of his feelings—complete aggravation. Unfortunately, the dog's mien was equally expressive—abject misery and forlorn hope.

The ragged urchin who had sold him the cur had sworn it was a 'purebred hunter', which Darcy had known was likely a gross exaggeration, if not an out-and-out falsehood. But Georgiana had looked at the speckled, downy little thing with an eager hopefulness quite unusual to her, and he had been unable to refuse.

As soon became obvious, the puppy had been parted from its mother too soon, and a frantic round of methods had to be devised to feed him. Georgiana had thrown herself into the project with desperate devotion, until at last, he began to thrive. And thrive. And *thrive*. Darcy guessed the dog to be part poodle or curly retriever, part Labrador, and part boarhound—or elephant. The dog's shoulder came to Darcy's thigh; his fur was dense and curly at his head, torso, and front limbs, whilst his back legs were nearly hairless. His thick, broad head, his chest, and his legs were densely furred golden masses, while his shoulders and back were coloured in blotches of chocolate and white curls. Georgiana had christened him Sir Derby, which name Darcy had objected to as entirely too dignified.

In all, he resembled an enormous bag of dirty laundry. A large, terrified bag, because he was unpredictably afraid of many things. For instance, a particular blanket's pattern weave might set him to shivering; he would take great detours to avoid passing near a Chinese urn that had belonged to Darcy's grandmother. A partially opened door was enough to freeze him in his tracks—he would neither move forward and push his way through nor back away, but only tremble and whine. Though still only a puppy, he was five stone of fickle cowardice.

Nevertheless, he loved many things another, prouder dog might genuinely treat with contempt; he adored cats, esteemed every horse in the Darcy stable, and had never met a person whom he could not immediately imagine to be his dearest friend. Georgiana had refused to consider leaving him in London, even knowing he would have to reside in the stables during their tenure at Netherfield—for of course he had his own bed and footman at their Mayfair residence. Darcy tried to protest sharing a carriage with fragrant doggy breath, but she had begged and...and he had little heart to deny her anything she wanted. He had ridden, and Georgiana —an expert driver—had taken the curricle with her dog perched happily beside her, tongue lolling, the entire journey.

"See here," he explained to the dog—patiently, he thought. "The one good outcome of our travelling arrangements is that I now have the opportunity to drive Miss Bennet home in my curricle. It seats two persons only—not two persons plus an immense mongrel. Neither of you drive, and thus my presence *is* required... although doubtless she would prefer your company to mine, did either of you possess the skill."

The dog continued to stare at him yearningly, adding a noise between a whimper and a groan in case he had not thoroughly communicated his loneliness and longing.

"It is fine weather for this time of year, and a fellow must take his advantages where he can find them. Someday, you will spot a pretty mastiff—or with my luck, an Irish wolfhound—to whom your heart will belong, and you will understand why, for now, you must *stay*."

In response, the animal lovingly laid his oversized head upon Darcy's boot.

"Has my sister been out to visit her dog today, Henry?" he asked one of the stableboys.

"Oh, yes, sir. She only left a quarter-hour or so afore you come. Brushed 'im and fed 'im, though I did offer to do it for 'er."

Darcy sighed. "I thank you. John has hitched the curricle for me. Will you take this misbegotten creature for a walk so that he does not watch me depart and treat the entire stable to a litany of grievous complaint?"

Henry was only partially successful in hiding his smile as he received the animal's lead. The dog glanced back a time or two as if to lament 'Farewell, beloved betrayer!' but trotted out happily enough with the stableboy. Shaking his head, Darcy climbed into his curricle and made his way to the drive where Elizabeth hopefully still waited.

Elizabeth wondered if she ought to simply start for home before Mr Darcy could reappear. She knew all the back paths and could certainly avoid being seen. Still, there were her hems to consider of this, her nicest, newest dress, which were already a bit dusty from her walk to the summerhouse on a nicely laid stone path. She could just hear Mrs Hill's opinion if she walked through the woods in it.

Besides, there was the matter of her cowardice, already too much on display this day.

The sound of horse hooves brought her attention to the drive. There he was, the arrogant Fitzwilliam Darcy, sitting tall, straight, and proud on the smart vehicle, handling the reins with ease. Why would he tease her as he had today? As if he *wanted* such an engagement to stand! He could not, not possibly!

And if he *could*, she could never find appealing a man who would treat his childhood friend in such a horrible manner.

Well, she admitted to herself, *I could find him appealing, but I would never allow myself to move forward in such thoughts. I quashed my attraction to Mr Wickham because he was completely inappropriate. I would never give way to a man with only half poor Mr Wickham's character, simply because he is wealthy and...large.*

The curricle was a gleaming affair, with a seat of burgundy-coloured leather and glistening brass rails. The pair of horses pulling it were beautifully matched, and for a few moments, Elizabeth found herself a little awed. The gentleman in his fine clothes and the curricle with its costly appurtenances was something for their obscure country village to see, and irrationally, she wished that Longbourn was a bit further than three miles out.

She glanced at Mr Darcy again, only to see his eyes widen at the sight of her...or was it something behind her? She turned to look, only to see some sort of bear... or monster...charging directly at her. She threw up her hands—as if *that* would do any good—only to be thrown off her feet by the marauding beast. *I did not know I would die today* was her last coherent thought before her head hit the paving stones and she knew no more.

Curses, loud pants, and something rough and wet upon her cheek awakened her.

"Blast it, Dubitz, get away from her, you ignorant mongrel!"

It was definitely Mr Darcy's voice, full of annoyance. *Mongrel*, he had said. *A mongrel.* She took the risk of opening one eye. The giant attacking beast—she would take his word for it that it was a dog—sat, cringing, a few feet away, whining unhappily. She closed it again.

"Do you see what you have done?" Mr Darcy's voice continued in stern lecture—he never raised it, and yet there was a certain force behind it she recognised as new to her ears. "How many times must you be told to *stay*? When will you learn any manners? I do not require the conduct of a gentleman, heaven forbid. I would settle for the comportment of a rabid squirrel! You are a degradation to your species, an inferior, no-account, good-for-nothing..." He appeared to run out of debasing appellations, and all the while, she felt her head gently lifted and soft fabric placed beneath it.

Another voice intruded—a young man's, out of breath. "I'm so sorry, sir. He caught sight of your vehicle and gave chase. I wasn't ready for the, um, strength of his wish to follow you."

"It is not your fault, Henry," Mr Darcy said shortly. "Please take him back to the stables, there's a good lad, and send for Mr Jones."

"Yes, sir, straightaway!" The voice—Henry's, it was to be assumed—sounded a bit frantic.

The next thing Elizabeth knew, she was hoisted in Mr Darcy's arms. This time, she opened both eyes fully. "I can walk," she said.

"Oh, good," he replied. "You are awake. I will not have to kill the dratted cur."

He sounded as calm as a summer's morning; his pace was swift, but steady. His expression was impassive. But there was something in his tone that told her he had not necessarily been joking.

"Was it a leopard? Or perhaps a Bengalese tiger? I once visited the Royal Menagerie with my aunt and uncle and saw one. I suppose my attacker could have been a lion, although a rather larger beast than possessed by His Majesty."

"And now you are babbling. I shall have to call in my physician from London."

A footman swung open the door, his face alight with excitement. Mr Darcy glared at him, again speaking very sternly, although his words were nothing but polite. "Miss Bennet has been injured. I shall bring her to the yellow chamber. Mr Jones shall be arriving at any time, Bertie. Please send him up immediately."

"Yes, sir," the young footman replied, appropriately chastened, really, by nothing more than the Darcy frown.

He turned the corner, continuing towards the staircase.

"You must be more patient with Bertie," Elizabeth chided, a distraction to keep dizziness at bay. "I suppose it is not every day that a houseguest is attacked by a bear. You will ruin your back. Set me down."

He only raised a brow, wearing the same expression as when she had suggested that he refuse her father's challenge. "Dubitz is my sister's dog, a mere puppy. He suffers from an excess of enthusiasm." He climbed the stairs as if he did not carry anything at all. Elizabeth was not a large woman, but neither was she a featherweight.

"If he is a mere puppy, I would hate to see his size when fully grown. But perhaps you mean to display him and sell tickets."

The corner of his mouth tipped in what was probably a smile; for some reason, she felt as though this were something of an achievement. Perhaps he *had* been upset, deeply upset, by his dog's misbehaviour? But it was only a suspicion; he certainly did not act as though he were, except for the lectures to the dog and Bertie.

He did not pause at the door but brought her directly into the yellow chamber, a room that Elizabeth had never before entered.

"Will you put me down now?" she asked.

"As my lady wishes," he replied, laying her gently upon the bed. She immediately sat up. If he had not scowled at her for it, she would have lain right back down again, for—whether from her accidental attempt at flight or from a long, fatiguing day—her head ached painfully.

"Now that you have gone to all the unnecessary trouble of hefting me up a flight of stairs and down a mile of corridors, let us go back the way we have come. The only thing wrong with me is that I am tired. The only thing I am in need of is a bed."

"Odd thing, I notice," he said blithely. "Here you are, in a bed chamber, which happens to surround your greatest requirement—a bed."

"I need *my* bed," she clarified.

He made a great show of looking up and down the bed posts and pressing down on the mattress. "I suppose this one is in some way deficient? Shall I heave you around to the various other guest chambers to examine all beds available?"

"You are not amusing."

His expression grew serious. "As a gentleman—no, as a *human being*—I take responsibility for the behaviour of any animal in my possession. Mr Jones, at a minimum, should give us his view of the case."

"I do not *wish* to see Mr Jones!"

"You do not trust his advice? You find him incompetent? If so, I shall send for my London physician."

Elizabeth sighed. She knew she was being surly, even rude; her head hurt, and she wanted to go to bed and sleep until the next sunrise. "If I agree, will you forget the whole stupid business of sins and challenges? It is the least you can do, after your savage dog attacked me."

He smiled at that. The sun shone through the window, limning him with light, his white teeth gleaming. He wore no coat, was standing in *her* bed chamber—well, it was not hers, but still—in his shirt sleeves! Plainly, he owed none of his physique to his tailor. Sir

William Lucas would have a gossip's field day if he got wind of *this* scrape.

"I believe your wits are as sharp as they ever were," he said, still grinning. "That is one worry put to rest. Lie down on that very comfortable bed, shall you? Await Jones's opinion, lest I think of several more sins I wish to be guilty of—which only means more work for you."

"You find yourself so amusing," she grumbled, plucking at a small tear in her now hopelessly wrinkled dress—but lying back down, nevertheless. "I shall send Mrs Hill to you when she sees the mess you have made of me."

He was quiet, not answering, staring out that window—probably watching for the apothecary's arrival, oblivious to the impropriety of it all. The room quiet—it seemed the whole house was. The chamber was warm and cosy after being so long in the sharper air of the out of doors. The bed truly *was* comfortable; it probably held at least three mattresses, and the counter-pane was luxurious. She only meant to close her eyes, to rest them. She fell rather instantly asleep.

Darcy heard her gentle snore and could not resist turning, going to her, watching her slumber, watching her breathe. He knew he had no business in here, and had the house not been in such a disrupted state, he would be causing yet another scandal. And yet, she was so dashed lovely, her dark hair escaping its confines, her cheeks pink from the wind—or perhaps Dubitz's apologetic tongue. She was far too innocent to know the thoughts and desires she inspired, but neither was she a milk-toast miss just out of the nursery. She was a proud, pretty, managing sort of female, with none of the over-bearing, arrogant qualities of his own relations. She would make a fine mistress for Pemberley and a wonderful sister for Georgiana—but those were not the merits he dwelt upon as he watched her, swathed in pale pink satin, lying in a patch of sunlight in the chamber adjoining his own.

Carefully, he removed her slippers and drew up the soft woollen blanket from the end of the bed to cover her and all that marvellous satin.

"You have made a far sorrier mess of me, my girl," he murmured, and left the room before he fell any harder in love than he already was.

5

Elizabeth woke to the fading sunlight of a dusky late afternoon. Stretching, she sat up. Her head hurt, still, but not unbearably. She spotted another tear in her new dress and sighed. By the end of the day, the thing would probably only be good for the rag bag. That was when she noticed she was not alone in the room.

"Miss Darcy," she said, a little surprised. "It was very kind of you to sit with me."

The girl only bit her lip in response. Elizabeth had never had any experience with someone as overtly bashful as Miss Darcy. Whatever the flaws of the Bennet sisters, diffidence was never one of them. Mr Wickham's words about Mr Darcy's younger sibling rushed back—'I wish I could call her amiable. It gives me pain to speak ill of a Darcy. But she is too much like her brother—very, very proud.'

Any fool could see that it was shyness, not pride. He ought not to have so openly denigrated the two Darcys, all while proclaiming that he never would; it had surely been disingenuous, at best.

After her aunt had gently chided her for showing too much interest in the handsome lieutenant, she had distanced herself from him in every possible way. With that distance, she had concluded—with a good deal of dismay—that she had perhaps given the man more credit for manners and charm than was likely deserved. But was not that, too, the fault of Mr Darcy? He had publicly insulted her, hurting her confidence in herself; Mr Wickham's open admiration had been a curative, a balm to her wounded pride. Besides, if he was not the man she had wished him to be, he still had not deserved the cruel treatment received at the hand of his enemy.

"You...you are feeling, um, somewhat recovered?" Miss Darcy asked, very tentatively.

"I am," Elizabeth firmly assured her. "It was never serious, not for a moment."

"Oh, but Fitzwilliam said you lost consciousness!" she protested. Her brown eyes, so like her brother's, filled with tears, and her apologies came in a rush. "I am so sorry! It is all my fault. My dog greets me in just such a ramshackle manner, and I have never punished him for it. I have never had a pet of my own, and I have too much enjoyed his eagerness. Fitzwilliam has requested many times that I teach him manners. I-I apologise, Miss Bennet, most sincerely."

"I should have braced myself instead of cowering like an idiot and allowing myself to be felled by a little harmless enthusiasm," Elizabeth said. While the dog *was* ill-mannered, it was its owner's fault—and that owner, in her inexperience, had failed to curb its zeal. Miss Darcy had not known better—but surely her elder brother had.

"Dubitz is an interesting name," Lizzy said, trying to

prevent a repeated litany of apology. "Is it German, perhaps?"

"Oh… Dubitz is not really his name."

"Excuse me. I thought I heard him called that."

"Well, yes. I mean, I suppose it actually *is* his name, more so than his real one." She blushed, and Elizabeth, touched by her genuine awkwardness, smiled encouragingly.

"I named him Sir Derby, but Fitzwilliam protested that 'Sir Dubious' was far more appropriate. Somehow, he became 'Dubitz'…I believe my brother began it, but I am as guilty, for it is all he answers to now." She sighed. "Are you truly well?"

"I am, indeed. I shall need to depart soon in order to reach Longbourn before full dark." She swung her legs over the bed's edge, only then noticing her feet were bare.

"Oh, you cannot leave!" Miss Darcy declared, sounding horrified. "Mr Jones said you must stay abed for at least four-and-twenty hours, to ensure you are not concussed!"

"I am certain I can stay abed from Longbourn just as easily," Elizabeth said mildly, looking around for her absent slippers.

"Oh, but…"

A door in the panelling—which Elizabeth had not hitherto realised *was* a door—opened, and Mr Darcy strode in as though the chamber were his. He seemed to take in the situation at a glance.

"Ah, I see our patient has already launched her next rebellion," he said conversationally, and not as if he were entering an unwed female's chamber in an extremely scandalous fashion.

"You cannot believe I mean to remain here," Elizabeth challenged.

"Why would I think such a thing? After all, the best medical advice within miles insisted it to be the proper recourse. So, naturally, I assume that you not only mean to leave but that you will no longer allow me to drive you and would, in fact, prefer to walk home in your bare feet."

Miss Darcy's brow furrowed. "Miss Bennet, my brother often expresses himself in, um, a rather ironic fashion. You must excuse—"

"You need not worry that I shall take a word from his mouth with the least degree of gravity," Elizabeth interrupted.

But Miss Darcy wrung her hands. "Please, will you not lie down again?"

"She cannot," Mr Darcy said gravely. "Miss Bennet suspects that I agree with the apothecary, therefore rendering her as honour-bound to *dis*agree."

"Surely not, Fitzwilliam!" the younger girl protested. "You must not tease."

"Your brother finds his own humour vastly amusing," Elizabeth said to the younger girl. "But with my sister and brother absent, clearly you can see that it would be improper for me to stay here. And besides, I have none of my things."

"B-but I am here, which, um, does not mean much as far as chaperoning, I suppose…but also Miss Bingley and Mr and Mrs Hurst," Miss Darcy added. "I promise, I would stay at your bedside all night, if only to ensure you take no harm as a result of my dog's ill manners."

"Oh, but my dear," Mr Darcy sighed. "To remain the night in the same house, no matter how immense, as the very eligible Fitzwilliam Darcy—even upon the insistence of Mr Jones—would practically announce to the neighbourhood her intention of capturing my interest. Which, of course, would wound her pride and swell my own—which is quite a sufficient size as it is, she has already informed me."

Miss Darcy appeared further distressed. "Oh, you must stop teasing, Brother! Miss Bennet is not accustomed to your odd ways!"

"I am already becoming used to Mr Darcy's little jokes, dear. While I cannot agree it is the most appropriate means of communicating, I can admire his commitment to overdoing it."

"Zounds! A direct hit," he said, clasping his heart in an exaggerated manner. "How insufficient are all my pretensions of teasing a woman worthy of being teased." He bowed to Elizabeth. "By you, I am sufficiently humbled."

Elizabeth snorted and was just able to prevent a smile from escaping. Miss Darcy was looking between them with some consternation, and she could not be blamed. Mr Darcy had never seemed to be a light-hearted, teasing sort of fellow. Oh, there had been the time he had provokingly taunted her—*with* Miss Bingley—that their 'figures appear to the greatest advantage in walking' and that he would remain by the fire to 'admire them', but then, most other times, he had seemed serious, preoccupied, and rather easily offended. She had believed him to be of Miss Bingley's stripe, looking down upon her and her family—less obviously, perhaps, but sharing her opinions. However, she did not really *know* him, did she? It was only that what she *did* know of him was not much good—except that he seemed to have a very kind regard for his sister, in allowing her free rein to keep dogs the size of ponies. She could think of little else to recommend him, and was unsure whether or not this one thing was to his credit.

His teasing, however, accomplished his purpose if he wished to prevent her from stubbornly refusing to remain at Netherfield for no other reason than his recommendation that she stay. *Am I that obstinate? It is possible. Provoking man! He brings out the worst in me!*

Another wave of fatigue passed through her; she really did not wish to argue. Her head *did* hurt, and one night in a home twice the size of Longbourn was surely innocuous enough.

"If you have writing materials, I shall send a note to my mother." She sighed. "In light of Mr Jones's advice, I suppose it is the easiest course of action for one night. Perhaps I can borrow something of Jane's."

Miss Darcy appeared relieved, retreating into silence once again. And though Elizabeth studied Mr Darcy's face for any triumph in his victory, his expression remained impassive as he left to inform the housekeeper —and the Bingley sisters, she presumed—of Netherfield's newest guest.

Elizabeth awakened early, as was her habit, and stretched, feeling the luxuriant softness of the mattresses and bedclothing—one certainly could not fault Miss Bingley her linens. Morning sun streamed in through the windows, and as the fire had been made up, the room was comfortably warm. She had slept the night away, thankfully free of dreams or illness.

She slipped out of bed, feeling much improved. Jane's nightgown hung loosely on her smaller frame, but in her note informing Mama of the incident and that she would be remaining at Netherfield for the night, she had requested fresh clothing to be sent over. She reached up to touch the tender spot on her head where it had hit the ground—feeling just a tad sheepish, and wishing with all her heart she had been braced for the impact of Dubitz.

She could not help but recall Mr Darcy's stern lecture to the dog—it *had* been rather amusing, she supposed.

The memory of other moments, however, caused any smile to disappear, her heart beginning to beat hard as she contemplated whatever peculiar challenges Mr Darcy might offer her. She did not *understand* him; she could no longer be sure of herself when he was near. It was simply impossible that she could have misjudged his feelings so greatly. *He disapproved of all of us last autumn! He hated us! But it will not matter,* she reassured herself. *Soon, I will be home, and I am certain my father will no longer be speaking of duels once I explain his misunderstanding. Then, perhaps I shall travel to Kent with Charlotte. Or even stay several weeks with Uncle Gardiner. I will remove myself from this impossible state of affairs!*

A sound from the corridor disturbed her thoughts, an unmistakeable voice—and yet she hoped she *must* be mistaken.

Mrs Bennet burst into her room. "Lizzy! My poor, dearest child!"

"Mama! It is so early! Why are you here?"

"A special licence! You must and shall be married by a special licence!"

Elizabeth closed her eyes, her dismay complete.

"I am *not* going to be married, Mama," she said calmly, trying to use Mr Darcy's stern inflections in order to make herself understood. "It was all a mistake."

"I daresay! But the trap is sprung, and you mustn't complain if the prize is a meagre one. It is natural to have second thoughts, now that you understand how scanty and bleak the harvest. He *is* a disagreeable sort of fellow, but Lizzy, I shall teach you just how to manage the farm."

"Manage what farm?"

"Do not be thick-headed, my girl. You are a woman now. Did you think it would only happen once? The sowing and the seeding! Laying in his crops! I do not pretend it will be your favourite chore. You must allow a good fifteen minutes at the first, but ten or even five is ample, once you grasp the lay of the land, so to speak. You have heard me criticise your imaginings, but now that is all to be forgot. Loose your fancy, indulge your imagination in every possible flight which the subject will afford. For myself, I always think of blancmange."

"Blancmange?" She was beginning to feel slightly ill.

"Oh, yes. I just imagine it there as a centrepiece of the course, quivering delicately upon its platter, its almonds mounding deliciously amongst its moist, creamy globules, and time simply flies without my noticing."

Elizabeth buried her face in her hands.

"You were very wise, my dear girl, to remain here. Your father might be inclined to allow the slippery worm to wriggle off the hook, but I shall never, not as I live and breathe, though the hook were baited with gold and diamonds. Your worm is *here*, and thus you and I shall *both* remain upon Netherfield soil until the maggot pays the piper. Here, together. I vow it!"

Worms and farms and blancmange! It was all too much, but then, Mama upon her high ropes was a Drury Lane prodigy. Elizabeth thought of Caroline Bingley and Mrs Hurst, of their snide looks and cutting asides. Mrs Bennet living under the same roof with them for even a day was impossible to consider. *It is past time to return home!* But as she opened her mouth to argue, a knock sounded. It was probably Miss Bingley arrived to criticise already. She felt her headache returning.

Mrs Bennet went to the door; Elizabeth, still in her nightgown, could hardly stop her. She heard a few moments of murmuring, and then her mother returned, handing a note over to her daughter. She appeared smug; Elizabeth had no doubt that she had already pried most of whatever information it contained out of whichever servant delivered it.

Her name was written on the front in a wide-spaced, too-careful hand.

My Dear Elizabeth,

By the time you read this, I suspect we shall have left Netherfield and be on our way to town. Mr Darcy, it seems, has business in London, so he and his sister shall be departing today as well, and as Miss Darcy quite depends upon our company, I am duty-bound not to leave her comfortless. I am certain that once he reaches town, he will not be in any hurry to leave. Many of his acquaintance—and my own, for we share all the same circles—are in London.

I regret that we cannot stay behind until you are fully recovered, but I trust your injury to be a minor one, and soon mended. Nevertheless, Mrs Fairbanks has been given instruc-

tions to see to your every need until your return to Longbourn, and Mrs Nicholls is preparing a broth she vows is a cure for any ailment.

I wish I could hear that you, my dearest Elizabeth, had any intention of joining us in London, but of that I despair. I do not know whether I ever before mentioned to you my feelings on this subject, but I will not leave the country without confiding them, and I trust you will not esteem them unreasonable. It is well known that Mr Darcy admires me greatly, and we will now have frequent opportunity of spending much time together in town. My relations all wish the connexion as much as does his sister, and my partiality is not misleading me, I think, when I consider myself most capable of engaging any man's heart. With all these circumstances to favour an attachment and nothing to prevent it, am I wrong, my new sister, in indulging the hope of an event which will secure the happiness of so many?

I do not pretend to regret anything I shall leave in Hertfordshire, except your society, my dearest sister, for a town life is much more to my liking, as well as Mr Darcy's; but we are family now, so will of course continue enjoying many returns of the delightful intercourse we have known, and in the meanwhile may lessen the pain of separation by a very frequent and most unreserved correspondence. I depend on you for that.

With sisterly affection,
C Bingley

Elizabeth's brow furrowed at the intelligence contained in this letter. So, Anne de Bourgh and now Caroline Bingley? Brides were literally lining up to marry the man! It was also most contrary to everything she knew of Mr Darcy's plans. But of course, it made her next actions clear. She could not possibly stay another moment at Netherfield with the Bingley sisters gone away, with or without her mother. She would appear as the worst sort of climbing ivy, as if she were claiming Netherfield in the absence of her sister in order to pursue its most distinguished guest. Getting in line behind Miss Bingley!

"It says they are leaving, does it not?" her mother asked. "Miss Bingley and the Hursts?" Elizabeth did not mistake the note of triumph in her voice.

"It does."

Mrs Bennet chortled. "As soon as your father told me what happened, I knew the situation to be a delicate one. No man likes a forced marriage—"

"Or woman!" Elizabeth cried.

"But it was not merely this affair upon which my caution was founded," she continued, as if Elizabeth had not spoken. "I can smell Miss Bingley's desperation from a hundred paces. She wants that dislikeable Mr Darcy for herself —I am sorry, dear, but dislikeable he *is* —and it is only her last remaining vestiges of pride stopping her from breaking into his chamber at night and doing some forcing of her own."

"Mama! It is evident that she is gone, no more to return, and…and evidently, Mr Darcy *with* her."

"Do not tell *me!*" she insisted. "She has always been jealous of you—especially for the way you care nothing about the things she most highly regards. If she knew of your engagement, the woman would do anything she could to prevent it from progressing. It was all I could do to stop Sir William from blathering it to the entire neighbourhood yesterday. But I make it a point to know my enemies, and Miss Bingley is a raging gossip. If a conversation is underway, she must know what it is about, and if Mr Darcy's name is mentioned, it is slops to a swine for her. I simply told Lady Lucas, when she was near, that Mr Darcy told *my* dear Jane that he was leaving immediately tomorrow to return to town to attend to his business there, and that he hated Hertfordshire and could not wait to leave it. I knew the Bingley chit would make haste to leave before he did, so she could follow him without *appearing* to follow him."

Elizabeth listened to this deviousness with some amazement. She had always considered her mother a silly woman; it had never occurred to her that Mrs Bennet might expend her wits upon the task of seeing her daughters married—to the exclusion of all else.

"If Mr Darcy is *not* returning immediately to town," she could not help pointing out, "Caroline Bingley shall surely soon discover he is not in London, if she is so desperate."

Mrs Bennet only shrugged. "What will it matter? She believes him to hate Hertfordshire and our society—as indeed he doubtless does. Why would she think him still at Netherfield? She will assume him gone to his home estate instead, and will spend her time trying to connive an invitation for the grouse."

"Why would you wish me to marry a...a worm who hates my home and family?" Elizabeth cried, at her own wits' end.

But to her great surprise, her mother took Elizabeth's face in her hands. "Listen to me, my daughter, as you would not when I tried to give you Collins. It is not *who* you marry, but what life your marriage brings you and your children after you. You could have done as you pleased with Collins and ruled him, his parsonage, and some day, Longbourn. This one is not so fat, so stupid, nor so ugly, but he is far less easily governed. Still, you are the quickest of all my girls—you will figure a way. You will *own* him and his thousands. Do you understand me?"

Mrs Bennet's intensity was rather overpowering; it was not the time, Elizabeth judged, to declare her absolute intention of avoiding matrimony.

"I understand, Mama," she said instead, with something like despair.

6

One helpful result of Mrs Bennet's arrival was that she had brought fresh clothing—and, Elizabeth noticed, she had freely scavenged amongst all the Bennet sisters' wardrobes. Lydia's new pelisse and three of her nicest dresses, as well as two of Kitty's bonnets were included in the overflowing trunk. She had every intention of returning to Longbourn immediately—thus, such a windfall was completely unnecessary. Still, she had always admired Lydia's yellow muslin and never been allowed to borrow it, as Lydia worried that Elizabeth's half-inch shorter height would somehow lead its hems to ruin. There was a temptation to wear it today.

Stop it, vain creature! she counselled herself. It seemed too much like an effort to dress for attention. For *his* attention.

Her mother, evidently, had already arranged her accommodations with the housekeeper and retired to them immediately. Only Miss Darcy was at breakfast, and after enquiring as to Elizabeth's health, that young lady had almost nothing to say. Elizabeth's conversational gambits fell flat, and after a short time, the girl politely excused herself.

In her own comfortable clothing, left to her own devices, she decided she may as well return home by foot, as she had attempted yesterday. Her father had always been able to turn a deaf ear to the worst of her mother's ideas, as well as her tantrums and nerves. It was to be hoped he would do so again, now that he was unaffected by yesterday's merrymaking, and she started off immediately.

It was too much to hope for two days in a row of perfect spring weather, however, and the clouds were rapidly gathering, the breeze turning into wind. Regretting that she had no umbrella, she kept an eye on the darkening sky and sped up her pace, thus nearly colliding with Mr Darcy, hurrying in the opposite direction, only drawing up short with a gasp when she glanced up to see his powerfully built form looming suddenly before her.

"Ah. I see you are running away to home already," he said evenly, as if meeting on gloomy forest paths were an everyday affair. "A bit of advice, if I might offer it— perhaps avoid your father today. If I had to guess, I would say he is not feeling quite the thing. I daresay he would as soon shoot you and me both, at present."

"You have been to Longbourn this morning?" she asked, incredulous. "You *walked*?"

"I enjoy a good tramp, and I believed the weather would hold but brought my umbrella if it will not." He lifted it to show her. "I said I would work to ensure you had choices. I thought to explain and apologise, and I believed that whatever was to be said was best said at once. Alas, he threw me, and my apologies, out of his home, unheard."

Yet another interaction with my family, lacking manners and propriety. She briefly closed her eyes, mortified.

Instead of offering criticisms, however, he only offered his arm; he was plainly still turned in the direction of Netherfield. And what, really, was the use of going home now, if her father was in no mood to listen and conciliate? She might as well stay with her mother for another day.

"I am sorry you were treated ill," she said at last, after they had walked some ways.

"In retrospect, I can see the timing of my visit was less than ideal," he replied politely.

"There is something else I ought to mention." She hesitated, feeling all the awkwardness of the confession. "My mother...well, she has come to be a chaperon to me at Netherfield. She seems to have had some sort of, um, premonition that Miss Bingley would be departing today with Mr and Mrs Hurst. As it appears they have."

"A premonition. I see."

She looked up at him sharply, expecting disbelief, but his face displayed its usual stolidity.

"They took their leave of me before departing, and I did not correct their impression that I would soon be gone as well. Is their absence why you decided to return home?"

Elizabeth bit her lip, but only the truth would do.

"My mother is set on the match. The *supposed* match between us. She only said nothing yesterday because, well, she did not like to-to...to say anything at Jane's wedding," she prevaricated, blushing, trying to think how to undo, in advance, any damage Mama might instigate in either manner or in pushing for an immediate wedding.

"Possibly your mother's removal from Longbourn further soured your father's mood. Shall I promise you that nothing she says or does will affect our agreement?"

"The challenges, you mean," she said, desperately wanting to turn the subject although not quite comfortable with the new one. "I expect I must prove bravery or wit. Shall I capture a wanted criminal? Or, perhaps, bait a bear? Not that I would agree to such an act—in my visit to the Royal Menagerie, I met a Greenland bear, you know. His eyes were very sad and very wise, and ever afterward, I could never approve of anyone provoking one of his cousins. It will have to be the felonious villain, I suppose."

She must not quite have succeeded in affecting nonchalance, for he looked down at her in some concern. "I promise, Miss Bennet, these challenges will be nothing dreadful. In fact, I have the first ready for you now."

The house had long since come into sight, and they walked up the terrace steps together, Elizabeth unsure she was quite ready for any contest, no matter how simple. She could think of nothing to say by way of protest, however, that would not brand her a coward.

As they reached the door, from an inner pocket of his coat, he withdrew a letter, her name written upon the front of it in the strong, even hand Miss Bingley had so admired.

"This is...instruction?" she asked.

He smiled. "No. Your first task is merely to read this letter with an open mind—and as I wrote it myself, to attempt to withhold your opinion of its author until after you have finished it."

"That is all?" she asked, brow furrowed.

He placed his index finger gently upon that furrow, smoothing the tiny wrinkle. "That is all," he said softly, and suddenly, he was so very close, his face only inches away from hers. She could smell the scent of his shaving soap, sandalwood and spices and...*him*. "No daring battles with highway robbers or Greenland bears required, my intrepid girl."

She shivered, and knew he saw it. His eyes, already a chocolate brown, seemed to darken...with something. The mischievous devil in him, perhaps, that he hid so well behind convention and stolidity. Taking the letter from his hand, she turned away quickly, darting into the house before she could change her mind and run all the way home to Longbourn.

❧❧❧

Elizabeth set the letter atop the large bureau in her chamber, where it called to her in equal tones of curiosity and dismay. Of course, he ought not to be writing to her, but had she pointed out the infraction, he would only have claimed that—at least temporarily— they were betrothed.

"Lizzy!"

Elizabeth spun around to face her mother.

"I could not find you earlier, and I feared you had returned to Longbourn! Oh, my poor nerves!"

"Mama, I really *must* go home, as soon as may be. I cannot stand the thought—" she began, but Mrs Bennet interrupted.

"What is that?" she asked sharply, her eyes fixed upon the letter from Mr Darcy, perched in plain sight upon the bureau.

Elizabeth snatched it, holding it tightly with both hands. "Nothing."

"Give it to me."

"No! It is not what you think!"

Arms akimbo, her eyes narrowed, she advanced upon her daughter. "What I *think* is that he is writing you letters, and probably has been for some time. This is just the evidence we need! You are too naïve to understand how easily a man of his wealth and property can do as he will, ruin a girl, then change his fickle mind! Proof of breach of contract is not so easily abandoned."

Elizabeth backed up until she hit the bureau. "Mama, whatever Mr Darcy's faults, he would not intentionally *ruin* me!"

"How happy I am that you think so, but his honour and three pennies will buy a loaf of bread. Give me that letter, as well as any others you possess."

Mrs Bennet proved relentless in her determination to have it, badgering her for some minutes without pause or reprieve. At last, Elizabeth had no choice but to explain the silly challenges that she had agreed to in order to release herself from the accidental betrothal. "It was all a foolish misunderstanding—he *never*… I did not allow him to-to…plant any crops! Papa did not see what he thought he saw!"

She expected her mother to disintegrate into tears and threats, as she had when Elizabeth refused Mr Collins. To her surprise, she did neither.

Mrs Bennet only looked at her—disbelief, astonishment, and frustration all in equal measure displayed upon her countenance. At last, eyes narrowed, she spoke.

"I can see that whatever *I* deem in your best interests, *you* will do quite the opposite. You are as stubborn as your father, throwing away all your opportunities in favour of some virtue or ideal. For all your wits, you are quite stupid, Lizzy, so I shall save my breath to cool my porridge. However, unless you remain at Netherfield *with me*, I am *done* with your sensibilities. Mr Darcy, evidently, has more patience with your nonsense than I do. If you go home to your father, I shall talk to everyone who will listen, demanding a wedding at the point of pistols no matter the risk to your reputation. Do I have your word that you will not sneak off to Longbourn the moment my back is turned?"

"It will not change the outcome, Mama," Elizabeth insisted. "I will not marry a man of weak character and vow to obey, for the rest of my life, a man I hate. I will rather go and live with my uncle, if he will have me."

Her mother shook her head incredulously. "I do not ask too much, do I, when I beg you to remain at Netherfield? Did I insist the banns be called? Did I visit the vicar, or even the magistrate, regarding the behaviour in which *he* has already indulged? *All* I asked was that you stay away from Longbourn! You have already promised Mr Darcy that you will see this ridiculous 'challenge' scheme through. Will you vow not to hide at home like a coward whilst you do so?"

Elizabeth bristled at the accusation of cowardice; it was the one sore spot she could not bear. There seemed no option except surrender to her mother's ultimatum, and, to be fair, she truly was not asking a great deal—especially compared to the harm she might do if crossed.

Mrs Bennet's apparent belief that being so much in Mr Darcy's company would change her feelings towards him was ridiculous, but any agreement certainly would not stop her father from visiting, if only he would. *He* might be able to reason with her.

"Very well, Mama. I will not go to Longbourn. At least, not until Mr Darcy's challenges are completed. We do agree on that, you know. The scheme is ridiculous."

Mrs Bennet nodded and, with a final, longing look at the letter, quit the room.

❈

Elizabeth yearned to throw that letter into the flames, but she *had* promised. Why she was so reluctant was a mystery—after all, what could it matter? Was she *nervous* about learning more of his feelings? Timidity? The idea was not to be borne, and she tore the seal open.

It was two sheets of paper, written quite through, in a very close hand. The envelope was likewise full, and dated only this morning.

> *Dear Miss Bennet,*
>
> *Since I understand it is only your justice that demands attention to this letter, I shall come right to the point: to address the weightiest of the accusations you have made against me—that in defiance of various claims, of honour and humanity, I ruined the immediate prosperity, blasted the prospects, and wilfully and wantonly threw off the companion of my youth, Mr Wickham. Of what he has particularly accused me, I am ignorant; but of the truth of what I shall relate, I can summon more than one witness of undoubted veracity.*

Bah. I have just re-read the above paragraph. It reads as stiffly as a steel brush. I am no expert at explaining myself. It comes as no surprise, perhaps? You shall think, doubtless, that I intend to fill this space with as many three and four syllable words as is possible—as of course, an excellent vocabulary is a sign of both judgment and honesty, is it not?

Instead of beginning again, I shall beg your patience, as I have already begun and discarded four attempts at putting this down on paper. I am determined this will be the final one, for I will waste all of Bingley's writing materials if I do not continue forward—even if the result reads not at all satisfactorily. (A six-syllable word—another point for me!)

First, a bit of history. Mr Wickham is the son of a very respectable man, who had for many years the management of all the Pemberley estates—and whose good conduct in the discharge of his trust naturally inclined my father to be of service to him. On his only child George Wickham, Father's god-son, his kindness was therefore liberally bestowed. My father supported him at school and afterwards at Cambridge— a most important assistance, as his own father, always poor from the extravagance of his wife, would have been unable to give him a gentleman's education. (I should strike out this portion of the sentence, as it is unnecessary to the point and reveals a certain acrimony towards a woman who is dead and cannot defend herself. Perhaps her husband's wages deserved increase, or perhaps he should have done a better job of assisting her with the household budget. But I cannot obliterate much before my letter resembles Bingley's scores and crosses and will rather ask, again, your forgiveness.)

My father was not only fond of this young man's society, he had also the highest opinion of him, and hoping the church would be his profession, intended to provide for him in it. As for myself, it is many, many years since I first began to think of him in a very different manner. The vicious propensities—the want of principle, which he was careful to guard from the knowledge of his best friend, could not escape the observation of a young man of nearly the same age with himself and who had opportunities of seeing him in unguarded moments, which my father could not have.

I just re-read that paragraph. I fear it inadequate. 'Vicious' suggests the physical violence of a robber holding a helpless female at the point of his pistol or the murderer who displays only savage brutality. It does not adequately describe a man who might blame his petty thefts upon the servants, or even the son of the household, or who steals the notes of another school-boy, pretending to have written the paper himself, or who professes to court a barmaid, even offering marriage, but breaks it off when the girl is found with child, claiming her to *have been unfaithful in the face of* his *'virtue'. In these instances, I am without proof, with only my word against his own. However, the evidence of repetition at the centre of these cases must have some merit—so many times, the only common-ality in the fraud, the theft, the disgraced, the shamed, is one name: George Wickham.*

My excellent father died about five years ago, after a lengthy illness; in his will, he not only left a thousand pounds to Mr Wickham but recommended he be given a valuable family living. Shortly after his own father's passing, however, Mr Wickham wrote to inform me that, having finally resolved against taking orders, he hoped I should not think it unreason-able for him to expect some more immediate pecuniary (five syllables—I hope you are paying attention) advantage, in lieu of the preferment by which he could not be benefited. The law, he believed, would better suit him.

As would vast quantities of cash. Elizabeth set down

the letter in shocked bewilderment at the sums mentioned. This was beyond anything! Mr Darcy had paid the man *thousands*! And then, after three years' passage of time with no contact except occasional reports of dissipation, idleness, and gambling—study of the law had been a mere pretence, apparently—upon the death of the living's incumbent, Mr Wickham had demanded its possession after all. How could he so blatantly, after receiving so much! With difficulty, Elizabeth continued reading Mr Darcy's words. To her, it seemed as if there was pain in every syllable.

Had I expected Wickham would return? I think I did, else I would not have made him sign documents giving up all rights to the living. I made certain, legally, that I could not be blamed for refusing to comply with his entreaty or for resisting every repetition of it. But I gave him that money knowing he would waste it. I did it, I think, because I hated him. A part of me revelled in his punishment. 'Look at all you have been given,' I told him. 'Whose fault is it that you have nothing left?'

I wanted him humbled. I wanted him disgraced. It was all the sweeter that he had done it to himself.

His resentment was in proportion to the distress of his circumstances—and he was doubtless as violent in his abuse of me to others as in his reproaches to myself. When I saw him that Tuesday afternoon last November, speaking with you on the streets of Meryton, my hatred for him burned as brightly as it ever had.

I have struggled to be as honest as I know how to be in this letter. If I cannot be accused of cruelty, neither can I be accused of helping him in any real fashion to change, to improve, or to atone.

Could it have been done? Was it an impossible task? I do not know. I did not try. I hated him. I still do.

For the truth of everything I have related, I can appeal more particularly to the testimonies of Mr Henry Saxelby, of West Smithfield, my esteemed solicitor, and also of Colonel Fitzwilliam, younger son of the earl of Matlock, who as executor of my father's will, has also been unavoidably acquainted with every particular of this transaction.

Both have been sent my request that they provide you with any information you require; the direction of each is included below.

You might possibly wonder why something of this was not told you in November. In retrospect, I emphatically wish I had. I suppose I felt it beneath me to offer any defence against someone I despised. I expected you, and your neighbours, to immediately take my part against him upon the basis of my name, my station in life, and other even more superficial differences. My pride, in other words, demanded I say nothing and simply fume instead. (As a tactic for winning affection, it possibly does not show my intelligence in the best light.)

As I again re-read my words, a certain bitterness of spirit is evident. I suppose it is due to the recollection of so much sorrow, degradation, and destruction. But I am attempting a more complete honesty with you, and perhaps with myself for the first time—and even so, I have yet omitted portions—some of his sins, and some of mine. It may be that I only now feel my own sense of blame, for the many times I covered his shame and paid his debts and looked the other way and pretended ignorance, all so that my father and his would never be disappointed nor upset. There are no heroes to write of, to be sure.

I will only conclude with my apologies for failing to inform you—and your neighbours—of the inherent risk of having any dealings with the fellow. In light of my regrettable silence, I hope that any to whom he owes his markers will apply to me for remuneration. They haven't a prayer of getting anything from him.

    Ever yours,

    F Darcy

7

Astonishment, apprehension, and even horror oppressed Elizabeth after reading the whole of Darcy's letter. She wished to discredit it entirely, repeatedly exclaiming, "This must be false! This cannot be! This must be the grossest falsehood!"— putting it hastily away, protesting that she would not regard it, that she would never look at it again.

But a sense of fairness forced her to reconsider, to instead read it through more carefully. Had not she been slightly repulsed by some of Mr Wickham's behaviour— in his way of encouraging her young sisters to participate in too-loud laughter and lightmindedness? He was charming and he was handsome but...had he not openly revealed deeply personal indignities to her, when essentially a stranger to him? She tried to recollect some instance of goodness, some distinguished trait of integrity or benevolence, that might rescue him from the attacks of Mr Darcy. No such recollection befriended her. Should she call him honourable or trustworthy because he could dance beautifully?

Almost as surprising was the entire absence of...self-righteousness, for lack of a better description, from Mr Darcy. He made no excuses for his hostility towards Mr Wickham. He had mocked such feelings, even, scrupulously putting forth a culpability that no one on earth would expect him to share.

Briefly, she considered writing to the men he had identified as his witnesses, but after a moment's reflection, she abandoned the idea. Mr Darcy would not have named them had they been likely to give her a substantially different report. No, she must make her own decision; she must judge for herself.

The nature of her friendship with Mr Wickham was of the shallowest sort. His behaviour towards herself, if he had never intended courtship, could have no decent motive. Either he had been deceived with regard to her fortune or had been gratifying his vanity. Neither had he paid any particular notice when she had withdrawn from whatever connexion they had shared. Or had he? Had not at least some of his attentions—light-hearted ones, to be sure—been transferred to her younger sisters? But whether they had been or not, there was nothing to recommend him in any of it.

Mr Darcy, on the other hand, had immediately put forth an expectation of marriage when they had been caught in an unfortunate circumstance. He had tried to speak to her father this morning, hoping to smooth things over. He had written her a deeply personal letter, including admissions he need not have shared. He was good to his sister, and although he had offered an unwelcome opinion on Mr Bingley's marriage to *hers*, he had also somehow seen to the repair of any damage. He had even suggested that her neighbours apply to him for what he expected to be unpaid debts from his enemy. What did he owe the neighbourhood? Almost without exception, he was disliked. And why had they disliked him? Because he had not behaved sociably and because he had, upon their first occasion in company together, insulted *her*, a great favourite of all.

No, any evidence of goodness was limited to his own side.

What ought she to do now?

She peered out the window of her chamber. The rain was coming down in torrents, precluding any walk she might wish to take to gather her thoughts, to calm herself.

Her dislike for Mr Darcy had been founded upon his conduct towards herself, Jane, and Mr Wickham. He was to be forgiven for the incident regarding Jane and now excused for any resentment towards Mr Wickham. That left only herself. Mr Darcy had requested that she meet seven—now six—challenges. Under duress, she had agreed, but past constraints no longer applied.

Could it be that he had wanted time to truly come to know her, or to allow her to come to know him? It seemed rather impossible that he should wish it! *And yet, I have been wrong, very wrong, in my every judgment of his character.* Could not even her hesitation to take up the challenges he had requested be seen as a symptom of her previous blindness? *Pleased with the preference of one, and offended by the neglect of the other, I have practically courted ignorance!*

There truly seemed only one course of action to take. She quit the room, intent upon searching for Mr Darcy.

Darcy sat before the library fire, an open book lying, ignored, upon his lap. He had made a resolution to cease brooding upon that which could not be changed, but the habit formed during the last five or so years could not easily be banished.

Had she read his letter? What did she think, if she had? The first iterations were so full of supercilious indignation, they had gone directly into the fire. Even so, he had been incapable of removing much of his hostility; he was a long way from forgiveness towards George Wickham.

"Mr Darcy!"

The shrill pitch of the voice startled him abruptly from his thoughts. Setting aside the book, he stood to face Mrs Bennet. "Madam," he said, bowing formally.

She had obviously been very pretty once and was a handsome woman still. It was only that so much *noise* emitted from her person. He had believed her to be a silly and ignorant female, and perhaps she was; however, she was also Elizabeth's mother. For that alone, he was honour-bound to find the good in her. He only hoped that his sister would not be subjected to any fits or tantrums in the brief time he expected them to share a residence—he would prefer Georgiana see only the best of Elizabeth's family.

"I have done what I can," she announced. "Lizzy is as good a girl who has ever lived, excepting, perhaps, being a bit stubborn regarding matters of matrimony."

"Only a bit?" he could not help but ask, suddenly seeing the humour in it.

"The very *slightest* speck," she insisted. "And it seems to me that one so disagreeable as yourself could make allowances for it. She has her father's quickness—I do not pretend to understand half of what they talk of. It is usually very tedious—but it ought to be music to *your* ears."

He nodded gravely, suppressing any temptation to smile. "Because I, too, am dull."

"Exactly!" she agreed, plainly pleased at his perception. "I have also succeeded in extracting a promise from her that she will stay away from Longbourn. She is the light of her father's life and can usually talk her way into or out of anything with him. If she took it into her head to refuse you—and I do not say she does, mind you, I am certain she will be sensible—you would have no chance of convincing him to overrule her. It is very important to separate her from Mr Bennet until matters are settled between you."

His brows raised at this unlooked-for assistance. "I thank you," he said.

"And so you ought. I say what I mean, but Mr Bennet claims I do not always mean what I say. Therefore, I wish to be clear now. It is the business of my life to see my daughters comfortably settled. When Mr Collins came to the point and Lizzy refused him, I nearly lost heart. I should have known she would be unable to suffer someone both ugly and stupid—she could have *ruled* that man, his parishioners, and someday, Longbourn. You, of course, are neither ugly nor stupid, and you *are* wealthy. If material comfort meant more to her, this would be to your credit. But perhaps you will find the gumption to put forth some effort to win her over. I cannot say. You *ought* to do it."

"And why is that, madam?" he could not help but ask, struggling for the serious mien that usually came so naturally to him, and only finding it in the alarm he felt at the idea of his beautiful Elizabeth yoked to his aunt's foolish parson.

Mrs Bennet rolled her eyes as if he were a brainless numbskull. "She is pretty, energetic, witty, an excellent manager, proper in manner, of good birth, and remarkably amusing to be with in company, unless she is conversing with her father about crop yields or astronomy or politics. You don't need more money, you need more spirit, boy! Or are you stupider than I believed?"

He had to bite his tongue to prevent full-blown laughter. "Perhaps a bit stupid," he agreed solemnly. "But I believe I am growing more intelligent the longer we speak."

"Good," she said, with obvious satisfaction. "*I* am her chaperon. I do not intend to make a nuisance of myself. However, if you hurt or misuse her, I do not need her father or duelling pistols. I was not born a lady. You will never know where my revenge will come from or when it will happen. You will, one future day, simply wake up dead. Am I understood?"

The urge to laugh doubled, but he had sense enough —and wish enough to remain alive—to suppress it. "Yes, ma'am. Understood, ma'am."

At this, she nodded regally and sailed out of the room with all the dignity of a queen.

When Elizabeth discovered Mr Darcy at last, he was alone in the library, looking a bit...bemused.

"Is all well?" she asked.

"Oh, yes," he said, although he seemed rather

distracted. But he politely pulled a chair for her closer to the fire, and seated himself in the one opposite.

"I read your letter," she said, coming straight to the point. But then, unfortunately, she did not know what else to say.

"Thank you," he replied. A long silence followed. He did not seem inclined to assist her with filling it.

"This reminds me of the last time we were alone in the library together, during Jane's illness," she said, recalling how rude he had been. It was no wonder she had formed no good impression.

He straightened, as if suddenly fully realising her presence. "Does it?" he asked, his eyes alit. "Were you imagining kissing me, as well?"

"What? No!" she cried, shocked. "You utterly ignored me, and thus I did my best to ignore you!"

He grinned piratically, a devil-glint in his eyes. "I can assure you, Miss Bennet, you have always commanded my full attention whenever you are near."

She could not believe his temerity, his insolence, his...passion. Blushing, she decided a subject change was in order. "Mr Wickham's behaviour," she began, and his expression instantly hardened. "I had already decided that he might not be so...hm, well-bred as I originally believed." She related the prank of dressing up Mr Chamberlayne in women's clothing and parading him around. "It is not that I am a killjoy. I think if my younger sisters were with friends of their own age participating in such a lark, I would hardly have noticed. It seemed a bit sordid, however, coaxing young girls to participate in outlandish capers with grown men—men who encourage them to laugh ever more loudly and drink far more punch than is wise."

"I am surprised your mother allows it. And your father."

Fleetingly, she was offended, but had she not complained to both her parents of the very same? "My father notices very little and believes it is all harmless foolishness. My mother...I truly think she wants Lydia and Kitty to wed officers and is happy to see them thrown together with anyone marriageable. She was in love with one as a girl, remembers him fondly." She sighed. Perhaps her mother might have been happier with Colonel Millar of the Hertfordshire regiment than she had ever been with Papa. "Besides, we do not have much in the way of a settlement, as you probably know. An eligible officer might be suitable." The words were spoken calmly although she could not help but feel some mortification. There was no point in prevaricating. If he was put off by the less elegant facts of her life, it was best to be clear now.

"Your mother is...an interesting woman. We had quite an informative conversation a few minutes ago."

Elizabeth closed her eyes, wishing she could disappear. She had hoped any such tête-à-têtes could be put off for some time and could only imagine what Mama had to say.

To her surprise, when she opened her eyes again, he was so close—practically kneeling at her feet—that she nearly gasped. His eyes were laughing. There was no other way to describe them.

"She offered to murder me if I behave in an ungentlemanly fashion."

Elizabeth groaned.

"I would like to kiss you now," he said, and her cheeks flamed. Despite his earlier words, it still seemed the last thing she had ever expected him to say, *especially* to her. Even more surprising was her instinctive response—an inexplicable interest.

"However, I do not wish to be murdered in my sleep by your avenging mama. I suppose her explanations were quite valuable."

"You are teasing me," she accused.

"Yes. But I am also being very truthful. You believed me? My letter, I mean."

She let out a breath she had not realised she had been holding. "Yes."

"Why?"

"Did you not wish me to?"

"I am only curious. You do not like me. We are, really, practically strangers to each other."

"Mr Bingley likes you. He knows you," she pointed out.

"That did not hold much weight with you yesterday."

"In such cases—as when I have been completely in the wrong—a good memory is unpardonable."

"I shall make a note of it. And what might your opinion be of kissing a person you have wronged?"

She gave him an arch look, unable to resist a return tease. "It is not as though I destroyed your property or stole your cook. Surely, you do not suggest we exchange kisses based upon a sense of guilt?"

"To be completely truthful, I would accept your kisses for any reason you felt so inclined to bestow them."

Her cheeks were burning again, the conversation well beyond anything proper, but she refused to back down. "Then I shall be completely truthful as well. Kissing is a wasteful exercise, something for men to enjoy and for women to learn to tolerate. I have absolutely no desire to develop the skill."

I have shocked him, she thought, before once again his expression betrayed nothing except casual interest. *I believe I have shocked myself.* But she should have known he would not be deterred.

"Perhaps you might provide more detail? What, exactly, displeases you in a kiss? I would by no means wish to suspend any pleasure of yours."

"Rather, ask what pleasure is to be found in such displays? Why would *anyone* like it?" *There,* she thought. *Let him chew on that and be disgusted with my opinions and my obvious experience. The sooner he learns I am not who he imagines, the better.*

"You are answering a question with a question. A woman daring enough to brave the topic is surely able to answer directly?"

At this appeal to her courage, she managed to look him directly in the eye, searching for any kind of mockery. At the moment, he appeared only mildly curious, and she dearly wished she had never said anything at all. But it seemed too late to withdraw from the conversation, as if she were fresh out of the nursery and could not speak as one adult to another. And then, in the memory of her one experience with kissing, anger suddenly flared. She would tell him *exactly* what she disliked.

"I do not like lips pressed so hard to mine that my mouth feels bruised. I do not like a tongue forced suffocatingly down my throat. I do not care for hands roaming my person as if there were a lost coin caught in my stays. I do not like it when a man who I thought was my friend, who I believed cared about me with at least a drop of affection, abruptly disappears in frantic animal spirits, and what is more, when *I* disappear. I do not like that I am no longer Elizabeth, not even a person, merely a thing to be acted upon."

It all came out in a rush, but now, her mortification complete, she looked away from him. She could not think of *any* conversation, *especially* with a gentleman, where the words she had just spoken might be acceptable. She had not quite realised, until this moment, how furious she still was about that 'kiss' until she had given herself permission to speak of it. She never had before, not even to Jane. She tried to think of how to make light of it, but unshed tears welled, ruining the nonchalant delivery she hoped for.

"I am likely being too dramatic. I probably only regret the loss of all that I ever *thought* a kiss would be, a mere illusion born of the silly novels read by silly girls who ought to know better."

Why will the earth never open and swallow one whole, just when one needs it to? she thought.

But his thumb only gently touched her chin, turning it so that she was forced to look at him. Instead of the derisiveness or disgust she had expected, a slightly angry expression twisted his brow.

"Do I know this sordid example of the male species —I dare not call him a man, for only a low swine would treat you thus—so that I might demonstrate the feel of my fist down *his* throat?" His voice was soft, and he appeared all the more dangerous because of it.

"You must find me to blame as well, for allowing it in the first place," she said, trying for dispassion and succeeding only in defiance, her chin raised, shaking off his gentle touch. "I wanted it to happen. It is my own fault that it did."

"I will tell you a great secret," he said, holding her gaze steadily, his voice lowered confidentially. "But to do so, I must now mention a circumstance which I would wish to forget myself, and which no obligation less than the present should induce me to unfold to any human being. I, too, have kissed another. Long in the past, of course."

She could not believe his response. He ought to be disgusted by her experience...oughtn't he? Instead, the danger in his gaze had passed, and playful mischief was back.

"And now you are laughing at me," she accused.

"Of course I am, darling girl. You are beautiful and exciting and possessed of an enquiring mind and a functioning brain. You did nothing wrong—it was your boorish lover who is to blame for the regrettable experience. While I believe your parents should have kept a better eye out, I would wager it was both your first kiss and your last."

"Why would I willingly repeat such an experience? When the time comes, I will suffer my husband and do my duty. But I need not anticipate such obligations before vows are spoken. I have more than learnt my lesson." She tried not to respond to his calling her 'beautiful' and 'exciting' whilst *she* bleated on like a dry, stuffy churchwarden.

"Do I know him?" he asked again, and whilst he did not betray his previous anger, something told her he was listening very carefully to her reply. Suddenly she realised—he suspected it was Wickham!

"You have been introduced," she said at last. "But

the, um, incident occurred two years ago, on my eighteenth birthday, and we have barely spoken since. He will be someone else's problem, and this is ancient history. How I wish you would forget the whole matter!" She could not have regretted her confidences, been more mortified by them, had she tried.

'Forget the matter', she said, as if forgetting someone assaulting her with brutal lust in her youthful first kiss was a simple sort of something to shrug off. *Bloody unlikely*, he thought. She spoke as if he could not remember every word she had ever uttered, right down to a *please* or *thank you*.

What he *wished* to do was hunt the scurvy animal down and spike his head upon the gatepost. He could see the scene from her past in his mind—Elizabeth, glowing with the pretty radiance of a girl on the cusp of womanhood, practising her newly minted skills at flirtation upon the supposedly safe personage of a childhood comrade, someone well known and looked up to since she was old enough to tell a male from a female. She, of course, had not taken into account the extent of her own beauty—luxurious dark curls, perfect skin, light, pleasing figure, wide, kissable mouth, eyes that smiled, laughed, sang, exulted—a thousand different emotions on unending, exhilarating, heady display. She should not have had to. The delicacy of her feelings ought to have been understood, even by a yokel.

What he wished to do was show her, here and now, what a kiss ought to be. He had often imagined it with her. Fireworks, brighter than Vauxhall at its most brilliant—red, glaring rockets of explosive passion turning midnight into noonday. But he was getting ahead of himself. Even if he did demonstrate to her that kisses could be neither ugly nor degrading, it would be far better for him than for her—because he loved her, and she did not love him.

"Have you seen the hermitage yet?"

"What?" she asked, obviously surprised. Had she expected he would harangue her over the matter? Be disgusted by one innocent trespass, as if she gave kisses away freely? He would not lie to himself—he wanted to flirt with her, tease her, *seduce* her into kissing him. But he would not; she was innocent as a lamb, in comparison to himself. It would not be fair.

"The hermitage in the park," he said, as if he were not dying to plunge his hands into her hair, to take it down so he could see. "Had you forgotten there was one?"

"No," she replied, adorably bewildered. "It is just...I did not expect the change of subject."

"I can see that the rain has stopped," he said, pointing to the nearest window, where a vividly blue sky and fluffy white clouds had replaced the previous wet gloom.

Her expression brightened, like fog parting for daylight. "Why yes, yes, I would like to. I mean, I have heard of it but have never been, nor been with anyone interested in finding it."

"It is worth the walk," he said, standing, helping her to her feet. "I shall get my coat—and perhaps you shall fetch yours—and meet you in the foyer in a few minutes?"

"I shall, yes. A few minutes."

He watched her go, but at the door she paused and turned, smiling at him in a way that caused a peculiar feeling to warm his insides. "Thank you, Mr Darcy."

"You are, of course, welcome. But I cannot guess any reason for your gratitude."

"I mean, for your understanding and for not...well, for withholding your most critical opinions during such a, um, frank discussion. For not saying anything unkind or insufferable."

"Ah, well. Give it time," he replied, smiling back. "The day is yet young."

8

Elizabeth went to bed that evening with mingled feelings of intrigue and suspicion. It was not so easy to surrender her prejudices, especially as she could not *understand* him. She had misjudged Mr Darcy, to be certain, but she had not been mistaken in *all* his former conduct. She had seen the annoyance he held for the behaviour of her younger sisters, her mother, even at times her father, before whatever mysterious errand had taken him away from Netherfield. How was it possible that he could be so changed, so tolerant, when he had once been so biased against them all?

Today they had explored parts of the park she had never before seen; he seemed to be something of an expert in various flora and fauna, surprising her. When she had questioned him, he had shrugged, saying that he was a farmer, after all. Him? A farmer? He was a landowner, certainly, but to declare himself a simple farmer was beyond imagination, and so she had informed him. It had become, like so many of their other conversations, an opportunity to challenge him. "What is this?" she asked him at a patch of greenery.

"Butcher's Broom," he had answered instantly. "Do you recognise this one?"

"Mouse-ear," she replied nonchalantly, secretly proud of herself. After six tries, she had finally stumped him, and she had whooped—it was nothing less—and done a little dance of victory around him, whilst he grinned and held up one of her arms—like the winner of a boxing match, he informed her. Then she had told him of her very unladylike desire to attend such an event, and he had demonstrated approved boxing stances learnt at Gentleman Jackson's, an establishment he, apparently, frequented when in town.

All in all, it had been a splendid afternoon. But a single question still begged for an answer: Just who was Mr Darcy?

One thing had changed, for certain. She eagerly awaited the next 'challenge' and went down to breakfast hoping to see him.

To her disappointment, once again, Miss Darcy was alone in the breakfast room—her brother apparently did not bother with the meal or took a tray, and of course, Mrs Bennet seldom rose before noon. Elizabeth tried, once again, to make conversation with the girl. And, once again, her efforts were fruitless. Was Miss Darcy's companion, whom she had learnt remained in London awaiting their return, able to extract a sentence or two per day from her charge?

"'Tis a fine morning, it appears," Elizabeth commented, looking out the window. "Perhaps we shall not have any rain."

Miss Darcy glanced out for less than a second, as if

the sunlight streaming in hurt her eyes. "Hm," she said, in what might have been agreement.

"The gardens are lovely," Elizabeth tried again. "In all the years I have lived near Netherfield, I never have truly explored them. I did enjoy seeing them yesterday, but there is a prettyish kind of a little wilderness on one side of the hermitage we did not explore. I should be glad to take a turn in it, if you will favour me with your company one of these afternoons?"

Again, the shifting of her eyes, this time ever so briefly towards Elizabeth before giving some sort of noise that might have been agreement, or might merely have been a grunt.

Had it not been for Miss Darcy's deep concern for Elizabeth's health after the incident with her dog, she might think her without any vocabulary—or ability to use it—whatsoever. Their longest interaction of the morning was her quiet few words excusing herself to return upstairs.

But Elizabeth soon forgot about Miss Darcy when a footman delivered a note to her in the distinctive hand she now knew well. It said nothing on the front except her name, but she quickly opened it, eager to know what challenge it held.

Instead of the many words of his previous challenge, this one used only a few.

Challenge Two. Allow me to teach you to ride. Meet me at the stables in one hour.

Her heart sank. He did not realise what he asked—to him, who had probably been riding before he was even walking, it must seem a small thing, inconsequential. He, the strong, competent, fearless male, could not begin to comprehend a deep-seated fear. He likely did not know what such anxieties felt like.

She could claim that she did not have a riding habit —which she did not—but somehow, she thought it would not stop him. He would probably have one fetched from London, from the supply he kept for his mistresses.

And where did that notion come from? she wondered.

It was doubtful Jane had taken hers, and they were close enough in size for her to manage somehow. But the very thought of going anywhere near a horse was an impossible notion. Perhaps she could feign illness? A rash? Her monthlies? She closed her eyes and began lecturing herself.

Imagine approaching Mr Darcy with stupid excuses about why you cannot mount a horse. Imagine the contempt in his eyes when he finally realises you are too cowardly to make another effort. Your accident was long ago, your previous attempt some years past, and you, who are so proud of your courage in other matters, refuse to face your fears again!

At last, there was nothing for it but to don Jane's habit and walk—slowly—to the lion's den...er, the stables. The habit was ludicrously military in style, with epaulettes at the shoulders and a ridiculously tasselled hat. Mr Darcy had arrived before her, of course—looking uncommonly sophisticated in his black woollen coat, buff leather breeches, and polished top boots, his tall hat making him appear even more imposing, with his already-lofty frame.

He stood beside a Thoroughbred hack that, rationally, she judged at perhaps fifteen hands. Nevertheless, in her mind, it grew larger with every step she took, until Mr Darcy appeared to be standing near an elephant. It was fitted with a ladies' side-saddle, distinguished by its fixed head pommel, there to steady her so that she did not slide from her precarious perch.

Do not think about the last time, Elizabeth Bennet! Do not remember the helplessness, the pain, the feeling that life, so barely begun, was over and finished.

But her feelings would not be repressed. She had tried again. Of course she had! *Not for years, however,* she reminded herself. *It was so long ago.* Lifting her chin, she forced herself forward until she was standing beside him.

New plan, she thought. *I will mount the elephant, trot once around the ring, halt, dismount—perhaps a ladder might be provided? Or a parachute?—then say offhandedly, 'Mr Darcy, as you can see, I already know how to ride. I simply do not enjoy it. You shall have to think of a different challenge.' Perhaps I shall add a dismissive little wave. And then I shall walk away as quickly as possible—without either breaking into a run or casting up my accounts. I can surely handle that much. A ride of a few minutes, no more.*

Her gloves contained her sweaty palms, but beads were forming upon her forehead—hopefully disguised by Jane's foolish brimmed hat. She saw no mounting block; he must mean to hoist her up. Vaguely, she was aware of a stream of instructions spilling from his mouth, but she could not hear a word he said over the roaring in her ears. She nodded and smiled and pretended to listen. *Five minutes, Elizabeth. You can stay mounted for five stupid minutes.*

He formed his own gloved hands into a stirrup, and she placed one booted foot upon them, tentatively reaching for the reins. The scent of shaving soap and leather and horse swamped her. At that moment, the mount shifted, and instead of allowing him to heave her onto the saddle, she twisted, throwing her arms around his neck and gripping him for dear life.

One moment, he had been explaining the fundamentals of horsemanship and reassuring Elizabeth that Sophie was the gentlest mare in the stables. Sophie was not, perhaps, the most ideal for a beginner, for all Bingley's horses were Thoroughbreds, better on the racecourse or the hunting fields than with a new rider. But he had intended to simply show her the basics, lead her about the ring, and then take her for a ride in his curricle.

Trembling, she buried her face in his neckcloth.

"Under most circumstances, I would highly encourage you to continue with all enthusiasm in clinging to my person," he said. "There is, unfortunately, a small matter of the requirements of air to flow through the passages of my throat and from thence, to my lungs. I shall not be gluttonous. I need not consume a whole breath. A mere thimbleful should suffice."

He could hardly credit her terror—she had always seemed so spirited. But since it appeared the horse was its cause, as he spoke, he quickly strode further away from it. The further he distanced himself from the animal, the better control she gained over herself. But they were nearly to the forested path—out of sight of the stables—before he felt he could slow.

She was taking deep, panting breaths; when he halted, she looked up at him and then quickly away.

"Put me down, please."

"I would not see you swoon."

"I am well. I apologise. Please, set me down."

"I must return Sophie to her stable. I beg you, await me here."

"Yes. Of course," she said agreeably.

He looked at her with some suspicion. "I will be a few minutes only. You shall remain in this spot."

"As you wish."

He carefully set her down. She wobbled a bit but was quickly steady on her feet. "It was nothing. I only need a moment of, um, quiet. Go. Restore Sophie to her stable."

Twice more, he cautioned her to wait for him. Then he turned towards the stables using his quickest stride. The first time he looked back, she stood on the path still, looking absurdly small and dejected. The second time he turned around, she was no longer anywhere in sight.

Elizabeth ran. She ran as far and as fast as she could. She wanted to run until she ran off the face of the earth.

But Jane's stupid riding costume was a bit too large and had a stupid clumsy skirt, forever catching on things, and even though the morning was cool, and the shadowy woods were cooler still, she grew hot and breathless. She was not even quite certain where she was—being not as familiar with Netherfield's park as her own. *Good.* Perhaps she would remain lost forever, having promised not to go home to Longbourn, since she could never face Mr Darcy again. She flopped grace-lessly down beneath a towering oak and tried not to think, to empty her mind and pretend she was someone else. *Pearl Harrington, perhaps, who will probably be Mrs Reginald Goulding by this time next year.*

Elizabeth did not envy Pearl, not really; she had dealt with the hurt long ago, and knew herself to be the wrong woman for Reggie. After all, if she could not bear his kisses, how could she bear his children? It was her pride that had been wounded, not her heart. If she must be rejected by her first love, it was best that she had been judged for her lack of fortune, not her lack of...of proper affection. How mortifying that, just as she was discovering she might be mistaken in her beliefs regarding said affections, she should make such a goose of herself. Mr Darcy was as different from Reginald Goulding as night was from day, and his kisses would have been different too. At least those old memories were no longer so distressing; what a shame that she would have no better ones to replace them.

Birdsong flitted through the trees, and the sounds of rustles and chitters as forest creatures returned to whatever activities she had disturbed gradually soothed her panic. It was peaceful here. A good place to live out the rest of her days. She could construct her own hermitage, and perhaps some intrepid explorer in a century or so would come across her hut and display it in a museum beside clay pots. *Ancient woman's habitat,* the placard would say.

After a time, however, she heard the sounds of a creature rather larger than a squirrel or rabbit crashing through the underbrush.

I hope it is a bear, she thought morosely, even though she had never heard of bears in the wilds of Hertfordshire. If she had to be eaten by a wild beast, she would prefer her carcass feed a bear rather than wolves or, heaven forbid, disgusting rats.

But it was Dubitz who came bounding towards her, with glad, excited whimpers and whines at the sight of her, as if she were his favourite person in the whole world. And then he did what seemed an odd gesture—he placed his enormous paws upon her shoulders, not leaping upon her but more like an embrace. It was quite a peculiar thing for a dog to do, but Elizabeth wrapped her arms around his ungainly, furry body and hugged him back. The tears came then, useless, weak tears, leaking into his silly topknot.

"Oh, Dubitz," she said. "I am such an idiot."

In response, he licked her chin.

"Would you like to run away with me?" she sniffed. "I have never been to Wales. Or perhaps Arabia."

He whined his eager agreement, adding another lick for good measure.

"Thank you," she said, smiling through her tears. "We shall leave a note for our families and friends— perhaps that we have gone to have tea with the queen, thus they must not worry. Arabia it is."

"Living in tents," Mr Darcy said, suddenly appearing in the glade like a great black shadow. "Sand in your boots and other, even less appealing places. It sounds very uncomfortable."

"Pulling up stakes whenever one has made a great fool of oneself. Simply pack up the camel and discover a new oasis where no one else has ever heard one's name —it sounds ideal to me." Dubitz, the fickle lover, left her embrace to gambol joyfully around Mr Darcy. She searched her pocket for a handkerchief and came up empty.

Mr Darcy seated himself beside her and handed over his. Drying her tears, she wondered why so often in his presence, she found herself wishing to evaporate into nothingness. Could she possibly humiliate herself any further? She tried so hard, always, to face life fearlessly, only to be caught short every time with him.

Dubitz abandoned them both in favour of a winsome butterfly, practically doing somersaults to gain its attention, as if to show her how silly it was to retain any worries over dignity.

"I apologise," he said at last into the silence, when it became clear she was not going to contribute to any sort of conversation.

"You did nothing wrong and have no reason to."

"I put you in a position of either confessing a deeply personal fear, or else attempting to do something you were in no way prepared to do."

"Oh. Well then, yes. It is all your fault, and we will leave it at that."

From the corner of her eye, she saw his lips twitch. And then, to her surprise, he brought one of his arms about her and tucked her into his side. "Dubitz was allowed an embrace. I am at least as comforting as he is."

She sat frozen; he was not comforting, not at all. From this position, she could feel the strength of his arms, the hardness of his chest, see the new growth of whiskers on his firm, clefted chin. Instead of fear, however, the sensation of being held by him was alluring, enthralling. Her hands were weak, mindless puppets to the desire she felt to glide them up his chest and press herself closer.

To be sure, you ought to assault him now, she reproved

herself with keen mental sarcasm, *while he thinks you an object of pity. Let us not forget how you have already embarrassed yourself with your opinions of kissing and tongues.*

"How did it begin?" he asked softly. "The fear, I mean."

"With hubris," she confessed, for even talking about one of the most painful episodes of her life was better than dwelling on these new, bewildering feelings she did not understand. "I considered myself quite the horsewoman. I was more skilled than my sisters, to be sure, and I enjoyed showing off my talent for trotting. And then one day, someone dared me to take a jump. I was a bit scared but too proud to admit it." She could still remember those feelings—Reggie laughing with John Lucas, teasing her for being spineless, her determination to excel at a skill Reggie admired.

"From a side-saddle? That was dangerous."

"Yes."

He frowned his disapproval. "You were thrown?"

"No, not then. I completed the jump, and I was crowing about it to Reginald—the boy who dared me—when...I am not exactly certain what spooked the horse, but Mr Hill found the swelling of an insect bite or a bee sting. I had not been paying attention to my seat in the moment he reared. My skirts caught on the pommel or tangled in the reins, and I was dragged..."

Elizabeth had to stop talking, reminding herself to breathe. She never spoke of those terrifying seconds or minutes—she had no idea of how much time had passed—before she lost consciousness. Witnesses had filled in the blanks of her memory, but all she truly recalled was wrenching pain and abject terror.

His arms tightened about her, and the warmth and

security of it somehow made the tears, so recently forced back, trickle out again.

"I was sixteen. I ought to be past it by now," she admitted, shutting her eyes tightly in the hopes that the tears would stop. Dubitz, as if sensing her distress, helpfully draped himself across her feet. "I did not, even, break any bones. Just an excruciating headache, a few bruises, and soon I was good as new."

"You could have died," he said gruffly. "I am uncertain if there is any 'getting past' such a terrifying accident." He did not loosen his hold. "And also, my lecture on overcoming heedless fears, which I thoughtfully prepared while searching for you, is rendered completely asinine. You have more than met this challenge, simply in your attempt to face such a thing. Dash it, Elizabeth, you could have died."

And his mouth lowered, and she thought *oh, kiss me, please,* and at the same time, *I cannot possibly be wishing to kiss Mr Darcy!*

But that mouth did not descend to hers; instead, he dropped sweet, small touches of his lips upon her tears, as if he could, somehow, take them into himself. He was so gentle, and so sympathetic, that she simply stilled in his arms and accepted his affection, absorbed it like sunshine. And then, one-handed, he withdrew the pins holding the silly hat in place and gently unwound her hair from the simple chignon in which she had tightly contained it, combing through her locks with his fingers until the masses of her hair flowed over her shoulders, down to her waist.

"Great gads, your hair is beautiful," he murmured. "I have wanted to see it like this. I have dreamt of it."

She blushed, feeling more beautiful than she ever

had in her life. Could it possibly be love, these feelings? Or simply the compassion of a good man? The cessation of humiliation, a reprieve from dark memories? Or the intensity of his admiration? Did it matter?

She had thought herself 'in love' with Reggie from her first assembly at age fifteen, when he had claimed her first dance. But perhaps falling in love was not a momentous initial attraction, but a growing realisation that one's life was simply happier, better, when in company with a certain gentleman. That had never been the case with Reggie; in his presence, she had always been painfully aware of all the things she was not.

Daringly, she laid her head upon Mr Darcy's shoulder, and they sat in the woods together and talked... simply talked, until trembling and tears were past. He told her of Pemberley, of what it had felt like to assume its control whilst most of his friends were still behaving as boys in town. She had nothing so earth-shattering to speak about—but he had a thousand questions for her regardless, about growing up with four sisters, about her relations, even of her favourite and least favourite foods. So, when he asked her how she had escaped her terrible encounter with the horse, she easily answered.

"Reginald Goulding got hold of the reins and somehow calmed the horse. I was unconscious by then, so I do not recall it. But I am told he carried me to Longbourn and then rode all the way to Hamblin for a doctor."

"Ah, I see. Was he, by chance, your first kiss?"

She turned sharply to look up at him. "How could you guess such a thing?"

He shrugged. "It only makes sense. You are not some

flibbertigibbet girl who would be free with your affections. He was your hero."

"Until he was not."

"I suppose that I can be thankful that he was not completely worthless when he was needed, even though he was an ignorant sapscull as a lover. I shall not plant him a facer, since he saved your life. But we must return to Netherfield, I suppose, before I surrender to the approximately ten thousand temptations I am currently wrestling against, especially the one which wants to make your experience with kisses a much improved one."

She looked into his eyes, those devilish, chocolate-coloured eyes regarding her so intently, and blushed again. "You already have," she said quietly. "At least...I think they were kisses."

Replying nothing, he helped her to stand, to find her hat, to brush off her skirts, whilst Dubitz pranced happily about them, eager to resume his walk. They did not speak as she took his arm and allowed him to lead her out of the woods and back to Netherfield—not until they were nearly at the terrace steps, Dubitz racing around them in excited circles all the journey back.

Mr Darcy stopped there, looking down at her. She held his gaze, feeling utterly caught within it.

"Just so you understand," he said in low tones, "I have not kissed you, not yet. When I do, you shall be completely certain that I have. I will return Dubitz to the stables now."

With a long-legged stride he walked away, giving a short, sharp whistle that not even Dubitz dared disobey.

At dinner that evening, Mrs Bennet waxed on about shopping in town at her favourite warehouses; she did not specifically mention wedding clothes, but her intent was obvious to Elizabeth. Mr Darcy bore it with civility, answering her inane questions with forbearance; Miss Darcy hardly seemed to notice there *was* a conversation. Elizabeth contributed what she could, although her thoughts were muddled with memories of not-kisses and being held in his arms —and such remembrances were not conducive to scintillating exchange.

After dining, they retired to the music room, where Mr Darcy urged a very reluctant Miss Darcy to play. She finally did so, and beautifully. Elizabeth was caught up in her playing—the girl was certainly more skilled than any master Mr Bennet had ever employed. She could even appreciate the opportunity to look her fill at the well-formed Mr Darcy, who was turning her pages. At his urging, she played another but then quickly returned to her seat, head down, not meeting anyone's gaze.

Unfortunately, Mrs Bennet, not to be outdone, urged Elizabeth to the instrument next; Elizabeth began a refusal, having no desire to follow such expertise as Miss Darcy possessed.

"Lizzy, you must play!" Mrs Bennet interrupted her protests. "All of my girls play, Mr Darcy. I insist upon such accomplishments. They are masters of all the feminine arts. Well, except for drawing. We hired a drawing master, and the only art he had mastered was drawing down his bree—"

"Mama!" Elizabeth squeaked, horrified, but Mrs Bennet waved this caution away.

"Oh, I did not put all the blame with Sally, our maid. She is still employed, is she not? I am never one to say that the fault lies with the female when it is the man who Tills the Fields of Forbidden Farms. Besides, she is an excellent worker, and good servants are so hard to find."

"Please, Mama, you must not speak of such things!"

"I would not, except with family. We are all *family* here, are we not?"

She had managed to capture the attention of Miss Darcy, unfortunately, who now watched them with curiosity. Elizabeth resisted the temptation to run from the room or dump the teapot over her mother's head. "I will play, if you will stop speaking!" she hissed.

Mrs Bennet smiled beatifically, leaning back on the settee with satisfaction. Elizabeth thumbed through the available music, looking for something she could play without embarrassing herself too greatly—much too conscious of Mr Darcy's eyes upon her. Fortunately, she found a piece she had once known well, one that she could probably fumble her way through.

After the first few stanzas, her fingers recalled the notes and she felt steady enough to whisper a few words to her page-turner. "If you could forget the last few minutes, I would deeply appreciate it."

"Forget what?" he murmured.

Smiling, she glanced up at him—and missed a note at his expression. There seemed such tenderness in it! *But I am likely imagining what I wish to see,* she thought. What man of his status could overlook such a mother?

The next morning at breakfast, Elizabeth was burning with curiosity regarding Mr Darcy's next challenge. She made the usual motions of attempted conversation with Miss Darcy, receiving the usual lack of result. Why, she wondered, did the girl even come down to breakfast, since she obviously had no intention of speaking to anyone? Georgiana Darcy was a mystery, to be certain, and she was not sorry when the girl quietly excused herself. It was not until she had departed, though, that another possibility entered Elizabeth's mind: Did Miss Darcy know about the supposed forced engagement between Elizabeth and her brother? And if she knew, did she object? Did her diffidence disguise hostility, although she was always so polite? It was one explanation; she must be aware of the difference between their relative stations in life, and had already been subjected to Mama's crassness. *Besides, if one of my sisters were to be forced by circumstance into an unlooked-for betrothal, I might feel upset by it! What had he told her? What had been her response? Should I ask him?*

When the message from Mr Darcy finally arrived,

Elizabeth took it out of doors to read it, finding a conveniently placed bench near one of the garden paths. She was fascinated by his willingness to play this little game, to tease her and intrigue her. After all, what else could be the point of the exercise?

Once again, the message was brief. And, in a different way, it was as unwelcome as had been the previous day's challenge to ride a horse.

Attempt to befriend my sister.

His very wording told her how difficult he believed the prospect. 'Attempt' to befriend Miss Darcy, as if he felt there was not much chance of success.

Annoyance filled her. Had she not, already, *been* attempting it? With no encouragement at all from the girl, of course! Talking to Miss Darcy was like speaking to a prisoner locked within a gaol; every word she pitched over the high barrier surrounding the girl's emotions *might* have landed, but one would never know it, much less see it happen.

Still, after a few moments of indignation, another thought took hold. In fact, she felt rather stupid for the amazement it produced. Had she been considering kisses, affection, even *love*…without following such thoughts to their natural conclusion? Had her wounded pride concerning everything to do with him blinded her to the depth of her own involvement?

Am I seriously considering marrying *Mr Darcy?*

He had, or very nearly had, told her he loved her. One would think he should be fighting tooth and nail to release himself from this engagement, the result of a foolish accident—her *own* hasty clumsiness. He could be maddening, it was true. She did not suppose, if they *did* marry, that it was the last time she would wish to box him in the ears. Nevertheless, he had instantly encouraged the betrothal. If he fought anything at all, it was only a fight to know her, to allow her to know him.

In other words, he had utterly set her every impression of him upon its head. Perhaps, however, she could be forgiven for her astonishment. Only three days ago, she had believed him to be her enemy.

On the heels of this epiphany, another occurred. *If I marry him, Miss Darcy will be* my *sister.*

The thought was somewhat off-putting. How old was she? In appearance, perhaps eighteen years of age...but something about her seemed younger. And she was certain Jane had informed her that she was not yet out—she almost certainly should have had a season if she had reached her eighteenth year.

Would he expect Elizabeth to bring her out? Surely not—there must be a more qualified relation who would be responsible for such matters. In fact, he might expect that same relation to put a bit of the town bronze upon his bride! He knew her only visits to London had been to Gracechurch Street near Cheapside, after all.

But *if* she married him, regardless of Miss Darcy's seasons or her future, they would always be sisters, related by that marriage. They must become friends, or learn to be. Did she want Mr Darcy enough to undertake the challenge of his unsociable sister?

Elizabeth had always hated the contention between her parents, the lack of understanding, even those sarcastic rejoinders from her father that she had so often found amusing. She wanted a peaceful home, insomuch as one could plan for such a thing.

Never forget, Elizabeth, her father often said, *when one takes a spouse, one takes on the spouse's entire family.*

Mr Bennet disliked Mrs Philips intensely, but what could he do? She was the elder sister of his wife, and thus the Philipses were welcomed at Longbourn.

Did Miss Darcy imagine, with disgust, the Bennet family descending upon Pemberley? Did she realise the foolish Mr Collins was Elizabeth's near relation? It was a humbling thought.

Were Mr and Mrs Collins still in Hertfordshire with the Lucases? Had Charlotte discovered that Elizabeth was yet at Netherfield? Had word of her supposed betrothal spread *past* the Lucases? Strangely, she felt no panic at the idea. It seemed her mind had been accommodating a possible engagement without her notice. But could she accept the brother over the sister's vehement objections? *Did* the sister object?

Well then. It seemed she had a sister to befriend. Or at least…attempt to.

After delivering his challenge, Darcy took to Bingley's study to attempt to shrink his pile of correspondence. He had expended a good deal of time that morning deciding whether or not to propose this particular challenge to Elizabeth. Several hours later, he still did not know whether he had made the correct decision.

He had seen her treat his sister with friendliness and civility. Georgiana, for the most part, retreated from any and all attempts at sociability and was especially anxious about coming to know Miss Bennet. She had been horrified, of course, when he had informed her that the dog had knocked her down. But the incident had put a damper on Georgie's fortitude, which was already so tentative.

Perhaps he ought to have told Elizabeth everything. He had wished to, of course. It had seemed wrong to do so while Wickham was still in the area, even though coming here had been Georgie's idea. He knew where Georgiana would spend *her* day—in her room, except when she visited Dubitz. Should he talk of her troubles to the woman he hoped would be his bride? Or would it prejudice her towards Georgiana, who was already difficult to know, and embarrass them both?

Determinedly, he applied himself to his letters. He then took Bingley's hunter out for a long gallop. He returned only just in time to ready himself for tea.

The ride had not lessened his worries about his sister. Nothing usually did. But as he descended the stairs, he caught sight of Elizabeth at the bottom of them. She smiled at him, and his mood, which had been worried and dismal, spun into an instantaneously cheerful humour. He offered her his arm to escort her into the large drawing room and would have offered her much more of his body than that, had it been at all appropriate for public display. And it seemed better to him, after all, to simply allow Elizabeth—so kind, so wise, so much better than he at every social grace—to do whatever she felt best regarding Georgiana, with as little interference as possible from himself.

By rising early, Elizabeth ensured that she would be first to breakfast the next morning. It had not helped their previous conversations, or lack thereof, that Miss Darcy was nearly finished eating by the time Elizabeth had filled her plate.

By the surprised look on the younger girl's face when Elizabeth entered, it was obvious that Miss Darcy had planned it thus, to avoid having to dine with others. Since there was no one else to avoid at breakfast *except* Elizabeth, it was a bit disheartening—but she was determined to try.

She began with a more direct approach, avoiding the usual topics of weather and health, as well as any question that could be answered with a mere yea or nay. "When did you begin playing? I admire your skill at the pianoforte," she said.

Miss Darcy mumbled a reply that might have been, 'Ages ago,' or perhaps, 'I do not know.'

"My sister Mary loves to play. In fact, she practises so much that the rest of us cannot, usually, find a time to use the instrument. At least, that is the excuse I give when my lack of expertise shows, as it did night before last."

"Hm."

This was going nowhere. Miss Darcy would not even meet her eyes. And yet...she recalled Miss Bingley's laudations and wondered if the girl was assaulted with the unwanted attentions of every young lady determined to reach Mr Darcy by means of her friendship. *Am I not doing the same? Not manipulatively, but might not such efforts seem identical to her?*

She resisted the temptation to sigh, and they both ate in silence. It seemed important to have more of a genuine conversation, but of course, it was impossible with the footman attending. Very soon, Miss Darcy would finish her breakfast and make her escape.

At last, Elizabeth said, "Miss Darcy, I know you are eager to return to your chambers but...but would you do me the very great favour of a walk in the garden first? I promise not to keep you out long."

For a few moments, she thought there might be no answer at all. But at last, Miss Darcy nodded, and Elizabeth secured an agreement to meet again at the terrace in a quarter-hour. Elizabeth waited to go upstairs herself until the younger girl left the breakfast parlour, just to avoid the discomfort of having to walk up the stairs together without a single word exchanged. Mr Darcy's challenge was not looking promising. Not at all.

❦

"Did your brother tell you that we are, for the moment at least, engaged?"

They had been strolling through a pretty garden path, and even though they had been quiet, it had somehow not seemed as awkward as their previous times together indoors. The morning was fine, and beneath their parasols, with only flowers for an audience, there was a sense of privacy and even tranquillity not to be found in the house.

Miss Darcy's head snapped up, staring at Elizabeth, her eyes wide with surprise.

"Ah. I see he has not mentioned it. It is a bit of a pickle, and I am its cause, I am afraid." She told her the whole story, sparing neither herself nor Mr Darcy. "Not to make an excuse, but I was very fatigued, on account of all the wedding preparations, and not really myself at the moment...or else, I am an up-and-coming harridan and will only grow worse as I age. I was trying to explain to him how large a muddle it all was, with Jane in a lather and refusing to leave on her wedding trip, and he was looking at me as I spoke, but...oh, my father often wears a similar expression when my mother is haranguing him—as though he is recalling something he read in the newspaper or the apple tart he had at tea—a vacant sort of look. When I see it, I know that, even if he were to parrot her sentences back to her, an essential part of him is not paying any attention at all."

This last was the hardest part to admit, especially to someone she would rather impress. "I-I *know* how unmannerly it all sounds, but I thought to deliver some cutting remark and flee, simply run away. Unfortunately, I tripped, and next I knew, I was toppling."

"Oh," Miss Darcy said, her eyes wide. "Oh, my."

"It gets worse," Elizabeth said, her cheeks pink with the recollection. "As I fell, your brother— being unprepared for a great tempest of a female to blunder into furniture—attempted to catch me. Stupidly, in the moment, I did not stop to think. He was suddenly atop me, and I did not, um, respond decorously. Just as I began to realise that he was trying to *save* me, at a very *inopportune* moment, my father and a couple of his cronies stormed the summerhouse." Her brow furrowed. "I do not know how they knew we were there in the first place, but they were in their cups and seemed to be up in arms from the outset. They drew the worst possible conclusions, and to avoid, um, more unpleasantness, your brother immediately proposed marriage."

"Oh," she said again, returning her gaze to the path.

"He says he will try to get us out of it," Elizabeth added.

Miss Darcy muttered something under her breath

that sounded almost like 'When pigs will fly.' Elizabeth quickly dismissed the idea, deciding she must have misheard another 'Oh, my.'

She took a deep breath, determined to finish. "I, obviously, do not frequent the circles you inhabit. My portion is small, and my father's estate is entailed upon Mr Collins—you probably met him at the wedding. My birth is well enough, but my mother...you have met her. She was not born a lady, and it often shows. *She* is determined that the marriage go forward, which is why she stays at Netherfield and insists I remain too. I would not blame you for objecting to the match on all counts."

"I-I wish nothing except my brother's happiness. It... it is not my place to object to his decisions," Miss Darcy said quietly. She looked over at Elizabeth for a long moment, as if she wished to say more. But her natural diffidence was real; clearly, it was difficult for the girl to express her feelings.

"Perhaps not, but your opinions on the matter *are* important to me. Your brother and I are beginning to become better acquainted. It remains to be seen if any wedding shall take place, but I am hoping that you and I could make an effort, at least, to form a closer acquaintance. Learn a bit about each other, and possibly even become friends?"

"I...that is, yes, of course, Miss Bennet." Her words were polite, but she sounded extremely uncertain.

"I hope you will call me Elizabeth. And while I do wish we might come to know each other, I have no wish to be your interrogator. If I ask something that you do not want to answer, please just tell me. I will not ever think you rude. I have four sisters—I think you have been introduced to them all—and we each have very different ideas about what constitutes good conversation. Lydia likes to talk of men, Kitty favours sleeves and bonnets, although men are a close second with her, Mary prefers sermonising, and Jane loves quiet, homely things, such as the exchange of menus and her stitchery projects."

In silence, they walked a little further, approaching the point where the path widened to allow for some rather unrestrained statuary before curving back towards the house. It would be an easy place for the younger girl to make her escape.

"I-I am Georgiana. What do *you* prefer to, um, speak of, Elizabeth?"

It was impossible not to feel greatly encouraged at this obvious overture, and she could have hugged her companion. She took her arm instead, leading her on a different path across the lawns. "Oh, I suppose 'a host of golden daffodils' or the 'Wisdom and Spirit of the universe'. Either will do! I love poetry and novels and even sometimes my father's farming journals...but am bored easily too, if matters grow too scientific or pious. I like to sew, although I am not so accomplished as Jane. The fun I have is in selecting the thread colours and imagining the finished work, not necessarily in the tedium of the actual stitches. Thus, I always have three or four such projects in progress, and around Michaelmas each year, I begin to be frantic that nothing will be ready in time for Christmas!"

Darcy glanced down from Bingley's study window and saw a sight so lovely he thought he might be dreaming.

It was Elizabeth and Georgiana walking arm in arm together, one in yellow, one in rose, their flowering parasols and maiden laughter and the beauty of the day making his heart swell with optimism as it had not done in a long, long while.

10

Elizabeth was feeling rather hopeful regarding the future. Last evening's dinner had been the most pleasant of any they had shared together. Granted, her mother's contributions had been of limited merit—she went on at great length regarding the improvements she had made to Netherfield's menus. Mrs Bennet seemed to be rapidly ascending Netherfield's throne, and Jane might find her rather difficult to depose.

Still, Georgiana had ventured a remark or two, and Mr Darcy had positively beamed at them both every time she spoke. Elizabeth turned her pages when they again retired to the music room after dinner, and then together, they tried a simple four-hand piece, in which Elizabeth's mistakes were not too noticeable and covered rather easily by Georgiana's skill.

It had been...fun, nearly, even if she must be so callously reminded of how little she had practised her playing in the last year or two.

The next morning at breakfast, she suggested to

Georgiana they take a walk into Meryton. "Two days in a row of fine weather is not to be disregarded. Besides, it is time I begin an embroidery for Mama's birthday, and we might as well inspect Edgerton's ribbon inventory while we are there."

It was also time to see how local gossip might be framing her stay at Netherfield, but she did not mention that and was pleased when Georgiana easily agreed to the outing. The ladies settled upon meeting for the walk in the early afternoon, their plans for the day happily arranged.

❦

The afternoon sun was shining brightly when they left for the town. "I should have asked if you might prefer taking a carriage," Elizabeth said, after they had walked for a time in companionable silence. "I am a great walker myself, but not everyone shares my enthusiasm."

"My brother is, um, somewhat protective. A walk, unaccompanied, seems a bit of a lark, actually. I cannot think of a time when I was ever allowed to walk to Lambton—the nearest town to Pemberley. But of course, it would be a much longer walk than this one."

They were the most words about her feelings Georgiana had ever uttered at once, and Elizabeth's first thought was triumph. It was followed, unfortunately, by a feeling that she might not be behaving exactly as was proper for a Darcy. She had not seen Mr Darcy yet today, had not shared their plans with anyone except Mrs Bennet. Her guilt at the notion of angering him sparked an immediate thread of annoyance. Was it not Georgiana's duty to report to him, not hers? She had been walking with her sisters to Meryton from Longbourn for half her life without any harm ever coming of it. The idea of bringing a maid or footman had never even crossed her mind, and taking a carriage more excessive still. And yet...

"We could return for the carriage and a maid, if your brother would not approve," she offered.

"Oh, as to that, I could have driven the curricle—I am an excellent driver. But...but a walk seemed lovely," Georgiana replied, still with a touch of shyness.

Elizabeth took her arm. "Really? Drive yourself? But that is wonderful!" She even proceeded to tell the younger girl about her catastrophic 'riding lesson', making a joke of her fears—and both were giggling by the time they entered Meryton.

Elizabeth smiled and nodded to her many acquaintances, but she introduced no one to Georgiana until they entered Edgerton's, where Pearl Harrington stood at the counter with Mr Edgerton. They spoke companionably for a few moments—or rather, Elizabeth did the speaking. But it was not at all awkward. She happily introduced Georgiana, feeling a complete absence of worry regarding any gossip their appearance in the village might provoke. They admired the selection of ribbons, and both picked out a few; Elizabeth also chose some new thread colours for the handkerchief she meant to embroider. Mr Edgerton wrapped their purchases, and they had hardly left the shop when Pearl excitedly approached them once again.

"Oh, Elizabeth—the lieutenant is at Willoughby's. Flirting with Miss King, no doubt, for she is there with her aunt. But do say you will come with me. I want him to attend our garden party—if he comes, it is sure to be a success." As she excitedly spoke, Elizabeth noticed Reginald Goulding a few feet away, glaring at Pearl.

This *was* a pickle. There was no question of *which* lieutenant it was to whom Pearl referred; gossip had pointed of late to Mr Wickham's obvious attentions to Miss Mary King. He was a popular guest, and when he was known to be gracing any event, a host of ladies, as well as other officers, were sure to turn up as well. But in no way would Mr Darcy want his sister exposed to Mr Wickham, not for any reason. At the same time, Elizabeth was not certain what ought to be said in the neighbourhood regarding the man—it was really a question for her father, she believed. Therefore, she made a quick excuse.

"I am sorry, Pearl, but Miss Darcy and I must hurry back to Netherfield. Mr Darcy is expecting his sister home shortly and would surely be displeased if we were to be late."

She felt a little discomfort for trading upon Mr Darcy's reputation for surliness; Georgiana frowned at her in some surprise. Thankfully, she was too shy to contradict her.

"Oh, pooh. Miss Darcy, surely you can explain to your brother—"

"Let the girl obey her brother's wishes, Miss Harrington," the young Mr Goulding interrupted, sounding seriously annoyed.

Pearl rolled her eyes at his brusque words. "If *he* were more amiable and pleasing, *he* might not spend his time envying one who *is*," she muttered, for their ears only. But thankfully, she turned back to Reginald, leaving Elizabeth to hurry Georgiana away.

Unfortunately, they must pass Willoughby's Linen-

Drapers on their return. Elizabeth could only hope that they would not see Mr Wickham, as they had not on their way to Edgerton's, but to be sure, she crossed the narrow street to pass on the other side, speeding up her already quick pace as they approached it.

They were unlucky, however.

"Miss Bennet!" Lieutenant Wickham's voice was all joviality. "It has been a long while, has it not? I hope, now that the grand wedding is past, you will have time to remember your friends?"

When contemplating the incident later, she realised she should simply have continued walking with no acknowledgement that he had spoken. But manners and expectation prevailed; several people were near, and in the moment, it had seemed less conspicuous to simply get the ordeal over with—a quick spot of conversation rather than giving him the cut direct, which would have meant endless, embarrassing enquiry later.

"We are in a hurry, sir, and cannot stop to chat," she said, coldly, she knew. But she saw he barely paid attention, saw the slight surprise upon his face as he noticed her companion—whom she had naively hoped he would *not* recognise.

"Why, it is Miss Darcy, as I live and breathe," he cried. "I had no idea you were in the area. Do I interrupt your ramble?" Immediately, he hurried towards them.

Georgiana, her arm in Elizabeth's, stiffened. Elizabeth saw the lieutenant look from herself to her companion, a definite calculation in his gaze. He was wondering, she supposed, how much she might have learnt of his true past, how her connexion to Mr Darcy might have changed. Georgiana, obviously, remembered him and almost certainly had been informed of his failings. It seemed most prudent to beat a hasty retreat.

"You certainly do," she replied, unable to summon anything more polite in response. "We are in a hurry today and must not stop." They continued walking, but to her chagrin, he fell in step beside Georgiana.

"You appear quite grown up since our last meeting, Miss Darcy," he said, all charm and affability. "Do you remember me? You cried, I think, to see me go on that last occasion. Such a darling little thing you were, so welcoming and friendly."

Georgiana answered nothing. She looked neither to the left nor to the right, but stumbled a bit upon a rough spot on the pavement. Elizabeth tightened her hold upon the girl's arm, concerned.

"Oh, that final sweet embrace," Mr Wickham went on, with rapt sincerity. "I recall it so fondly. Did you think, my dear, that we would never part? I thought so. I believed I would be the next thing to family, always. But of course, if I had been given the living I ought to have had, it would have answered all my ideas of happiness."

Georgiana remained silent, and Elizabeth, annoyed, tried to extract her from another rehearsal of his woes.

"I have heard, from good authority, that there was a time when sermon-making was not so palatable to you as it seems to be at present—that you declared your resolution of *never* taking orders, and that you received recompense accordingly."

"Did you? I suppose your information is not wholly without foundation. You may remember what I told you on that point, when first we talked of it."

"I only remember a single point of view, casting others not present to defend themselves in an ill light."

The street was bustling, her friends and neighbours practically surrounding them. They had almost reached the edge of town—nearly to her aunt Philips's home. Should she whisk the girl inside? But her aunt's interrogations could be more exasperating than Mr Wickham's, and of course, he was often welcomed there—nothing would prevent him from following them in. It seemed best to keep walking.

"Come, come, Miss Bennet, do not let us quarrel about the past," he said, still jovial. "It is the future which concerns me now. Surely, Miss Darcy, *your* memories of me are only happy ones?"

A sound escaped Georgiana at last, something between a gasp and a sob. While there was nothing in his words which ought to have been so harrowing, it was suddenly plain to Elizabeth that he was, somehow, poking at her. Rage filled her; it was bad enough that he had defamed the brother, but the sister whom he deliberately goaded was a gentle, fragile thing.

What she might have said in reply, however, she would never know. Their quick steps had taken them past the green, nearing the point where the road split in two directions. A polished black curricle rounded the curve, with Mr Darcy driving it. A vast relief filled her at the sight of him. He would put this wretch in his place!

Halting his cattle, and, leaving the reins slack, he leapt from the vehicle. When he reached them, he held his arm out to his sister. She let go of Elizabeth's to take his. His face was utterly white; Mr Wickham's, she saw, was utterly red. It reminded her of the first time she had seen them together, very near this exact spot. After a moment, Mr Wickham touched his hat, but Mr Darcy granted no such acknowledgement. He only looked at

Elizabeth, and it seemed to her that fury limned his countenance.

He glanced up at her aunt Philips's home—they were practically upon her doorstep. Elizabeth could only hope she was not watching from her front parlour window. "You will await me at your aunt's home, Miss Bennet. I will return for you very shortly."

Without waiting to see if she had anything to say to this directive, he hurried his sister to the curricle. Moments later, she watched him turn the vehicle where the road widened and then disappear in a cloud of dust.

Mr Wickham looked at her, again with that assessing air. "I am surprised to see him returned to the area, and with Miss Darcy, too. He is a very kind and careful guardian of his sister—some might say, *too* careful, *too* attentive. I would not like to be a female under *his* protection, for he is a most jealous overseer. So likely to misconstrue the most meaningless encounters."

But Elizabeth was in no mood for his insinuating remarks. "Really? Is that the best you can do to defame him? He does not like you. He has no reason in the world to like you, and you know it. He is her guardian. It is his right—nay, his duty, to remove her from your presence."

His face, which she had once thought so handsome, turned obstinate and peevish.

"I see you, like so many others, have succumbed to the lure of his wealth and reputation. His father loved me, and Darcy allows his jealousy to rule his reason. I daresay the old man loved me more than his own son! If his father were alive, he would *order* him to give me the living!"

She looked at him in disbelief and then laughed—for

it seemed comical that this man would accuse Mr Darcy
—of all people—of his *own* sins. "Talk of jealousy! You
will whinge about your ill treatment forever, will you
not?"

He looked at her in some distaste, but she could not
prevent another chuckle as she pictured Mr Wickham in
clerical garb.

"The very idea of *you* giving s-sermons!" she said,
struck by the hilarity of it, covering her mouth, trying to
prevent herself from going off into whoops.

"Miss Bennet, is this fellow bothering you?"

It was Reginald Goulding, his expression in a full
glower now—and she realised how the scene might have
appeared to an onlooker. He probably thought she was
sobbing, and she quickly sobered.

"He is not," she replied. "However, I would prefer to
be talking with just about anyone else in England. How
does your father do, Mr Goulding?"

Mr Wickham had again grown very red in the face; he
touched his hat—which salutation, like Mr Darcy, Reginald did not return—turned on his heel and strode away.

Neither did Reginald answer her question regarding
old Mr Goulding's health. "A sorry excuse for a man, he
is. I never did like him, for all the ladies fluttering about
him like bees on honey. Miss Harrington says it is envy,
but it is not. What have I to envy? He owes Whitford six
shillings, has plenty of excuses about when he will bring
it round, but I say he is a slouch, and Whitford will be
the poorer for it. Are you engaged to Mr Darcy?"

His question—which had come so abruptly and unexpectedly at the end of his rant—wholly surprised her. Had
Pearl expressed the same question, she would have had a

quick and meaningless retort, but of all people, he was the *last* person she had expected to probe. They had talked of nothing more personal than the weather for years.

"If there is ever an engagement to *anyone* to announce, you may be certain your family will hear of it," Elizabeth said—sounding stilted to her own ears.

"That is no answer," he replied. "My father insinuated an attachment, but will not confirm it."

The entire conversation seemed remarkable. Was *Reginald Goulding* truly badgering her for these intimacies?

Before she could think how to reply, Pearl, quite out of breath, joined them, hearing the last part of his words. "Mr Goulding, you are not quizzing her about that silly betrothal rumour, are you? Everyone knows that arrogant Mr Darcy would never propose marriage to anyone less than a duke's daughter, and hinting of his admiration for Eliza is only one of your father's little jokes. I do not understand why you keep on so about it!" She turned quickly to Elizabeth. "I noticed you talking to the lieutenant—did you happen to mention my garden party?"

"You and that ridiculous party!" Reginald fumed. "You would invite Napoleon if you thought it would bring three more! Why your father allows that scoundrel in his home, against my every suggestion—"

"*You* are the one who is behaving ridiculous!" she cried.

Elizabeth took the opportunity of their bickering to back away and, when they failed to notice her retreat, turned in the direction of Netherfield and began the walk back. There was no question of going to Aunt

Philips's home; she would only ask a hundred questions if Mr Darcy called for her there.

She had briefly begun to think that perhaps a marriage to him might be an idea worth contemplating. Now, walking alone on the road, she reconsidered.

While she certainly could not blame him for his desire to remove his sister from Wickham's company, her own presence there had scarcely mattered to him. True, he believed refuge available in her aunt's home, but why had he not extracted both of them, if he felt the lieutenant so villainous? It would not have been difficult —he could have sent the blackguard on his way with a look, put them into his curricle, and then either led the horses or even allowed Georgiana to drive them back! *I am not a large woman. I could probably have squeezed onto the seat with them both!*

She had not felt herself in the slightest danger; indeed, he would have known she was not. But had Georgiana been in any, either? No, not at all. In Mr Darcy's moment of great dismay, he had cared *only* for his sister's welfare. His face when he had *ordered* her— for it was nothing less than a command—to stay with her aunt had been a cold mask. He probably blamed her for bringing Georgiana into Meryton at all. Evidently, his escort of 'Miss Darcy of Pemberley' was the only *important* matter.

I am merely Elizabeth Bennet, daughter of two nobodies, and nothing compared to his sister.

The embarrassment of the thought goaded her into a quicker pace.

Well, he cannot command me. It is best to know now that his feelings for me are so shallow, she told herself.

Unaccountably, however, she felt quite desolate. Oh,

to be able to return to Longbourn! *If only I had not given my word!*

Although she had not been in Meryton for long, it was apparent that the topic of her betrothal was *not* first on everyone's lips. Reginald had inexplicably bleated on about it, but Pearl had been quick to discount it. *I suppose my past abuse of Mr Darcy, so often, to so many, has been my defence. We could, apparently, be marooned alone together on an isle of the sea and still be thought an unsuitable match!*

After several minutes, she saw the approach of a vehicle on the road ahead—Mr Darcy, returning for her. His expression appeared stony, icy, angry, as if she had planned an *assignation* between Wickham and his sister. The coldness in his face trickled across the distance still separating them, right into her heart. It was just the miserable sort of thing a person of low morals might do —take a fragile, persuadable young girl like Georgiana and lead her into such an encounter.

Does he think so little of me?

He had wanted time, he had said, time for her to come to know him.

I know enough now, I think.

11

Darcy had accompanied his sister back to the house without his fury abating a single whit. Georgiana had remained a frozen statue all the way home, ignoring any of his attempts at comfort. As soon as they arrived at Netherfield, she practically leapt out of the curricle and raced to her chambers.

Why had Elizabeth taken such a risk going into the town, knowing as she did that the villainous Wickham was as likely to be there as not? Without even a maid or footman to lend them countenance! It had never occurred to him that she might suggest it! The very sight of the man was enough to spark rage, and to see him in company with the two most important women in his world had sent his temper soaring. Grimly, he had turned back towards Meryton; the only reason he had left her with her aunt was so that they could have this out in privacy.

However, off in the distance, he saw the lone figure of a woman, walking in quiet solitude on the country lane. There was no doubt of who it was, the bright blue colour of her dress identifying her as Elizabeth. There was also something dejected in her attitude, noticeable even from this distance—so unusual to her spirited demeanour, so the opposite of her lively disposition.

She knows nothing of Georgiana's humiliation, he reminded himself. How he wished he had revealed the episode!

But then something else occurred to him, only recalled in this moment. Elizabeth's expression as she had faced Wickham, seconds before she saw Darcy arrive; it had been one of unmitigated fury. He *knew* that expression. He had witnessed it himself, more than once. It calmed his own rage several degrees, remembering it.

A possibility blossomed in his mind—the two girls, walking alone to Meryton, obviously in the process of becoming good friends. Might Georgiana have shared *something* of her recent distress? Probably not the whole of it, but perhaps Wickham's importuning, and the awful effects of realising he cared only for her fortune? Ladies *did* confide in each other, much more often than a fellow might. And Georgiana had desperately needed such a friend.

He pulled up when he was but a few yards from her and hopped down. Her expression told him nothing. "You did not wait at your aunt's, I see," he said, giving her his hand to boost her into the curricle.

"No," was her only reply, situating herself as far from him as the seat would allow—which was not very far at all.

He climbed back in and took up the reins; he could not turn the vehicle around upon the narrow lane, and besides, it was a perfect day for a drive and for them to have a civil, private conversation regarding what had happened. He would avoid accusation, he decided handsomely. But they would come to a right understanding about where she might traipse off to alone, with or without Georgiana.

After a few moments, she spoke. "Any connexion, making such a match…it is ludicrous to imagine, as I am sure you would agree. It seems utterly impossible that it could even have been discussed."

His mood lightened another degree. So, Georgiana *had* confided in Elizabeth! But then why had she continued into town where the villain might be?

"This knowledge came to you very recently, I suppose," he guessed aloud. *Too late for her to prevent the meeting with Wickham, at the very least.*

"Oh…yes," she agreed.

Anger filled him at the very idea of his sister's near elopement. "It *was* ludicrous. Ludicrous and illogical and completely impossible. I cannot think, now, how it got so far as it did." He clutched the reins too tightly in his emotion, hating the recollection of Georgiana's attachment to the scoundrel, and then had to force himself to ease his grip for the sake of his cattle.

"Neither can I." Elizabeth's voice was colder than he had ever heard it.

Wickham has the same chilling effect upon me.

"The match could never take place, of course. Honour, decorum, prudence, nay, interest forbid it. Georgiana would be censured, slighted, and despised by everyone connected. The alliance would be a disgrace, considered only the upstart pretensions of one without family, connexions, or fortune—a patched-up business and hardly to be endured."

She gasped, but perhaps she had never considered just how low any connexion with Wickham might bring his sister, and so Darcy continued on in the same vein. Perhaps he should also explain about Mrs Younge and how she had abetted the scheme.

"I had truly supposed that I could trust that my sister would be safe with—"

"I think you have expressed censure enough. No one is entirely blameless," Elizabeth interrupted crisply.

He gave a great sigh, considering. She was not wrong. He ought to have hired Georgiana's companion himself, rather than leaving it to Lady Matlock.

"After all is said and done, the situation *is* entirely my responsibility. And I should have shared my misgivings with you earlier."

"That might have been wise."

Her tone sounded odd; he glanced over at her, but her expression was mostly hidden by her bonnet. "In regards to my sister, I am accustomed to a higher standard of discretion."

She stiffened, and he hoped she was not taking offence at his former silence. He simply had got into the habit of great protectiveness where Georgiana was concerned. "If you have any questions on the matter, please, feel free to ask me anything at all."

"Oh, I think 'the matter' has been over-talked and over-thought enough as it is."

It was with relief that he heard her words. He had no desire to speak of Georgiana's past. "I apologise for leaving you. I believed your aunt adequate protection for the few minutes I planned to be gone, and I wished to discuss this privately. I am certain you can understand the importance of removing Georgiana from Wickham's vicinity as quickly as possible."

"Naturally."

Her tone sounded a bit...sarcastic. But surely he imagined it. "It was always my intention to come back for you as soon as I had *her* safely to Netherfield."

"Of course."

They drove in silence for some minutes.

"The road widens just beyond the bend, if you recall. You can turn the curricle around there," she said at last.

He *did* recall it but felt no particular urge to hurry her back to Netherfield. A few minutes ago, he had been enraged and distressed, but now, the whole scene was beginning to pale in importance beside the opportunity to spend time alone with Elizabeth. It was exhilarating, really, to be driving out with the woman he loved—such a simple thing to do, a skill he had learnt as a boy and honed as a man—suddenly rendered exciting by her mere presence. They had both been upset by the unpleasant encounter; now was the time to put it behind them, to restore their equanimity. He would think about how to restore Georgiana's...later.

And so he kept driving, passing the wide spot.

"What are you doing?" she asked.

He glanced over at her but could only address her hat; she did not look at him. "It is a fine day. Would you like to drive on for a bit? The weather is perfect for it."

"Absolutely not. Please, turn back at once."

He started at the hostility of her tone; finally, she turned to look at him. He read incredulity and...resentment, for it was nothing less, in her gaze.

Was she angry that he had left her there in Meryton

with only Mrs Philips for protection? But then why had she set off utterly alone? Or was it something else?

"I might ask why, with so little endeavour at civility, I am thus rejected," he wondered aloud, as he considered another possibility. "Or do the horses frighten you? We could exchange the curricle for a different, less open, vehicle."

"You could not have made me the offer of a drive in any possible way that would have tempted me to accept it," she snapped, her cheeks pink with temper. As if to emphasise her aggravation by putting physical distance between them, she clung to the board at the side furthest from him.

It must be the abandonment that has got her on her high ropes. However, she ought to have a little more compassion for Georgiana's predicament, and she ought *to have remained with her aunt,* he thought, with a bit of his own resentment, and opened his mouth to say so—except at that moment, something in the distance caught his eye. He narrowed his gaze to be certain, and—recognising just who was approaching—he swore. He only knew one family with a carriage that particular shade of green. With a jerk, Darcy halted his horses, manoeuvring them about in a manner much less proficient than his usual expert handling.

"You call *me* uncivil! Perhaps you might accept my refusal in a more gentlemanlike manner!" Elizabeth cried.

He could not take the time to respond—the road was barely wide enough to turn here, and he had but a few moments to perform an about-face towards Netherfield. He only just managed to do it without dismounting.

He glanced at his passenger. "You may wish to brace

yourself," he said grimly. "I am about to spring the hors-es." There was not a chance in heaven or hell that he was willing to meet the owner of that carriage, Mr Thomas Bennet, while driving out with his daughter—especially as they seemed to be in the middle of a small disagreement. Something told him that if she met her father at this moment, he would have a devil of a time extracting her from Bennet's clutches.

His team broke into a canter, and he heard her exha-lation of surprise. But when he hastened them into a full gallop, she gave up her pride, quickly moving to cling to his arm.

"Why are you doing this?" she cried. "Have you gone mad?"

Darcy grinned, unable to help himself, as she pressed into his side. "Believe me when I say that I am looking after our best interests, milady. If that behindhand coach catches a glimpse of us, I shall be in for it."

She tried to glance to the rear but quickly brought her eyes forward once again as he took the turn leading to Netherfield at a reckless pace. "You *are* mad," she hissed. Once he had rounded the bend and put some distance between them, however, and knew his rig to be out of sight of the main road, he slowed.

"I apologise," he said immediately.

She straightened, and he felt her lift her fingers from his bicep one at a time, as if she must force herself to let go.

"I will have bruises from your grip, I think," he said, smiling, flexing his arm in a dramatic fashion.

She did not return his smile.

"Now, my dearest," he said coaxingly, "you were never in any danger. You cannot think I would ever allow you to come to harm." He pulled up and around the curving drive at the front of the house, slowing the horses to a smooth halt.

She leapt from the curricle, not waiting for his assist. Witnessing her glaring up at him, her beautiful eyes flashing, he found himself thankful she was not holding a pistol, for it looked as if she might be quite willing to fire it. Her temper merely excited him, if only she knew it.

"Do *not* call me 'dearest'!"

"Darling?" he asked. It seemed the gallop had truly upset her, but he could not resist a tease.

"Not that either!"

"My precious little cabbage?"

"Why, you...you..." Elizabeth struggled to form words around her outrage, her mouth gaping, and obviously at a loss, she turned on her heel.

"It is French," he called. "*Mon précieux petit chou*. If we were *en France* now, you would be falling into my arms."

"Arrgh!" was all he heard as she stormed away, and he was chuckling as he urged his greys on towards the stables.

Elizabeth hurried to her room, seriously wishing to strangle someone.

Not *someone. Him.* How could he call her a pretentious upstart with whom a marriage was an impossibility in one moment and then ask to take her on a drive, calling her his 'precious little cabbage' the next? Did he truly believe what he had said? Whyever would he say it if he had not? She would not be treated in this cavalier manner! She had watched her mother be mocked for her upbringing and conduct all her life, and she would not knowingly imprison herself in such an unequal alliance. Pacing this chamber would not change anything. It was time for action.

Enough was enough. She had promised she would not go to Longbourn, but she had—and quite purposely —never promised that she would remain *here*. Marching to her dressing room, she dragged out her trunk and began pulling out clothing and undergarments.

"What do you think you are doing, young lady?" Her mother's voice startled her from her internal ragings.

"Leaving here," Elizabeth declared defiantly. "I will not go to Longbourn, since I did promise. But I will take *the post* to Gracechurch Street if I must. I cannot stay in the same house with that man!"

For the second time that day, Elizabeth witnessed clear calculation in another's gaze.

"You have had a lover's quarrel, have you?"

"Absolutely not. We are *not* lovers and there was *no* quarrel. We came to an understanding that we are not suited to each other."

"Does *he* understand this? Or only you?"

"I cannot speak to his limited understanding of caring behaviour, kindness, or proper address. I only know that I cannot bear it another minute!"

"Lizzy, Lizzy, Lizzy. Men are simple creatures. If they do not behave as they ought, one must train them to behave better."

"Training! Is that what you have done with Papa?" she asked sarcastically.

Her mother blinked, as if the retort was unexpected —but she quickly recovered, rolling her eyes in apparent disgust. "In ways that you are not privy to, yes. I should not have to explain these things to you. It *ought* to come naturally. I suppose you have read too many books, which have drained your mind of all the most important accomplishments. It is unfortunate. Nevertheless, I am a storehouse of wisdom—put that dress down! You are *not* packing. For all your supposed intelligence, you are a complete nodcock when it comes to the language of love. Come out of here. Follow me. Now sit down, and listen instead of talk, for once in your life."

Elizabeth followed her mother to the sitting room, taking the chair she indicated. She knew better than to disobey Mrs Bennet when she was in such a fulminating sort of mood, but she knew *nothing* would change her mind.

"We will have to start at the very beginning. Whenever you enter a room where he is likely to be, seating is of the utmost importance."

"Seating! Mama, he can sit in the Thames for all I—"

"Hush! I am still your mother, and until you make a home of your own, you *will* pay attention! As I was saying, when entering a room which will contain the male in question, you must discover the very best of your available seating options. Ideally, you will choose a small settee, and then pat the seat beside you as soon as you have his attention, so he knows he is welcome. There are very few who have heart enough to be really in love without encouragement."

It was Elizabeth's turn to roll her eyes, but her mother was not finished.

"Once he is seated, with every gesture, you must touch him. Oh, I do not say to drape yourself over him like a greatcoat. You must be subtle. Emphasise your remarks with little flicks of your fingers upon his person. Incline yourself towards him whenever possible, and speak lowly, so that he must lean towards you in return."

"This is ridiculous!"

But Mrs Bennet would not be interrupted. "Hush—this conversation is important to your future happiness. You claimed your father's observations were in error. Has Mr Darcy kissed you yet?"

"Mama!"

"It is a simple question. Yes or no?"

"No!" Her cheeks flaming with mortification, Elizabeth decided she would rather swallow her tongue than admit to the *not*-kisses she had experienced with him.

"Good. You may allow it—but not often. Only when there is a definite chance of being interrupted, which will further cement the honourable expectation of marriage. Shortly after he puts his tongue in your mouth, interruption or no, you must end it. There is to be no grazing or gleaning in the fields before the harvest. Keep the barn door closed."

"That is disgusting!"

"After your wedding, you will recall this conversation and feel remarkably foolish. Well, unless he is an idiot like your father, in which case, we shall have to speak more upon the subject. You can do a great deal with most men. Or would you prefer I speak to him and set him straight on certain matters?"

"No!"

"Did he say something stupid?"

"Wh-what?" The abrupt question bewildered her.

"Did he tell you something stupid? Insensitive? Tactless? Unfeeling?"

Elizabeth opened her mouth in protest, then shut it again. At least her mother was no longer speaking of *tongues*.

"Yes. Yes to all those things."

Mrs Bennet nodded shrewdly. "I thought as much. I ought to have begun with this lesson: all men are missing a key part of the brain. He cannot help himself."

"Missing...what?"

"Oh, you know, the part of the brain that thinks out, 'if I say this, her obvious response will be that'. They cannot imagine but that every pearl of wisdom or wit occurring to them is worthy of telling, and probably repeating. The stupider it is, the more likely they are to say it. They are all the same in that sense."

"I do not—I *will* not live with a man who is an idiot."

"There *is* no such unafflicted creature. You must not blame him for it—or rather, you must include all men in your blame. They are born with the defect. After all, what man would go into battle if he thought out the consequences? Would he not more likely say, 'you know, these fat generals will not be the ones six feet underground if I brandish my musket in that other fellow's face' and promptly run the other way instead?"

Elizabeth was about to protest, and then she recalled the enthusiastic grin on Mr Darcy's face when he had sprung his horses at a mad pace.

"Well, perhaps there is some truth in what you say. But must we suffer such thoughtlessness all of our lives? It is not to be borne!"

"You will *train* him, Lizzy, and do a better job of it than I have ever done with your father. You will reward him for good behaviour and punish him for bad, and he will learn. And there are...compensatory blessings. I *can* tell that your Mr Darcy will be one of those rare gentlemen who has the means of rewarding his wife, in ways that most other men cannot."

"I do not care about his money!"

Mrs Bennet clucked her tongue. "Not that, stupid girl! There are other ways!"

"What other ways? And how could you know?"

"You are not ready for that lesson yet. Work on the first."

"Punishing him for bad behaviour? How is that even possible?"

"Start with the easy part. Reward him for good. If you look hard enough, you can usually find *something* to approve in what they do."

Elizabeth sighed, slightly disturbed by the thread of reason in her mother's advice. She was also feeling the beginnings of a headache.

"And one more thing, my girl. When dealing with men, you must *always* keep this in mind. Three simple words: lower your standards."

"What? Mama, I would never—"

"I do not mean your standards for your*self*," she interrupted. "Never suffer yourself to be treated poorly or abused in any way. But quit expecting a man to behave like an insightful, sympathetic, considerate female. He never will, and you are just *asking* for disappointment to believe he might."

"You allow Papa to speak to you unkindly!" she accused, finding her mother's advice quite the opposite of her experience.

Her mother waved this off. "As I said, you shall do better than I at training him. Besides, I do not listen to half what your father says, and if it amuses him to tease me, and relieves my feelings to rail at him, why should anyone else care?"

With that, she stalked into the dressing room, bore out Elizabeth's trunk, and quit the room while Elizabeth could only stare in astonishment and watch her—and her trunk—depart.

12

E lizabeth managed to get through the rest of the day without catching the post to London. Dinner was a quiet affair. Georgiana did not appear, Mr Darcy relating her excuse of a headache. He was not his usual self. It was a rather curious conclusion to draw, when she had believed, not long ago, that his 'usual self' was a Friday-faced bore. She might have said it of him even a few days past.

Tonight, she called his mood 'quiet' and 'preoccupied', and Elizabeth wondered whether he was stewing in anger towards her for the meeting with Mr Wickham, or if Georgiana was. Of course, her mother was of an eloquent disposition that evening, interrogating him minutely upon his estate, his London home, and whatever other assets she could discover of him. Once, she would have thought him disgusted by her mother's questioning; tonight, she believed him to be barely paying attention to either Mama's questions or his own answers.

After the tedious meal, she excused herself to her

room, even though it was still early. She had paced for an hour before she realised that she was waiting, waiting for that connecting door *from Mr Darcy's chamber* to open, for *him* to open it, so that she could demand answers of him and so that they could come to some sort of...something, whether it be an end or a beginning. She had to force herself to hurry to it, to lock and remove the key. She nearly dropped it out the window to likewise remove the temptation to use it! What had become of her good sense? Her virtue, even?

And why was it that a simple conversation with a man with whom one was—at least temporarily—betrothed seemed so difficult to manage?

Well, it would not be, not really. Tomorrow, first thing in the morning, she would send him a note asking for a walk. She would get to the bottom of his inexplicable, hurtful, and occasionally amorous behaviour, or go mad in the attempt.

❦

Georgiana was not at breakfast. Elizabeth waited for her for well over an hour, but she never appeared. She tried sending a note to Mr Darcy, but the maid came back with word from his man that he had gone out, and he had no idea when his master might return. She was not quite bold enough to present herself at Georgiana's chamber door—what if it was Elizabeth she was avoiding? Had Georgiana decided that Elizabeth would make a poor sort of sister? Was that the reason behind Mr Darcy's brooding of the evening before? It seemed the likeliest answer.

So, she went for a walk herself—to the stables to

visit Dubitz. He, at least, was overjoyed with her company. She obtained his lead and allowed him to escort her to the most enticing smells of the park. It was difficult to remain in her confused, morose mood on such a fine morning and with such an enthusiastic companion, and by the time she returned to the house, she was, if not happy, at least determined to be patient and withhold conjecture until Mr Darcy returned.

But she entered the house to a small commotion. "Lizzy," Mama called, from where she was standing at the window of the drawing room. "A chaise and four is driving up the lawn! It is too early for visitors, and I do not recognise the carriage nor the livery of the servants. Oh my goodness! Heavens above! Mercy me!"

Elizabeth peered out the window and quickly understood her mother's awe. The vehicle resembled something a king might ride in pageantry for a parade. From one end to the other, it was a gilt-encrusted monstrosity of Grecian gods vomiting cherubic legions, the effect too bright for the eye to rest upon. "The horses are post," she commented unhelpfully.

Mr Darcy appeared then, his hair curling damply around his ears. He met her eyes as he entered, tucking a note—was it the one she had sent him?—into his coat pocket and looking...eager? Whatever had been troubling him the evening before, he did not seem troubled now.

"Has the Regent trotted over to Hertfordshire for tea?" she wondered aloud. "Or perhaps a coronation?"

Mr Darcy joined them at the window, and Elizabeth could have sworn she heard a muttered oath.

"My lady aunt," he murmured. "Lady Catherine de Bourgh. Why in blazes is she here, I wonder?"

Mrs Bennet eyed Elizabeth, nodding emphatically towards the smallest settee in the room. But it seemed unlikely that any useful flirtation could ensue under the critical eye of his aunt, so Elizabeth took the nearest seat instead, a single chair; Mrs Bennet, frowning, sat across from her. Mr Darcy remained at the window.

It was not long before the housekeeper entered, bringing two familiar visitors and a third one unknown.

"Charlotte," called Elizabeth in surprise. "We were not expecting visitors so early."

Charlotte blushed and muttered something unintelligible, but her husband pushed himself into the room, bowing to Mrs Bennet and Elizabeth.

"Do not worry yourselves," he announced. "Her ladyship will not think the worse of you for being simply dressed. You need not be embarrassed."

Embarrassed by their morning clothes? What was he about? Elizabeth glanced over at Charlotte, but her friend had seated herself as far from the company as was possible, and her attention seemed absolutely fixed upon her lap. The unknown aunt, however, entered the room with an ungracious air, sitting without saying a word. She was a tall, large woman, with strongly marked features, dressed all in black. The only colour she wore was a jewel encrusted collar, a gaudy thing that sparkled haughtily at her throat. Now that all were seated, neither Mr Collins nor Mrs Bennet had anything to say.

Interrupting the awkward silence, Mr Darcy said very stiffly, "I am very surprised to see you, my lady. I hope all is well at Rosings?"

"It is," she replied, then continued in a voice laced with contempt. "That girl, I suppose, is Miss Bennet."

"She is," Mr Darcy said. "This is her mother, Mrs Bennet, and—"

She interrupted him, turning directly to Elizabeth. "Miss Bennet, I require a turn through the gardens. You will favour me with your company."

"My aunt seems to have forgotten one or two of the niceties of polite conversation. Miss Bennet, meet my aunt, Lady Catherine de Bourgh. Lady Catherine, Miss Elizabeth Bennet," he said, his tone very dry.

"I know all about *her*," Lady Catherine sneered. "*And* who is her mother. *And* her uncles and aunts."

"Oh, yes, uncles. You met my uncle Gardiner," Elizabeth put in, turning back to Mr Darcy. "He was the one to whom Jane turned, once her heart was crushed by your unwelcome recollections on her wedding day."

"A very sensible gentleman, as I remember," he said. "Do you think your sister will ever forgive me?"

"Knowing Jane, she has not only forgiven you, but probably decided to name you godfather to her first child," Elizabeth replied. "*She* is the kind one of the family."

"Enough!" Lady Catherine interrupted, looking from one to another of them with displeasure.

Mr Collins looked appalled. "I apologise, your ladyship," he said. "My cousin is usually—"

But her ladyship had no interest in her vicar's apologies and cut him off.

"Miss Bennet? Shall we?"

Elizabeth resisted the urge to turn to Mr Darcy for reprieve and—albeit reluctantly—agreed. After running to fetch her parasol, she attended her ladyship out of doors. But she had no sooner stepped onto the terrace, when Mr Darcy joined them.

"I have no need of your company, Darcy," Lady Catherine snapped.

"And I have no need of yours. Yet here we are." He held out his arms for the ladies to take. Lady Catherine refused, but Elizabeth was glad of having it. Obviously, his aunt had decided upon hating her—but the aunt was Mr Darcy's problem. Whilst she had no need of a man to fight her battles, neither should she have to fight *his*.

"You, plainly, have forgotten upbringing, manners, and every decent behaviour," she accused her nephew.

"I promise, Aunt, to recall them again once you demonstrate any. I shall speak as spoken to until you act like the lady you are. I warn you now, if you speak to Miss Bennet with any further degree of insolence, I shall return you to your carriage, if I must pick you up and put you in it myself."

Elizabeth had to press her lips firmly together to keep from smiling—his conduct was so deliciously unexpected. She managed to keep her expression sober, but she could not help lightly squeezing his arm in approval where she rested her hand upon it. His gaze moved sharply to her, and she returned it innocently.

Lady Catherine, evidently, decided not to test his word, and addressed him instead of Elizabeth. "You can be at no loss, Darcy, to understand the reason of my journey here. Your own heart, your own conscience, must tell you why I come."

"On the contrary. I have been racking my brain to account for it."

"Mr Collins has reported that you have very nearly tied yourself to a—"

Mr Darcy stopped walking and glared at his aunt in

such a manner that she quickly rethought her phrasing. After a moment, she tried again.

"Darcy, you know that your entire family has considered you engaged, almost from the cradle."

"Engaged?" Elizabeth asked, looking up at him interestedly.

"Only if my entire family has selectively flawed hearing," he replied, giving his aunt a look of vast displeasure that she seemed, somehow, to easily disregard.

"It is an engagement, or a misunderstanding?" Elizabeth asked. "What a fascinating tale to tell one's children."

"He has been formed for my daughter!" Lady Catherine insisted. "They are destined for each other by the voice of every member of their respective houses."

"Except my voice, which happens to be the only one which is never consulted nor heard, and which has been adamantly opposed to this scheme since I was old enough to speak," Darcy reproved mildly.

"My mother says that a man's brain is missing a certain important capacity for reasoning out the consequences of his actions," Elizabeth said helpfully, leaning around Mr Darcy to speak to his aunt. "Which seems to me a good enough excuse for excluding him from the marital decision altogether."

Mr Darcy frowned down at her. "Surely you do not believe that."

"In the guiding principles of arranged marriages? Or in the design of your brain?"

"I am almost your nearest relation in the world, Darcy," Lady Catherine interrupted. "I am entitled to know your dearest concerns."

"Do share them with us both, Mr Darcy," Elizabeth agreed.

He stopped walking again and faced Elizabeth directly. "Let me be sure I understand. You believe I should share the state of our, er, connexion, with my aunt?"

"She is, apparently, entitled to know. *I* did not make the rules."

Lady Catherine regarded them both suspiciously. "*Miss Bennet*. Tell me once and for all: Are you engaged to him?"

"Oh, you must not worry, your ladyship. Mr Darcy has explained everything. A match could never take place," Elizabeth replied in her sweetest tones. "'Honour, decorum, prudence, nay, interest, forbid it. Georgiana would be censured, slighted, and despised by everyone connected. The alliance would be a disgrace, considered only the upstart pretensions of one without family, connexions, or fortune—a patched-up business and hardly to be endured.'" She looked directly into Mr Darcy's eyes. "Or something like that. Is that not your own stated opinion on the matter, as of yesterday?"

His mouth opened in what appeared to be astonishment. Lady Catherine seemed pleased.

"You have misunderstood me," he protested.

"I cannot see how. Your point seemed *exceptionally* clear."

Lady Catherine grew suspicious once more. "Fitzwilliam Darcy! Such an alliance *would* be a disgrace! She just admitted it! Her name would never even be mentioned by any of us! But do not deceive yourself into a belief that I will ever recede. I shall not go away till you have given me the assurance I require."

But he ignored her to continue addressing Elizabeth. "I was not speaking of *you*. Heavens, woman—even had I entertained *any* such sentiments—which I do *not*—I would hardly tell you so harshly. I am a gentleman, at least. You cannot believe I would say that of you, *regarding you*, under any circumstance?"

Elizabeth shrugged. "I can believe *she* would," she said, indicating the fuming Lady Catherine. "And there are always your brain issues to be considered."

He grinned at her then, the devilish rogue boldly gleaming from his eyes, and she knew she was in very great danger of losing her own reasoning. How had he ever hidden it?

"You can hardly blame my aunt," Mr Darcy explained. "What mother would not wish me as her son?" He reclaimed Elizabeth's arm and began walking back towards the house at a rather quicker pace.

Elizabeth heard his aunt scurrying after them, berating them the whole while.

"Darcy! I am ashamed of you! What honour and credit do you do your illustrious name? And how will *Miss Bennet* give Georgiana a season, I wonder?"

"Did you have a come out?" he asked politely.

"Oh, yes," Elizabeth replied. "I attended my first assembly at age fifteen—I had a new dress and everything. I took Hertfordshire by storm, you may be assured."

"I suppose Goulding claimed your first dance," he said, and was there a sour note in his tone?

"Who else?" It was her turn to grin.

"How could this creature even *begin* to understand the office of Mrs Darcy of Pemberley?" her ladyship called, panting a little.

"Mrs Darcy will have her own office? Not simply a sitting room?"

"Mrs Darcy may have her own wing, if her happiness requires it," he said.

"Or two wings? I have always wished to fly."

"Are you both mad?" Lady Catherine said disgustedly from somewhere behind them. "Darcy, you are drawn in! She has used her arts and allurements—"

"Not nearly enough," he muttered.

She elbowed him, but he only tucked her arm more tightly in to his side. She lightly gripped his arm, for the first time noticing just how muscular it was. She had clasped it the day before in the curricle but had been too…frightened was not quite the right word, although there had been some of that. Despite her fear of horses, exhilaration and anger and joy had formed a convoluted turmoil in her soul when he put the horses to a gallop. The ride in his smart vehicle had been quite a breathtaking experience.

Now this, the sensation of holding his bicep, was bringing the best of those feelings back to the surface. There was something very exciting, suddenly, about the feel of it beneath her fingers. She felt him flex his arm beneath his coat, and her breath caught.

Was this flirtation? It somehow seemed more. But doubtless, every foolish girl thought so.

Lady Catherine's harsh wheezing could be heard, even further behind them now.

"You are walking too quickly for your aunt to keep up."

"That is the idea."

She could not help the little giggle that escaped.

His voice lowered. "When we pass the statuary,

instead of taking the left turning back to the house, we must take the right, and if we increase our speed, we will be out of sight of both garden and house before she can reach it."

"What is that you are saying, Darcy? What is it you are talking of? What are you telling Miss Bennet? Let me hear what it is."

They had reached the statuary where the path curved, briefly hiding them from their interested audience. Elizabeth did not question his directives; rather, as they rounded the bend, she let go his arm and took off running. For a short while, she was a girl again, escaping from whatever authority and justice might ruin her fun. She did not ask where they were going, or why, or even wonder whether it was wise. She only ran, her parasol catching the wind like a sail.

Of course, his legs were longer, and he quickly outpaced her. When he made for the woods, she followed, only slowing once they were long out of sight of prying eyes. She closed her parasol before it tore on low branches. And then they were both laughing.

"I cannot imagine what your aunt must think of me," she said, after her breath caught up with her lungs and laughter quieted.

"You seemed extremely unconcerned about her opinions a few minutes ago," he remarked.

Her smile faded. "It was nothing less than impertinence. I was insulted, but I ought to have demonstrated a shred of dignity instead of allowing her to goad me."

He waved this off. "It would not have mattered. She was determined to be uncivil. Here, take this turning to the left."

She did, for the first time realising that he had an

actual direction and purpose to this escape. They walked for a distance, with him occasionally moving brush aside, as the path was narrow and overgrown. But they had probably walked no more than a quarter-hour when they suddenly came upon a forest glade.

She gasped at the sight. It would have been rendered beautiful by merely trees, sunshine, and grassy knoll, but to this was added rugs, pillows, and a large picnic basket. He looked at her, smiling rather sheepishly, and withdrew a note from his pocket. It was not the one she had sent him after all, the one she had written, brisk and cold with demands that they talk. "Challenge number four," he said.

Opening it, she read:

Share a picnic lunch with me.

13

Elizabeth looked at Mr Darcy. "Your note to me was much more gracious than mine to you."

He looked at her soberly, the devil in him concealed once again in whatever private part of his soul he kept it, every inch the gentleman.

"I believe your note was rather polite, considering you believed I called you a pretentious upstart yesterday. And now you know how I spent the early morning hours. It took time to find someplace suitable for picnicking out of sight of the house or gardeners, and then, because I was aiming for discretion, I did not ask any servants to help, beyond Mrs Nicholls with the meal. I had to make more than one trip back and forth from the house. I meant to bring you here for a luncheon, but perhaps as a late breakfast it will work as well."

"Should we really remain here and leave our guests to my mother? Will your aunt summon Georgiana?"

"Believe me, my sister is adept at hiding when she wishes to hide. Lady Catherine will have no success in that quarter, should she try. Your mother is perfectly capable of entertaining them, else they can entertain each other."

She liked his confident view of Mama, and if he did not worry about their visitors, she would not either. It had touched her heart, that he would search these woods, and do all the work himself to make a private moment for them to be able to speak freely with one another.

But he did not immediately talk of anything serious. Instead, he removed his hat and gloves and began unpacking the basket, producing tasty little sandwiches, biscuits, a fruit tart, and even a delicious lemonade. Elizabeth, who had not realised she was hungry until that moment, happily partook of the repast. He ate a little but soon stretched against a boulder, rugs and blankets spread beneath him, pillows at his back, looking for all the world like her notion of an Arabian sheik—and she told him so.

"We only need dancing girls and scarves to complete the picture," she teased.

His smile reached his eyes. "If you are volunteering, I am more than happy to return to the house for costuming. I do not know how many scarves I will find, however. Do you think cravats will do the trick? I will gladly donate all of mine to the cause."

She tossed an apple at him, which he caught neatly, and she opted to change the subject to one that remained pressing.

"If *I* am not the pretentious upstart, who is? I do not understand your remarks of yesterday."

The smile disappeared, and he sighed heavily, closing his eyes briefly. Birdsong was the sole sound in the grove. Finally, he spoke. "I already informed you of my past association with Wickham. That part of the story, I felt, was mine to reveal. However, it was not the end of our dealings."

"He did something else? *He* is the 'pretentious upstart'? But..."

"Yes." He stared up at the sky, as if there were words to be found in the clouds; his expression darkened like an approaching storm.

"You need not tell me if it is too personal," Elizabeth offered, seeing how difficult it was for him to talk about it. She was curious, of course, but despised the thought of forcing a confidence.

He sighed again. "It concerns Georgiana. From something you said, yesterday, I mistakenly drew the conclusion that *she* had told you some part of the tale herself. Having said this much, I feel no doubt of your discretion. I ought probably to have told you from the beginning."

"Georgiana? But she is still a child! Is she even as old as Lydia?" She certainly seemed much younger than Elizabeth's youngest sister, even if her figure was rather womanly.

"She is just past her sixteenth birthday. But yes, in some ways, she seems much younger. She has always been very retiring, much happier with her music and drawings than with companions her own age. My father left her guardianship to both myself and my mother's nephew, Colonel Fitzwilliam. He is only a few years older than me, and it seemed clear that Father wished for the colonel's mother, Lady Matlock, to influence Georgiana's upbringing. This, she was more than happy to do. I am ashamed to say, we were both content to leave her to it."

"So, your sister was what…ten or eleven years old at the time of your father's death?"

"Yes."

She put her hand upon his. "I cannot think of a young man whom I would have wanted placed in charge of *my* life, especially at such a young age. So youthful a girl surely needs a mother figure more than a brother."

He glanced at her hand before taking it in both of his and absently twisting the garnet ring on her finger. "That was my feeling, but of course, it was also very convenient for me. Colonel Fitzwilliam also was much occupied with his military career. But you have never met Lady Matlock."

"Please tell me that she is nothing like Lady Catherine."

He squeezed her hand, a brief smile flitting over his face. "No, nothing. Lady Matlock is very staid, very dignified. She is not warm, although she is not unkind. But Georgiana also had a very good governess and was happy enough, I think. However, my aunt worried that, socially, she was not progressing as she ought, so she let the governess go and put her in school, hoping to help her come to know other young ladies her age. About a year ago, she was taken from school and an establishment formed for her in London, and then last summer she went, accompanied by the lady who presided over it —a Mrs Younge—to Ramsgate."

"Why did Lady Matlock remove her from school? Was she unhappy there?"

"I do not know whether she was happy or unhappy," he said, sounding a little sad. "It is what is done. A lady is educated in the running of a home, and once she completes her training, she is given a home to run. I do not know what friends she made, or did not make, whether she loved it there or missed her former home at Matlock. Her letters spoke of the minutiae of her days and little of what she thought of them. Lady Matlock had discharged her duty, and beyond writing to Georgiana regularly, I did not step in and take it up. I did not perceive the need, even though I knew my sister still was very young—an age when I, myself, had yet two parents who were concerned in my upbringing."

There was such regret in his countenance; a cold feeling filled Elizabeth at the idea of Mr Wickham's involvement.

"There proved to have been a prior...acquaintance between Mr Wickham and Mrs Younge. By her connivance, he was given complete freedom to court Georgiana, to convince her of his love, and to press for an elopement."

"What? Oh, no! How did you prevent it?"

He studied her ring, as if it were the most fascinating jewel in England, instead of meeting her gaze. "There was something new in her letters. I am not sure what. Whatever it was, I became concerned, and joined her unexpectedly a day or two before the intended elopement. Within an hour of my arrival, she confessed the scheme."

"You were there when she needed you. You *did* keep her safe."

He did not appear reassured. "She had only known him as a child, to whom he had been carelessly kind. I explained to her the whole of Wickham's motives. I told her, in detail, the various schemes he had worked upon me and upon our father over the years. I told her of the women he had ruined, the gambling debts I had paid, the fortune he had lost, the degradations he had undertaken to keep from prison. I sketched his character with excruciating detail. Oh, I kept her safe from him. I rid her of a man who only wanted her fortune and revenge upon me. And in one fell swoop, I rid her of any shred of self-assurance she possessed."

Elizabeth's heart broke for his pain, for Georgiana's; at the same time, she experienced another shaft of fury at Wickham, for his lies, for the destruction he had caused.

"Thank goodness you arrived yesterday when you did," she said quietly. "He was taunting her. I did not realise why what he said was hurtful, but I could tell he was somehow being very cruel. His wording was innocuous, but now that I know the story, it was unconscionable."

"That was my other errand this morning," he said coldly. "I went to speak to Colonel Forster, to tell him one of his officers was making a nuisance of himself in the neighbourhood. He told me that the regiment is soon removing to Brighton, that Wickham asked him yesterday if he might go immediately, and that he was given permission to do so. If he is not gone yet, he soon will be. He dares not risk my further displeasure by remaining."

"I wonder whether he will pay his debts before he leaves, or what his commanding officer thinks of him after your information."

Mr Darcy only shrugged. "Likely he will desert. Besides, he is hardly out to protect England from enemy invasion. He is hiding from his creditors. He may hide elsewhere."

Elizabeth let go of his hand to clench her fists. "That is the least of what he deserves. What a despicable rogue! Is this why Georgiana will not come downstairs? Does she blame me for practically delivering her up to him? Oh, I could cheerfully shoot him!"

His expression lightened as he took hold of her clenched fists and used the momentum to pull her into his arms. "Easy, my tigress."

She stared up at him, troubled. "Do not tell me to be easy, when you have just revealed that surely the wickedest man who was ever born tried to-to make away with your sister, a mere child! For her to always know that her first, precious love was wasted upon a scoundrel!"

"Most 'first loves' are nothing to celebrate," he said.

Her interest was caught immediately. Elizabeth knew she must pull away, but the strength of his embrace was too tantalising. Her mother's advice had encouraged her to touch him, to enjoy, just a little, the raw masculinity so properly clothed. Still, she doubted her mother's advice extended to remaining alone with him in an isolated grove, where no one was *ever* likely to interrupt.

"Mine certainly was not, but then, you know all about it. It is only fair you tell me about yours," she challenged, imagining him twirling some diamond of the first water across a ballroom floor. He said nothing, but his eyes hooded, and there was that devilish mischief again in the gleam. Why she was unafraid, she could not say.

"I may have forgotten," he murmured.

"A daughter of nobility? The betrothed of some

ancient earldom, young and lovely, sacrificing herself for family honour and fortune?"

"Far less romantic, I am afraid. Lucy, a pub owner's daughter in Lambton."

She was genuinely astonished. "But…but love? How impossible! How would you have made conversation with her? How could any real connexion be formed, with one who could not possibly understand you, your life and your responsibilities?"

He smiled then, becoming more dangerous still. "I was seventeen years of age. I did not imagine *talking* to her."

It took her just a moment to understand. She pursed her lips disapprovingly and would have pulled away, but he laughed and tightened his embrace.

"Then it was not love," she scolded.

"I suppose you are correct. I told you it was nothing to take pride in."

"You did not…" She could not quite bring herself to finish the sentence.

"No, I did not," he reassured. "I was not raised by fools. My father was careful to explain the false power I would hold over servants and tradespeople and villagers. Likewise, he helped me comprehend how ruinous such a connexion would be—to me, to them—how disappointing, unfulfilling. But then, he understood love better than most men, I think. He adored my mother. He was several years her senior, and it was devastating for him when he lost her to illness. He wanted me to have something real, something like they shared."

"Your mother was the daughter of an earl," Elizabeth mused. "I wonder what your father would have thought of me." She had not meant to say it aloud, and wondered at her own boldness when the words escaped. He had not asked her to marry him, not truly, and she was still a bit bewildered by the idea of it. *Was this love?* But Mr Darcy did not appear to notice her chagrin.

"He would not have understood, not at first, not until he grew to know you."

"Fearing you had wed the barmaid from Lambton," she said drily.

He sighed. "*I* did not understand, at first. I behaved as if you were a different species than myself. And then Georgiana..." he trailed off.

"What?" She tried to move away, to see his face, but he clutched her to him, as if to prevent her. Just as quickly, however, he released her—as if restraining her had been most unconsciously done. She did not move.

"Tell me," she demanded—just as if it were her right, as if he were hers to command. She looked up at him expectantly, meeting his gaze beneath the rim of her bonnet. And just as if *she* were *his*, he wrapped his arm around her, delving his fingers beneath it, into the hair coiled at her nape—almost absently, as if he caressed her this way daily.

Dangerous, Elizabeth, a voice inside her head warned.

Shut it, she told the voice. *I need to see him. I need to hold him. I can trust him.*

"Tell me," she urged again.

"I did not ask my aunt to find Georgiana a new companion. I thought I could do a better job of it—or that surely I could do no worse. Mrs Annesley was older, more...motherly in nature. I brought Georgiana with Mrs Annesley back to London and then promptly threw myself into Bingley's project of finding a country estate to lease. I knew my sister was not fully recovered. I supposed that hiring maternal attention would fix things."

"It did not? She was not...good?"

"Mrs Annesley was not the problem. Georgiana was, simply, more troubled than any hired companion could possibly cope with. I had been looking forward to the ball at Netherfield with what was probably an overly enthusiastic regard. I was going to ask you to dance, you see, and spend thirty minutes flirting with you."

Elizabeth's head popped up, and he pressed it back down to his chest, placing the briefest of kisses upon her nose. "I had no intentions then, of course. I found you irresistibly delightful and completely inappropriate."

Indignant, she tried to move, and again he restrained her. "Come, Tigress, let me finish. Besides, I misspoke— there was nothing inappropriate about you, *per se*, only your family, all who managed to put you to the blush far too often. You and Mrs Bingley must always be excluded from every criticism."

"Is this your idea of charm?" she asked wryly.

"This is my idea of distracting myself from what I would rather be doing right now," he muttered, giving her a look that was so blatantly admiring, she blushed. But she could not resist taunting him.

"Oh, I am back to being the barmaid again, am I? Am I using too many words?"

He looked at her, only looked, and there was the hellion in that look, tantalising, resisting the restraint he usually wielded.

"You, my dear, play with fire," he murmured lowly, his eyes glittering, and she felt a combination of fear and thrill, an urge to coast her hands over his broad chest, to...explore. And an urge to run. There was that, too.

"Georgiana?" she asked quickly, instead of doing either.

He regarded her for some moments before continuing. "Yes. I received a letter from Mrs Annesley, putting me on notice that unless I came at once to visit Georgiana in person, and judge for myself what ought to be done with her, she was finished with us both. Of course, I was furious at the woman for being, as I considered, demanding and overly dramatic. And for ruining my plans to have thirty minutes of your uninterrupted attention."

Elizabeth smiled to herself. The only man she had wished to dance with that night was Mr Wickham, who, providentially, had not attended. It was all for the best that Mr Darcy had not appeared either.

"Unfortunately," he continued, "Mrs Annesley was most correct to have summoned me. Georgiana had ceased caring for herself in any manner, or allowing others to care for her either. Mostly, she refused to leave her bed, spending all her time sketching hideous drawings of great monsters eating—well, never mind that. But she needed help, most desperately."

Elizabeth sat up, and this time he did not try to stop her. "What did you do?"

Remembered frustration and bleakness crossed his face. "At first, I tried simply demanding more of her. It seemed to help in the beginning, but too soon, she ceased caring *what* I said." His brow furrowed. "That is not exactly correct. She told me later that she *wanted* to please me, but the smallest effort felt simply too difficult to even attempt."

"She had fallen into a melancholy then?"

"She had fallen into *something*. I spoke with our

physician, and he in turn spoke with a few of his trusted colleagues. Along with some wildly idiotic notions, two suggestions were presented—Bedlam or Bath. Obviously, I was not going to incarcerate Georgiana in Bedlam. So, off we went to Bath, to take the waters."

"I have always wondered whether there was any good to be found in those cures."

"I am not certain there is. The change of scenery was good. We took only my man and her maid, and I leased a small but lovely house in one of the crescents, with no live-in servants, only a couple of dailies and a woman to do simple meals. I hoped that being on our own, more or less, would be beneficial. At first, I urged her to drink some foul-tasting water that was supposed to be restorative—until I realised that she would do more of what I asked, in the way of getting out of bed and taking meals with me, in order to *avoid* drinking it. She did, finally, take the waters once, but I was never able to get her to do it again."

"The situation sounds...daunting,"

"Yes. I was terrified."

Elizabeth looked at him in some amazement. If someone had tried to tell her, even a few days ago, that this man could feel something so...*human* as terror, she would have scoffed. The softness, even vulnerability in his tone fit not at all with her initial impressions. *Just who is Fitzwilliam Darcy?* she wondered again.

"One day," he continued, "I finally managed to coax her into taking a walk with me to one of the gardens. A young boy—obviously well on his way to becoming a stalwart member of the criminal classes—was selling his 'purebred hound' pup. A mere ball of fluff. I knew it must be a mongrel, but it was the first sign of interest

Georgiana had shown in anything at all. I bought the mutt on the condition that she take him out for walks daily. Had no idea he would grow to the size of a small pony," he grumbled.

"Not quite that," Elizabeth murmured, hiding a smile.

"Very nearly. But at least the required walks helped us into a routine of sorts. We ate a breakfast of cheese and toast, and we would usually take the dog to walk in one of the gardens or parks if the weather was passable. Then we would return to the townhouse, and she would brush Dubitz, and I would talk."

"You?"

"You needn't sound so incredulous."

"You are not known for being an avid conversationalist."

"I prefer to listen more than I speak. Besides, much depends upon those whose company I share—have you noticed any deep silences this afternoon?"

"I am properly honoured," she replied, grinning.

He kissed her nose again. "Minx. I had to talk because she would not. And during the course of all my talking, I finally spoke to her about you."

"Me?"

"Indeed. In an odd way, you might say...you brought her back to me."

❧ 14 ❧

Darcy remembered that frightening time with an awful sort of clarity. After the advent of Dubitz, he could coax his sister to take walks, as he had just described to Elizabeth—indeed, she performed the chore uncomplainingly. But other than monosyllables, she offered little in the way of discourse.

And so, he had tried to talk.

At first, he spoke to her of the weather, or of whatever was featured in the newspapers delivered daily from town, or the business of his solicitors and stewards as received in his letters. Little seemed to reach through whatever fog she existed within.

One gloomy, rainy afternoon, the weather preventing all but a brief turn out of doors, he had felt almost as if —even though his sister sat directly across from him— he was alone in the room. Battling something like despair himself, he sorted through the mail forwarded from London. In the pile, he had discovered the letter from Bingley, inviting him to stand up with him at his wedding to Jane Bennet.

His first emotion, upon reading it, was fury.

He had tried to forget Elizabeth, and his frustration with his inability to do so came to some sort of pinnacle at the sight of her sister's name linked with Bingley's. It had seemed such a daft decision, wedding someone so unsuitable, so much a selfish choice made without reference to his familial duty. With a sudden loss of his vaunted control, he had voiced his exasperation, his love, and his disappointment—for it was nothing less—to the shell of his sister who sat across from him, staring at nothing.

"It will not be repressed," he had protested. "Why will my admiration and love for her not simply fade? It makes no sense! Oh, she is pretty enough—more than merely pretty, actually—just not the pink porcelain sort of prettiness that one sees painted so often, like her elder sister's good looks. Her birth is well enough for the Bingley match, at least—she is the second-eldest daughter of a gentleman. Her manner is proper. But her family is dreadful—taking every opportunity to expose themselves as vulgar! Her mother is but the daughter of a solicitor, and I believe she has an uncle in Cheapside—both facts of which must materially affect her chances of making a decent match. Not to mention, she has *nothing* —nothing! Her father's estate is entailed away—to Lady Catherine's vicar! It is why, I suppose, she is not married already. One cannot imagine any other reason.

"Not that she is *overfond* of propriety. Why, her sister took sick—a brief illness, a slight fever only—and nothing would do for her but to walk three miles in the mud and showers to nurse her because their horses were needed on the farms and no carriage was available. Bingley has lost his mind, having anything to do with them! And yet, he can hardly be blamed for succumbing to the lure of it. I do not doubt Miss Elizabeth helped the match along somehow. Magnificent, headstrong girl!"

He had rambled on in this vein for some minutes—half admiring, half complaining. And when he had finally paused for breath, Georgiana spoke.

"Do you hate her? Or do you love her? I really cannot tell," she had said.

"Neither can I," he had muttered. And then he realised...Georgiana had asked him a question—two of them, and spoken beyond the bare necessities of mono-syllabic communication. It had begun that way, her opening to him. And the more he spoke of his infatua-tion with Miss Elizabeth Bennet, the more she had to say.

❦

"Me?" Elizabeth asked. "Why in the world were you speaking of me?"

"I was thinking about you," he said nonchalantly.

She raised a brow. "Very well. Why were you thinking of me? Exploring the idea of a different species, as you said? Was the species a mongrel one, I wonder?"

Her tone was casual, but he was not stupid—he could hear the ice crackling at his feet.

"It was a dangerous one," he said. "The sort of species that captures a man—a man who was minding his own business, doing a favour in helping lease an estate for a friend, courtship the very *last* thing on his mind—and will not release its hold."

"Like a bog, you mean," she said.

He kissed her.

He had wanted to do this since the first moment he had seen her again, greeting guests for the wedding of her sister, energetically bustling with every preparation so that all would be perfect. She had stayed behind the scenes, more or less, never still, always occupied, working herself to the bone, no doubt. He had wanted to take her in his arms so he could look, simply look, hold her still, and then touch his lips to hers, to feel their softness meet, to bind them to each other in avid connexion. And now, mere days later, alone with her in this enchanted glade, he ceased resisting.

His mouth met hers, softly. Hers was tentative, uncertain—but she did not pull away or shove at him. He was not an idiot, like Reginald Goulding—drat his hide, who probably had waited years to take her pretty mouth and then tossed away his opportunity in a savage flare of lust. But he acknowledged the difficulty, for every part of him fired into thrilling desire. To compensate, he made himself fix upon the sensation, the sweetness, the taste of honey, fruit tart, and Elizabeth. But she was addictive, drugging, and he gently deepened the kiss, protecting her from his need, still, but wanting more of her. Wanting *her* to taste *him*.

"Elizabeth," he breathed against her mouth. "Tell me I am not alone in this passion. Tell me I am not the only one caught." And in response, she opened to him, let him in, and he groaned, knowing he must stop before common sense—already in short supply when she was near—fled the countryside entirely. Her hands crept up his chest, and he thought, *the devil with sense*, and deepened the kiss. The straw of her bonnet scraped his forehead, and his hand moved to its strings, ready to unpin and untie. But just before his brains entirely combusted, a sound penetrated the delicious fog. It was not the sound of birdsong nor spring breezes batting at clouds and trees. Abruptly, he sat up.

"Wha-...what is the matter?" she asked, looking flustered and rosy and so beautiful he ached with it. The noises seemed to be getting closer, a sort of thrashing through the brush. Dash it, what approached? It might be a pack of wolves or rabid badgers. Or perhaps two bucks fighting over an attractive doe. He could sympathise with the inclination.

"I believe someone has commenced a fox hunt on Bingley's grounds—rather a wrong time in the year—and the hounds are headed this way," he said. "Or perhaps, the entire Royal Menagerie."

Elizabeth suddenly perceived what Mr Darcy obviously had already, and scrambled away from him. Hurriedly she stood, brushing at her skirts, casting about in all directions for approaching marauders.

But the intruding beast—his lead dragging, brambles stuck in his fur, and what was surely a wide grin upon his silly face—was only Dubitz, joyously proclaiming his glee at finding them, leaping upon them both with enthusiastic kisses while upsetting crockery and scattering plates. Mr Darcy managed, finally, to capture his lead, and demanded he sit with such a forceful air that the dog reluctantly obeyed. Mr Darcy looked at her, chagrin upon his handsome face.

"Dubitz!" called a voice, not far distant. *Georgiana!*

"And, it only wanted this," Mr Darcy said with some

disgust. Hurriedly, he hooked the lead over the nearest scrubby bush likely to hold it, shoved the remainder of the plate of sandwiches under Dubitz's nose, and without warning, grabbed Elizabeth's hand.

"Run," he said.

For the second time that day, Elizabeth ran. They aimed for the opposite side of the clearing, which, being a very small one, was quickly traversed. Unfortunately, their destination was also more overgrown, and as Elizabeth lunged forward, a tree branch snagged her bonnet —still pinned snugly to her head—and she made a squeak of protest. Caught, she somewhat frantically tried to extricate herself; but Mr Darcy slipped in behind her, stilling her hand. "Hush," he whispered in her ear, nudging her with one finger pointed in the direction from which they had just come.

They were but twenty feet away from their picnic site and only partially hidden. In fact, had Elizabeth's gown been any other colour than a deep shade of green, they might have been instantly spotted. Georgiana had appeared in the grove, her dismay obvious.

"Oh, Dubitz! How could you?" she cried.

He glanced up from his sandwiches, barking a happy greeting.

"You are *not* a mighty hunter," she disagreed, extracting his lead from the bush. "You have destroyed this meal—although I cannot imagine why it was left unattended. Some creature was bound to find it. Oh, dear!"

She tugged him away from the plate, and he immediately pulled in the direction of Darcy and Elizabeth. "No, Dubitz! Stay!" Gaining a better grip on his leash, she glanced in the direction of the missing picnickers—fortunately not glimpsing them.

Dubitz tried to return to the plate of sandwiches.

"Bad doggy!"

He cocked his head and peered up at her innocently, as if wondering how she could possibly vilify him. She sighed, tugging him away from the meal. He licked her hand, assuring her of his love despite her dreadful temper.

"Very well," she conceded. "Mediocre doggy!"

Elizabeth felt Mr Darcy all along her back, large and warm, as he worked at the tangled bonnet. Moments later, she felt it carefully lifted from her head—it must have been sorely snarled indeed. But he did not move, only stood there, and she could not fix her attention upon whether Georgiana—or Dubitz—would eventually discover them. Finally, she gave in to temptation, leaning back against him. As if he had been waiting for the signal, he wrapped his arms around her. She felt his lips on the curve of her neck, raising gooseflesh, and she wanted to turn in his arms and feel, once again, those kisses. They had been *nothing* like Reginald Goulding's—obliterating any previous experience.

In the clearing, Georgiana cast her eyes about once more, but Dubitz jerked on his lead—yet again in their direction—and she firmly turned him about, heading back from whence they had come. When all was quiet, Elizabeth glanced over her shoulder, looking up into dark eyes. He looked stern, almost angry.

"Your sister has departed, it appears," she said unnecessarily, a little uncertain. "Is something the matter? You look unhappy."

"Not at all. I am unused to dealing with such an

onslaught of, er, admiration," he said somewhat cryptically, giving her his arm as they strolled back to the picnic site.

"What would you have said to her if she had discovered us?"

"Oh, well, as to that, she *did* discover us. She must have recognised your parasol. And besides, it was her recommendation to have a picnic in the first place. I simply did not wish her to be embarrassed, as she would surely have been. This is the first time she has left her rooms since the confrontation with Wickham."

She placed her other hand atop his arm to stop him. "I have been worried about her—fearing she might be blaming me for yesterday's experience."

"No—Georgiana never blames others, even when they are at fault. She heaps blame upon herself, and far in excess of what is necessary."

"Do *you* blame me?"

He sighed, turning to face her fully. "Of course not. I blame myself. I withheld necessary information from you. You are accustomed to walking anywhere, at nearly any time, unaccompanied. I knew this. Your independence of spirit is part of what attracts me to you. I wonder, even, how to keep you safe without crushing it."

"I hardly have a habit of running headlong into danger."

He appraised her with an aggressively male look, one that made her very aware of him, and of herself, and recalling those heated kisses. "You, my love, are in very great danger right this minute, if only you knew it."

She thought she understood what he meant, and blushed. "You must not kiss me again. Mama warned me against displays of affection in areas of too great an isolation. I am certain she would *not* approve of a forest glade."

For a time, he replied nothing, only straightening the mess that Dubitz had made of their picnic and resettling himself upon the rugs; she wondered if she had sounded prudish, young, and inexperienced. But after a few moments of feeling foolish, she was struck by a prickle of annoyance.

"I am no green girl, yet I cannot help but see the wisdom in Mama's words. I simply want my choices to remain my own."

He appeared somewhat taken aback. "I hope you will always speak your mind to me, Miss Bennet. I swear to you that I perfectly understand your mother's point. I admit, I hope she also explained that it is not the affection itself which is a problem, but the too-free exercise of it before the protections of matrimony. In too many situations, a woman is blamed when a man misbehaves. I apologise that you felt required to remind me."

But she waved his apologies away, very willing to turn the topic. "I suppose you ought to call me Elizabeth, at least when we are private. It seems silly to insist upon formalities when I have been so...very informal."

"I already have, have I not? In certain moments of... forgetting?" He looked a bit rueful. "I am honoured, Elizabeth. Most of my acquaintance calls me 'Darcy' but Georgiana has always called me 'Fitzwilliam'."

"Which do you prefer?"

"Either one is an improvement over 'bottle-headed buffoon'."

She gave him a contrite look. "I believe you misheard. I only asked if you were 'leaving so soon'."

He laughed, and she was caught by the sight of it. He was so unfairly handsome!

"I am happy to hear *any* name of mine upon your lips," he assured.

Elizabeth could imagine times of calling him 'Darcy' and times of calling him 'Fitzwilliam'—and then was rather shocked by these imaginings.

"There is a certain look you get," he said, "that leaves me with a nearly overpowering urge to disobey your mother. We must change the subject. Tell me something you have always wished to do but never had the opportunity."

She stared at him in some surprise—it was a most unusual question, in her experience with men. Most wished only to talk of themselves, expecting polite nothings in return. "What if I said I wished to study Latin?"

"Do you? I am certain I have several texts I could loan you, if so."

He hadn't even raised a brow! She had borrowed such a tome once from her father's library, and even he —who was usually so liberal regarding what books she studied—had objected, fearing she would turn into a bluestocking.

"Not really, as it happens," she admitted, and decided to tell the truth—although he would likely be shocked. "Something much simpler, and yet so difficult. I would like to learn to swim."

"Not so difficult. I should think you would be a quick study."

"You know that young ladies are never allowed anything of the sort! I cannot tell you how many times have I been rowed out on a hot summer's day, listening to the gentleman who is doing the rowing speak about how much more amusing it is to swim *in* the lake than to sit upon it."

"Even once would be too dull," he said, and began to speak of swimming, of 'strokes' and methodologies. It was obvious *he* would have no objections. From there, their conversation diverged to the ponds, rivers, and streams at Pemberley, to her opinions on living in the country and London, to her relations near Cheapside—it seemed incredible; there was almost nothing he did not wish to know about her, about her feelings and opinions. But at last, he sighed and looked at his pocket watch. To her surprise, it was nearly noon—they had been out for over two hours.

"Shall we clear our picnic?"

"Are we finished here so soon, then?" she asked, with an impish expression. She could hardly believe how quickly she had gone from lecturing him to teasing him, from despising him to eagerly accepting his affection. Although she did not completely *know* him—neither, she was beginning to believe, did she completely know herself.

"Minx," he called her again—a name, she was learning, that he used when he wished to kiss her. However, he picked up the nearest rug and began rolling. "It is only the beginning, my loveliest Elizabeth. Only the beginning. Just heap the crockery into the basket whilst I fold the rugs. I shall return for it all later."

They packed everything away in companionable silence, which lasted until they were on the path back to the house.

"Will you find a way to reveal to my father the truth of Mr Wickham? Not Georgiana's experience, of course…but I would not have him believe that you are at all to blame for his troubles."

"As you did." But he winked at her, interrupting her immediate protest. "It is already done. I have written to my solicitors. They will send your father enough credible proof that even he will not be able to deny it."

Elizabeth was happy to speak of something else. "The picnic was Georgiana's recommendation, did you say? Could it be that your young sister is advising you in this courtship?" she teased.

A slight smile played upon his lips. "What courtship? You accepted these challenges to rid yourself of me, as I recall."

Her sidelong glance was pointed. "I hope you do not think that I allow just any man kisses."

"Are we courting then?" he questioned, threading her arm through his, her bonnet dangling from his other hand.

"It is most unfair of you to ask me that. A woman does not decide whether a certain man will court her or whether he will not. She only has rights of refusal. And besides, you evade the question. Does your sister advise you?"

He shrugged. "Why should she not? She, at least, has been in love, although she plainly has abominable taste in men. Who better to counsel me regarding what actions might appeal to a young lady? Granted, I drew the line at bringing along a book of sonnets."

Elizabeth giggled, reciting, "'I have seen roses damask'd, red and white, But no such roses see I in her cheeks; And in some perfumes is there more delight, than in the breath that from my mistress'—"

He stopped abruptly, pulling her swiftly into his

arms, his expression raw, the secret devil in him on full display—it took her breath away.

"In a few minutes, we shall be in sight of the house," he murmured. "Is this public enough?"

She stretched up her arms to wrap around his neck. "And just private enough, too," she replied, as he bent to take her mouth with his. For long moments, she simply experienced the sensation of it. Sometimes careful, delicate, sometimes exploring, demanding—and when she followed his lead, learning from him, she felt the change in him as he pressed her ever closer. When he finally drew back just a little, she felt as though her very essence had been exposed to the open air.

"*Your* breath is of rose petals and springtime, if you were in any doubt," he said, his voice rough. "Likewise, if you are in any doubt of my intentions, I *am* courting you, my Elizabeth. And to be clear, my sister did not advise me on the kisses. To see you is to want you. I always will." He looked at her again with that secret intensity he wore so well, and she shivered beneath the warm afternoon sunshine.

Suddenly, however, he gentled his smile into something approaching his usual polished elegance, as if caging an untamed ferocity within—perhaps in several cages. Perhaps he hid the entire Royal Menagerie within his staid and implacable gentlemanliness. Somehow, she would not have been surprised.

❧ 15 ❧

Darcy approached the house feeling equal parts anticipation and contentment. Elizabeth would be his wife; there was no longer any question of his intentions between them. Hopefully, his aunt had seen the futility of her interference and departed swiftly once her prey—er, her nephew—had escaped her clutches. He would visit Mr Bennet again tomorrow, he decided. Perhaps tonight he would present Elizabeth with a necklace that he had long been desiring to give her, a Darcy family heirloom and a physical sign of those intentions. Whether she married him or not, he could never imagine it upon any other. Not that he had any doubts about her willingness to marry him; her kisses had told him all he needed to know about her feelings. She was everything he had always wanted and ever needed—he simply had been too dim to realise it, at first.

He climbed the steps up to the flagstone terrace, arm in arm with his Elizabeth—and halted abruptly.

A group of people stood there, obviously awaiting

them. Standing in the middle of them was Mr Bennet, arms akimbo, frowning. Mrs Bennet, appearing extremely displeased, was mid-protest. "Mr Bennet, you cannot be serious!"

He shot her a look of contempt. "Do not flaunt your ignorance, my dear. You do not know how these men prey upon the unsuspecting. If this is your idea of supervision, we are dealing with a situation beyond your touch."

A situation you have ignored these last five days, Darcy thought with his own contempt. From his dealings with Mrs Bennet, he expected her diatribe to continue—but she snapped her mouth shut. Her husband had successfully quelled her.

A pompously smiling Mr Collins—with his longsuffering wife—pulled Mr Bennet forward. Darcy's aunt was nowhere to be seen.

"Elizabeth Grace Bennet, where have you been?" Mr Bennet called.

"My middle name—never a good sign," Elizabeth muttered.

"Shall we leave?" Darcy murmured back.

"Where would we go?"

"Scotland?" he suggested.

Elizabeth gave him a look. Even though it was apparent her father despised him more than ever, his heart lightened. He knew this look already, one chiding him for inappropriate words or behaviour. The one nearly demanding he kiss her.

"Our daughter will not remain another minute in the same house as *him!*" Mr Bennet announced angrily as they approached. "Collins, for once in his life, has offered a useful suggestion."

Mr Collins looked as if he might protest Mr Bennet's wording, but Mrs Collins spoke first.

"Perhaps, Eliza, you would accept my invitation to visit our home, as you could not during the winter," she said. "Now might be a good time."

༺༻

Somehow, the arrangements were made swiftly. Elizabeth could hardly take it all in.

"When Collins appeared upon my doorstep expressing his concerns, I realised I should have sent you away sooner," Mr Bennet informed his daughter privately.

Mr Collins had been responsible for this? Why should *he* be concerned about anything? "Since when do we listen to Mr Col—"

But Papa interrupted. "A miserable match with such a man as Mr Darcy is not to be borne. A visit with Charlotte will be just the thing."

"What you interrupted in the summerhouse—it was not what you thought! Mr Darcy never, in any way, acted otherwise than in the most gentlemanlike manner. I was the one who—"

"A gentleman! Hah! He would not know a gentleman if he hit one with that fancy curricle of his!"

"But Papa, surely, as Mama has pointed out—"

"Your mother has set her heart on a wedding, I am certain. But she cannot see past his wealth. He would make an even worse husband than Collins—he would trample your spirit and make you wretched, without even providing the amusement of idiocy."

"The gossip—"

"What little gossip there is will soon die down. No one can believe it anyway—everyone knows how you dislike each other. Darcy will swiftly lose whatever little interest he had in such an unequal union. While I suppose it is to his credit that he was willing to do the right thing, the idea of you trapped in such an unhappy marriage has grated upon me."

How earnestly did she then wish that her former opinions had been more reasonable, her expressions more moderate! But his opinion was fixed, and he was convinced that any softer feelings she had developed for Mr Darcy were grounded upon fear for her reputation within the community. She was to leave with Mr and Mrs Collins in a hired carriage that very day, even though it meant they would not arrive in Kent until well after dark. He had already ordered her trunk packed and, what was worse, was determined to stand sentinel to Darcy. Wherever he went in the house, Mr Bennet meant to follow. They had not been, would not be, allowed any private leave-taking.

A soft knock interrupted her final packing and desolate thoughts. "Come in," she called, expecting her mother.

But it was Georgiana, blushing, who hastily entered. "I only wanted to add my farewell, and that of Fitzwilliam. He would have given it himself, had it been possible."

Elizabeth swallowed a lump. "I am sorry my father is being so unreasonable."

"Think nothing more of it," she said, and looking around as if she was fearful of being overheard, spoke in a rush. "I-I have a note for you, from my brother. I promise there is nothing in it of-of an inappropriate nature."

She held out a small, folded piece of paper; Elizabeth took it and put it in her pocket. "Thank you, dear. I have loved beginning to know you. Please tell Mr Darcy…" she bit her lip against tears and tried again. "Please tell *Fitzwilliam* that I hope to see you both again. Very soon. And Dubitz too, of course."

Shyly, Georgiana smiled. On impulse, Elizabeth added an embrace, which was returned. When the younger girl slipped from the room, Elizabeth felt an inkling of hope for the future.

Elizabeth had of course wished to read the message immediately, but Mrs Bennet suddenly entered, full of complaints about Mr Bennet's inability to see sense and reason when it was staring him in the face. For once, she and her mother were in complete agreement.

The note was a weight in her pocket and a burning curiosity in her heart, but she had no opportunity to open it until the first horse change at Pinchfield, when both Mr and Mrs Collins exited the carriage.

It was disappointingly brief. '*Challenge Number Five*' was all it said. Still, it made her smile, even as she had hoped for something more…romantic, and gave her heart, somehow, during the interminable journey to Hunsford. Mr Collins preached endlessly regarding the certainty of an upcoming wedding between Darcy and Anne de Bourgh, naming several instances wherein the great man had 'proved his love' by deeply interesting himself in his cousin's health and well-being.

"I think you will like our home, the Hunsford Parsonage. It is so nicely situated, with views of the park to the east and west, as well as our lovely garden behind, and all within walking distance to such a pleasant little village," Charlotte said, obviously attempting to soften her husband's overbearing opinions. "I wish it would not be dark when we arrive, so you could see the plantings—our neighbours often remark upon them."

"You will find my home enchanting," Mr Collins chimed in. "The views of the park are magnificent from every window. My garden is the delight of my neighbours—'what a delightful garden' they often say. Such a charming village, at such an easy distance!"

How did Charlotte put up with his nonsense? Elizabeth glanced at her friend, but she remarked nothing upon his parroting of her every thought. What might it have been like to try and live with this fool?

I would never have been able to keep my tongue between my teeth; I would not be able to help trying to improve his conversation. And yet, what good would her efforts have done? It had not escaped her notice that whilst Charlotte called it 'our home' and 'our garden', with Mr Collins, it was all 'me, my, mine'.

Perhaps he means to show me what I rejected. Unbidden, however, came the recollection of her scolding to Darcy for his damage to Jane's feelings after her wedding. Perhaps he had not taken her own feelings quite so seriously, at first, as she might have wished. Still, the differences between the two men were so vast, she could draw only one conclusion.

Had I married Mr Collins, eventually, I would have murdered him and gone to the gallows unrepentant.

The house was a very sturdy, tidy affair, agreeably sized, suiting Charlotte very well. It quickly became apparent that other than meals, Mr and Mrs Collins spent little time together. If Charlotte had a love at all, it was for this home, for her favourite parlour, for her henhouse and her needlework. The doings of church and village were her helpmeets, keeping her busy and contented. One or two agreeable parish matrons called within a day, and with the exception of certain vexatious interruptions from her husband, Charlotte seemed well on her way to a satisfying life.

"I am glad to see you so happy," Elizabeth said sincerely to her friend two days after her arrival, as she penned a letter to Jane and Charlotte to her mother, in the cosy parlour on a windy afternoon. "We have not seen her ladyship. But I suppose you are not too often obliged to endure her."

Charlotte turned a rather disapproving look upon her friend. "I assure you, Eliza, Lady Catherine is a very respectable, sensible woman indeed, and a most attentive neighbour. Many weeks, in fact, we dine at least twice at Rosings."

"I do not think I would want much, if any, attention of hers."

"You naturally did not see her ladyship at her best," Charlotte replied, the note of reproval still in her tone.

"What think you of this proposed match between Mr Darcy and Miss de Bourgh?" Elizabeth could not resist asking. "Your husband seems to think it all but a certainty."

"I believe Mr Darcy has a decided preference for

you," Charlotte openly disagreed, much to Elizabeth's surprise. "However, Lady Catherine must not be blamed for taking up Miss de Bourgh's part. Mr Darcy would make an excellent husband."

"I suppose. However, wishing is one thing, but she was intrusive and rude. You did not hear her in the garden."

Charlotte set down her pen. "From what I understand of the situation, Mr Darcy made his lack of intentions towards Miss de Bourgh clear to Lady Catherine and her daughter a number of years ago, before he was of an age to consider marriage to anyone. Thereafter, little was ever mentioned upon the subject, and Mr Darcy did not fix his interests elsewhere. Meanwhile, he has always been an attentive relation, and it would appear Lady Catherine's hopes grew with every passing year he remained unwed. It must have come as quite a shock to her, learning that her hopes were forlorn ones, after all."

There is only one way she could have learnt it—from your *husband—probably via* your *father!* Elizabeth wished to point it out, but she refrained.

"Still, when you think of it, neither Miss de Bourgh's marital prospects—nor even Mr Darcy's— has anything to do with me. If I were to die tomorrow, they are no more likely to wed than if I live to be ninety. And no less likely, either."

"A great deal more likely, I should think," Charlotte countered. "Tell me—is there an official betrothal yet?"

Elizabeth was instantly wary; she had no idea whether she could trust Charlotte to withhold information from her husband, and the last thing she wanted was another visit from Lady Catherine.

"We are not engaged. It is far too soon to speak of betrothals!" But she felt her cheeks pinkening and feared Charlotte saw more than she wished to reveal.

"You two certainly seemed comfortable together at Netherfield during our visit."

"Do you mean while Lady Catherine was interrogating me? Mr Darcy was appalled and embarrassed by her behaviour and escorted me away from her."

She did not remember any embarrassment on his part—some annoyance, perhaps, couched within his sarcasm.

"And stayed away for some hours," Charlotte added, brows raised.

"I stayed away until I was certain she was gone. You did not hear her discourtesy. She was awful!"

"Now, Eliza, one cannot expect her ladyship to accommodate such disappointments without expressing herself however she deems fit. She is sister to the earl of Matlock, you know."

"No, I did not know. Does that give her permission to behave abominably?"

The fact was, her rank gave permission for far worse. Elizabeth knew it. But she could not help wishing it otherwise.

"We must be patient with her. If there is an attachment between you and Mr Darcy, she will learn to accommodate the match, in time."

"I am surprised you invited me here, with such disapproval as Lady Catherine has for me. Will she not resent you, and possibly even Mr Collins, for it?"

"Now, this is where you are wholly absurd, Eliza. It was her ladyship's idea. She practically ordered us to bring you to Hunsford. It is why Mr Collins went to your father."

"What? How can this be?"

"In the moment, I suppose she was not overfond of the idea of you and Mr Darcy in the same county, much less the same house. But of course, I have been wanting you to visit this age, and I do not suppose, if Mr Darcy has decided to have you, a different location for a few weeks will change anything," Charlotte said complacently.

Elizabeth found herself annoyed. It was all well and good for Charlotte to assume things would take their natural course, regardless of a separation. *She* had never been practically torn from the arms of her lover, at the behest of an arrogant aunt. On the other hand, Charlotte had never had a lover at all, only the pathetic Mr Collins; she could not be expected to understand. Well, Lady Catherine had managed to plant her here, but she would find she could not keep her. *Challenge number five, indeed.*

"It seems incredible," Elizabeth pushed a little. "And you will miss your dinners at Rosings, for I cannot believe she will take any notice of you while I am here."

Charlotte only shrugged, changing the subject. "Oh, I had nearly forgotten. I received a pattern for lace from Mrs Tilson—you met her sister yesterday, and I expect she will stop in soon. I have been wanting to show it to you." With that, Charlotte brought forth stitchery projects in various stages of completion, and the afternoon was spent in their admiration, saying no more about either Lady Catherine or courtships.

But Elizabeth could not help but be puzzled by it all.

Darcy was puzzled by the invitation.

Naturally, he had meant to pay a visit to his aunt. He had figured to give it a week before he did so—giving Georgiana time to settle in their Mayfair home and ensure she was well and comfortable before leaving her alone again with Mrs Annesley. She seemed content enough, he thought, glancing at her from across the table where he had joined her for breakfast, a meal he usually took much earlier in his rooms. Without a word, he handed over Lady Catherine's summons.

After a moment's perusal, she frowned up at him. "This makes little sense, if Elizabeth is still at the vicarage."

"My thoughts exactly," he replied.

"Perhaps she wishes to convince you of the error in your choice of female."

"By comparing her to Cousin Anne? Will she put them beside each other and watch Elizabeth's smile and wit fascinate me? I am likely to forget anyone else is in the room."

Georgiana smiled at this depiction. "It does seem a rather daft thing to do. Will you go?"

"I was going regardless, simply not this soon. I shall probably take Colonel Fitzwilliam with me. We may as well see what our aunt has in mind."

"That is the last thing I would ever want to know," Georgiana said. "Dubitz and I shall await you here. Give Elizabeth my love."

⚜

He and his cousin, Colonel Richard Fitzwilliam, arrived at Rosings Park late the very next evening. To Darcy's mild surprise, his aunt said absolutely nothing regarding Elizabeth. She did remind them, repeatedly, of Anne's fortune and prospects, even mentioning her 'pleasing figure' once or twice—causing a flare of alarm in both gentlemen.

"Lock your chamber door," the colonel muttered.

"As if Lady Catherine has no spare key," Darcy replied under his breath.

"Barricade it," was the colonel's response.

It was too late to call upon the vicarage, but Darcy planned to make it his first order of business upon the morrow.

Thursday morning, he awoke far too early in his impatience for the day to begin. After attending to some correspondence, he decided to seek out another likely picnic spot amongst the forested paths in the park. He could not arrange one immediately, more was the pity; the colonel was keen to meet his choice of bride, and undoubtedly Lady Catherine would demand his attention every moment she could.

To that end, I should probably escape the house now so that my reunion with Elizabeth will not be in company. I can return later for my cousin and all the necessary, more tedious introductions.

Matching thought to action, he slipped out of the house, taking a back path towards Hunsford, a short-cut through the garden. He had only gone a little distance, however, before he was abruptly startled into halting by the sounds of voices on the other side of a tall hedge.

"He is here. You must prepare yourself to act," Lady Catherine's voice announced through the shrubbery.

"Your ladyship's plans are, of course, excellent ones,"

came the anxious tones of her vicar, Collins. "However, I am certain you can appreciate the difficulty of—"

"How difficult could it be?" she interrupted. "I will arrange the most complicated share of the assignment. I will have Darcy in the centre of the maze today at two o'clock. All you need do is bring Miss Bennet nearby without entering it and then protest her attack upon your person—loudly enough that Darcy hears your horrified objections."

"It is only that, as a man of the cloth, I am—"

"You are *my* vicar, are you not? Your loyalty is to *me*, is it not?"

"Why yes, madam, of course! It is only—"

"She shall likely practise her arts and allurements upon you the entire time she is in your company, and you shall be well-primed to fight her off. Now, it is of the utmost importance that you be as explicit as possible. Be certain to complain of her hands clambering upon your posterior, and when we appear, act as if she has been plying you with kisses. Wet ones."

"What? Why, my lady, I cannot possibly—"

"Heavens, do not be so missish! You are *saving* my nephew from a most unfeeling, selfish trollop who cares only for his fortune. Would you *like* to see him imprisoned in such a match?"

"Of course not, madam," Collins replied, managing to sound supercilious, nervous, and resigned. "It shall be as you say."

Darcy's first thought was to take hold of the pair of them and bash their sanctimonious heads together. How dare they conspire to injure Elizabeth in any way! He would not have believed in the ruse, regardless, but that dearest, loveliest Elizabeth might be offended by its performance was intolerable.

Their voices were already moving away, however, and by the time he reached a break in the hedge, they were out of sight. Perhaps it was best that he wait, after all—he was so outraged, he might require Fitzwilliam's intervention to avoid violence. With a narrow-eyed gaze that promised retribution to the plotters, he made his way, instead, to his beloved.

❧ 16 ❧

It took Darcy hardly any time at all to traverse the mile or so to the parsonage—his anger gave his feet impetus to practically fly there. But as he approached, off in the distance, he saw a bright yellow speck. He knew that speck, watching as it rapidly, purposefully crossed a path leading into a forested—and very private—part of the park. Grinning, he changed direction to intercept it.

He was perhaps a dozen yards away before she saw him. For a moment, she stilled in surprise. And then, in the most exciting, sweetest moment of his life...she ran to him. He moved, opening his arms, and at last, at last, he held her within his embrace; their mouths met hungrily, happily, with laughter between kisses.

"Has it been a year? It feels so," he said, holding her dear face within his hands.

"A decade, at least."

Her wide, pretty smile hit him somewhere deep within; he had to kiss her again, a long and wistful sort of kiss—only a small part of what he wished for. "When will you marry me?" he demanded, kissing her cheeks, her closed eyes, the sensuous lobe of her ear.

"I do not believe you have asked me yet," she pointed out—and nipped his chin. It made him feel rather desperate, and certainly diminished his common sense, as she wrapped her arms about his neck, and he pulled her in more tightly.

"Marry me, will you," he commanded. "Marry me *now*." He had to stop himself from too frantic a display, his feelings spiralling towards the folly of a reckless desire.

She laughed. "That was not a proposal, you clunch. I was hoping to see you on bended knee."

He pulled them both down, rolling so she fell atop him, heedless of grass stains upon his coat. "I bent my knees," he explained. "Who knew it would be so enjoyable?"

The kisses grew more dangerous then, and more exquisite. He knew she was innocent of her effect upon him, and it was up to him to protect her—but it was devilish difficult. Only a lifetime of making the harder choices—whether it was applying himself to his studies or learning the management of his estates or hurrying to his sister instead of staying for a ball to dance with the girl he was falling in love with—gave him the discipline needed, the discipline such a spirited beauty deserved.

"I beg you to marry me," he breathed, between kisses. "I implore you to take a clunch for a husband and make what you can of him."

"What an offer," she said, kissing his lower lip. "But really, with my lack of fortune, I suppose I cannot do much better." They both chuckled.

He sighed, his hands coasting along her back. "Your

mother would *definitely* disapprove of any of what I feel like doing at the moment, and your father would simply shoot me. I must return to Rosings, but not before I tell you of my aunt's plotting."

"Plotting? What is this?"

He helped her up, brushing at her skirts whilst she extracted pine needles from his coat collar before explaining the situation and how he had discovered it. His only means of preventing her from marching back to the vicarage and emptying a chamber-pot over Collins's head was to reveal the response he had formulated upon his walk to Hunsford. "Of course, you shall not walk with him anywhere at all. Simply refuse, for what can he do? I predict he will arrive alone to the maze and attempt to apologise to Lady Catherine for your absence —he will not dare to do otherwise. I will have the truth of their intentions out of him quickly enough and give them both a dressing down neither will soon forget."

"How could he agree to take part? He is *supposed* to be a man of God! I wish I could shoot him!"

"No court in the land would convict you if you did," he said. "But I will see him beg your forgiveness."

"I cannot believe I am residing with a degenerate who would participate in such a monstrous scheme!"

"You have spent your last night in his home, I promise. I will whisk you away from Rosings once I have administered his punishment."

"And what of your aunt?" Elizabeth replied, indignant. "She is willing to invent falsehoods, plotting to destroy my character in order to break us apart! It is unconscionable!"

"Lady Catherine will have an audience of both her daughter and the colonel to her perfidy. It will be more humiliating for her, as Fitzwilliam will certainly inform the earl. I will ensure she never dares anything of the sort again," he promised. "Your relations in town—the Gardiners—will they welcome you, do you think? I will send an express immediately, if so, and hire one of the maids to accompany you."

"Yes, of course," she said, obviously still furious. "But I had better include a note, explaining what I can. They knew of my dislike for you and would be alarmed to receive such an unusual communication."

He pulled her again into his arms. "Dislike, in the present tense?"

Her hands went to his chest, and she looked up at him, her big eyes suddenly unhappy. "I wish I was everything you deserve in a bride—wealthy and dripping connexions like jewels. I wish your aunt was not correct that I bring nothing to you. I hate that some will believe she is right to do anything in her power to stop it, and I have not an argument to contest her interests."

He stroked his thumb across her soft cheek, shaking his head, smiling down upon her. "You bring more than I ever imagined I could have to this match. I have enough wealth should we have a dozen dowries to provide—how much more could a man need? It seems to me that gaining a wife who is clever, lively, loyal—and whose kisses take my breath away—is asking Fate for too much." He touched his lips lightly to hers, not daring to grow carried away again, and had the pleasure of seeing her expression soften and sorrow flee.

"I have a proposal."

He raised a brow at her.

"I *will* walk through that maze with my cousin."

He frowned, opening his mouth to protest, but she

interrupted him. "I am their intended victim. I have the right to be there, to witness their punishment. I think we should follow my father's example of how one should confront a challenge, since it was he who sent me into this madness." She went on to describe a few ideas of hers, which might, indeed, create a brilliant comeuppance for the pair, then reached up to touch the curls at his nape, sending shivers down his spine. "I hope you do not believe me incapable of dealing with Mr Collins, no matter what he attempts to say." She gazed up at him, a smile in her eyes along with a certain wistful expression as she stared at his mouth.

"There is that look again. It is dashed near irresistible," he complained. "How is a man to guard against it? You could ask me for anything at all, and I would be helpless to refuse."

"Would you teach me to drive your curricle?" she asked, and he laughed.

"Thank the Lord I did not bring it. Yes, yes, but first you must learn—again—to ride, lest you use too heavy a hand on the reins. I will find a pony for you to practise on. Something an infant could manage." She swatted him, and he laughed again. He could not recall laughing so much in years and years.

After confiding in his cousin and further refining their plans for the encounter, Darcy had decided that the most circumspect behaviour would cast their aunt in the worst possible light. Hence, they spent what was left of the morning playing the parts of attentive guests. He and Fitzwilliam did not, as they had planned, visit the vicarage. He sent his man to collect Elizabeth's note to her Gardiner relations and thereafter to see to sending his express to Gracechurch Street.

Why, he wondered, did his aunt believe her daughter ought to marry him? Anne had nothing to say beyond the commonplace, showing no more than the vaguest interest in him—or Fitzwilliam either, for that matter. She was not shy; she simply could not have cared less about either of them.

He had been curious as to how her ladyship proposed to lure him out to the maze, but she simply announced, in her usual overbearing fashion, that she had planned a tea at the maze's centre at two o'clock, at which she expected their presence. And that was that.

Even though her plot was a stupid one, and he did not wish for Elizabeth to be importuned in the slightest fashion, he could look forward to its denouement with some eagerness. Not only would he see Elizabeth again, but he would be able to extract a bit of justice for her and, best of all, take his immediate leave of Rosings. He could hardly wait.

⚜

Elizabeth saw no reason to make anything easy for her cousin in his role of deceiver. How far Charlotte might approve of her husband's infamy, she could not guess, but when she failed to come down for breakfast—the result of a megrim, Mr Collins explained—Elizabeth had her suspicions. Alas, she was beginning to believe that if Lady Catherine ordered her to stay abed for the day, Charlotte would simply do so, with no questions asked.

"Cousin Elizabeth," Mr Collins declared in a too-animated tone as the time approached for his deceit. "I cannot stand to see such a lovely day ruined by my dear Charlotte's illness. You must be bored. May I show you the maze at Rosings Park? It was designed by Humphry Repton and is well worth seeing."

She glanced up from the handkerchief she was embroidering for Darcy. "No thank you, sir," she replied politely. "I will wait for Charlotte's health to improve, that we might all see it together."

He coloured, appearing nonplussed. "I-um, that is, my wife has had the pleasure many times. Allow me the honour of escorting you."

"You are too kind, but I wish to finish my stitchery. It is a gift, you see, and I would rather not go anywhere before finishing it."

"B-but...you must!"

Elizabeth raised a brow. "Must I? And why is that?"

"I did not mean...that is, you do not...um, I say, it is fine weather. A walk would be just the thing. Good for the health, you see."

She let the silence stretch for long, awkward moments, as his face turned various shades of purple. Finally, she agreed. "Very well. Allow me to fetch my parasol." She took her time about it, changing her bonnet to a different one and putting on heavier half-boots in case she had the opportunity to step on his toes. When she finally returned downstairs and saw him pacing the entry anxiously, she hid a smile.

"There you are!" he said hastily, opening the door.

"Oh! I do believe I forgot my shawl. I shall fetch it—"

"No! I mean, the weather is quite warm. Look! Very warm. Rather hot, even!"

"Hot? Oh, perhaps we should wait for a cooler day."

"No, no, no, not hot, not at all. Not chilly, either. Just perfect weather, perfect!" A bead of sweat cascaded down his brow.

"Well then," she said, gliding out the door, "what a day for an outing."

Mr Collins chattered incessantly all the way to the maze—which was rather a long ramble—as if, were she allowed to get a word in edgewise, she might turn around for home. She was mightily tempted, to be sure, but could not resist witnessing the comeuppance they had planned for him. They ought to achieve *that*, if nothing else.

When they entered the maze, his stream of words finally dried up; he continually retraced his steps, slowing and then speeding about rather frantically.

"If we cannot find the centre, we might as well turn back," she said graciously.

He did not even bother to answer, beginning to mutter directions to himself. "Right at the armless cupid, left at the pineapple on a post. Or was it right at the pineapple? I am certain it was right. Now where have they hidden that girl with the bird?"

"Was it Repton who designed these marbles?" she asked. He gave an annoyed look at her for having disturbed his recitations, and he quickly returned to his muttering. After a few minutes, she pointed out a statue they had already passed at least three times. "Is that the girl with the bird?"

A slender marble maiden set atop a post, her arms outstretched, a bird perched upon her shoulder, seemed to point in the opposite of their current direction. "Yes, yes, that is it," he replied, mopping his brow with a large handkerchief. "This way."

Soon thereafter, she could hear the murmur of voices, and as they turned a corner, she saw it—the roof of a pavilion, peeking just above the next hedgerow, a magnificent arch of formed shrubbery leading to their destination.

"Ah," she said obligingly, and paused. "It appears we are almost to the centre. I hear others who have also reached it—"

"Move your hands away from me, Miss Bennet!" he called, in an unnatural falsetto that barely squeaked from his throat.

But as he began speaking, Elizabeth filled her lungs and screamed—and not a childish, fresh-from-the-nursery sort of scream, but a full-throated, ear-piercing screech.

There came the sound of feet pounding, and Darcy and a man she presumed to be Colonel Fitzwilliam rounded the corner. Lady Catherine and a very thin, younger version of her ladyship—Miss Anne de Bourgh? —rapidly followed behind. At the sight of them, Collins lost his head completely, grabbing Elizabeth as if to use her as a human shield.

"What in the name of almighty heaven is happening here?" Darcy roared.

"It is obvious enough, Darcy," replied the colonel. "That fellow is attacking the young lady."

"What? No!" cried Mr Collins and Lady Catherine, almost in unison. The other lady said nothing whatso-ever, looking from one to the other as if mildly puzzled.

"Collins, name your friends! Fitzwilliam, will you stand with me?"

"Of course, of course. Nothing else to be done," the colonel agreed.

"What is that you say?" Mr Collins sputtered squeakily.

"You will meet me and answer for your dishonour," Darcy said coldly.

"What? This is impossible! I do not agree to-to meet you. Never! I would never! It is against the law!"

"Oh, no need to worry about that," said the colonel reassuringly. "Local magistrate is the best of good fellows. Will hush the matter up in two shakes. His constables as well. Wouldn't be the first body they helped bury, for the price of a pint or two. They understand these things. Honour and all that."

"You cannot mean...I would not choose—"

"Oh, absolutely—naturally, it is your choice of weapons, since Darcy called you out. Just between ourselves, I would not choose pistols if I were you. A crack shot, is Darcy."

"P-p-pistols? But-but-but..."

"I am just as good with swords as pistols, I daresay," Darcy interjected helpfully. "Boxing might be fair. Haven't been to Gentleman Jackson's in a month of Sundays. Not sure if I could beat you to death, but of course, I would give it my best effort."

"Fitzwilliam Darcy! I demand you stop this nonsense immediately!" Lady Catherine cried.

"It is much too late for that," the colonel said, shaking his head. "Gone too far. No honourable way to withdraw."

Darcy nodded. "No other outcome is possible, at this point." He turned sharply to his aunt, his face very close to hers, cold fury on his brow. He looked rather terrifying, Elizabeth had to admit. "Did you have anything to do with this plot, ma'am? Were *you* its instigator? We both know this weakling would never have acted, except upon your direction!"

"I-I did not mean—it was not s-supposed to-to…" she stuttered weakly, for once looking rather lost and almost feeble.

"Oh, Mama. You were very wicked!" the other lady—who *must* be Miss de Bourgh—cried.

"You have played with fire, and now your puppet will burn," Darcy said harshly. "We are gentlemen. Gentlemen must live by gentlemen's rules, and his death will be on your head, not mine. May God have mercy on your soul."

Lady Catherine sputtered bursts of protests like a leaky teapot, while Collins whimpered long-winded ones. "But I am not—that is, not having been raised as a gentleman, although well-schooled in a manner similar to and having the appearance of a gentleman, the next thing *to* a gentleman, but not exactly one… or rather a variety of one, but not of the classic variety—not one who follows a traditional sort of conduct, but a more modern mode of peaceful gentleman-ship—"

"Shut it!" the colonel ordered, as if Collins was a new recruit in his service. "Another word and I shall run you through with my dress sword!"

For the first time, Elizabeth noticed that the colonel was wearing his full military costume, complete with medals, insignias, and fobs. Somehow, she doubted he usually attended tea in such state—but it was quite wonderfully impressive.

Darcy took his watch from his pocket. "Shall we meet in an hour?"

"An hour? An hour!" Collins shrieked.

The colonel speared him with a look that quelled it.

"Plainly, Miss Bennet can no longer stay in the same household with her attacker. She must be taken to her nearest relations. Darcy, would you perform the introductions?"

"My apologies, Fitzwilliam, of course. Miss Bennet, my cousin, Colonel Fitzwilliam of His Majesty's army, youngest son of the earl of Matlock. Colonel, Miss Elizabeth Bennet, of Longbourn in Hertfordshire."

"Very pleased to meet you, Miss Bennet. I am sorry it is under such distressing circumstances."

Elizabeth curtseyed low, saying nothing for fear of bursting into laughter.

"Where do your nearest relations reside, Miss Bennet?"

"London, sir," she managed. "Near Cheapside."

The colonel nodded solemnly and turned to Darcy. "We should allow three to four hours to have her safely delivered before dark. Can the duel even wait an hour, do you think?"

"Only just. Name your seconds, sir! At once!"

"B-but I...I...I..." Collins could not seem to form a sentence.

Fitzwilliam clapped a heavy hand upon his shoulder. "Mind you, it must be no one who would gossip. We must keep this between ourselves."

"Call on Olmsby, Fitzwilliam," Darcy snapped impatiently. "I daresay he would act for him, and he will know to keep his mouth shut. The two of you can tell us where to meet."

"Excellent idea. I will go to him directly."

Mr Collins looked from one man to the other. They were both tall and broad-shouldered, their faces wearing identical, deadly serious expressions. He glanced pleadingly at his benefactress, but she looked, for once, help-less. There was no mercy to be found here.

He dropped to his knees at Darcy's feet, beginning to sob. "I am so sorry, so very sorry. Please, please, forgive me. I will never approach Miss Bennet ever again, for any reason. Only say you will pardon me. It was all a misunderstanding, a mistake. A terrible mistake. Please!" Tears dripped down his face and onto his bulging waistcoat.

Elizabeth *almost* felt sorry for him. Darcy and the colonel had issued the same challenge as her father had, but with a significantly more dangerous impression in the performance.

"Darcy, what say you? The offender has apologised. Can you accept it?"

"The apology of a worm," he hissed. "Miss Bennet, you have been grossly offended by this scoundrel. The apology belongs to you. Can you forgive it?"

"I only wish to be safe," she replied meekly. "I never dreamt I was in danger at Rosings."

A look of alarm passed over Lady Catherine's face; obviously she had begun to perceive her future reputa-tion as an aggressor against innocent maidens, should Elizabeth relate the tale she now possessed. "Oh, Miss Bennet, you never were," Lady Catherine protested. "You would not want any others to find out about this! It could reflect poorly upon you!"

"What did you say?" Darcy roared. "Did I hear a *threat* to *her* in your words?"

"Never," Lady Catherine vowed, her eyes wide with alarm. "I swear it!"

"You have brought shame upon our entire family. I have already asked for Miss Bennet's hand. You had best hope that she decides in my favour and that every further communication from you is a pleasant one. If not, expect the cut direct next time you are in town. From me and all who side with me."

Lady Catherine gasped; sister to an earl she may have been, but Elizabeth guessed that in a public dispute, she and her daughter would not fare so well as Darcy, especially as he obviously held the Matlock loyalty.

"Thank you, sir," Miss de Bourgh said, coming to her mother's rescue in a surprising display of dignity. "It is a most generous offer. We will not test your patience any further. Come, Mother," she ordered, and taking her by the arm, firmly led her away. Once or twice, Lady Catherine looked back confusedly, but her daughter brooked no resistance. She was resolutely marched out of sight.

"I believe we have just witnessed the changing of the guard," the colonel murmured, sounding somewhat awed.

"As for you," Darcy said in awful tones, turning back to Collins—who shrank from his still obvious fury— "there is only one acceptable punishment. Miss Bennet, cover your ears, please. What I am about to say is not suitable for a delicate maiden like yourself."

"Thank you, sir," she said meekly, covering her ears in an exaggerated manner that blocked nothing of the sound of his voice.

Collins hunched over as he cringed at Darcy's feet. "I will do whatever you wish to prove my remorse, if you will only accept my apology!"

Darcy hauled him up by his neckcloth. "Anything?" he challenged.

He really is amazingly strong, Elizabeth thought admiringly. Collins was not a small man.

"Yes!" Collins squeaked.

He brought his face right up to the vicar's. "You will not touch your wife *intimately* unless she asks you to—not unless it is her idea *entirely*. You will not expect *anything* from her beyond the duties of house and parish. *Do you understand me?*"

It was all Elizabeth could do not to giggle aloud; this portion of the 'punishment' was utterly Darcy's invention.

"Y-yes, sir."

"Do you? Do you?" Colonel Fitzwilliam bellowed from directly behind him, with all the gusto of an army officer accustomed to shouting over the furore of battle.

Collins fainted dead away.

D arcy put his arm about Elizabeth's slender waist. "I apologise, my darling, that Collins laid hands upon you. I never dreamt he would dare touch you, not in any fashion."

She regarded him smilingly, waving this aside. "He hardly meant to—only your fearsome presence startled from his head whatever little wit he possesses." She looked down upon the vicar's inert form. "How shall we get him home?"

"Leave him," the colonel muttered. "He can find his own way when he wakes."

"I am not sure he can," Elizabeth said. "He could not find his way through the maze with a map. Even I could tell we were going in circles and was forced to point out clues."

Darcy shepherded them away from the fallen vicar, leading her swiftly out of the maze. The colonel obviously knew the way as well, walking several steps ahead to give them some semblance of privacy. "Making his way home, dearest, is his own problem. Are you packed?"

"Yes, but I will have to return to the vicarage for my trunk. Whatever shall I say to Charlotte?"

"I would tell her she married a nincompoop."

"She already knows *that*. Desperation must be her excuse. She does not like her elder brother's wife, and feared for her future rather more than I ever realised, I think. I do pity her, but I do not possess her nerve, or her foolishness. I cannot decide which it is."

"Probably a little of both."

"What does your cousin think of this whole matter?" Elizabeth asked.

"Colonel Fitzwilliam thinks our aunt has lost her mind and that her vicar never had one. He was happy to assist in whatever way he could."

"I cannot help but wish our introduction was not heralded by my screeching like a banshee."

"Our ears are still ringing," Darcy agreed, and she gave him a stern look. Glancing up to ensure his cousin was out of sight, he stopped on the path and pulled her into his arms. After kissing her thoroughly, he said, "He is bound to love you, because you are a spirited, sweet, sensible girl who will make me happy. You could not have played your part in this silly affair with better assurance."

"I do not understand what your aunt expected to gain," Elizabeth said—several minutes later, after the violence of her returned affection was satisfied.

He sighed. "Lady Catherine is spoilt and selfish. She is accustomed to having her way, and she wants me for Anne—how much she has wanted it, I have plainly underestimated. But like the child who grabs for a favourite toy, she did not think it out. Not only does she not know you, but she does not even have the slightest understanding of *me*. It is ludicrous to think I would ever believe you would throw yourself at the ridiculous Collins."

"Plainly, she does not know her vicar very well either," Elizabeth agreed. "Had I wanted him, I could have had him. He proposed to me and was refused only a day or two before he suddenly remembered he was in love with Charlotte, instead."

"Somehow, he must have forgotten to mention that to my aunt."

She giggled, a sound he adored, as they exited the maze.

"Ah, I was just wondering if I was needed for another rescue," the colonel remarked good-naturedly, from his position just beyond the maze entrance. "Forgot the way out, did you Darcy? A few wrong turns?"

"My memory is not what it once was," Darcy allowed. "However, you could have been better employed in having the carriage brought round rather than fretting over our whereabouts."

But at that moment, the Darcy carriage trotted up the lane and into sight; the colonel laughed, a hearty, full-bodied chortling. "Your slightest wish, of course, is my command."

"Well played," Darcy approved.

"I cannot take credit. Your man, Pennywithers was waiting here when I emerged. Devil of a mother hen, is Pennywithers."

Elizabeth was somewhat surprised by the banter between these two cousins. Her first impression of the colonel had been of a stern, warrior-like man, battle-hardened and humourless. Which, she supposed, he might be when the situation called for it. But this jovial, teasing fellow did not match up to that impression in the slightest.

"Forgive me, ma'am," Colonel Fitzwilliam said, suddenly addressing her. "Forgot my language. I hope you did not make too much of my aunt's nonsense. I can assure you the rest of the family is only half as mad."

"How comforting," she replied, and he chuckled again.

A maid awaited her in the Darcy vehicle, a quiet girl named Susan who had been hired in the village by the mother-hennish Pennywithers. Darcy and Colonel Fitzwilliam, it seemed, would be riding to London in escort—a little disappointing, but very proper. The carriage pulled up to the gate of the parsonage, the steps were lowered, and she hesitated before the door.

Pennywithers, riding upon the box with the Darcy coachman, would undoubtedly fetch her trunk should she request it. Rather than encounter Charlotte, she could write to her, and think out more carefully what she did and did not wish to say of the matter. Yet, the anger at her friend for the supposed 'megrim' had dissipated entirely—indeed, if Elizabeth had to put a name to her current disposition, she would have to call it…relief, tinged with sadness.

Perhaps, in the furthest corner of her mind, she *had* felt guilty for refusing to marry Mr Collins—for failing to preserve her family's home and her children's inheritance. Hence, she had continually looked towards Charlotte at every stupid remark from her husband's mouth, seeking some sort of validation for that refusal, as if it mattered any longer. And now that she knew with absolute certainty that the husband surpassed 'foolish' and tumbled headlong into complete nincompoopery, she felt only relief that she had sought a different fate—with a good deal of compassion for Charlotte, who could envision nothing else. She must give her farewells in person, for she could never imagine visiting Hunsford again; she would miss her old friend.

She exited the carriage, hurrying into the house and straight up the stairs, tapping on Charlotte's chamber door.

"Enter," came a muffled voice.

Charlotte was sitting at a little desk, her back to the door, writing materials at hand. She had not turned, probably believing it to be Ruth, her maid-of-all-work.

"I must leave," Elizabeth announced.

Charlotte swivelled upon her chair, her surprise evident. "Eliza? What is this?"

"I am leaving. Mr Darcy's carriage has been put at my disposal, and I will go to my uncle Gardiner."

"But...why so short a visit? Have you been summoned to your relations?"

Elizabeth studied her closely; Charlotte's expression held confusion, but they had been friends for many years —there was mortification in it as well. Most likely, Mr Collins had been incapable of keeping his lips entirely sealed, and in this case, she could not expect her usual habit of looking away and pretending ignorance to shelter her. She might not know exactly *what* had happened, but she knew *something* had.

Still, although it was not in Elizabeth's nature to

encourage such deceit—neither could she blame Charlotte overmuch. Her friend would never have guessed that her ladyship's scheme would be such a distasteful one. Besides, Elizabeth was leaving, while Charlotte must remain here, more or less, until Papa died. As Mr Bennet was in the pink of good health, and as *his* father would likely be alive today had he not had the misfortune of possessing a recalcitrant stallion with an unfortunate habit of tossing its riders—and as his paternal grandfather, whom he closely resembled, had lived to the age of ninety—one could presume Charlotte must live in the shadow of Rosings for many years to come.

"In a manner of speaking," Elizabeth replied. "I thank you for your hospitality, but I must depart immediately."

Charlotte looked as though she wished to protest but did not quite dare.

Elizabeth searched for something encouraging to add. "You, um, do have a beautiful home, Charlotte. I wish you very happy."

It was weak, but nothing else came to mind. Elizabeth left her sitting there and made the arrangements for her trunk to be brought down. Somewhat to her surprise, Charlotte joined her at the entry. She looked as near to tears as Elizabeth had seen her in many years.

"I am so sorry your visit was cut short," she said, and Elizabeth knew her apology was for much more than that. "I am so very sorry."

"I am sorry as well," Elizabeth replied, and meant it. Impulsively, she added, "Charlotte, your husband..." She tried to think of how to form the words, how to explain the impossible penalty Mr Darcy had administered; but her friend nearly cringed, obviously expecting to hear of something embarrassing and shameful.

"You must know your husband has been up to something. Well, it was not something good. He gambled. He gambled and he lost." Her next words came out in a rush. "Lost, to Mr Darcy that is. Until you give your permission, he cannot seek you out."

"Why would Mr Darcy seek me out?"

Elizabeth stifled a giggle. "No, not Darcy. Mr Collins. He does, um, seek your *private* company, at certain times of *privacy*?"

Charlotte flushed. "Yes," she replied shortly.

"Well, he cannot, that is all. Not unless it is *your* idea, with *your* full cooperation and permission."

"My what?"

"You heard me," Elizabeth said, having no desire to repeat herself. A short silence followed.

"He-he will say I am undutiful," she whispered.

"And you will boldly wonder aloud if you ought to write to me and ask *my* opinion. Believe me when I say, he will *not*, um, press."

Charlotte's mouth gaped...and then...a smile dawned, lighting her whole countenance.

"Be sure to write often, dear, whether or not you feel to mention personal subjects," Elizabeth entreated. "You have friends and must never forget it."

"I will," Charlotte assured, and suddenly spoke in a rush. "Elizabeth...I wished to do much more to promote your match with Mr Darcy after I watched how he followed you about at Jane's wedding breakfast. I promise, my father did everything he could. But later, Mr Collins was absolutely set against us mentioning a word of the...the incident at the wedding between you two, more's the pity. I just know that if we had been free to say more, you likely would be betrothed by now. I do apologise."

Elizabeth stared at her in startled surprise. Charlotte was apologising for *not* gossiping? Suddenly, the mystery of who had sent her father, Sir William, and Mr Goulding after her and Darcy seemed explained.

"No apologies are necessary," she managed, as she climbed into the carriage.

Charlotte stood at the gate, smiling and waving, until long after she was a tiny dot on the horizon.

⁂

The drive to London was rather tedious, but the Darcy coach-and-four was a comfortable one, and the journey was accomplished in well under the four predicted hours. Though they had no private time together, she and Darcy shared looks, little smiles, and of course, she rejoiced in the frequent views of him riding, which caused a certain breathlessness in her bosom.

He is mine, she thought, with mixed feelings of glee and disbelief. *I am his*.

It was impossible but seemed to be true.

The carriage pulled up at the front of a stately, elegant home; her uncle could afford to live at a 'better' address—as in, one with more consequence; but his property was a fine one and convenient to his warehouses. As the coachman let down the steps, she glanced over at Darcy, who was looking at their surroundings with an assessing air; she felt certain that he would find nothing lacking.

He and the colonel escorted her up the walkway and

rapped upon the door. A neat maid showed them in, but her aunt quickly made an appearance.

"Oh, Lizzy, how good to see you!" Mrs Gardiner said, giving her niece a kiss and looking at the party expectantly; Lizzy performed the introduction to the colonel, and her aunt led them to a lovely parlour, serving such refreshments as showed the greatest hospitality. Mr Gardiner, she explained, was expected home at any moment. Indeed, shortly thereafter he arrived, and several minutes of pleasant conversation followed.

At length, her uncle delicately enquired as to the 'incident' drawing her away from Kent, and Mr Darcy gave a highly expurgated account which nevertheless managed to communicate that both his aunt and Mr Collins were guilty of some incivility towards Elizabeth.

"It must have been so distressing for you both," Mrs Gardiner commented graciously, showing no sign of curiosity, while Mr Gardiner quickly sought to change the subject. The visit proceeded in the most agreeable fashion; Mr Darcy begged to be able to present his sister to them on the morrow.

"Will she bring Dubitz with her?" Elizabeth asked, and Mr Darcy groaned. They were therefore required to retell the story of Elizabeth's introduction to Georgiana's enthusiastic companion, as well as enlighten the colonel as to the character and disposition of the newest Darcy.

When they prepared for departure at last, the Gardiners and the colonel contrived to give Elizabeth and Darcy a few moments of privacy in which to exchange their farewells.

The second they were alone, they were in each other's arms.

"Tomorrow seems so many hours away," Elizabeth lamented, shivering when Darcy found a place at her nape which she felt throughout her whole body.

"I will get a licence," he murmured roughly. "We shall marry immediately. I cannot bear to be parted from you. I only wished to give your father time to receive the paperwork from my solicitors regarding Wickham, or I would not have allowed it at Netherfield."

Elizabeth sighed. "I still need Papa's permission. I ought to have written him volumes' worth of praises to your character and virtues, so that he understands how mistaken I was—and he is. Nevertheless, it would be still better to speak to him in person."

"I will go to him at once."

"No—that is, of course, yes, eventually. But what I mean is, he needs to hear my feelings directly from me. At Netherfield, I was too astonished, and of course Mr Collins had stirred him up into the boughs. It is to be presumed that he has calmed down from his temper by now."

"Collins, that prat," Darcy muttered in disgust.

"Agreed. If my uncle can arrange it, I will return to Longbourn tomorrow."

"Tomorrow? But I had hoped to have you and the Gardiners dine with us tomorrow—at the London home of which you shall soon be mistress," Darcy said. "The day after which, on Saturday evening, we could all visit Vauxhall—have you ever seen the fireworks? And then it is the Sabbath—I will admit to coveting your appearance at St George's upon my arm. Say you will remain until Monday, and Georgiana and I will both accompany you home to Longbourn."

"Elizabeth," Mrs Gardiner called. "Mr Darcy's carriage has been brought round."

"She means our scant moment of privacy is at an end," Elizabeth sighed.

He brought his mouth down upon hers, and she returned his kiss, meeting his enthusiasm with her own.

"Monday it is," she gasped, wondering for how long he would be able to render her breathless within moments.

Forever, I hope.

18

Friday evening, Thomas Bennet sat alone in his study, his emotions in a turmoil. He was not at all certain he had done the right thing in sending Elizabeth away to Kent. It was his wife, for once, who had borne in upon him the foolishness of the act.

"For heaven's sake, Mr Bennet, if you were so determined to keep your eye upon Lizzy, why did you not simply bring her home?" she had asked, sounding exasperated.

And try as he might, he could not fault her logic. Darcy had departed Netherfield when Lizzy had, so he now had no way of knowing whether the man was in pursuit of his daughter or had dropped the whole matter and made his escape.

Blast! I ought to have brought Lizzy to Longbourn! I should have known the gossips would overlook the incident at the wedding breakfast. If Mr Darcy truly was serious in his intentions—unlikely as it might be—why, they could then proceed in a more conventional fashion.

He did not like the man—no one could—but one

could not deny it to be a brilliant match for Lizzy. The thought of his favourite daughter *forced* into it had been repugnant and disgusting. But if she wanted Mr Darcy... well, that was another matter.

She *had* seemed rather taken with him when protesting her removal from Netherfield, but equal in her arguments had been the opinions of her neighbours. Guilt, he knew, did as little to promote future joy as a handsome face.

Devil take that Collins, reminding me of my faulty degree of chaperonage at the very moment I felt my own self-reproach!

A rap on the door heralded the entry of his good friend, Goulding—who often popped in just before the dinner hour, as Mrs Bennet's table was a great deal better than his own bachelor household's. The interruption was a welcome respite from his thoughts. Unfortunately, Goulding was quick to bring up a topic equally unappealing.

"Everyone is a bit dull, what with the regiment's imminent departure," he said. "Bound to be, I suppose, but things seem a bit flat."

"Tell me!" Bennet snorted. "Try having a daughter who was invited to depart with the Forsters and join them in Brighton! She does nothing but bemoan her ill fortune in having too strict a parent."

Goulding shrugged genially. "Colonel Forster seems a good enough fellow, even if his wife is a bit of a feather-brain. My mother lives in Brighton, you know. Born there, and returned as soon as my father died. Always claimed we in the south were too full of ourselves, and Brighton society more accepting."

Bennet vaguely recalled Goulding's mother, although

it had been many years. A tiny woman. Dignified. He nodded his agreement.

"Pretty girls like yours probably find husbands more easily there, what?"

This might be true, Bennet reflected. Lydia was a taking sort of girl. Empty-headed, but popular and pretty. Of course, she was just as likely to fall flat on her face and embarrass herself—but who would really care about the happenings on a brief trip eighty miles away? She would return, at worst, wiser for her experience, and at best, with an offer of marriage. Best of all, if he gave his permission for the holiday, Longbourn would be peaceful once again.

"Mrs Bennet does not want her to go—but only because she believes that Elizabeth *will* marry Darcy, and that all of Darcy's influential relations will be in attendance, and that none of her daughters must go anywhere until after this imaginary event takes place."

Goulding scratched his balding head. "As to that, I suppose she might have a point. But I am certainly glad nothing came of the, um, trouble at the wedding. Darcy did offer to do right by her, and Lizzy would not have had much choice but to go along, had the gossips gotten hold of it. Frankly, Bennet, I cannot see the match. Not him pursuing it if he does not have to—talk of high in the instep! Nor her with such a dead bore."

They were both quiet as they considered it. It *was* unlikely, Bennet knew, for *either* of them to foster an attraction beyond the unfortunate circumstance, which of course was a huge relief. Such a man could never make his Lizzy happy. He would throw up her poverty at her with every argument, and she would writhe under the tedium of his dullness.

In the shared silence, they both startled a bit at the tap on the door.

"Come," Bennet barked.

Mrs Hill entered, looking anxious. "An express for you, sir," she said, handing him a letter. "The boy is still here—will there be a reply?"

He glanced down at it, and his brows raised as he noted it was from his cousin, Collins—the last person he had *ever* expected to invest in an express. Had something happened to Lizzy?

He tore open the letter and tried to read; in his panic, the words refused to form coherent sentences. It took some moments before he was able to force his trembling hands to still, and his trembling brain to quiet enough to comprehend its message.

The colour drained from his face.

"No, Mrs Hill," Bennet choked out. "There will be no reply."

❧

The housekeeper waited a long moment before reluctantly departing, plainly eaten with curiosity and concern. Once the door shut behind her, Goulding was not so reticent.

"Good gracious, man, what is the matter?"

Without a word, Bennet handed over the letter, dated that morning.

My Dear Sir,

I believe it my duty to give you the speediest intelligence of a situation beyond my control. Your daughter has earned the attention and admiration of a young gentleman who is, to all appearances, blessed with everything the heart of a mortal can most desire—splendid property, superior kindred, and extensive patronage. Yet, in spite of all these temptations, let me warn my cousin Elizabeth—and yourself—of what evils you may incur by a precipitate closure with this gentleman's proposals, which, of course, you will be inclined to take immediate advantage of. I have recently learnt he lacks the approbation of an important figure, one who has known him from the cradle; Lady Catherine de Bourgh does not look upon him with a friendly eye.

In confidence, I shall share that for many years, it was the dearest wish of her heart that he wed her own daughter; in fact, she planned and hoped for a union of their great estates. It is only recently that she has learnt of the greatest objections to his character; she now terms the very idea of a match disgraceful, openly stating she would never subject her only daughter to such an awful fate.

While Miss Bennet was yet under my protection and care—not to mention that of Mrs Collins—there was no cause for alarm. However, the gentleman (and I use the label with only the bitterest disappointment) has managed by means of gross deception to remove her from our watchful eyes. Only yesterday, he detached her from those who might be powerful enough to safeguard her, hurrying her to those relations in Cheapside—who, as I understand it, would never be able to stand against him. Having a personal, private knowledge of the enormity of his guilt, despite the nobility of his kindred, I am inclined to think him naturally bad.

I cannot suppose what argument of mine might soothe so severe a misfortune. My only motive for cautioning you is to prevent a grievous affliction to a parent's mind. I beg you, however, to keep my name from any future discussion of his suit. He has threatened to make a public example of Lady

Catherine and her daughter if she breathes a word of his disreputable conduct, and he has the influence and fortune to do it.

Indeed, if he were to learn of my warning, Lady Catherine assures me that my death would be a blessing in comparison to his wrath.

I am, dear Sir, your most dutiful servant,
William Collins

"It cannot be true!" Goulding exclaimed, dismay filling him as he read. "I judge it a pack of lies! It must be!"

"He is a vicar who takes his office most seriously," Bennet replied, his voice thick with horror. "I cannot conceive of him hoaxing me."

But Goulding remained unconvinced. "Darcy is a gentleman, though. He is a good friend of Bingley's. Seems impossible."

Bennet shook his head. "He certainly made himself scarce all winter, never visiting Bingley once. We all heard Wickham's complaints. I received a packet of lawyerly nonsense from Darcy's solicitors, with a note from him repudiating Wickham's claims. I have yet to delve into it, but 'the gentleman doth protest too much, methinks'."

Goulding, having an equivalent distaste for 'lawyerly nonsense', nodded his agreement. "'Tis suspicious, to be sure."

"Mr Darcy is the sort of 'gentleman' who would act in defiance of honour and humanity, who would ruin a man for the sake of a few hot-headed, youthful arguments. Such a man might very well be...depraved."

They looked at each other in alarm.

"I must fetch her from the Gardiners, at once. I can

be to Gracechurch Street early enough tomorrow morning."

But Goulding laid a hand on his sleeve. "To do what? Bring her here? If he is determined to have her, what good will that do? How can you refuse such a man as him?"

Bennet's shoulders slumped; they both knew the answer to Goulding's questions.

❦

William Goulding tried to think. He had always been fond of Bennet's second-eldest daughter. In fact, there was a time when Reginald had made noises about wishing for a match with her. Lizzy was a good girl, smart, sensible, the kind of wife Reginald needed to keep his head out of the clouds and upon estate matters —and yet, she brought so little to the marriage! The Gouldings were prosperous, though, and had it not been for his mother, he might even have given his approval. But Mother was a fearsome sort, with the strongest ideas of what was suitable in a wife. His own Dorothea had been his third choice, after Mother had vetoed the first two in the most vehement fashion. And she had been right, had she not? He had been very happy with her selection—which had also immensely swelled the Goulding coffers—and faithful to her until the day she died. The very idea of crossing his maternal parent made him shudder. She would find nothing to object to in Pearl Harrington, with her ample dowry.

And yet...Lizzy. Such a winsome little thing she had always been. She would have made an excellent daughter. He might always mourn the loss of her, even if Reginald himself had moved on easily enough.

Suddenly, he snapped his fingers, stating aloud the thoughts just now occurring to him.

"I have it! We shall send Lizzy to my mother in Brighton. She's not what you would call permissive—daughter of a marquess, you know. Fine home, too big for her, all alone there, and the company will do her good. But she knows how to make all within it toe the line, I tell you. Ideal chaperon. I shall send her an express. No, no, no time to waste. Better still, I shall leave at once, explain to her the situation in person. Send Lizzy along as soon as you can, Bennet. It will all be right and tight, I will see to it m'self."

"Leave to Brighton? At this hour? You cannot be serious! It would be impossible to expect such a favour, from you or your mother, especially on no notice!"

"Very serious indeed. Mother has been complaining since my second cousin, Isabella, her companion of the last ten years, married Mother's physician. Terribly distressing for her—had to find a new companion *and* a new doctor. She took on my cousin Mildred—but Mildred left after a few weeks. Said she could not abide Mother's ideas."

"Your mother's...what? Are her ideas strange ones?"

Goulding snorted. "No, no, no, she only has her little book club, a bunch of old ladies who get together to complain about men and recite poetry, rubbish like that. One can hardly understand a word of it. It does not mean a thing—an amusement to pass the time. I suppose Mother will want Lizzy to listen to her blather —she does go on a bit. But how difficult could listening to her be? Simple enough to think of something else whilst she rambles. I have done it all my life."

"It does sound…safe," Bennet admitted.

"Safer than a babe in its cradle, I daresay. Mother will introduce her around—she knows everyone worth knowing. There is good society to be found in Brighton. 'Tis bound to be the best thing for both of them."

"I suppose, as soon as Darcy realises my daughter is not a pigeon ripe for the plucking, he will give it up and move along to his next victim," Bennet pondered aloud. "It should not have to be for long—be sure and tell your mother that this shall not be a permanent situation."

"No, no, no, of course not. Still, I would not be at all surprised if they take to each other, and Lizzy chooses to stay the summer. Quite a lot of entertainment to be had. Benefits." He felt very satisfied with his solution. Mother would love Lizzy; everyone who knew her did.

Bennet slowly nodded. "It would be a fine holiday for my girl. For that matter, I might as well send Lydia along with the Forsters. Mrs Bennet will refuse to believe in Darcy's depraved character, not if it means surrendering her dream of a wedding even grander than Jane's. It is time to quash that notion once and for all. I will owe you for this one, Goulding."

He held out his hand; Goulding shook it, smiling genially.

"Never fear, my friend. All of your problems are about to disappear, poof."

"Poof," Bennet repeated. "Disappear to Brighton."

Aunt Gardiner was talking, and Elizabeth knew she ought to be listening. But she had wakened that morning to a delivery of yellow roses, and the sight of the vase upon the breakfast parlour table, overflowing with delicate, perfect blooms, had captured her attention instead. Her usually practical, straightforward mind was twisting in pirouettes; before breakfast she had started a letter to Papa explaining why she was no longer in Kent, but found herself continually losing her place amongst the sentences, as day-dreams of Darcy took the place of sense and reason.

"Lizzy?" her aunt asked, plainly repeating herself.

"I apologise, Auntie," Elizabeth sighed. "My mind wandered. Could you please repeat what you just said?"

But her aunt only smiled. "I am not so old that I cannot remember what new love is like," she said. "It is an exhilarating time."

"Love," Elizabeth repeated, testing the word upon her lips, and finding it to be the right one. "Yes, that is it exactly. I love him, Auntie. It is so difficult to believe that once I hated him. Am I fickle? How could everything have changed in so brief a time?"

Aunt Gardiner glanced at the roses. "Are you worried, dear? Worried that your feelings will diminish?"

"No," Elizabeth replied firmly. "No, I am not. I *have* experienced infatuation. I did not love Reginald Goulding, I only loved the *idea* of him. I had no interest in learning about him, about who he *really* was. The attraction to Wickham was even worse, and shallower still. It was almost, I am ashamed to admit, a competition in the neighbourhood which I wanted to win—'who can draw the most attention from the handsomest man in the regiment?' After you spoke with me about his unsuitability and I distanced myself from him, I did not suffer the slightest pang. In both 'romances', I was only concerned about myself, about what *he* would mean to *me*—how *I* would look upon his arm, how the other girls would envy *me*."

"It is different with Mr Darcy?"

Elizabeth sighed. "I will not deny that I should be proud to be seen with him. But it is more. Every moment we are able to spend in conversation, the minutes pass like seconds. I want to know everything, from what he was like as a boy to his favourite meals. The most mundane detail seems fascinating, somehow. And the odd thing is, he feels the same way. I have not always been certain, but I know now—we are creating a foundation upon which the future can build."

"'Tis a wondrous time," Aunt Gardiner said, nodding and smiling. "It will not always feel so...intense—else one would never be able to accomplish the smallest tasks in life. And there will be times in the future, I promise, when you shall look at each other and say to yourselves, 'Who is this angry, foolish person?' But as you try your best to be loyal and caring, and as he tries his best to be loyal and understanding, I also promise that you will overcome those difficulties and grow together, as you obviously wish."

"'And the two shall become one'," Elizabeth quoted softly. "It sounds so—"

She did not complete her sentence, for the parlour door burst open and there stood her father, red-faced and breathing hard.

"Papa!" Elizabeth cried.

"What a start you gave us, sir!" Aunt Gardiner said.

"You are still here," Mr Bennet gasped, wiping his

face with a large handkerchief, looking as if he had run all the way from Longbourn. "I began to think I might be too late." Seeming to lose all his vigour, he sat heavily in the nearest chair. Elizabeth went to him at once, kneeling before him.

"Papa...are you ill?"

He only shook his head.

His manner was so unusual to his nature, her alarm increased every moment.

"Please, tell me what is the matter. Can I fetch you anything? Tea? Might I fix you a plate?"

"No, no. I am only relieved," he said. "I feared you would have put yourself beyond my power to provide aid before I could arrive."

Elizabeth and her aunt looked at each other in puzzlement.

"As you can see, I am quite well. I can explain why I had to leave Kent—you see, Mr Collins—"

He held up his hand, halting her explanations with the imperious gesture. "Never mind it. I do not need to hear the tale. I know you were not to blame, and indeed are a victim of whatever ignominy transpired."

"Yes, this is true," Elizabeth replied. "What *is* the matter, Papa?"

But he turned to her aunt instead of answering.

"Margaret, can you have Elizabeth's trunk brought down?"

"What? But Papa, we have made plans for this evening! Uncle was to return me home on Monday—very soon."

He turned a look of disapproval upon her, such as she was unused to receiving from him. "Then it is to be assumed you have not fully unpacked. I daresay your aunt can have all your things brought downstairs without too taxing an effort."

Elizabeth saw that he was in no mood to argue; evidently her aunt realised it as well, for she excused herself to see to Elizabeth's belongings.

"I will write a note to Mr and Miss Darcy, cancelling our plans," she said, unable to keep the disappointment from her voice.

"You will not!"

"But Papa! It would be most impolite—"

"I wish never to hear that man's name again."

"But why? This is incredible!"

His mouth tightened. "He is an over-proud, unpleasant, unprincipled fellow, completely unworthy of you, Lizzy!"

She was determined, this time, to argue better for the love she believed in, rather than allow her father and fate to rip them apart.

"He is perfectly amiable! You do not know what he really is."

He rolled his eyes. "I know that he is not good enough for you."

"Papa, this will not do. I must tell you how ardently I admire and love him!"

"I am sorry to occasion you pain, Elizabeth, and I hope it will be of short duration. Doubtless, recollection of the bitter feelings which you have expressed towards him in the past will assist you in overcoming these fancies in the future."

"I admit I was guilty of listening to Mr Wickham's tales, but they were lies. All lies!"

"And who informed you of this dishonesty? Mr Darcy? Ah, yes, I can see by the look on your face!" His voice rose, his face reddening again, in anger this time. "You are naïve. It is plain to see who was the better man. Everyone knows what Wickham's misfortunes have been."

"His misfortunes!" repeated Elizabeth contemptuously. "Only according to him! And Mr Bingley, your own son-in-law, made it clear that we knew not half of the story." She had no right to reveal Georgiana's experiences with the scoundrel, and she would not betray a confidence. "I am not at liberty to provide details, but trust me when I say that the only misfortune is that Mr Darcy was ever required to be in the same country with the fiend!"

Mr Bennet snorted. "'Twas *Mr Darcy* who reduced him to his present state of poverty, comparative poverty. It is *Mr Darcy* who withholds the advantages which were designed for him. *Mr Darcy* deprived him of that independence which was no less his due. Mr Darcy has done all this! And yet you defend him? Can you not see, Lizzy, that you have been taken in by a master deceiver?"

Elizabeth felt her temper flare but tried to regain her composure. "How can I convince you of his goodness? He is caring and thoughtful and a wonderful brother to his young sister and a great favourite of the earl of Matlock. You do not *know* him. Pray do not pain me by speaking of him in such terms."

"You are mistaken, Elizabeth. There is nothing you can say that will change my opinion of him."

"But this is your opinion of *me*? A naïve simpleton, incapable of judging the character of the man whom she would agree to marry?"

He sighed, his anger obviously abating, but his words, when he spoke, were implacable. "From the very beginning, from the first moment I may almost say, of my acquaintance with him, his manners impressed me with the fullest belief of his arrogance, his vanity, and his condescending contempt for us all. I had not known him a month before I felt that he was the last man in the world whom I could ever be prevailed upon to agree to a marriage with *any* of my daughters. Even Mary." He tried a smile at his tasteless little joke.

It was all she could do not to scream in frustration. Mrs Gardiner returned then, followed by a servant carrying the requested trunk. Their eyes met, and she saw her own helplessness to convince her stubborn father reflected in her aunt's. The tears she was trying desperately to supress escaped. "Papa, please, listen," she whispered.

He turned away from her, plainly uncomfortable with an emotion his daughter seldom displayed. "You have said quite enough, Elizabeth. You will come with me."

She gave her aunt a brief, wordless hug, then followed him out the door and into the drive where the coach awaited, gathering her arguments to resume during the journey to Longbourn. But he handed her inside without entering himself.

"You will not be returning home for some time," he explained from the carriage doorway. "John Joseph will see you safely to your destination. Once you are settled and I receive a good report from, um, where you will be staying, I promise your circumstances will ease, and it will be a fine holiday for you. Forgive me for an action that only another parent who loves his deluded daughter could understand. In time, you will thank me."

He shut the door.

For a very few seconds, Elizabeth stared at the closed

door in amazement, a thousand protests upon her tongue. Even as the coach began moving, she wrenched at it, attempting to throw it wide—meaning to leap out. *I will not go! He cannot force me!*

But it would not open, although she tugged with all her might. She scrambled to the window, her shaking hands slow to raise it.

"Auntie!" she screamed. "Auntie!"

Her aunt ran towards the moving carriage, but her father detained her—only for a moment or two, but the carriage was already gaining speed. By the time he released her and she ran forward again, Elizabeth only had a moment before her voice would be lost in the hubbub and traffic.

"Tell him to find me!" she cried, as loudly as she could. "Tell him it is the sixth challenge!"

19

Darcy held the ring up to his eye, inspecting it for flaws; as expected, he found none. It was an emerald that had once belonged to Queen Elizabeth, given to his ancestor for some heroic duty never recorded in its history; Darcy himself had a rather good idea of what the earning of it had likely entailed, and heroism had nothing to do with it. Still, the thing was exquisite and barely worthy of the lady whose finger it would soon grace.

"Excuse me, sir," his man, Pennywithers said. Only Pennywithers would interrupt him here in his study when he had specifically asked *not* to be disturbed. Of course, Pennywithers had known him since he had been breeched, which greatly affected his deference.

He had not wanted to be disturbed because he was working on a draft of the instruction he meant to provide his solicitors regarding Elizabeth's settlement. He must make it very clear that she was to be treated with as much respect as if she had been an heiress or even a princess. His men of business could be a bit...

protective of his assets, which in the courses of conduct was a good thing—for the most part. But when it came to his tenants and now, his wife, they required guidance.

"Yes, Pennywithers," he said discouragingly.

"You have visitors, sir."

"I recall specifically begging not to be interrupted," he reminded.

"Indeed, sir. I shall instruct Hulbert to tell Mr and Mrs Gardiner that you are not at home."

Darcy stood so quickly he nearly knocked over his chair. Ignoring the triumphant look upon Pennywithers' face, he only asked where they had been put, feeling a sense of alarm entirely out of proportion to circumstances. He had seen Elizabeth only the previous evening, he reminded himself. She had toured his home, been introduced to his household, and been eagerly looking forward to tonight's expedition to Vauxhall.

"In the green drawing room, sir, although Hulbert would have chosen the blue."

"Well done, Pennywithers." The blue was a small parlour at the back of the house, for Hulbert was a dreadful snob—probably smelling trade on Gardiner's shoes, despite the fact that Elizabeth's uncle was as elegant and mannerly as any gentleman. He would have to ensure that the Hulberts treated his wife with the respect she and hers deserved, and that Pennywithers influenced the hire of a lady's maid for Elizabeth; his man would be an excellent ally for her in entering this new sphere. The green was elegant enough to be respectful and cosy enough to be welcoming—it had been his mother's favourite.

"Welcome," Darcy said as he entered. Mr Gardiner had remained standing by the fireplace, while Mrs

Gardiner was perched upon the edge of the chair nearest him. Both looked solemn, and his sense of alarm returned. "May I offer you refreshment?" But he closed the door behind him without ordering any.

"No, thank you sir," Gardiner said. "We would have sent a note except—"

"Except that I insisted upon coming in person," his wife interjected. "I simply had to be certain, for Lizzy's sake, that I represented the events of this morning as carefully and-and as clearly as possible."

Gardiner, he noticed, moved to his wife's side, placing a comforting hand upon her shoulder. She looked a bit...shaken, although her voice had been steady. Darcy's alarm increased.

"What has happened?" His tone came out sharper than he had meant it to, and he tried to soften it. "Is Elizabeth well?"

"Oh, I am certain she is," Mrs Gardiner quickly reassured. "Her father arrived about an hour ago, perhaps a bit longer. To take her home, we thought. Lizzy did her best to reason with him, imploring him to allow her to stay. It was futile." She bit her lip.

"I tried talking to Bennet as soon as I received Margaret's message and hurried home—attempting to discover her destination. He was not to be reasoned with. Actually, to be plain, sir, not everyone in Meryton and its surrounds is an admirer of yours," Gardiner added uncomfortably.

"Wickham," Darcy nearly spat.

Gardiner scratched his head. "That is a good part of it, of course. My brother believed every word the fellow said. My wife hails from Lambton, however, and she holds the memory of your father in great esteem. She found it difficult to believe his son would be so depraved as to be guilty of-of his particular accusations. Wickham has recently left the area, however, gone to Brighton with his regiment, Bennet claims. He said he has not seen him in a few weeks, but *something* has suddenly riled him to his core. It has put him against you, sir, I am sorry to say. Nothing I said in your defence seemed to penetrate."

"Of what Wickham has accused me specifically, I am in ignorance. I can guess, however." In as few words as possible, he outlined the gist of his history with Wickham, omitting reference to Georgiana. "I tried— although only once—to converse with Bennet regarding the matter. But my timing was poor." It was the day after Bennet believed Darcy had forced himself on Elizabeth, and he had been unable to speak to him. "I had my solicitors send him physical proofs. I suppose he refused to read it through."

"I am uncertain it would have helped. Bennet is a decent man, but stubborn. Lizzy is his favourite, and I fear your initial opinion of her last year did not set you in his good graces."

Darcy closed his eyes. "I was an idiot," he admitted. "A week had not passed from that assembly before I felt Elizabeth to be the handsomest woman I know. Her destination today was not Longbourn?"

"Unfortunately," Mrs Gardiner said, "we do not know where she was taken. I followed her and her father almost to the carriage when he seemed to be stopping to have a word with her at the carriage door. Thinking to give them privacy, I moved away. But instead of seating himself inside, he shut her in it—and I saw him wedge a-a stick of some sort into the crevice of the carriage door—clearly fixing it so that she would be unable to open the door from within. That was when I became alarmed and ran towards the vehicle, meaning, I think, to pull it out. But I was not permitted."

"He set his hands upon her," Gardiner said, looking furious. "He will not do so again."

"Only for a moment," she soothed, putting her hand over her husband's. "It slowed me enough, however, that any attempt to catch up to her was futile. But she called out to me...a message for you, I am certain, although it makes little sense. 'Tell him to find me,' she said. 'Tell him it is the sixth challenge.' I know not what it means, but I hoped it would give you a clue to her whereabouts."

He smiled bleakly, as his heart broke at the thought of her locked into a carriage against her will. "I rather think it means she had no idea *where* she was going," he sighed. "I will go to Longbourn at once, and I *will* discover her whereabouts."

"I do not think Bennet went directly home," Gardiner said. "He told me he meant to take a bit of a holiday himself, and was annoyingly sly."

"His coachman, John Joseph, drove her. My guess is that he gave instructions for the man to take her to a certain destination and then meet him elsewhere," Mrs Gardiner put in.

"The Bennet carriage is rather a distinctive shade of green, as I recall," Darcy said.

"Too bright for Bennet's taste—he was not very happy with the result after having it painted last year."

Darcy nodded. It was something to go on, but he still grit his teeth in frustration. "Does he believe he can conceal his whereabouts from me forever? He must return home sometime."

"He seems to believe you will tire of waiting," Gardiner replied.

"And *lose* her? What nonsense! A decade would not be long enough for him to hide. But I will find her if I have to tear England apart, and we will be married the day she is of age, if he will not agree to any earlier one."

Mrs Gardiner beamed with approval. "We will write to Mrs Bennet, and I am confident she will tell us the moment he returns to Longbourn. If she knows of any place he might be taking, er, refuge, it will not be long before we know it as well. He hates being away from Longbourn and is sure to talk himself into returning much sooner than he implied." She hesitated. "I know my brother Bennet has made no good impression upon you, and certainly he is in the wrong—but I am confident he believes he is doing his utmost to protect his daughter."

Darcy slumped a little. He had never *tried* to make any good impression upon Mr Bennet, not really. And while the man was behaving in a melodramatic fashion, a small part of him could appreciate how much trouble he had gone to in the process. Most men would probably hand over their daughters solely on the basis of the Darcy fortune, whether or not he was a bottle-headed buffoon or the worst sort of reprobate.

"You are, of course, correct. Elizabeth is worth every effort of Bennet's to protect her, and my every effort to recover her. Thank you for any intelligence you can gain from her home—your assistance is deeply appreciated. And thank you for taking the time to tell me of this in person. It was most kind of you to come."

They said their farewells, but at the door, Mrs Gardiner turned back. "Mr Darcy, I do not know whether I ought to mention it...but I am certain Lizzy would wish you to know. She told me of her love for you—declaring it quite fearlessly. I believe she tried very hard to make her father understand, as well. It was through no fault of hers that she was unsuccessful."

It touched him deeply to know that she had named her feelings aloud, and that they matched his own. "I hope soon I can declare mine for her to the world. And then, I hope it will not be long before you and your family come to Pemberley as our guests—for a lengthy visit. This summer, all things willing."

Her eyes lit; if she was from Lambton, she knew Pemberley. At least he had that to offer; it would be difficult to repay such kindness as she and Mr Gardiner had demonstrated.

Once they were away, he went in search of Georgiana. Finding her in the music room, Dubitz lying near her feet, he told her all that had occurred.

"Do you intend to drive the length of England on a possibly futile search?" she asked.

"I *cannot* sit upon my hands and do nothing. I suppose chasing green carriages about the countryside does sound rather a 'forlorn hope', especially because in a few weeks I will be able to thrash the inhabitants of Longbourn for the information I need. Bennet cannot stay away forever. Gardiner judges he will return sooner than he implied."

"Thrash them? Truly?"

"Oh, you know," he said, waving his hand expansively, "attack them with the Darcy stare, possibly accompanied by the Darcy frown."

She still looked worried, and he felt a pang of longing for Elizabeth, who would have laughed. "I do not expect you to go," he assured. "It might even be a rather arduous journey, as well as pointless. I intend to travel light and use such help as the inns can provide."

"Oh, absolutely I will go—as will Dubitz. We should see if the Gardiners have a handkerchief of hers, something with her scent."

Darcy could not help smiling, feeling a little better. "You have only yourself to blame, Sister. It was you who urged me to go to Bingley's wedding, to discover whether my feelings were love or only frustration."

She shrugged. "I love you. You deserve every happiness. Whinging about her to me was not going to help you discover it." And she smiled, just a tiny smile, but it boosted his spirits immensely.

Georgiana might not completely understand teasing, but she was no longer trapped within the abyss of her own sorrow. "As I have always maintained, you are the expert on matters of the heart. I defer to you in these situations. But I am unsure what Elizabeth will think about the bold nature of my rescue if Dubitz becomes the hero of the piece."

Dubitz, hearing his name, demonstrated his valour by giving his hand a gallant lick and a bark of satisfied agreement.

By the time Elizabeth arrived at their destination, she was exhausted. John Joseph had certainly *not* kept her locked in the carriage—indeed, he had opened it a few miles beyond London, at an inn where he stopped to change horses and take on his cousin's daughter, who had acted as maid for the journey. She was painfully shy and very little company, however—and certainly no one who could provide aid.

Of course, Elizabeth made several attempts to get him to reveal their destination. It was no use. If there was one word which described their longtime retainer, it was 'stolid'. How had she ever used the descriptor for Darcy, its very opposite? John Joseph would do exactly as Mr Bennet had ordered him to do, no more and no less. Besides which, he had a tendency to believe Elizabeth was still approximately aged five.

"I am being taken against my will! Please, I beg you, John Joseph, if you have a care for me at all, tell me our destination!"

"Now, now, miss, don't be in a taking. Do just as your pa wished, and you'll be right as rain and home again soon enough," he would say, nodding and smiling and paying no attention whatsoever to her distress or even her tears.

He could not prevent her from speaking to innkeepers and the hostelry at every posting inn; nor did he try. But she could hardly tell them she was being kidnapped and risk any consequences to the loyal servant. She could only speak to those to whom it was safe to speak, identify herself, and hope that if Darcy came this way, she would be remembered so he would know he was on her trail. She had not a doubt he would follow if he could.

John Joseph drove slowly, making the journey interminable, but she comforted herself with the assurance that wherever she landed, there was bound to be paper and pen, was there not? Considering herself as good as betrothed, she would write a letter to Darcy and post it as soon as she could, telling him exactly where to find her. It took her far too long to realise Brighton *must* be their object, but as she had never before travelled this far south, everything was strange. And she still had not any information regarding her final destination.

It was after eight o'clock when they pulled up a meandering drive at the top of an incline, the sea's waves loud in her ears as she stepped wearily from the carriage and saw her destination at last. At least, she saw its enormous, shadowy outlines and the reflection of brilliant light from its entry. She would be residing in a mansion, it seemed. She had never heard of her father knowing *anyone* in Brighton, and for it to be someone of such elevated means was incredible.

The entry was marbled, featuring a magnificent stone staircase curving up into heights unknown, lit by a crystal chandelier with at least forty candles. She blinked as she realised the gentleman in formal-cut coat, pale buff pantaloons, and striped stockings was none other than her father's dearest friend.

"Mr Goulding?" she questioned, astonished.

"Quite, quite," he replied, nodding benignly. "It has been a long day for you, eh what? Mother has gone to bed—never stays up past eight o'clock unless she wishes to—but have no fears on that score. She was delighted to learn of your impending visit. Delighted! You are as welcome as welcome can be. Please stay as long as you like!"

"Oh, but...it is very kind of her, I am sure, but I greatly desire to return home as soon as poss—"

"Nothing to that, nothing to that," he interrupted. "But you haven't seen the town yet! Home will be waiting for you when you've had your holiday, there's a good girl. And here is Whitby, Mother's own maid, come to help you settle in. A tray will be sent up, rest assured —nothing but the best of everything at Sea Terrace. And you have had such a long day."

John Joseph, obviously, was not the only one who believed her an infant. And yet Mr Goulding was so garrulous, so concerned about her long journey, so solicitous, she could find no opportunity to object—and indeed, she was too tired to try harder. She allowed herself to be led upstairs, washed, fed a repast of soup, toast, and tea, dressed in one of her own nightgowns, and tucked into bed as if she really was still in the nursery. It was luxurious, to be sure; but as she sank onto the thick mattresses, her last thought was of Darcy, wishing she was near him, hoping he had discovered her trail.

⁊⁊

Darcy did not set out immediately. Instead, he called upon his man of business, Digweed, explaining the need to find the direction Elizabeth might have travelled. It was of the utmost importance that it be a discreet search, but neither could he go off in twelve different directions at once. He could not even be certain she had left London—although Gardiner had been confident, due to Bennet's distaste for town, that she would not be found in the metropolis. He must have a direction before beginning!

Digweed—a man of remarkable talents and myriad connexions from every walk of life—quickly launched into action. By Saturday evening, he had two potential leads. Both were carriages painted in a distinctive shade of green, both carrying a dark-haired young lady with her maid. One, heading for Birmingham, had given no name; the other, heading south towards the coast, *had* given the innkeeper her name, but the busy man could not remember whether it had been 'Elizabeth'.

"Coulda been 'lizabeth, coulda been Betty Butter-bean," he had informed Digweed's man.

In the end, Darcy chose to follow the Birmingham carriage for the simple reason that he was well acquainted with the various roads and inns along that route, as he traversed a similar one every time he travelled between Pemberley and London. Likewise, he was well known in the area and could expect to receive answers to his questions without much resistance or suspicion. If the nameless lady was not Elizabeth, he would discover it that much more quickly.

It was possible that neither path would lead to her; however, when they finally met again, he was determined to give her a report of his efforts—however fruitless—to find her. She should never be in doubt of his feelings. Besides, he missed her. He wanted her. What else was there to do but search, while awaiting her return?

20

E lizabeth hesitated before the door of the room which had been pointed out to her as the breakfast parlour; she had no idea where Mr Goulding might be, and she was reluctant to come upon the mistress of this grand home without a formal introduction.

"Come, Miss Bennet," came a voice from within, possessing unmistakably imperious tones of command. "I must have you eat. I hate to see you standing about by yourself in such a stupid manner. You had much better eat."

"I apologise," Elizabeth answered quickly, moving into the room and curtseying to the elder woman seated at the table, a plate of poached eggs and plain toast set before her. "I was searching for Mr Goulding before I intruded upon your breakfast. I am Elizabeth Bennet."

"Of course you are. I am Lady Lavinia Goulding. You may address me as Lady Lavinia. My son departed early this morning," she explained, directing Elizabeth to the sideboard with a nonchalant gesture of her beringed fingers. She was a small woman—tiny, almost—with grey ringlets piled so high upon her head, it reminded Elizabeth of a drawing she had seen once of a volcano erupting, silvery molten masses of curls. Her skin was lined with age, but her eyes were bright and clear as she scrutinised her houseguest.

Elizabeth could not prevent her expression of dismay. "Truly, he has departed? Oh, dear."

"He *said* he had to hurry home to his son. Hah! As if Reginald cares two shakes whether his father is gone three days or sixty."

It *was* a weak excuse, and her own disappointment was great. She had missed a final opportunity to beg that she be taken up with him and returned to Longbourn, which had been her first plan. But her ladyship did not appear to notice Elizabeth's dismay and continued speaking.

"Either he could not bear hearing any more of my opinions regarding the many ways in which he might improve himself or else he wished to avoid seeing you again. Which is it, do you think?"

"I cannot imagine why he might wish to avoid either of us."

"Whitby said you desire to return home."

Whitby? Oh, yes, the maid who helped me settle in last night! Still, while not exactly encouraging, Lady Lavinia's words brought a surge of hopefulness that she, at least, might not treat Elizabeth as a child.

"I am grateful for your hospitality. You do not know me and cannot have wished for my incursion into your household. Your ladyship has been most generous, and yes, I hope you do not take it amiss that I greatly wish to return home as soon as is possible."

Lady Lavinia raised a brow. "As I suspected, William's tale of a maiden in distress was only half of the story. But you are not quite a stranger. Although it has been a good ten years since I left Hertfordshire, I remember your parents well. Now, fill your plate, sit down, and tell me why my son has dumped you so unceremoniously—and so unwillingly—upon my doorstep."

Elizabeth did as she was bid. With the prodding of several astute questions for detail, she even found herself retelling the story of her initial encounter with Mr Darcy at the assembly, then of overhearing him at Jane's wedding, and the misimpression her father, Sir William, and Mr Goulding had thereafter received at the summerhouse—and hence, her father's unreasoning opinion of Mr Darcy.

Lady Lavinia laughed uproariously, the sound incongruous from such a small, venerable appearing creature. "I remember George Darcy," she said. "If the son is anything like the father, I should say it would be astonishing to find him caught in an embarrassing circumstance."

"As to that, I cannot say," Elizabeth replied, "not having known his father. However, the Mr Darcy I knew during his first few months at Netherfield and the man I have come to know since are persons so wildly different as to not be the same man." In the face of Lady Lavinia's deep interest, Elizabeth found herself retelling the 'adventure' at Lady Catherine's. She did not name names—after all, her own cousin was as guilty as

Darcy's aunt, and as little as she was fond of either, family must be afforded some protection. Again, the lady found the tale deeply amusing.

"I like you, Miss Bennet. Have you ever been criticised for reading too much?"

"I am not so great a reader that I should very often be censured for it! I take pleasure in many activities. Reading is but one of them."

"You have been, or you would not rip up at the idea so immediately. It is all part of it, you see." Lady Lavinia smiled in an annoyingly knowing fashion.

"Part of what?"

"Part of a man's world, Miss Bennet. A woman is not to be too educated, or she is a bluestocking; if too well-informed, she is a gossip. Too competent, and she is a calculating schemer; too much smarter than a male, and she is a cunning shrew. You cannot deny it. My father was a forward-thinking man, and I, his favourite, was the blessed recipient of his knowledge, his library, and a nice portion of his fortune. He did not approve of my suitor, the senior William Goulding. He did the best he could to protect me, in my settlement, when he could not make me see reason and understood I was determined to have William regardless. It was William's fine physique, I think. I have a weakness for men who need no buckram padding to lend them shoulders. So, of course, my children are a disappointment."

Elizabeth took a small bite of plum cake to cover her surprise; she could hardly follow her logic or think how to respond. "Mr Goulding is a very good man, I know."

"Oh, I did not say they were not *good*. What they are is *dull*. They thrive amongst convention. My daughter,

Lady Colyear, will not allow her daughters to visit me without bristling at my every word of advice. She does not wish them to grow 'odd' like her mother. She wants them to net purses and paint tables and speak only of the weather. You must know my grandson Reginald—he is the image of his father. And his grandfather, for that matter."

It was all Elizabeth could do not to blush as she murmured her agreement. She had never considered Reginald to look *anything* like his balding, rotund father. Had Mr Goulding, once upon a time, possessed the noble bearing of his son? It seemed incredible.

"Never had an original thought in any of their heads," her ladyship continued. "The Goulding blood is imbued with an inordinate dose of tedium nearly impossible to overcome. *I* could not do it, no matter how I tried. Had his mother lived longer, Reginald might have been saved. Alas, she did not. I suppose you are determined to marry George Darcy's son?"

"I, um…yes." There was no point in dissembling.

"I thought as much. I remember George's shoulders. If the son resembles the father, I suppose it is to be expected." She nodded to herself. "Have you any honour?"

Honour? This woman is very unusual, Elizabeth thought. Her confusion must have shown in her expression.

"Oh, I know there are those who say that females may not possess it. A man's world it may be, my dear, but we ought to have our own self-respect, integrity, our notions of character—every bit as important as any male. Does your word of honour mean anything?"

"Of course," Elizabeth replied, a little offended.

"Good. I thought as much when I first set eyes upon

you. It is the chin, you see. Men would term it 'stubborn', but *I* call it independent. In the future, whenever a male accuses you of obstinance, know that you are only thinking for yourself instead of parroting some man's ideas." Frowning, Lady Lavinia picked up her teacup. "Now, let us come to a clear understanding. Promise me that you will not write to your beloved Mr Darcy or send him word by any other means for...let us say two weeks. Not so very long a time, is it? During that period, you will read one or two books which I suspect will never be found in your father's library...or George Darcy's, for that matter."

"Two weeks?" Elizabeth asked faintly. It sounded like two decades.

"I am an old woman, Miss Bennet. You have many years left, God willing, but I do not. I failed miserably at influencing my own children and have never been allowed to inspire my grandchildren. I would like to inspire you."

"Inspire me to what end?" *What a bizarre conversation!*

"To think! To possess one or two opinions not spoonfed you by your parents or your husband-to-be. To learn a few things I daresay your mother never taught you. The men would call it 'unconventional' or even 'dangerous' thinking. I call it 'necessary'. At the end of two weeks, I vow to have my own carriage and servants deliver you anywhere you desire in all of England."

"But...why?"

"I admit that my motives are selfish ones. I long to bring some fresh spirit into this dull home for a few brief days. Whitby never will participate in a decent conversation—too snobbish, you see. She possesses strong ideas of who I ought to speak to and what I ought to say, and berates me with a disapproving stare if I break with her rules. It quite puts me off my digestion."

It was at this moment Elizabeth noticed the silent servant had entered the breakfast parlour, escorting a squat, fat pug on a lead. As soon as his bulbous eyes landed upon Lady Lavinia, he began whimpering and straining at his leash.

"The mistress has an odd sense of humour," Whitby sighed, bending over to release the pug. The dog promptly waddled over to Lady Lavinia, whining until he was hoisted up and fed from her ladyship's plate.

"His name is Mirth," Whitby murmured to Elizabeth as she left the room. "He hates everyone but Herself."

Elizabeth glanced back at the dog happily gobbling bites of egg. He noticed her looking at him and growled.

"Now, now, Mirfy-poo, Miss Bennet promises not to harm me. Such a good guardian you is!" The sight of the stern, elderly lady babbling to the fat pug as if he were an infant further added to the ludicrousness of the entire situation.

The dog bared his teeth at Elizabeth, then nipped Lady Lavinia's finger in his haste to wolf down the proffered bite. Plainly, his guardianship was primarily concerned with protecting his breakfast.

"And if I will not promise?" Elizabeth asked, returning to the subject at hand.

"I pray you will not be so boring as to require me and mine to watch you like a spaniel on a scent, hide all the writing materials where I doubtless will never find them again, and sit at home like prisoners staring at each other until your father feels like fetching you."

There was really not much choice, as she considered it. The old lady had put a reasonable time limit to her stay, asking very little in return. Besides, no matter how silly she sounded now—chattering in an affected manner to her plump dog—no matter how much she appeared merely a tiny woman with ridiculous hair, Elizabeth had no doubt that if she decided to become the Warden of Sea Terrace Prison, Lady Lavinia Goulding could do it.

"Mr Darcy may find me," Elizabeth said. "I have no doubt he will search."

Her ladyship shrugged. "Apparently, when my son hatched this plan with your father, they decided that he would not return to Longbourn for several days, in case Darcy decided to press. And of course, your suitor has no idea that Mr Bennet's neighbour is involved. William can keep his mouth shut, whatever his other failings."

This is true, Elizabeth considered, disappointed in the extent of Papa's plans. What could Darcy be thinking now? Had he gone to Longbourn, only to be thwarted? Had this given him a new disgust of Mr Bennet? *Had* he tried to follow her? *Would* he come? Her allegedly stubborn chin lifted. He would try. She just knew it.

"I will you give you my word," Elizabeth said. "With one caveat. If Mr Darcy does find me—whether in one day or ten—I will go with him immediately. I will not wait."

Lady Lavinia nodded. "I suppose that if he goes to as much trouble as unearthing you would require, he might be a worthwhile sort. Or else only pigheadedly stubborn."

"In that case, I shall prefer to think of him as independent-minded," Elizabeth replied.

Five days after starting to Birmingham, Darcy found himself returned to his London home. His efforts had been wasted; in a stroke of rotten luck, they had been searching all of Birmingham before finally discovering that the target they pursued was not Elizabeth, but a middle-aged female who should never have been mistaken for a younger woman.

He and his sister were so tired, they had gone directly to bed. When a new day dawned however, early as it was, he found Georgiana already in the breakfast parlour.

"Up and about at this hour, Sister? I thought you might sleep until noon."

"If I were foolish enough to do so, it would be my own fault if I was left behind."

Darcy considered the long hours of travel on minimal sleep they had just endured; also, while no one had discernibly objected to their questioning, they had roused some distasteful curiosity. "I can hardly believe you wish to leave again."

She looked down at her plate, and for a moment, he thought she would not answer. But her newfound direct-ness held. "Since almost the first moment you mentioned Elizabeth, you have been...interested in my opinion. I had always placed you on a pedestal, I think— a man who needed no one. A man who would never make a mistake. But suddenly you have become...very human." She smiled. "And not always the brightest light in the candelabra, when it comes to the fairer sex."

He smiled back. The more he encouraged her, the livelier she grew. Truth to tell, he had not, really, been predisposed to take much of her advice in the beginning; he had only felt obliged to do so to make up for his caustic words in the matter of Wickham. Nevertheless, it had not taken him overlong to see results from it—in her confidence, in Elizabeth's responses to Georgiana's suggestions. The picnic at Netherfield had been an act of brilliance; for that alone, he would owe his sister for the rest of his life. He was learning, slowly, the person she truly was. It was a gift, never to be taken for granted.

"Fortunately, your ill opinions have not bruised my pride too much. I am a resilient sort. I promise not to behave too abominably towards poor Elizabeth if you wish to remain in London while I continue the search."

Her smile grew wider. "She would make me an excellent sister. I do not wish to risk it."

He laughed. "And now you tease me, just as she would. I shall be sorely outnumbered when we find her, I think. It is a good thing you are fine company," he said, and had the satisfaction of seeing her beam at the compliment.

"When do we depart?"

"I sent Digweed a note last night, and I expect him at any time. He has been investigating the southern route whilst we wasted time on the road to Birmingham. We will set off after his call, once I pen a note to the Gardiners to keep them informed."

Georgiana hesitated, looking down. "I know you did not enjoy travelling with Dubitz. The incident with the runaway squirrel...well, I can leave him, if you would rather. I suppose he was not overly useful as a tracker."

For one moment, Darcy imagined riding in his carriage without a dog's hot breath panting in his ear. Retrieving him from his chase of the squirrel had cost them at least an hour. But he knew the beast gave his sister courage, and whatever else one wished to say about him, Dubitz had enjoyed himself immensely, only once growling ferociously at another traveller—whose looks and general manner, Darcy had agreed, *were* quite suspicious.

He smiled ruefully. "Tell your dog to be ready to leave within the hour."

Lady Lavinia was *most* unusual. She had begun by introducing Elizabeth to several of her friends, paying calls and inviting them to tea. They were not all grey-haired matrons of society like herself. Miss Cecilia Siddons was probably a year or so younger than Elizabeth, while Miss Herschel looked to be in her seventh decade. While all were respectable, Elizabeth detected a good deal of difference in the fashions and fabrics they wore—from the plain, dark wool of Mrs Blanchford to the elegant silks of Lady Roden. But it was the topics of discussion which most astonished her.

They sat in the saloon, talking desultorily and drinking tea and eating dainty little sandwiches and biscuits, just like any of a hundred such gatherings Elizabeth had attended, when Lady Lavinia's first question rang out.

"What is beauty, and why or why not should it be pursued?"

"Did not Plato maintain that it was instinct? We can detect the form of loveliness in painting, in sculpture, because we first recognise it as an abstract concept," said Mrs Cooke. "We naturally seek it out, admire it, even prize it."

"Plato believed that love itself was a desire for beauty," added Mrs Sharpe. "'Tis why the handsomest man in the room is the object of most women's attention."

"'Taught from their infancy that beauty is woman's sceptre, the mind shapes itself to the body, and roaming round its gilt cage, only seeks to adorn its prison'," recited Miss Bendish.

"Miss Bendish is proud of her ability to parrot Wollstonecraft," said a middle-aged woman—Mrs Stanhope?—"but *Vindication*'s point was not simply to argue the narrow confinement of opportunity such a fixation on beauty creates for women, but an objection to the harm it does to both men *and* women when society measures worth based solely upon it."

"There is nothing wrong with a decorative man, I say. Until they open their mouths," said Lady Roden. The other ladies laughed.

Elizabeth had never heard of this Wollstonecraft, and even the little she knew of philosophy did not help her much. The views of Plato, Aristotle, Socrates, Edmund Burke, and many others were discussed in elevated detail; Elizabeth felt quite out of her depth, remaining quiet. But Lady Lavinia's piercing gaze finally lit upon her.

"Elizabeth, what do you think of beauty?"

"I have never truly considered the question."

"Balderdash!" Lady Lavinia replied. "You have *considered* it with every assembly you ever attended. Were you not, in the beginning, insulted by your Mr Darcy because of his disregard of your own beauty? You were 'not handsome enough to tempt him', as I recall." She proceeded to repeat the story of Elizabeth's first encounter with Mr Darcy, to the great interest—and amusement—of the other ladies.

Elizabeth had not expected such a hostile strike from this quarter; her instinct was to excuse herself immediately. However, she could not countenance cowardice and narrowed her eyes at her hostess. "I suppose that is one way of looking at it. However, one might also be insulted by the judgment that 'beauty', or Mr Darcy's opinion of it, should be *the* determining factor for one's eligibility to participate in a country dance. Civility demanded the acknowledgement of at least an appropriate excuse. Good manners are an outward expression of inward beauty, are they not? Or is mutual respect to be discarded in the face of such a judgment? Did he not render *himself* unattractive thereby?"

To her surprise, Lady Lavinia beamed at her, rubbing her hands together with apparent glee. "Did I not tell you she was a clever one? Her education has been incomplete, it is true, but she is as quick as they come."

The other ladies were smiling at her approvingly. *This was some sort of test? But I have, apparently, passed it.*

"What a shame my grandson was too stupid to see it," Lady Lavinia sighed. "I would guess, Elizabeth, that you stood out like a daffodil in a coal pit in that tiny corner of tedium that is Meryton's surrounds. Reginald might have snapped you up, when he would not have stood a chance, had you a greater selection."

"As flattering as your opinion is, I have no fortune, my lady," Elizabeth answered wryly. "His selection necessarily included only those who do."

"Balderdash!" she repeated. "I admit there are those

who *must* marry a fortune—often due to their own ignorance, self-indulgence, and indolence. The Goulding men are unoriginal, to be sure, but there is no lack of understanding when it comes to finance. They certainly can marry where they please. He could have had you, I daresay, and I would have had a granddaughter I could tolerate." She sighed again heavily.

Elizabeth was startled by the notion. She recalled, with absolute clarity, the 'incident' on her eighteenth birthday, which had coincided with a large party at Haye-Park. She had worn a new dress to it, a gift from her parents, and had—as Lady Lavinia had just accused—spent much time on her appearance. Reggie Goulding had been entranced. She had known it, felt it. When he had asked to show her the garden in the moonlight, she had happily slipped out with him into the darkness.

She had welcomed his kiss—at its beginning. But too swiftly, his mouth had battered at her, heavy and bruising, his tongue suffocating, his hands roughly handling her person. He was no longer Reggie, a dear friend, and she was no longer Elizabeth, who thought she might love him. Still, she had delayed her response a bit, hoping it would get better, hoping the dream of love might not shatter so completely. But the longer she let it go on, the more she disappeared, until she had finally shoved at him in a near-panic.

"Stop!" she had cried. "Leave me be!"

Fear lent strength to her pushes until he staggered back. He had stared at her for several seconds, the sound of his breathing harsh in the silence of midnight.

"My family would never permit the match," he had panted at last, wiping his mouth on his sleeve. "You are the next thing to penniless. Forgive me."

Too shocked, too upset, Elizabeth had hardly taken heed of his words.

"We should return to the party before our absence is noticed," he had said.

She had begun walking back at once, practically stumbling, and avoided him for the rest of the night. Avoiding him in the future was effortlessly done—he never again gave her the slightest indication of interest.

Of course, she had examined the encounter from every angle later. She had decided she was glad to be penniless. He had disappointed her, in nearly every way.

Now, she wondered. *If he had ever again seriously pursued a courtship,* might *I have accepted him?* Despite the kisses she had hated, none of the objections of Mr Collins applied; Reggie was neither stupid nor ugly, his fortune and face handsome. She might have been able to talk herself back into being 'in love'—at least for a time. With his veneer of beauty, what if she had judged Reggie's flaws to have been acceptable ones? Ultimately, she would have found herself stuck with a ham-handed lover who never cared a whit whether she ever learnt to swim or drive a curricle; he would likely be appalled by the notions in the first place. She might then have devoted herself to the pursuit of happiness for her children, as her mother had—hopefully in a more competent fashion, but just as relentlessly. A substitute for—or a pastime within—her own life of tedium.

Blancmange, she thought. She would have come to understand...blancmange.

"Are you well?" Georgiana asked.

Darcy turned to her, trying to soften the frown he knew he wore into a less angry expression. "I had a fifty-percent chance of choosing correctly," he said. "It is frustrating to know I failed."

"You are not so far behind as all that. Mr Digweed's men have done much to figure the actual route. We would have had to stop at multiple inns and ask a lot of questions to come to the same conclusions. As it is, we know she is in Brighton somewhere. We will be there tonight, and tomorrow we can begin the true search."

She was right, of course, but it did not ease his frustration. "*Late* tonight. Who knew it would take so long to move a household?"

"Yes, it was a slow process—but you will be able to use your men to assist in the search, run errands, and help set up housekeeping. We do not wish to rely solely upon the few servants Lord Middleton will have at a closed house. A few extra hours now will save much time later."

Darcy scrubbed his hands through his hair, returning to his original point. "I was trying to be so thorough, so meticulous, yet I utterly missed Digweed's letters at the mailstops we chose," he grumbled. "It was rotten luck. He might have reached us with the news more quickly."

"His rider would have caught up to us eventually, had we not already turned back. The important thing is that we are no longer searching blindly, but in possession of her location." Dubitz, at her feet, added an enthusiastic woof of agreement.

He forced a smile for her benefit. She was correct in that they would at last be on Elizabeth's trail, albeit a week behind her. Apparently, she had left her name at every posting stop on her journey, making her easy to follow once her track was discovered. The last *known* stop had been ten miles from Brighton, and she had specifically told the innkeeper there her destination. Of course, he did not know where in the town she might be, and Digweed had not yet learnt it, but unless she was being held prisoner, locating her ought not to be an impossible undertaking.

He *would* find her, if he had to beat on the door of every house in Brighton.

⚜

The ballroom was large and crowded. Lady Lavinia had insisted they socialise, and although Elizabeth was not particularly interested in dancing with strangers, she strove to be amenable and gracious to her hostess. This was the third such affair she had attended in as many days—and it was by far the largest. She had already read most of her ladyship's reading assignments—including Mary Wollstonecraft's treatise. Her father might not be over-pleased with Lady Lavinia's selections, but she thought and hoped that Darcy would not mind. She would love to hear his opinions upon some of these ideas—and she believed he would want to hear some of hers. It was, she had realised, his ability to *see* her that she had first fallen in love with, and his personal beauty, although immense, was much further down in importance. Despite her interest in Lady Lavinia's 'education', she missed him more now than ever. Obviously, he had been unable to trace her—a needle in a haystack. He must be so worried! It was another part of why she was here—the more people who came to know her, the easier it would be for him to find her if he did happen to come this far south, although her hopes for quick rescue had mostly faded.

Seven days down, seven more to go, she thought.

One other thing was certain: her father would have a great deal of trouble bustling her away in a carriage ever again—to say nothing of regaining her trust.

The orchestra was playing a waltz, a slow tune that would never be called in a Meryton assembly. She had already danced a couple of sets, once with the elderly but kind Lord Roden, as well as the middle-aged Mr Sharpe. When the waltz had been called, she quickly made herself scarce in a lady's retiring room to avoid having to refuse a partner, only reappearing when she was certain to be safe from an invitation to dance. She was determined to dance her first waltz, whenever that might be, with Darcy.

Suddenly, she heard nearby a familiar laugh—a laugh she would recognise anywhere: youthful, exuberant, and much too loud.

"Lydia!" Elizabeth called.

Lydia turned, saw Elizabeth, and waved frantically. Elizabeth now could also see her partner: George Wickham. Her stomach turned. Lydia looked to be gesturing to her, but instead of approaching, Wickham deftly waltzed her away in the opposite direction. In the crush of couples, she quickly lost sight of the pair.

It was concerning, to say the least. Lydia had about as much sense as a goose with half a head and certainly should not spend any time in company with the dissolute lieutenant. Her mother had mentioned Lydia's invitation for a holiday in Brighton with the Forsters, but her father had been set against the idea. Once again, it seemed her sister had managed to have her way.

How does she do it? I cannot convince Papa that I ought to marry a man with ten thousand a year, and she persuades him to allow her to traipse off half a country away with Harriet Forster as chaperon! Harriet, who is barely twenty!

Lady Lavinia was very nearby; Elizabeth wondered if she ought to inform her of her younger sister's presence and perhaps try to gain her help in finding the Forsters. But she could not be sure whether her ladyship would be sympathetic, and besides, beyond warning her sister about Wickham's nefarious nature, what could she do? Lydia was so contrary, warning her might even make him seem more attractive. She bit her lower lip.

Lydia has nothing to offer him, she reminded herself. *She has no fortune, and thus, can be in no danger.*

"Why, Miss Bennet! As I live and breathe, it is good to see you!"

Captain Denny approached her, a warm smile of greeting upon his face. Lady Lavinia, hardly a strict chaperon, glanced over at him but only nodded, resuming her conversation with Lady Roden, taking no interest in Elizabeth's potential dancing partner.

After exchanging pleasantries with the captain, Elizabeth asked her questions. Had he seen Wickham and Lydia? Where might they be now? Were the Forsters here somewhere? Where was their residence?

Of course, in return, she must provide some explanations; she disclosed that she had come unexpectedly on holiday to Brighton to visit Lady Lavinia Goulding, adding that Lydia had no idea of her coming here—but that she had seen her on the dance floor and unfortunately lost sight of her. He answered her queries easily enough; yes, he had arrived with his friend, Wickham, but he had not yet seen her sister or the Forsters this evening. He provided the Forsters' direction, promising he would give them hers. A country dance was called, and he begged to partner her; she reluctantly agreed.

In vain, she searched for her sister amongst the other dancers; yet she could not help also watching the captain. Although very eligible, in comparison with Wickham, he was positively homely. Still, he was also kindly and gentlemanlike, from a good family in Suffolk. Elizabeth felt a pang of guilt; she had been just as bad as everyone else, judging a man upon his outward appearance.

Nevertheless, it *had* been he who brought Wickham into their midst—and he could not be *completely* ignorant of Wickham's nature, could he? Should she tell him just how ill was her opinion of Wickham, how awful the idea of him being anywhere near her sister? And yet, the thought of broaching the subject of Wickham's character with him, even delicately, filled her with a combination of unease and distaste. It was difficult, she found, to maintain her usual banter throughout the fleeting, frequent moments they were close enough to speak.

The dance would soon draw to an end, and they would have only a brief opportunity for more conversation. With all her heart, she did not want to say anything, but *something* must be said.

"Mr Denny," she began, slowing as he steered her back towards Lady Lavinia. "As I said earlier, I saw my sister Lydia on the dance floor with Mr Wickham. She saw me, I know she did—she even started towards me. But Mr Wickham saw me too, and what is more…" she hesitated, noting Denny's puzzled look. Was he so completely innocent of Mr Wickham's character as he appeared? No matter; it was her duty to press. "What is more, Mr Wickham led her purposely away from me, as quickly as he could. I have not seen either of them since, and despite the crush, I ought to have."

"He could not have seen you in the crowd," Denny protested, sounding sincere. "I cannot imagine *any* reason why he would not approach you directly. You were always a great favourite of his. You worry overmuch."

She stopped where she was, on the edge of the dance floor, turning to look at him directly. "Can you truly imagine *no* reason why a respectable lady might find him an inappropriate companion for her young sister? No reason whatsoever?"

Two bright spots of colour flared on his pale cheeks, and his eyes shifted away from her. "I know he has perchance, in the past, on occasion, not very recently, had one or two incidents wherein he, er, behaved in a manner, um, not as, um, forthrightly as I, myself might prefer. Nothing to do with anyone respectable, of course," he added hastily. "His own business...and her, er, the other party, um, not perhaps reliable or in my confidence."

Her heart chilled as her eyes narrowed. "Mr Denny, I can assure you that the lieutenant does not limit his degenerate behaviour to the disreputable. Whatever imaginary act of friendship you choose to defend your association with him can be no business of mine. Still, I expect that you, as a man of honour, could bestir your-self to ensure that my gently born, very *young* sister is safe."

"I am certain she is in no danger!" he cried, looking appalled. "The very idea!"

"I have every reason in the world to think ill of Mr

Wickham. Might I remind you that it was *your* introduction that commenced their connexion? How can you help feeling an interest in her protection, or refuse to make such enquiries as you are able to ensure her welfare?"

Bowing formally, his expression was one of deep offence and even revulsion. "I thank you for explaining so fully. Of course, I shall do whatsoever is in my power to seek them out," he said stiffly. "I bid you a good evening." He strode away.

After that encounter, Elizabeth returned to Lady Lavinia, experiencing all the distressing feelings of having committed publicly a social *faux pas*, yet at the same time wondering if she could have done more, pushed him even harder.

"What is the matter?" her ladyship asked, looking at her houseguest sharply.

"Not a thing." Elizabeth struggled to sound nonchalant. She took the seat beside her and recommenced searching the dancers for Lydia; when a young man—previously introduced to her by Mrs Cooke—asked for the set, she politely declined, declaring the heat had affected her.

Lydia—and the Forsters, for that matter—remained elusive, no matter how carefully she looked. Lydia's green dress ought to have stood out amongst all the pastel pinks and whites, but there was no sign of it.

Lady Lavinia continued her conversation with Lady Roden for only another set before suddenly rising; Elizabeth stood too, looking at her enquiringly.

"I do not attend these events for my health," she snapped. "If you are determined not to have any share of the amusement, far be it from me to forego my own bed."

Elizabeth hesitated a moment, considering begging Lady Lavinia to stay, explaining fully the situation. But in the end, she decided against it. A number of her ladyship's friends were nearby, and this was a confidential matter. She had been keeping a sharp lookout for Lydia and her chaperons for what seemed a full hour now, with no luck. No, she would call on the Forsters tomorrow and speak to Lydia herself. If Lydia seemed unwilling to pay any heed to her elder sister, she would ask for a private conversation with Colonel Forster and try to demand that Wickham be kept away from her. There was nothing else to do here tonight.

Her ladyship said not another word until they were ensconced in the carriage, her maid a silent shadow beside her.

"Very well, Elizabeth," she said. "The entire population of Brighton is no longer listening, hoping for a tit-bit of gossip. You needn't mind Whitby—she possesses more secrets than Westminster and will not inform me the half of what I demand to know. That officer with whom you danced your last—was he rude? I have noticed many a pretty uniform masking vulgar insolence."

"Oh, no," Elizabeth replied. "I fear I was the one who was impolite. Or at least, I broached a subject with him that no proper young lady would ever mention. He was very offended."

"Pooh!" she replied. "Mark my words—if a man decides what a woman should or should not say, you can count on it being the wrong decision."

It seemed, in the dark and quiet of the carriage, silly to withhold the tale of Wickham's perfidies. If it did not help, how could it hurt? She did not name Georgiana, only called her an acquaintance, but related the whole of it so that her ladyship would fully understand Elizabeth's concerns.

"But your sister has no fortune to abscond with," said Lady Lavinia. "She cannot be of interest to such as he."

"I know that," Elizabeth sighed. "And yet...why, when they saw me, did they hurry away, apparently even leaving the ball? It was not Lydia's idea to avoid me, I am certain. Why did I never see Colonel and Mrs Forster?"

"You did not search every corner."

"But I know them! They are gregarious and sociable. They would not hide in a corner! Could they have allowed Lydia to attend without adequate chaperonage?"

Lady Lavinia's lips pursed in a thoughtful frown, only just visible in the reflected light of the carriage lanterns through the windows. "I daresay we had better pay a call tomorrow," she said, "and let the Forsters know our expectations regarding the watchful care of your sister."

Elizabeth felt deep relief—along with gratitude. Her hostess would lend much countenance to any conversation with the Forsters. "Thank you, your ladyship."

The older woman reached across and poked her in the knee. "You are no longer alone here, girl," she said.

"Please cease behaving as though you are friendless. I may be an old lady, but I am not without influence. You did not choose to come, but you *will* choose when you go. After arrangements are made for your sister, we shall make yours for departure. I ought not to have forced you to stay, even if you did learn a thing or two. And you will always be welcome to return."

Elizabeth reached across to take Lady Lavinia's gnarled hand in her own. "Thank you," she said again—but much more quietly. The lump in her throat did not allow for a noisier reply.

22

Elizabeth was in the midst of a dream. Darcy was swimming, hand over hand, muscles rippling within a murky screen of water that she continually—and unsuccessfully—attempted to penetrate. Thus, she was disappointed when an interruptive force shook her out of it.

"Miss," called a disembodied voice from the darkness. "Miss, wake up, please."

The hazy wisps of the dream refused to reassemble, and reluctantly she opened her eyes. In the dim firelight stood Lady Lavinia's woman.

"Whitby?" Elizabeth asked, her voice sleep roughened.

"Yes, miss. You must be up at once. It's a rare pickle you're in, if only you knew it. I've got Hetty here to help you dress, but you must be quick about it."

Elizabeth rubbed her eyes, trying to make sense of it. "What is the time?"

"Near eleven, miss. Herself be waiting for you in the yellow drawing room, if you please, miss."

She had only been asleep an hour or so, and the unusual interruption erased the effects of slumber; hastily, she submitted to Hetty's waiting hands, hurriedly dressing in the gown pulled out for her. By the time she reached Lady Lavinia's favourite parlour, she was nearly beside herself with alarm. What could be the matter?

The first person she saw was her ladyship, standing beside the door. The look of pinched distress she wore was in stark contrast to her usual imperious expression.

"Elizabeth, there you are at last. We have a visitor, and I fear you must hear what he has to say before another minute passes."

"Who?" Elizabeth implored, more alarmed than ever. "What is this about?"

"It is your sister," came a curt male voice.

Elizabeth turned towards it. "Mr Denny!" she cried. "What are you doing here? My sister? Lydia? What has happened?"

"I took the liberty of sending over a note to the Forsters before I retired," Lady Lavinia said. "I informed them of your presence in Brighton and our expectation of visiting them in the morning. Apparently, it arrived on the heels of your acquaintance, Mr Denny. I think we ought to listen before we ask more questions."

The formality of her words called Elizabeth's mind to order, and she clamped her mouth shut against the demands for answers filling her head.

Mr Denny bowed awkwardly. "I apologise for the lateness of the hour, and any imposition."

"You may also suspend all pretty speeches. The facts as you understand them, if you please. Repeat what you told me upon your arrival."

His cheeks flushed, his tone stilted, and he avoided meeting anyone's gaze. "I made a few enquiries concerning that subject about which you were so adamant, regarding the whereabouts and safety of your sister. I discovered that Colonel Forster and his wife did not attend the ball due to an ailment of Mrs Forster's, and Miss Lydia attended under the auspices of another officer and his wife. By the time I found her chaperons, they admitted they had not seen her for an hour at least."

Elizabeth closed her eyes, regret that she had not made a larger fuss about Lydia's earlier disappearance swamping her.

"I then began asking around amongst the other officers with a bit more urgency," he continued. "And...a friend, or rather, someone who knew someone who was an acquaintance of—"

"The point, Mr Denny," her ladyship interrupted sternly.

"An elopement," he blurted. "I did not wish to believe the, um, rumour, but went immediately to the colonel's home with it. Unfortunately, upon a brief search, they found most of your sister's belongings gone and a letter from her stating an intention to be wed to the lieutenant in Gretna Green."

Elizabeth's heart began racing. *Such an imprudent match! And to Mr Darcy's worst enemy! Marrying the deceitful Wickham!* It was in every way awful.

"Colonel Forster is tracing their route." His voice was stiff with embarrassment. "An express has already been sent to your parents. I apologise for doubting your, um, conjecture regarding Wickham. He shall henceforth be no friend of mine. I begged to be of service, and the colonel sent me here to explain matters as best I could. He was anxious to be off and hopeful that, as they would not have such a lead as they believed they would, he might be able to catch up to them."

Elizabeth struggled to formulate all her questions and her fury into any type of coherence, but Lady Lavinia spoke first.

"Mr Denny," her ladyship demanded grimly. "You know the miscreant well, I take it. Are they, in your opinion, for Scotland?"

Elizabeth gasped at the implication.

Denny's cheeks reddened. "It...that is, um, I did not hear of any other destination—"

"I did not ask what you did or did not *hear*. I asked your truthful opinion. Did Wickham mean to marry the child?"

"I do not know," he replied, withering a little beneath her stare.

"Neither did I ask what you *know*," she persisted relentlessly, her eyes boring into him. "You may *not* hide behind polite pretence, you selfish imbecile. What do you *think*, man? If you had to guess, and your honour depended upon guessing correctly—which it *does*, I might add—which way are they headed? The Great North Road to Scotland? Or—"

"London!" he burst out, as if the words were forced from him against his will. "I would expect him to hide in town, where he claims to have so many friends. He has too often stated his intention of finding himself an heiress to wed, and, well, I do not believe his feelings towards Miss Lydia are, um, of a strength to overcome that desire. He is pockets-to-let, at the moment," he finished miserably. "Owes me a bulls-eye, myself."

"Based upon what you have told me thus far about Wickham, it is as I feared," she said to Elizabeth. "Well, my dear, shall we follow them to town in my coach-and-four—bound to be much faster than some rented hack—and attempt to intercept, whilst the men chase their tails?"

There was no time for tears, or for the part of Elizabeth that wished to scream her fear and sorrow—she *must* find Lydia before the pair were able to reach the metropolis and disappear into Wickham's dissolute world.

"Yes," she said simply.

***

Darcy was beyond weary by the time he reached a hostelry some ten miles before Brighton. Having begun the journey so late in the day, and travelling so slowly with such a large party, his frustration had risen to new heights. They had stopped only a few miles back to change horses, but there had not been enough decent horseflesh available; what there was, Darcy had given to his servants so that they might reach the borrowed Brighton home more quickly.

Georgiana dozed, her head resting on Dubitz's curly fur. He did not want to stop, but his team was tired. As much as he wished to proceed past it and directly to Lord Middleton's fine Brighton mansion, put his sister to bed, and begin afresh in the morning, he could not justify the abuse of horseflesh.

As he waited, it occurred to him that this inn also happened to be the last known stopping point on Elizabeth's southern journey; she had not only left her name here but revealed her destination. While there was no reason to think Digweed's men had not thoroughly canvassed the place for every crumb of information, there was no reason, either, to be certain they had. If interviewing the stablemen here did not help to find her, neither would it hurt.

She must be so close! His mind had devised scheme after scheme to uncover her whereabouts. Digweed had a man in the Brighton area somewhere, also searching— very discreetly, of course. He hoped he could be forgiven for so deeply desiring to find her himself.

Georgiana sat up and stretched. "Have we arrived?" she asked sleepily.

"Not as yet—almost, though. Give me a few minutes to ask a question or two, and we will be onto the last leg of our journey." He opened the door himself, not even having forbearance enough to await the footman. And then, in an act of impatience far greater than that of his master, Dubitz suddenly leapt off the seat, scrambled out the door, and was away before Darcy could even think to grab him.

"Dubitz!" Darcy bellowed, but the dog had run out amongst the tangle of carriages, chaises, hackneys, and cattle. In the darkness, in the shadows cast by lanterns, even in the barking of stable dogs, he simply...vanished.

"Brother!" Georgiana cried. "We must find him!"

"I will," he replied, cursing inwardly. "You stay here with Frost."

"I have to help search!" she protested.

It would be all he needed, to lose Georgiana too. It was *not* a genteel crowd beyond this carriage door. "Dubitz might return," he said. "If you are not here, he will not stay. You know he will not."

She bit her lip, obviously weighing the benefits of arguing the point against the delay it would entail. "Very well. Please, please find him quickly!"

After a brief word with Frost, he hurried out into the stable yard, loudly calling his wayward dog by name.

⚜

Elizabeth sat across from her ladyship in the darkness, her worries too great to put into words. Lady Lavinia suffered from no such insufficiency.

"Perhaps you think I spoke too harshly to the captain," she said.

Elizabeth, in her grief and despair, had thought no such thing, but made no answer.

"Men like him make me sick. He is a disciple of the typical male's eleventh commandment: 'Thou shalt look the other way'. Hiding behind their camaraderie, pretending not to notice when their friends commit abominations…and the most he will do if his comrade 'ruins' your sister is withdraw his polite conversation and perhaps refuse to introduce him to any more innocent victims. He will *not* help see that Wickham makes reparations. He will not lift a finger to help recover Miss Lydia. It is none of his concern."

The dowager pursed her lips as if in disgust with men everywhere. "Even Colonel Forster, who is under a moral obligation to attempt to find your sister, will call her damaged goods, as if all that makes Lydia Bennet a human being is confined to a few square inches of her person. Make no mistake, she is a stupid girl—but she has been taught to be stupid. Your parents have taken pride in her ability to capture the attention of males, have they not?"

"My mother is the one who..." she began to argue, but could not continue. The books her ladyship had insisted she read had helped her to see Mama in a new way. Essentially powerless, thinking beauty was the only tool a woman had—for it had been the only one *she* had ever found—and despising the intellect of her husband, who used it only to humiliate her, she believed beauty to be her only ammunition in her fight to achieve stability for the future. Jane and Lydia, the prettiest of the sisters, had been the hardest hit by Mama's relentless focus on outward appearances. It was a miracle Jane had survived it; Lydia...had not.

"Yes," she said instead.

"Whatever you wish to say about *my* daughter, she at least was taught that she was a person, important in her own right, irrespective of whether some man wanted her. That she chose to be a *dull* person was no fault of mine."

Elizabeth wished she could argue, could protest. Her father had not taken any pride in Lydia's flirtatious manner, to be sure—but then, he had taken no pride in Lydia for any reason whatsoever. Elizabeth would never forget his deep disappointment at her birth. He had not emerged from his book-room for days, and she now believed he had never been able to completely overcome his resentment. Lydia might have been a foolish girl regardless, but his singular lack of attention could not have helped, and only led Mama to compensate with greater attention and even less discipline.

The carriage pulled into the yard of The Fork & Lightning, a large posting inn where Lady Lavinia's coachman had hoped the runaways might have stopped. Thankfully, her ladyship did not object when Elizabeth stated her intention of asking around herself, only instructing her footman to 'keep her out of trouble'.

Her first impression was of noise—even at this late hour, there were so many hacks, carts, and coaches rumbling, stablemen calling, stable boys answering, horses neighing—and stinking. Despite lanterns, the place was full of shadows, and she was glad of the burly footman, Vincent, who trailed close behind her. The arrivals and departures were of most interest to her, but she was required to come near to each carriage to see anything, even quite shamelessly looking in open doors and trying to peer in windows. She could not afford any pretence of polite disinterest.

Near a chaise, a bickering older couple gave her a look of disapproval when she poked her nose into the open door of their vehicle. "See here, mind your own self," the man barked at her, but Elizabeth noticed the woman's attention—equally disapproving but fixed on a point beyond herself. Following the line of her gaze, she saw the source of her censure. A young couple was locked in each other's arms, the two involved in a kiss— and it was no courtly, demure suitor's buss, but a passionate display, *wholly* improper. Several of the inhabitants of the inn's yard seemed appreciative as well, as the accompanying whistles and catcalls attested. Neither appeared to notice or care about the spectacle they made, and Elizabeth nearly looked away in embarrassment. And yet, there was something about...about the young lady's hat.

That hat is mine! Elizabeth realised.

"Lydia!" she cried, hurrying towards her sister. The kissing couple broke apart.

"My luck," muttered George Wickham, "has, perhaps, run out." He faced her glare with an insouciance Elizabeth found infuriating.

"Perhaps you would care to explain what you do here with my young sister?" she hissed.

"'Tis none of your business!" Lydia exclaimed. "Just...go away, Lizzy. I am a woman grown, and I will make my own decisions!"

"A woman grown? An interesting argument. Hmm, allow me to recollect the date of your birth, Lydia. I certainly cannot remember you turning one-and twenty! But perhaps you possess a letter from Papa giving his permission to ignore that small fact. Show it to me, and I will take my leave of you both!"

Her sister flushed. "George, let us go, now. I am *finished* with this conversation."

Elizabeth whirled on him. "I swear to you, if you enter that carriage with my sister, I will call for constables. I will call rape, I will scream as loud as I am able in defence of her, and I will make a scene so unholy none here will ever forget it, whether or not *she* wishes it!" Vincent stepped up behind her, adding menace to her words.

"Never fear, dear lady," Wickham said, with a mocking, courtly bow. "I would never be so uncivil as to disobey any desire of yours. Lydia, darling, go with your sister."

"George! I will not leave you, George!" Lydia wailed. "Lizzy, you are ruining everything!" She looked between Vincent and Wickham, obviously weighing her odds of remaining with her lover. Suddenly, with desperate intention, she screamed, "Find me, George!" and set off at a run into the shadows.

Lydia could run like the wind when she wished, and there were a hundred places to hide. "Vincent!" Elizabeth cried. "You must go after my sister! Do not allow her to escape!"

Wickham began laughing, leaving Elizabeth with the uncomfortable realisation that she would be left alone with him; she glanced back towards Lady Lavinia's carriage. But hardly a moment passed before Wickham's coachman approached. "I's ready ta go," the man said impatiently, addressing them both.

Evidently in the dark, he could not tell the difference between herself and Lydia.

"One of this company shall be going no further. Take down my sister's trunk," she ordered.

Wickham, still chuckling, must have realised the coachman's error; quickly, he drew an arm about her waist.

"My bride has cold feet, but I am certain I can warm them up again once we are on the road," he said, his tone ingratiating, and what she supposed he thought to be seductive. "Sweetling, I am not blind. You wanted me once. Allow me to remind you."

Elizabeth shoved against Wickham's grip. "I am *not* his bride! I will be going nowhere with him. Let me go!"

He stumbled back a little, freeing her.

The coachman looked at them both with disgust, gesturing towards his vehicle. "I's paid ta drive ta Clap'am. Git in, or don't. I be leavin' now."

"We were always good friends," Wickham said, grabbing her hand. "Now we can be better. What a cosy little drive we should have. Come now, I favoured you once as well, I cannot help but remember."

She tried to yank her hand away, but he did not release it. She pulled harder.

Suddenly, within all the shadows, apart from all the strangers and all the traffic—hacks, carts and coaches rumbling, stablemen calling, stable boys answering, horses neighing—she heard one word, one name ringing out over the din and gloom.

"Dubitz!"

23

Dubitz's large form bounded between herself and the weaselly Wickham; his fanged teeth bared, and he growled low in his throat. Dropping her hand, Wickham took a hasty step back, regarding the beast warily. Even the surly driver paused from mounting the box to regard the scene with new interest.

Elizabeth laid a hand upon Dubitz's dear, curly top knot. "Take Lydia's trunk down. Now, if you please."

Wickham peered between her and the dog, as if weighing whether he should make an escape. Elizabeth paid him no further heed, for a broad-shouldered male in a tall beaver came into view at that very moment. She felt the smile breaking from her face, as if a deep freeze had suddenly melted, thawing her, letting her feel again, her heart leaping, her very body rejoicing, coming alive. But Darcy did not look at her, all his attention fixed upon Wickham. How much had he seen?

"Is this young lady disturbing you?" he asked, his

voice at its smoothest, haughtiest pitch. "Is her aggressive dog misbehaving?"

Wickham looked at him mistrustfully, as if not daring to believe he was there to take his part. It was a wise suspicion; there was something not quite *safe* in Darcy's calm, flat address.

"He wished me to join him on his journey," she explained helpfully. "I have interrupted his elopement with my youngest sister. He was having surprising difficulty taking 'no' for an answer."

"I never did!" Wickham protested. "She misunderstood!"

Darcy looked at him, just looked, and Wickham seemed to wilt. Darcy spared another glance for the driver, who without a word of argument, clambered up to release one of the two trunks.

"Perhaps you were afraid to be alone with your thoughts," Darcy said evenly, still not looking at Elizabeth and with no sign that his temper was engaged. "Perhaps you might have been forced to reflect upon your entire sorry life. I can see how unpleasant that would be."

Wickham slowly backed away a step, and then another. The driver looked from one man to the other, dropped Lydia's trunk, and scrambled back to his box. With hasty movements, he urged the horse forward.

Wickham lurched towards the departing vehicle with his mouth agape. "Everything I own in the world is on that coach!"

"My heart breaks for you." Darcy began shrugging off his coat, and Elizabeth recognised the emotion behind his outwardly staid and even temperament—fury, certainly, but also a certain diabolic glee. The devil in him had been freed—and was anticipating a good thrashing.

"I will hold your coat," she said, grinning at him, and he looked at her for the first time. He grinned back.

"I have missed you," he said, his voice low and tantalising. "You are not to disappear again."

"Since you command it, I suppose I might refrain."

Wickham saw his opportunity for escape in their distraction. He made his move, darting off in the direction of the disappearing coach. Before Darcy could make chase, Dubitz launched himself after him. Wickham was fast, but Dubitz found a speed hitherto unused except when chasing squirrels. With a mighty leap, he caught his prey mid-stride, hitting him square on the back. Down Wickham went, directly into a large, steaming pile of horse manure. Dubitz plunked down upon his back, a doggy smile of triumph upon his face. Every time Wickham tried to lift his face from the filthy ordure, the dog growled ferociously, until he simply gave up and lay in it, unmoving.

"That is so very fitting," Elizabeth remarked, laying her hand upon Darcy's arm in a staying motion as he made to follow his dog.

Darcy frowned, a bit of frustration showing at last. "The repulsive toad thought you were helpless. He supposed he could do whatever he wanted. It is past time he was taught a lesson. A painful one. Besides, why should Dubitz have all the fun?"

"We have more important matters. Lydia has run off," she said, dismissing Wickham entirely. "Lady Lavinia's footman is in pursuit, but I do not know if he was able to catch up to her or what he could do to hold her if he did."

"Who is Lady Lavinia?"

She quickly began an explanation of the situation, but after a few moments, she realised she was wasting her breath. While he watched her intently, something told her he paid no attention whatsoever to what she was saying.

"You have not listened to one word I just said," she complained.

"How can I?" he asked. "You are so beautiful, so real…so very…right *here* before me." He reached for her.

What might have happened next, she could not know —she might have been as bold and brazen in her affections as Lydia, except for a stern voice of reason mixed with a familiar whinging.

"Ah, there you are, Elizabeth. I take it this creature belongs to you?" Lady Lavinia asked.

Elizabeth thought, at first, that the 'creature' she spoke of was Dubitz, who continued to periodically emit low growls from his position upon Wickham's back. Lydia's wails, however, soon informed her otherwise. Her ladyship stood with one hand cinched tightly upon her sister's ear, Vincent hovering in the background closely enough that Lydia dared not try and break free.

"She is my sister, yes," Elizabeth replied ruefully.

"If only we had not departed so quickly!" Lydia wailed. "I begged that we should wait until Thursday, for I wanted to attend the masquerade—I had *such* a beautiful costume for it, no one would ever have recognised me! But dear Wickham said that we would have no other chance now that *you* are in town, and since Harriet did not go to the Halifax ball tonight, it *did* seem an ideal opportunity for escape. Oh, you have spoilt my whole life, Lizzy! We were to go to Gretna Green, and it would have been *so* romantic!"

Elizabeth clenched her teeth against the sheer number of responses she wished to make. Darcy must think her family beyond redemption! "Your fare was to Clapham. It does not seem the most direct route to Scotland."

Lydia only shrugged. "Well, we would have gone *eventually*. When his business in town was finished."

Lady Lavinia twisted her ear, and Lydia shrieked. "Stop speaking nonsense, girl. Your lover used you for sex, and you have made a tale of romance out of it. Very imaginative, I suppose, if you intend to write novels for a livelihood. Not so useful in keeping yourself alive and free of disease, however. I only hope he was good at the business. You might be able to pen a decent love scene, if so—I despise when the heroine swoons instead of coming to the point, so to speak. That is, unless he has infected you with the pox and you die before your eighteenth birthday. But perhaps you can write quickly."

Lydia, staring in wonder at the bluntness of this speech—and perhaps fearing another ear twist—subsided into wide-eyed silence.

"Lady Lavinia Goulding, I see you have already made the acquaintance of my sister, Miss Lydia Bennet. This is Mr Fitzwilliam Darcy. And his dog, Dubitz, currently, um, observing Lydia's abductor."

The group all turned to look at Wickham. He turned his excrement-smeared face—cautiously—towards Lydia. "Help me, love."

Her face showed a mixture of astonishment and revulsion. "Ew! What is all over you? Is that—"

"For once, a man whose outward appearance

matches his inward character," Lady Lavinia interrupted Lydia's outcry. She turned back to Darcy. "Took you long enough to find her, boy." She nodded then, peering at him through the shadows of the dim yard. "He has his father's shoulders," she sighed.

Darcy raised a brow at Elizabeth. "Lady Lavinia *Goulding*?" he asked incredulously.

"Yes," Elizabeth replied.

He shook his head with some irritation. "I should have known."

⚜

There was no time, and certainly no privacy, for anything she wished to say to—or do with—Darcy. He retrieved Dubitz, bending to say a few low-voiced words to Wickham. Most of what he murmured was unintelligible to the group—but Elizabeth thought she heard the words 'will never find your body' within them. At any rate, despite Dubitz's departure, Wickham remained in the muck, unmoving. They left him to it, Lydia whinging about their 'cruelty' but making no move to actually go near her fallen, fetid lover.

Georgiana, Darcy explained as he escorted them back to Lady Lavinia's carriage, was awaiting him in his, and he needed to remove her to a borrowed home—which, apparently, was not far from Sea Terrace. He would call after breakfast tomorrow, he assured Elizabeth, and only squeezed her hands tightly before departing, practically dragging his *very* reluctant dog. Elizabeth was much in sympathy with Dubitz; it was horrible to see him leave after such a brief, wholly unsatisfying reunion.

But in the meantime, they had their own business.

An express must be sent directly from The Fork & Lightning to follow the one that had already been sent to her parents, with a report of Lydia's recovery from Wickham's clutches.

"The Forsters must wait until morning for their news," her ladyship decreed. "Imagine, allowing a pretty, romantic girl like your sister to travel alone in Brighton without the strictest of eyes upon her. 'Tis amazing she was not importuned by a dozen impatient fools."

Elizabeth glanced sharply at Lady Lavinia, trying to discern in the darkness whether she was being sarcastic; she appeared perfectly serious, however. It was strange, indeed, that she was not lecturing Lydia within an inch of her life—certainly she had never hesitated to do so with Elizabeth. It was not until much later, after the ever-useful Whitby took Lydia away to bed, that she had any opportunity to ask why.

"You were very kind to Lydia," Elizabeth said. "After you were done twisting her ear, that is. I, myself, wished to keep on twisting. Had she managed to succeed in running away—why, that blackguard never would have married her. She has no portion to speak of, and my father has little set aside to force the issue. She might have ruined us all. It was so thoughtless!"

Her ladyship only sighed. "You must *think*, Elizabeth, as your sister has obviously never done in her life. To the first man who offered to do it for her, she acceded her entire will. For pleasure, yes, but mostly to escape the responsibility of thinking for herself."

Elizabeth frowned. "I would say she has never taken *any* responsibility for that."

"Obviously she had to, once she was in Brighton. At even the shallowest levels of society, there are rules, there is a pecking order, there is competition. Away from home for the first time, she suddenly was no longer 'Miss Lydia', to be treated in a certain, well-established fashion with the threat of a papa—even a lackadaisical one—overlooking one's shoulder. Mrs Forster was not up to the task of providing any guidance, it appears."

"She is very young." Elizabeth suddenly felt drained of any energy.

Lady Lavinia nodded. "If we wish for her to turn to *us* for that guidance, we must not completely antagonise her. For every teaspoon of discipline, we must offer a cupful of restorative, an increase of understanding, lest she esteem us her enemies."

"It is a very generous view. Still, do not you think she ought to at least understand—or be *brought* to understand—that an elopement with a man by whom she could not even guarantee the promise of marriage was the stupidest idea in the world?"

But the elder woman only shrugged. "*You* understand it. It is because you are willing to think for yourself, despite every incentive not to."

Could it be that what seemed so obvious to her was really so obscure? It was Elizabeth's turn to sigh; her father had been, always, the biggest influence in her life, while he had barely given Lydia a thought. "I had incentive, at least more than Lydia. My father respects thoughtful discussion, and I learnt to please him early."

"It always comes back to the men, does it not? You had best be certain your Mr Darcy is no fool. Although I do already give him points for persistence." She smiled knowingly. "You both exercised the utmost restraint tonight, and I am grateful. It is so long past my bedtime that I can hardly remain upright. I could not have borne having to deal with weeping from you or tantrums from him." She patted Elizabeth on the shoulder and made her way to the stairs. "You are a sensible girl, Elizabeth. That is not romantic, but it is much more comfortable for those who must bear with you."

However, a half an hour later, Elizabeth lay in bed, tired beyond measure and still swamped by regret.

Sensible! Ha! Little does she know how I hated leaving him after so few minutes together. I wanted to stamp my feet like a child and cling to him like a lovelorn Lydia. And now I lie here like an imbecile and fret over a parting of only a few hours' duration.

It *was* stupid, but after all the problems they had encountered, it seemed as though fate was already planning to again tear them apart. *Where will I be taken next? Wales? America? Could I borrow Dubitz from Georgiana and set him upon anyone who tries to whisk me away?*

Finally, she quit her bed in favour of seeking the fresh ocean breeze—an incredible expanse of which was available to her by climbing one flight of stairs and opening a door to the lovely rooftop terrace for which the home was named. It overlooked a vast beach and silent lanes, as well as a carpet of stars beyond the quiet glow of half a moon.

It is peaceful here, she thought. But in the next minute, she attempted to calculate the distance to the Darcys' borrowed home.

It might as well be in London.

In a nearby alley, a dog howled forlornly. *I sympathise with you, doggy,* she thought. *You sound like I feel.*

"Muzzle it, beast." A familiar low voice floated upwards in the break between waves.

She ran to the wrought iron railing. "Darcy?" she called down.

He looked up, shading his eyes as if against the noonday sun, plainly trying to spot her. She could only make out the dimmest silhouette and had no idea if he could see her at all. Her every determination fired.

"Wait right there! Do not move!"

She ran lightly down the stairs, her slippered feet making no noise, pausing at her room only to throw on a wrapper over her night rail. In a very few minutes, taking no thought for propriety or practicality, she was letting herself out via a side door nearest the lane where he would, hopefully, still be waiting. Her whole soul urged her to run to him, and run she did, without hesitation.

He caught her mid-flight, lifting her from the ground in his strong arms, whirling her around in sheer exultant joy. "My love, my love, my love," he whispered, over and over. Their mouths met, and it seemed so incredible that she could possibly pour out her depths of feeling into a sole point of contact, lip to lip, a kiss that felt more like a touch of his spirit to hers.

"I want to marry you. Here. Now. I cannot bear to be parted from you again," he murmured roughly, between kisses, whilst Dubitz leant heavily against her.

"I know, I know," she answered. It was not until her lips felt almost bruised that they finally broke apart, a chill wind blowing right through her thin nightwear. "Come sit in the parlour with me. We can slip in and take shelter from this wind." Dubitz whined his agreement.

"Devil take it, Elizabeth, I apologise. Here I am, selfishly devouring you while you shiver. I am a brute."

She grabbed his hand and led him up the steps and through the side door she had left open. It was not long before they were in a back parlour, Darcy shrugging off his coat and draping it over her. After building up a neat flame, he waited patiently until it was truly burning before adding a log. When he was finally satisfied, he sat down beside her, stretching out his long legs, Dubitz at his feet before the blaze. She laid her head upon his shoulder, and for long moments, they simply luxuriated in being together at last.

"Will Lady Lavinia throw fits if we are discovered here?"

She smiled. "I do not suppose she will, but even if she does…well, she will say nothing to my parents. Lady Lavinia does not think exactly like most people do. At least she believes now that you are highly likely to marry me."

"I have heard of Lady Lavinia Goulding," he replied. "So, she will not be too strict in her opinions of an engaged couple spending time alone together? That is as well."

"Well, not for that reason precisely. She approves of you, I think, or at least your steadfastness. As much as she approves of any man, I suppose. Also, she fancied your father."

He turned sharply to look at her, as if to discern whether she was serious.

"She said you look very much like him."

"I have been told that, yes."

In the drowsy silence to follow, her thoughts tumbled one over the other.

"It is not the challenges, is it?" she asked, for the question had been upon her mind since completing the reading her ladyship had thrust upon her. "This connexion between us? The hunt, the competition, the-the game of it all. I would not blame you if it were—or would try not to. We are friends, I think, and always will be. But if it *is* the challenge, I would prefer not to marry you because it is so much more than that to me. For a connexion to be so unequal would be heart-breaking."

She liked that he did not immediately protest, or worse, smother her questions in kisses—as he could most assuredly do. He was very good at the lovemaking part of this affair, she had noticed. Expert, even, and she had no wish to consider how he had gained that experience. No, instead, he held her hand, pressing a kiss upon it. Nevertheless, he seemed to take a ridiculously long time to answer, and she was beginning to worry by the time he did.

"Make no mistake," he said finally. "I have thoroughly enjoyed at least some of these challenges. I like that you think well of yourself, that you did not fall into my arms simply because I crooked my finger at you. That you challenged me at all."

"Oh, well, the part where I fail to fall into your arms whenever you come near me seems to have passed."

A sly grin touched the very corner of his lips. "To a man such as I, who grew to adulthood having anything and everything he had ever desired, I think there was a good deal of both resentment and curiosity in my heart concerning you. From your stay at Netherfield onwards, you would not behave as I expected or even wished. I wanted you physically, but more, I wanted to hear what next you would say, to see you every day, to understand your opinions. I wanted *you* to *want* me, first and foremost, and rather than simply accepting that you did not,

I told myself that you were...misbehaving. If I pursued the connexion, I would have to expend a good deal of effort in your training."

Her eyebrows rose. "As you have Dubitz? I notice you are quite the expert at this 'training' business."

He pulled her over to face her directly. "You see, that is what I mean. I say my sincere but ill-spoken thoughts, and you respond with an intoxicating mixture of sarcasm and honesty. Who can guess what you might say next?"

"I would hate to be predictable."

He bestowed another kiss, but one more pensive than passionate.

"When I first began to speak about you with Georgiana, she could not tell whether I loved you or hated you. I was in a low mood of self-recrimination, of doubt. I had royally botched my role as her guardian, as I have already explained. If I could not even succeed as a brother and adviser, guiding *her*, who already loved me, how could I begin to be a husband, to know and nurture *your* mind and heart? I thought endlessly about it, about what love and hatred might really be or mean, but I remained hopelessly confused until I saw you again at your sister's wedding."

"What is it then?" she asked, sitting up so she could see the flames reflected in his dark eyes, the wild side of his nature obvious and exposed. She had named it a devil, but perhaps she had been wrong. An untameable force, not wicked, but certainly neither docile, easy, nor compliant. The restraint and impassivity he displayed to society were a part of him as well, but it was not *all* of him, nor even most. He was ardent, witty, and teasing; he was disciplined, introspective, and attentive. At this moment, she did not care; he was Fitzwilliam Darcy, and she loved every bit of him. She scooted closer, unafraid, her arms going around his neck. "What is love, and what is hatred? What are all the answers to all the deepest questions of the universe?"

"I still cannot explain," he replied, as he pulled her across the remainder of the small space left between them. "But when I look into your eyes, it simply does not signify. Wherever you are, that is where my questions all have answers. In sickness and in health, in good times and bad, till death do us part." His mouth descended upon her own, and such uncertainties ceased mattering to either.

❦ 24 ❧

Elizabeth did not waken until the sun was high in the sky. She stretched, feeling pleasantly, deliciously, completely happy for the first time since leaving her uncle's home. Darcy would arrive in the early afternoon, instead of just after breakfast—he was insistent that she sleep as long as she was able, since the clock had been striking four before he—and his dog—had reluctantly departed for their own beds.

Neither had Whitby wakened her, which struck her as slightly more unusual. The household had expected Darcy shortly after breakfast. Still, everyone had likely slept late after their adventures of the night before. She thought about seeking out Lydia, who—knowing her sister—was still abed; they had put her only a few rooms away from her own. However, she decided against facing a sulking Lydia on an empty stomach.

She rang for assistance, taking her time about readying herself for the day. At breakfast, no one made mention of her missing suitor, but perhaps they were taking cues from her own lack of concern. Nothing, in fact, could disturb her; not Lydia's irritability when she finally appeared downstairs an hour later, nor Lady Lavinia's complaints regarding unspecified 'goings-on' when 'rational people ought to be sleeping'.

Elizabeth had to smile; she should have known that her ladyship would discover every secret. She could not care and could trust in her discretion—one would always be safe in any home of Lady Lavinia's.

It was teatime when Darcy arrived, Georgiana in tow, apologetic for their tardiness in making an appearance. Lady Lavinia was at her most gracious, inviting them to stay. Darcy's manner towards all was perfectly formal and correct; the only sign he gave of being more than a distant acquaintance was taking the seat beside her upon the settee, Georgiana on his other side.

At least I had the good sense to choose to sit upon it, she thought. *Mama would be so proud.*

Lydia, unfortunately, was at her worst, her behaviour more closely resembling a spoilt infant's than that of a young lady. She did not respond to anything said to her, only sitting in sullen resentment. Elizabeth's newfound serenity was sorely tested, and she might have lost her patience, had not she been prevented by some severe looks from her ladyship.

Lady Lavinia's reasons for tolerating such conduct seemed weak, especially as her patience only encouraged Lydia. *She ought to allow me to discourage it!* It was beyond embarrassing, especially before Darcy and her—hopefully—soon-to-be sister. *And why,* she also wondered, *did he bring Georgiana with him? Could ever a tableau be more awkwardly situated?* A hostile, unashamed Lydia who had attempted to elope with Georgiana's former lover, a man whom Darcy despised, sitting with them over tea served on Sèvres porcelain. What could there possibly be for *anyone* to say?

To her surprise, it was Darcy who found a means of opening the conversation—and his words were not at all what she had expected.

"I had a childhood friend who was far more gifted with charm and address than myself." He looked directly at Lydia as he spoke, his expression grave as usual—but his tone was kind, without any hint of the disgust he *must* feel. "I was as drawn in as anyone. When we were young, I enjoyed Wickham's pranks, his sense of adventure. It was only as we grew older that I began to feel his notions of amusement might not be so diverting as he believed. It was one thing to filch a pasty from an ill-tempered tradesman who had so many; it was another to take it off the Widow Saunders' sill, whose only meal that day it was. He simply could not see any difference. If he wanted something, he took it. I gave up trying to explain or argue with him while still in school. He graduated from pies to purses and then, finally, to the unprotected. If he wanted a female, if he could get away with the taking, he would take. My friendship was only useful to him in clearing the destruction left in his wake. But I continued to shield his misdeeds for the sake of my father and his, even though it meant deceiving them both, I am sorry to say."

Lady Lavinia looked down her long nose at him. "Do you feel guilty for lying to your father, or for providing Mr Weakling the respectability to continue hurting young girls?"

"Or older ones," he sighed, and Elizabeth saw it then—his pain, the blame he shouldered, obvious despite his quiet, straightforward manner. He did not answer the question but continued to speak.

"Upon my father's death, I paid Wickham a thousand pounds, with an additional three thousand to sign away the clerical living designed for him. Upon the death of Pemberley's vicar afterward, I would not give the living to him, nor pay him once more for it, as he demanded. I hoped our paths would never cross again. But when they did, I pretended to myself that they had not. He saw my interest in your sister, Miss Lydia, of that I am certain. Thus, he set you up for merciless heart-break, knowing you were too innocent to comprehend his villainy. I ought to have given him another three thousand and saved you from his machinations. I apologise."

Lydia drew a breath and, by her still-sullen expression, clearly meant to be disagreeable. But Lady Lavinia interjected her own opinions before she could.

"She is too young and naïve to believe you, Mr Darcy. Men like Mr Wastrel delight in those who are exceedingly inexperienced, and who cannot recognise a scoundrel."

Lydia looked at her as if she wished to argue, opening her mouth again to say something, but Elizabeth beat her to it.

"I believed in Mr Wastrel's...er, Mr Wickham's lies against Mr Darcy." It was part of why she was so angry at Lydia, she suddenly realised—because Mr Wickham's ability to hurt her sister had been heightened by Elizabeth's own words. "What is more, I repeated them to you as well as to others, doing my best to destroy a good man's name. Even after learning of Wickham's deceit, I told no one and left you to believe he was a man of decency, his reputation intact so he could ruin you at his leisure."

Lydia barely glanced at her, returning her gaze to Mr Darcy, her expression still angry. "I know what you are about. He said you would do this, say anything to make him appear a rogue in my eyes."

"You are wasting your breath, both of you. At least until she is more mature and able to tell the difference between an honourable man and a reprobate," interjected her ladyship.

"I am no child!" Lydia cried. "Everyone wants to treat me as a child!"

"Is that what Mr Ne'er-do-well told you?" Lady Lavinia asked. "Oh, let me guess. I suppose he offered to help you 'become a woman'? How *very* generous of him. And what were you to gain from the bargain, beyond a few moments of dubious pleasure and possibly the pox?"

"I will be—*would* have been his *wife!*"

"Why do you think it? Because he *said* so? Did he give you a ring? Speak to your father? Give you any assurances beyond *words*, so easily spoken and so easily denied?"

Lydia turned bright red, her mouth snapping shut.

Lady Lavinia sighed. "If you have relations with a man, it becomes possible, even likely, that you will become impregnated with a child. If your companion is disloyal, if he has other lovers, especially prostitutes, he is likely to give you a disease or two. If you are lucky, the disease will only kill you."

"George would never!" Lydia cried.

Lady Lavinia opened her mouth to answer, but to the surprise of the room, Georgiana did instead.

"Yes, he would," she said softly. All eyes turned to her. "You are not the first girl he has lied to," she added quietly.

Lydia looked at her in astonishment. "But he hates you."

"Perhaps he does. But he pretended to love me." Her cheeks flushed, and she stared at her feet.

"He said you were exactly like your brother, proud and arrogant."

"Oh, yes." Lady Lavinia snorted. "She is plainly the image of Hybris, goddess of insolence, hubris, reckless pride, and outrageous behaviour in general. Anyone can see it."

It was so plainly the opposite of shy, gentle Georgiana Darcy, so obviously a blatant untruth, even Lydia had the grace to look abashed.

"After his attempt to elope with me was foiled, he sought me out in secret," Georgiana softly continued.

She glanced at her brother, whose expression remained stoic. His impassivity seemed to give her the courage to continue. "George was very angry that I had changed my mind. He told me that he and his-his prostitutes—he used a coarser expression—that they would laugh together about me. About my...naivety. About how stupid I had been to ever believe he could love someone like me."

Elizabeth's heart broke for the young girl. Darcy placed his arm about her shoulders in silent comfort.

Lydia appeared uncertain now, and Lady Lavinia clearly knew when a point had been made.

"Well, we all know that this Mr Worm is a gross deceiver," she said, as if speaking of prostitutes and elopements was *de rigueur* for afternoon teas. "We can at least agree on that, I think. Miss Lydia, would you care to pour?"

⁂

To Elizabeth's amazement, her ladyship shifted the topic of conversation rather easily to a subject of great interest to both younger ladies—fashion. Lady Lavinia 'just happened' to have placed periodicals out, including a recent issue of the delightful *La Belle Assemblée*, to which she subscribed from London—featuring the latest in sleeves, hems, and trims. Her possession of such publications was rather a surprise, since she dressed in styles at least a decade out of date, and she probably subscribed for the sole purpose of forcefully criticising everything she deemed too 'modern'. Lydia, of course, could not remain silent, and even Georgiana could hardly resist the debate regarding bound sleeves.

"What does the description say? Oh wait, do not tell me. 'Before dressing, the young lady must roll herself in suet and sage. Salt and pepper her to taste, wrap her in sheep's gut, and smoke her until she's ready to eat.'," her ladyship snapped, to the disgust of Georgiana and Lydia, who both were quite taken with the sleeves' sausage-like appearance.

"It gives new meaning to the phrase, 'linking arms'," Darcy murmured.

Elizabeth smiled, watching him from beneath her lashes. Georgiana had moved to the chair nearest Lydia, to better take her part in the sleeve debate. No one was paying the least attention to their quiet whispers. "You brought your sister to meet my sister. I find myself astonished."

"Why? They are of an age. Surely you do not believe Miss Darcy of Pemberley has behaved any better than Miss Lydia of Longbourn?"

"Your sister is repentant and mine is not."

"Ah, yes, 'repentance'. There is a word I would bet your cousin Collins enjoys, although he, along with so many others, likely uses it incorrectly. In the Greek—the language of the gospels—the word was translated 'metanoia'—'meta' meaning 'after' and bearing the concept of 'shifting' or 'change'. I forcibly *shifted* my sister's direction, just as you have forced yours. Does that constitute regret? Does my sister regret the loss of George, or angering me, or perhaps only the heart-ache of betrayal? Can one *force* repentance? And what do her regrets have to do with whether or not she is a worthwhile friend to your sister, or anyone else?"

Elizabeth stared at Darcy, frankly shocked by his opinion.

He smiled, the barest hint tugging at one corner of his mouth. "You have just begun on a path I have already travelled. The road to 'Nothing Is As I Once Thought' awaits."

"It sounds an adventure," she murmured. "And not a very comfortable one."

He shrugged, almost imperceptibly. "I found you on it," he said, lowly. "Perhaps not always comfortable, but always exciting."

⚜

The visit ended amicably enough, with an invitation to dinner for them at Darcy's borrowed home the following evening. Just before their own dinner, a large bouquet of exquisite blossoms arrived at Sea Terrace accompanied by a small note that Lady Lavinia wordlessly handed over to Elizabeth.

Written in a strong hand was inscribed, *'You are in my every thought. FD'*. Her heart fluttered, just a little, but Lydia's envy spoilt a bit of her exhilaration.

"I suppose you think yourself so fine, Lizzy. A smart, fancy man sending you smart, fancy flowers."

"Do you think I ought to refuse them, Lydia? That would be sensible." Elizabeth rolled her eyes.

"Tell me that Mr Waggish at least sent *you* flowers a time or two before you handed over your person to him," Lady Lavinia snorted.

"His name is *Wickham*," Lydia protested.

"His name is Mr Stingy if he could not be bothered to buy you flowers. What were you thinking, girl? Do not sell yourself so cheaply! I daresay if you had taken a bit of time and used a bit of sense, the men would have been tripping over themselves for your attention!"

Lydia's expression grew stony. "'Gifts' and 'tripping' are for girls with dowries."

"Is that what he told you? Your oldest sisters have a similar portion to you, do they not? They seem to be doing well enough."

Lydia glared, and Elizabeth felt a stab of sympathy. "It *is* incredible that Jane found Bingley and I have attracted the attention of a good man such as Mr Darcy," she said gently.

"All without making fools of themselves over the men," her ladyship added—unhelpfully, Elizabeth thought.

"I notice *you* have no one paying attention to you, you dried-up old thing!" Lydia snapped viciously.

"Lydia Frances Bennet!" cried Elizabeth, horrified, but her ladyship cackled…gleefully?

"It is the first thing she has said since she arrived that someone did not tell her to say. Perhaps she has a mind of her own, after all."

"I would say she has been following her own mind far too often!"

"No. She has failed to use her brain utterly, allowing some idiot man with a pretty face to fill her head with nonsense, to tell her what to think and how to think it. Can you reason at all, girl, or are insults the best you can do?"

Lydia made a noise of disgust and flounced up the stairs, whilst Lady Lavinia chuckled quietly to herself. Elizabeth only shook her head, wondering at both of them.

❧

The following day, Elizabeth had barely finished her morning ablutions when Whitby entered her chamber after a quiet tap on the door.

"You are wanted in the blue saloon," she said. "Immediately."

She seemed especially solemn, even for her.

"What is it, Whitby?"

The lady's maid appeared to hesitate. "Your father is here," she said after a moment. "Please come, and at once, miss."

Elizabeth donned the dress closest at hand, sighing. "I suppose he is here to collect Lydia."

"I suppose, miss," she murmured, assisting with the buttoning.

There was something...doubtful in her tone, but really, what else could he be there for? She was to stay with Lady Lavinia for the immediate future, by her father's decree, and Lydia must be taken home to face—hopefully—*some* sort of discipline. Surely her ladyship would not reveal their bargain, nor even the presence of the Darcys in Brighton. Of course, Lydia was unlikely to keep her mouth shut, but as she knew nothing of Elizabeth's expulsion from the Gardiners' or her father's anger at Darcy, speaking of them would probably not be her first inclination.

Perhaps, even, Papa wishes to make amends with me?

If he does apologise, I shall accept it and put our differences behind us. After all, I do not expect to live at Longbourn for an extended period, and I have a wedding to plan.

The thought of reconciliation was a heartening one, and she nearly skipped down the stairs, a smile upon her face. She entered the saloon still wearing it. For a moment, her father smiled back as if happy to see her, but abruptly, his face sobered. She looked around for Lydia, who was nowhere to be seen. However, Mr Bennet was not alone. Lady Lavinia, dressed all in black, sat enthroned upon her favourite chair, appearing her most regal. And on either side of her were her son, Mr William Goulding and his son, Reginald Goulding.

The men stood awkwardly. "Sit, Elizabeth," ordered her father.

She sat, suddenly filled with unease as she looked at their solemn faces.

"You have summoned us, William," her ladyship said. "Pray tell us what has you all in a lather."

Mr Goulding cleared his throat. Reggie, she noted, looked at anything and everything *except* her.

"Mother," Mr Goulding said, "I received your latest letter with some surprise."

She raised a brow. "You ought not to have been surprised. I have been a most regular correspondent."

His cheeks flushed. "Why, yes, um, of course. What I meant is, something you wrote in it. Something I found most unexpected."

"Perhaps you would refresh my ageing memory," she said imperiously. "I recall nothing out of the ordinary."

"You *said* that Reginald was, um, *had* been, rather, um, misguided, for having been a neighbour to the Bennets all these years and yet having failed to secure the hand of Miss Elizabeth Bennet."

Elizabeth opened her mouth in astonishment, but it was Lady Lavinia who answered him.

"Misguided? Pshaw. I called him an outright fool. Elizabeth Bennet, refined, pretty, and possessed of a brain which actually functions, a nearly ideal choice of a wife, was right under his nose, and he was too blind to see it!"

"I did not miss anything!" Reginald cried. "She has no fortune! Father told me that you would not approve!"

"Did he *ask* for my approval? Was it refused? Was I *invited* to Haye-Park to *meet* a prospective bride?"

"For goodness' sake," Mr Goulding sputtered. "I-I did not exactly say that, Reginald. You know our conversation was nothing so formal...more an offhand discussion of the difficulties associated with—"

"You *said* Grandmama would cut your still-beating heart from your chest and serve it for tea if I married her! You *said* she would string you up by your—"

"Here, here, now, I am sure I do not recall anything so, um, uncouth—"

As they continued to bicker over who held the greatest share of blame for the 'miscommunication', Elizabeth looked to the room's other occupants for some sort of explanation. Her father was plainly uncomfortable and embarrassed; Lady Lavinia wore a rather sly smile upon her face, as if she were entertained by the argument in progress. Elizabeth struggled to contain her questions, her astonishment, for the entire conversation was completely useless. Her interest in Reggie Goulding had gone up in flames upon her eighteenth birthday. Why would they bother bringing the subject up now, after all this time?

"Daughter," Mr Bennet said, clearing his throat and speaking loudly enough to interrupt the squabbling Goulding men. "I have excellent news. Whatever discussions occurred in the past, current circumstance has changed. Mr Reginald Goulding has asked my permission to make you his wife, and I have given him my blessing. The problem of this...hmm, entanglement with Mr Darcy is resolved. You may come home at once, giving your mother the delight of planning another wedding...and me, the delight of knowing a most beloved daughter will live nearby for the rest of my life."

✤ 25 ✤

Elizabeth stood, speechless, shock and disbelief nearly overwhelming her.

Old Mr Goulding cleared his throat. "I want you to know, dear Elizabeth, that I have always looked upon you almost as a daughter to me, and when I saw your grievous affliction at the hands of a gentleman, I could only sincerely sympathise with you—and all your respectable family—in your present distress, which must be of the bitterest kind because it proceeded from a cause which no time can remove."

Lady Lavinia rolled her eyes. "Your father would be *so* proud of you, William." He preened, completely missing her sarcasm.

"*I* can remove it," Reginald declared. "Your stain shall be wiped clean with my honour!"

"Oh, for the love of Saint Lucy," her ladyship muttered.

Elizabeth gaped at her father. Had there been some confusion with the letters posted via express the night of

Lydia's interrupted elopement? Did they believe it was *Elizabeth* who had run away with Wickham?

"Papa, I believe there must be some grave misperception at work here. Shall I call for Lydia?"

But the moment she mentioned Lydia's name, he flared up. "There is nothing so difficult to understand! I shall speak to your younger sister in my own good time, and I will thank you to keep your attention on the situation presently before us. It only remains for you to accept the joyous and generous proposal offered by our dear friends and neighbours. Elizabeth?" He raised his brows and inclined his head towards the Gouldings.

Elizabeth glanced at Lady Lavinia, hoping for succour, but the wretched woman, her expression a mix of humour and challenge, only smiled as if to say, 'How will you extract yourself from this one, eh?'

She finds this amusing! Papa, plainly, will not listen—as this is everything he wants. Never mind that I would hear about my supposed sins for the rest of my life while the Goulding men explained my good fortune to me. Never mind that I love another.

She stood, turning to Reggie. "This is impossible! What of Miss Harrington? She must have expectations!"

Reginald flushed. "We have decided that we would not suit," he said stiffly.

We? Elizabeth wondered. *Or you?*

"*Elizabeth,*" Mr Bennet said sternly, a definite note of warning in his tone.

She thought quickly; if she flatly protested, an argument would ensue, and while her father would be ultimately unsuccessful, he had proved stubbornly devious thus far in getting his own way. What might he do next…hire armed guards to spirit her to America? She could not trust him to look out for her or to believe her from within the blindness of his sentiments. Neither was she stupid enough to fight with them all, an action which would only push three obstinate men into mulishly defending their inflexible opinions —and thus make her own escape more difficult.

"I...I..." she swayed on her feet, and then collapsed into a full-blown faint. In order to make its execution realistic enough to fool her father, she had to fall hard, which hurt, rather. But the rug was thick, and she had counted the cost. Fortunately, all the Bennet girls except for Mary had seen the wisdom of practising a good swoon.

She lay face-down—naturally, for fluttering eyelashes were a dead giveaway—while the men scrambled to do nothing useful. All she needed to do was escape this room; if she could get beyond the door, she would run. She had the name of the street where the Darcys were staying, and she would ask about until she found it, and them. The unknown factor, of course, would be Lady Lavinia; the odds of *her* having been convinced of the truthfulness of this performance were somewhere between 'slim' and 'none'.

"Hush, all of you," her ladyship announced in her usual acerbic tone.

It was all Elizabeth could do to keep herself still as she waited for the elder woman to pronounce her fate, else do something drastic—like pour cold water on her or shove salts under her nose.

"What were you thinking, Bennet?" Lady Lavinia asked instead. "Do you routinely force engagements without warning upon your daughters?"

"What? I did not…that is, there is no…we have been neighbours for years!" he sputtered.

"How lovely for you. Would that you could marry each other. Plainly, you and William have settled everything to your personal satisfaction, without an iota of consideration for the girl who must live with your edicts. The three of you may take yourselves elsewhere," her ladyship declared. "I am certain you have another life you can disrupt whilst Miss Bennet recovers. I shall send for my physician in the meanwhile."

"She does not need a doctor! Lizzy has never fainted before in her life! Perfectly healthy girl!"

"Um…Bennet," Elizabeth heard old Mr Goulding mutter. "Usually best to clear out of Mother's way when she's in a taking. No reasoning with her."

"Out!"

Her father grumbled, but then came the welcome sound of retreating footsteps followed by the click of the door latching. She did not move.

"You make a lovely rug, Elizabeth, but do get up. The door is a heavy one, and we shall not be overheard."

Since there was no sense in continuing the pretence, Elizabeth sat up, looking at Lady Lavinia with some bitterness. "I thank you for your endorsement, your ladyship, but in future, I would prefer you limit any commentary regarding my suitability as a bride."

"You may thank the Goulding men for twisting what was meant as a learning opportunity into a pickle. Although believe me, if I thought there was the smallest particle of hope that you could be happy with my grandson, I would lock you in this room until a parson and a special licence could be fetched. Alas, he might be even stupider than his father."

"How kind of you to take my feelings into consideration."

"It is self-preservation. It is not wise to push a clever girl such as you into a corner. I would be required to have Whitby taste my food for the rest of my life."

She is doing it again, Elizabeth realised. In her perverse way, her ladyship managed to help one feel...better. Stronger. Even when one was angry at her for penning idiotic letters to her offspring.

Sighing, Elizabeth made to stand, freezing in place when the door opened. But it was only Whitby.

"Whitby, there you are. Miss Bennet requires her things to be packed, and you had best call Bickerton, for he will need to have the carriage brought round to the Crescent to deliver her to her betrothed."

"Hetty has the packing in hand," Whitby replied, with her usual prescience. "I had an idea you might be leaving this morning, Miss Bennet."

"My father will be prevented from noticing my departure, I hope?" Elizabeth asked, after the servant departed to summon the carriage.

Her ladyship sighed, as if deceiving the three men was some sort of hardship, instead of, as Elizabeth well knew, the most fun she would likely have this year and probably her every intention since they walked out the door. "I suppose I must, since I brought this onslaught of male ineptitude down upon you. An excellent swoon, by the way."

Elizabeth stood, shaking out her skirts. "Where is my sister?"

"Your father requested that I have her remain in her chamber until he was ready to depart. I am unsure as to whether or not William or Reginald knows of Lydia's, er, adventures. My guess is 'not', but her foolishness is undoubtedly at the heart of your father's sudden desire to see you safely and immediately wed."

"Oh, perfect," Elizabeth said. "Since you already have her under lock and key, perhaps Reggie can marry Lydia instead."

Her ladyship chuckled. "In two or three years, she might do for him. He needs a female with initiative and daring, to counteract the thick strains of tiresomeness in his blood. You are certain you will not change your mind? Reginald is a good-looking boy, with his grandfather's *physique*. You could make something of him, I am certain."

For a moment—and despite the elder woman's sardonic humour—she appeared...sad, somehow. "However fine his shoulders, Reggie cannot compare to Mr Darcy. He...he *sees* me, if that makes any sense."

"But I notice my grandson is 'Reggie' to you."

It suddenly seemed appropriate to tell of her eighteenth birthday, as she had never told anyone, not even Jane. Even Darcy had heard only the most expurgated account.

"Somehow, the men in this family are impossible to underestimate," the dowager sighed after hearing the tale, and Elizabeth laughed. In a surge of kind feeling, she also admitted to her of his daring rescue when she was thrown from her horse.

Lady Lavinia shook her head in disgust. "Fool. He held your esteem in the palm of his hand, and he had to ruin it all by behaving as...himself. I can see that intervention in his future is a necessity, lest he descend beyond tedium and into brutishness. Ah, well. You had best hurry. Take the servants' stair, and Bickerton will be waiting. Whitby will have given him Darcy's direction, and he will lead you to the other side of the hill, where the carriage cannot be viewed from the house, so you may make your escape. But do not dilly dally. I shall not lie about your whereabouts, only delay telling anyone anything. You must be gone from Brighton within a couple of hours." She appeared unfeeling, imperious, and completely unaffected, but Elizabeth knew better by now.

She put a hand upon the older woman's arm. "Thank you, ma'am. For everything. Mr Darcy would thank you too, if he were here."

"Hah! Wait until you tell him your new opinions on giving the vote to women! He will not thank me then, I wager!" She cackled, her good humour plainly restored at this notion, as Elizabeth slipped away—smiling too.

The housekeeper at Number 100 Manchester Street looked down her nose at Elizabeth. "Mr Darcy is not at home, miss."

Elizabeth glanced down at herself; in her hurry to dress this morning, she had donned her oldest frock. Her belongings had been packed with such haste, she had no idea where in the trunk was her reticule. Lady Lavinia's coachman had not waited, as the massive home was perched upon a hilltop with a busy, curving street running past it, and the carriage had been blocking traffic. Apparently, a shabbily dressed young lady—whose only companion was a trunk, lacking calling card, maid, chaperon, and any notice of her arrival—was hardly a welcome sight at the imposing residence.

"I will wait," she replied. But the woman was already shutting the door.

Elizabeth put out her hand to stop the door from closing, and the housekeeper's mouth opened— undoubtedly to protest or call a footman to eject her from the premises—when the sweetest sound in the world reached her ears.

A bark.

She turned to see Dubitz racing towards her, his lead trailing. She held out her arms, and he leapt up, his paws upon her shoulders in a doggy embrace, his panting breath warm in her ear, seemingly happy to remain that way for as long as she would allow it. As she held his warm, furry bulk, she did not know whether to laugh or cry. She was conscious of the curious and bewildered stares of passers-by and the housekeeper, but could not make herself leave his protective, comforting warmth.

"Um…miss," the housekeeper began, trying to reassert control of the situation.

Dubitz's big head turned towards her, and he barked at her. Loudly.

She backed away a step.

Elizabeth laughed, even as tears escaped and trickled down her cheeks—and that was how Darcy found her a few minutes later. His brows raised.

"Do not give me that look," she sniffed. "It has been a difficult day."

He snapped his fingers, and Dubitz reluctantly folded himself at her feet; his lead was handed off to a footman. With one Darcy glance, the housekeeper's demeanour instantly changed into respect and an offer of refreshments, and before many minutes had passed, Elizabeth was ensconced in a grand drawing room, with hot tea and biscuits served on finely patterned porcelain, Darcy seated a respectful distance from her.

"You may close the door behind you, Mrs Fowle," Darcy said, so sternly that the woman practically tripped over her feet in her eagerness to carry out his order.

Elizabeth looked at him, feeling a bit sheepish. "Your housekeeper did not think much of my arrival upon your doorstep lacking kith or kin."

"She thinks you a young relation of mine, flown from home. 'Young relation'—those were her very words to Tincton, the butler. I am certain she believes me the elderly uncle reprimanding you with overbearing censure."

He looked so peeved at this misperception that she instantly felt several degrees better and more able to relate her ridiculous tale.

"Are you ready to hear what my family has done this time to cause a new disruption?"

"Actually," he said, his tone perfectly nonchalant, "I have several ideas of what I wish to do right at this moment, most of which would cause Mrs Fowle to hand in her notice at once—and one or two which might have the same effect upon you. None of them involve talking about your family's foibles, however."

She blushed, but nevertheless moved over to sit beside him on the settee.

"Dangerous, Elizabeth," he murmured, even as he enfolded her in his arms. "I have not seen you for several hours. I found myself envious of Dubitz."

"I am not afraid of you," she said, snuggling in.

He kissed her then, and despite his pronounced desire, his obvious passion for her, his lips were gentle and sweet.

"Now, tell me what new turmoil your sister has managed to inflict before I forget all my best intentions."

"It is not my sister," she sighed.

"Who, then?"

"My father brought Reginald Goulding to Brighton to marry me."

She had managed to shake his usual unflappable calm, she saw, feeling him straighten. She sat up anxiously and related the morning's confrontation in detail.

"We need to leave within the hour, I think. Lady Lavinia said she would wait a couple hours before telling Papa where I fled, and to whom. That was probably at least an hour ago. Will you take me away? Will Georgiana agree to go?"

But he made no immediate move to leave, to ring for trunks to be packed and carriages to be called. Instead, he stared straight ahead in obvious contemplation. The longer he stared, the more anxious she grew. After several minutes, it became clear that he had no intention of whisking her away to Pemberley.

Her heart froze.

Finally, without a word to her, he stalked across the room to an escritoire, removing writing material. He wrote something upon it, obviously brief, sanded, folded, and sealed it.

Please be writing a note to Georgiana, she thought, her mind racing. *Or arranging accommodations for me? Perhaps you mean to put me up at a nearby inn, hiding me from my father until the danger is past?*

But rather than take the letter elsewhere, he went on one knee before her, laying it upon her lap, watching her intently. Her frozen heart moved to her throat. She could not bear to look at the note, wary of all the things it could say.

Your family is too much trouble.

You are *too much trouble.*

Go home with your father.

As he watched and waited, a flare of anger pushed its way through her fear. Why would he not simply *speak* whatever words he had to say? Almost defiantly, she looked down.

Written across the front of the envelope in the firm, bold penmanship she had come to know, he had written '*The Seventh Challenge*'.

A challenge? *Now?*

She stared at it, wondering what it meant; a reckless, rash part of her wanted to rip it open and find an offer to take her to Pemberley—or even Scotland—to be wed, and the devil take the hindmost. But the panicked part of her brain told her that he must be tired of yet another obstacle from her father. Her family had been nothing but a trial to him, and he was Mr Darcy of Pemberley, with wealth beyond measure and the blood of earls in his veins. *The best I can hope is that he might send me and a borrowed maid back to my uncle's, to await my twenty-first birthday.*

Cautiously, she picked up the letter.

"It is the final remaining challenge," he said gently. "I meant to use my last one for...well, never mind. It is a hard thing I will ask now."

The deep freeze began moving through the rest of her soul, a sense of despair filling her. He loved her, she knew…but that did not mean he was anxious to have anything to do with her family. Why should he feel anything for them, except contempt? *She* loved them and could not help but wish that her father, who had always been the most sensible adult in her life, had managed to remain that way.

What she wanted to do, truthfully, was throw herself into Darcy's arms. She wanted to hold him, wanted to keep him close. And she also wanted the simple gift of her family in her life, despite the annoyances they brought with them. It was foolish to believe she could have both.

But there was nothing to do except face what came next.

Hesitantly she opened the note, reading the two words inscribed therein.

Trust me, it said.

❧ 26 ❧

Elizabeth peered up from the paper, confused. "Trust you?" she asked. "I already do. It is my father I do not trust."

"I do not believe we should leave Brighton," he announced. "We must face your father, here and now, and make it clear that his control over your future is finished."

She had not prepared herself for *this* proposal, for the most obvious of reasons.

"But it is not!" she cried. "Until my next birthday, yet several months away, I am his... his *property*, to do as he will. You would not understand because once I marry you, I become *your* property. Men have all the say, and I am to be silenced by whomever *owns* me." Almost, she could not believe the bitterness she had just voiced—but it had spilled out, unnoticed until it overflowed.

He looked at her, astonished, she thought, before he masked it with his usual impassivity, moving from his position at her feet to sit beside her.

"I see you and Lady Lavinia have held...conversations."

It was Elizabeth's turn to be surprised, and her expression must have shown it, for he added, "She is well known for many of her opinions regarding the rights of women. I daresay your father did not know of her, er, reputation before he sent you to her."

"It is true, is it not?" she asked resentfully, waiting for him to disagree or—as her father did when he no longer had a valid argument—quit the conversation.

"It is," he said, somewhat to her surprise. "It is not, however, the whole truth."

Here it comes, she thought, bracing herself. *The reasons why he, and men everywhere, must remain at the head of every female.*

"I told you what happened with Georgiana. I appeared in Ramsgate only a few days before her planned elopement with a scoundrel. I prevented it, as was my right as her guardian. However, I also believed—without ever truly considering it—I possessed the right of...of her feelings, for lack of a better description. I felt entitled to change them, by whatever means necessary. I belittled her judgment. I humiliated her with my opinions upon her lack of sense and reasoning. I decimated her character. Or at least, that is the way my words felt to her, however I meant them."

Elizabeth could hardly fathom him speaking in such a manner...but then, Georgiana was a very *soft* soul. She recalled how Lady Lavinia had slipped in backhanded compliments within her diatribes. A 'cupful of restorative', as she had termed them. Georgiana might require a jugful.

"When Georgiana's companion, Mrs Annesley,

expected me to fix the situation I had created, I supposed I could undo, with opposite words, the damage both Wickham and I had caused. Unfortunately, the human spirit does not work that way. The law cannot govern the soul. Wickham had badly damaged her pride, but I crushed the fragile underpinnings that remained, and all the rights in the world could not restore who she had once been."

He had spoken of that time, of his terror while his sister seemed to slip away further and further from his reach. A melancholy, she remembered.

"I do not say it is right, the way things stand," Darcy said, taking her hands. "Your opinions and judgment have been abused by the father you love. But I promise you, dearest, that I have learnt my lesson...or at least, I have begun to learn it. I put myself in your hands. I shall be as-as transparent as I know how to be. Because *I* trust *you*. You are not powerless, my love, not within our connexion. If you give yourself to me, it is only because I first give myself to you." Then he grinned. "Too, there are my brain issues to be considered. Who else would have me?"

Slowly, her frozen fear began to melt, until she found herself smiling back. "Mama *did* advise me to lower my standards, as far as the male species is concerned."

"Your mother is possessed of an inherent wisdom I cannot but admire."

"She possesses something." But then Elizabeth sighed. "It is easy to tell you that I trust you, but I suppose...the proof is in the doing."

His deep brown eyes held compassion and tenderness and humour. "I am your weapon, my dear. Point my rights, my wealth, and my bloodlines at whatever target you choose. What is mine is yours. I vow it."

The world could be a very unfair place, as well she knew. Men like George Wickham could emerge unscathed while the woman who loved them suffered. Her father, in the name of loving benevolence, had inflicted much distress and insecurity upon her. But not every man was a Wickham or a Bennet. If she loved this one as much as she thought she did, and he loved her the same...well, perhaps they could bring about a bit of change upon their little corner of this unjust world.

"Very well," she said. "You may aim it all at my father. I do trust you. Or...I am beginning to." She reached up to place a kiss upon his chin.

The look he gave her caused a trembling deep within, an alchemy of longing. "I wish we were already married," she sighed.

"Soon," he promised. "Perhaps you ought to join Georgiana in the music room, and then await me upstairs. I do not wish you to be exposed to your father's, er, *opinions* until we have an opportunity to come to a right understanding."

"I am not afraid of my father," she said defiantly.

"He is the one who ought to be afraid, my lovely, fierce tigress," Darcy said, his big hands framing her cheeks. "He stands upon the brink of losing your respect. However, I believe that I will have an easier time preventing that from happening if he does not feel obligated to posture in front of you."

Papa will not behave well, regardless, she firmly believed. Would he behave even worse if Darcy took him down a peg or two before his favoured daughter? *Probably*. For selfish reasons, she would prefer to watch it happen, but there really was no telling how foolish he might act if she was a witness; if she ever meant to try and mend things between herself, Darcy, and her father, she had best not do anything to goad him to greater folly.

Could she trust Darcy to succeed in a contest of wills against Mr Bennet, with or without her presence? There was only one answer: *absolutely*.

"Very well," she agreed, somewhat grudgingly. "But what if he brings along the Gouldings and the three of them together try to—"

He set his lips to hers, joining their mouths fully and deeply. It was a kiss of comfort, of tenderness, of reassurance.

"Trust me," he whispered.

And because she did, she left him to it, and went to find Georgiana.

🙬🙖

Darcy stared across the gleaming surface of the ebony table separating him from Elizabeth's father. At least the man had been prompt, appearing on his doorstep within the hour. Darcy had had Tincton escort Bennet into this most ostentatious of drawing rooms—in a home devoted to the ostentatious. While not to his own taste, the elaborate marquetry furniture inlaid with spring flowers— with birds and scrolls of acanthus surrounding them— the gold cut-glass and ormolu mounted chandeliers above them, the elaborately framed portraits of distinguished ancestors staring sternly at them, all equalled a picture-perfect demonstration of one word: power.

Lord Middleton, his uncle's crony from whom the property had been borrowed, enjoyed his gilt and crystal to a ridiculous degree and belonged to the same school of decorating thought as Lady Catherine. Still, Darcy appreciated a subtle reminder of wealth and influence as much as the next man, and could not miss the way Bennet's eyes flitted around the room or the fidgeting of his normally insouciant posture.

"Where is my daughter? Do not think your money will permit you to hold her captive!"

Darcy allowed a slightly scornful smile. "There is only one man who seems to be having trouble keeping hold of Elizabeth, and it is *not* me."

The older man's cheeks flushed. "How dare you refer to her so cavalierly—she is *Miss Bennet* to you!"

"She shall possess your surname for only a short while longer, and then she shall be *Mrs Darcy* to all."

"Over my dead body!"

"That can be arranged," Darcy replied coolly, rather amused by being cast in the role of villain.

"Dare you threaten me?" Bennet cried.

"Oh, I would dare much for Elizabeth's sake. For example, she has requested that I attempt a reconciliation with you, and I have agreed to try. But we are both finished with your highhanded manoeuvres and entrapments. Your parental tyranny is henceforth no longer required."

"You despicable cur! My cousin warned me of your scandalous, dastardly ways!"

Darcy raised his brow. "Your cousin, William Collins? Would this be the same cousin who plotted to discredit your daughter by claiming that *she* attacked *him*? Did you not even think to *ask* Elizabeth why she might have fled so precipitously from the home of her longtime friend, Charlotte Collins? Did *nothing* seem amiss to you? Are you so pig-headed that you would believe the word of that imbecilic buffoon over that of your daughter?"

He saw doubt flicker in the older man's eyes—but distrust quickly overcame it.

"Even if nothing he said was true, she is not yet of age and will never receive my permission! With you, only a life of misery awaits her, and all your riches cannot change the truth of that! She knows nothing of the continuous insult, the hopelessness that looms in any future with you! In the time I have remaining, I will do all in my power to discredit the false image you have deceived her with, to prevent her from ruining her life!"

"And you believe the man who offered this morning to 'wipe her stains with his honour' could bring her happiness instead?"

Bennet had the grace to look slightly ashamed. "Never mind him. She need not marry Reginald."

"Unquestionably, she need do nothing she does not wish. Did you not receive my letter with the information from my solicitors regarding Wickham, showing proof that the aspersions he cast upon my character were nothing but lies?"

"I did. It is beside the point. You could not have made me the offer of your hand in any possible way that would have tempted me to accept it."

Beating his head upon the wall seemed a more fruitful occupation than a rational conversation with Thomas Bennet. "If you know the truth in this matter, upon what basis do you form your wretched opinion of my capacity as a husband?"

"I have every reason in the world to think ill of you. You know I do."

"I admit that my first words to Elizabeth were uncalled for and unkind, spoken thoughtlessly and without reason. I have apologised to her for them, and she has graciously accepted my apology. Why will not you?"

"Because I would not see her subjected to the misery, the agony of such an *unequal* match!"

Ahh. Now, at last, we come to the heart of the matter.

"An interesting point of view. Tell me, do you fear I would scorn and despise her for her upbringing and relations, treat her with contempt, even mockery? Do you believe I would refuse to accord her the respect and devotion she deserves?"

"Yes!" Bennet roared, leaping from his seat as if he was ready to attack. "That is exactly what I believe! At present, she is a shiny plaything, dangling just out of reach. Once the challenge of 'winning' her is finished, she shall find herself trapped with a man she can neither esteem nor respect in a life guaranteed to make her wretched."

The devil in him wanted a fight. Darcy stood as well, pacing straight to the other man, his eyes boring into him. Bennet retreated a step.

"*I* am not the man who is guilty of mocking his wife, belittling her, treating her with disdain for all the things she is not. For the man who is, look in the mirror. Not at me. Never at me. You are correct that I do not deserve Elizabeth. Unlike your example, however, I shall spend the rest of my life attempting to. If she makes mistakes, simply because she has yet to learn the endless rules of a position she was not born to, I will *never* hold them against her. I shall use all my strength—of position, of wealth, of wit, of character and kindness, to lift her, to raise her up. I have sworn to her that I shall keep *my* vows to love." He drilled a finger into Bennet's chest with each successive word. "To honour. Cherish. Respect. Take the blame for your own sins, man. *They are not mine.* Do you understand?"

Darcy was taller, more fit, and definitely more imposing, but for a moment, he thought Bennet might strike him. And in that moment, balanced upon the precipice of fury, he hoped the older man *would* start something, so that Darcy might finish it.

But Bennet suddenly seemed to droop. As if to avoid meeting Darcy's gaze, he paced to the window, staring out over a piercingly bright view of the sea.

Darcy's own anger collapsed as he recognised himself, staring out the windows of Netherfield to avoid looking at what he wanted most. He had wasted enough time already.

He made his voice as calm and reasonably respectful as he could manage. "Sir, my solicitors have drawn up a proposed marriage settlement. The papers are here on the table. After you have had a chance to review them, please join me, my sister, and Elizabeth for breakfast—I shall have Mrs Fowle escort you to us whenever you are ready."

Darcy left him there without waiting for a response.

27

Elizabeth found the role of one who 'waited and watched' a difficult one, and although resigned to it, her feelings of distress upon abandoning Darcy to her father's obstinate will left her apprehensive and impatient. She forced herself to sit in the music room, to quietly listen to Georgiana play. The younger girl had only smiled at her entrance, accepting Elizabeth's stilted explanations without question. But the tunes she played without pause were rich, soothing melodies, as if she intuitively understood the affection, anxiety, and anger possessing Elizabeth's soul. Gradually, as she listened, her pounding heartbeat calmed, her tension easing as she gazed out the sea-facing window.

By the time Darcy entered the room, she found herself meeting him with equanimity, standing to greet him. But he stayed some little distance from her, clasping his hands behind his back, the expression upon his face annoyingly aloof. Georgiana continued to play.

"All is well, I think. Or at least it will be," he said.

She raised her brows at him. "And?"

The corner of his lip tipped up in brief humour. "And no broken bones, no pistol wounds, no meetings at dawn."

"Unless you fail to tell me immediately, in detail, exactly what happened."

Georgiana called out from the pianoforte. "My brother is doing that annoying taciturn thing he does, which obliges one to wheedle information from him whilst he decides how much of it you are allowed to hear."

He shot his sister an exasperated glance. "I do not require wheedling. I am simply gathering my thoughts."

"This is not the time for a manly, rational, unemotional discussion," Elizabeth put in. "I hated knowing you were facing a situation alone that I ought to have shared with you."

He gave her his crooked smile again. "Now you can understand how I felt from the moment you were whisked away to Brighton."

It was true enough, she knew. How awful it would have been to have *him* disappear like that, without a clue to his whereabouts!

"Which is why it cannot happen again," he continued. "Even my manly, impervious-to-all-emotion character cannot take it. If not for Georgiana, and the need to appear sane in her presence, I should have run about England tearing out my hair."

"But it is such very nice hair," Elizabeth replied, able to smile for the first time. "I would hate to return to a patchy-headed betrothed."

For a moment they just gazed at each other, smiling, until Georgiana cleared her throat. "Should I leave you two alone for a few minutes?"

Elizabeth laughed, and Darcy gave his sister a side-long glance.

"Regardless," he said, taking up his explanations again, "I think your father has a better understanding of how I intend to treat the wife who I love than he did at the beginning of our conversation."

Georgiana stood. "I really do wish to give you both a few minutes of privacy. There is probably more left to say than you wish me to know, while you are already approaching more than *I* wish me to know."

Darcy turned his smile upon her. "Perhaps you could see Mrs Fowle about bringing up some refreshments. I do not think any of us have eaten breakfast as yet, although I have invited Mr Bennet to join us for the meal shortly."

As soon as she was gone, Elizabeth turned back to him. He stood a few feet from her, appearing indomitable and unruffled, as always. But there was something troubled in his stance still, although she could not put her finger on it.

"Please, tell me just what you said to him and what he said to you."

Happily, he did tell her, apparently omitting nothing.

"Collins told him what?" she exclaimed.

"I know. I believe, upon further reflection, Bennet could admit that he had no basis for believing that hypo-critical oaf. Nor did he, truthfully, disbelieve my solici-tors regarding Wickham." It was, he explained, her father's concern that Darcy would look down upon her, in time, due to their differences in fortune, upbringing, and blood. Darcy told her of his rather ardently expressed suggestion that it was Mr Bennet who was guilty of such unjust treatment, especially towards his own wife.

"Truly, you said that to him?"

"I did. But Elizabeth, his concerns are not completely invalid. I do not know if I will always be as reasonable as I ought to be. I did not know I was wounding Georgiana so deeply until my words were already spoken. I may—undoubtedly, will—make mistakes in the future, probably hurtful ones."

She moved closer to him, only the arrangement of the armchairs now separating them. "We cannot know what we do not yet know, can we?"

He gave her a look she read clearly, a 'you are making little sense' sort of look.

"Your very fear that you might at times be wrong reassures me," she clarified. "A man who never believes he could be wrong can never *be* wrong, at least in his own head."

"Or woman?" Something in his posture eased, she noted.

"Or woman. For instance, I did not realise that I was capable of so intense a prejudice towards a certain prosperous gentleman from Derbyshire. Mr Wickham's manipulations were so obvious in retrospect! But now that I have learnt that *any* opinion of mine may be fallible, it leaves a bit of room for them to change."

"Only a bit?" he asked, his expression solemn while mischief lurked in his eyes.

She held up her thumb and forefinger spaced a bare half-inch apart, giggling.

He strode towards her, skirting the barrier of chairs with definite intent, and had nearly reached her when the noise of a throat clearing halted them both.

Behind Darcy, Mr Bennet stepped into the room, Mrs Fowle behind him with a tray. After glancing at him, Darcy moved close beside Elizabeth, close enough that she could feel the heat from his body. Wordlessly, he directed the housekeeper to leave the tray, and she silently slipped away.

"Papa," Elizabeth said quietly.

"Elizabeth," he replied. He scratched his head, seemingly nonplussed. Had his hair silvered more since she saw him last?

"Please, be seated," Darcy said. He looked at Elizabeth, raising a brow. She nodded, and he gave her his half-smile. "Do come and eat when you are finished talking. A footman will be just beyond the door, ready to direct you to the breakfast parlour." With that, he strode from the room, closing the door quietly behind him.

She sat upon a beautifully upholstered chair, and her father seated himself upon the matching settee. He scratched his head again, still quiet—and very unlike himself. She busied herself pouring out cups of tea, finding some comfort in the familiar routine, in preparing his exactly as he preferred.

He took the cup, but then stared at it blankly.

"How do Mama and my sisters fare?" she asked finally.

"Oh...well enough, I think," he said at last, seeming grateful for the opening. "Had a bit of a scare, of course. A bad few hours. We were very grateful to receive your express."

So you repaid me by trying to force a marriage to Reggie Goulding? she thought, but did not say.

But it was as if he heard her anyway. "I believed you always had a...a certain fondness for Reginald."

She sighed. "I did, until my eighteenth birthday, when he forgot every vestige of gentlemanly behaviour. Once was more than enough."

His head snapped up, and she saw his horror.

"No, no, it is not what you think. Well, it *is* what you think, but—" She scrubbed her hands across her face. "He stopped." Now they were both in agonies of embarrassment, but she pushed past it. "I should have told you at the time, but I was in no danger from him, I had no desire for any kind of future connexion with him, and I did not wish to in any way impede your friendship with his father. The only thing he truly hurt was my childish image of his character."

"Empty-headed gudgeon," he muttered.

"Yes, or so he was at the ripe old age of nineteen years, and he is only one-and-twenty now. Perhaps he will improve in time. For someone else, anyway."

He looked up at her. "I was referring to myself," he said. He smoothed his neatly trimmed beard. "As I recall, you once tried to tell me what truly happened in the summerhouse during Jane's wedding breakfast. I was not then ready to listen. Perhaps you would be so good as to explain now."

She did so, omitting only a very little. He chuckled when she told of railing at Darcy for his thoughtless remarks regarding Mr Bingley's past *amour*, but when she told him of Jane's threat to take refuge with the Gardiners instead of leaving on her wedding trip, his eyes widened.

"Dash it! You do not say!"

"I certainly do. As for what you and your friends witnessed, it was nothing more than my own clumsiness causing both of us to fall in a heap. Fortunately, Mr

Darcy effected a reconciliation between Jane and Mr Bingley, somehow quickly making things right between them. In the days following at Netherfield, I discovered that he is not nearly so arrogant as I had believed. He has no improper pride. Possibly, he possesses an improper sense of humour, but then, so do you." She also related in detail the cruel hoax Lady Catherine and Mr Collins had attempted to enact and how it was that she, Mr Darcy, and his cousin turned the tables on the plotters.

Mr Bennet just shook his head in bewildered astonishment. "Lizzy, after all this, I must give him my consent—indeed, I dare not refuse him. I now give it to you. I have just reviewed the settlement he proposes to make upon you. It is...beyond generous, almost to the point of foolishness. You will be wealthy far beyond anything I could have imagined. But *will* he make you happy?"

"I am already happy. But will Mr Darcy add to that happiness? Can I trust him in the most important ways a wife can trust her husband?" She reached across to take her father's hand. "Yes. Yes, Papa. I can. I do."

He squeezed it. "I have made a mess of things, I know. Will you ever forgive me?"

Elizabeth smiled. "I will, upon one condition. When you go home to Mama, you must tell her that she was right, and you were wrong. You must apologise for failing to listen to her. Humbly."

He began what might have been a protest but suddenly snapped his mouth shut. "I suppose I must then," was all he said.

28

The wedding of Elizabeth Bennet to Fitzwilliam Darcy was held within six weeks of the Brighton dénouement. The bride wore a dress of fine white muslin, and over it a soft silk shawl—white shot with primrose—with embossed white-satin flowers, and on her head, a small lace-trimmed cap to match. While the church affair was a quiet and simple one, as per the desires of the bride, Mrs Bennet was once again allowed free rein for her breakfast, requiring—again— the use of Netherfield's largest dining parlour.

Once more, the two eldest sisters sought a private moment alone after the many courses had been served and many toasts drunk to the health and happiness of the newly wedded couple.

"Oh, Lizzy, I am so happy for you and Mr Darcy. That our husbands are such good friends... it is like a dream come true."

"Our happiness pales in comparison to our mother's. Thank you so much for allowing Mama to overrun your home and servants," Elizabeth said. "I wanted a much smaller celebration but—"

"You needn't tell me." Jane laughed. "This is a great secret at present, but Lizzy, Bingley intends to give up the lease on Netherfield in favour of purchasing property nearer to you and Mr Darcy. They have been discussing what is available and believe that we will be able to live within thirty miles of you by Michaelmas."

"That is the best wedding present you could have given me," Elizabeth cried. The sisters embraced, neither caring much about wrinkling their lovely new dresses, so overjoyed were they at the thought of being near neighbours for the rest of their lives.

Without warning, as though they were thrown back in time, the strident sound of the Bingley sisters' voices interrupted their sisterly affection.

"Mr Darcy and my brother both could have had so much more!" Caroline hissed. "I simply cannot keep a smile pasted upon my face any longer. It is a tragedy! My black crape would be more appropriate. We should all be in mourning for the losses endured this day—loss of blood, loss of fortune, loss of family connexions!"

"It defies explanation!" Louisa Hurst commiserated.

For just a moment, Jane's face expressed dismay. But Elizabeth took her sister's hand, and Jane's expression smoothed; the sisters glanced at each other in mutual agreement and stalked together to the adjoining drawing room, Elizabeth about to fling open the partially ajar connecting door. But there, they suddenly halted as another voice rang out.

"Bingley, do you grieve at waking daily to the lovely, caring wife of your heart?"

Elizabeth and Jane peered around the door to see

what Caroline and Louisa had failed to notice upon their own entry: the library was already occupied.

"I do not, Darcy. Neither do I wish I had instead a shrew mindlessly nagging me about new dresses or attending some *ton* ball, in between mouthfuls of disapproving, meaningless gossip."

Darcy nodded and, in a contemplative tone, asked, "Have you ever thought, 'oh, if only I had several thousand pounds more, smiling at me from across the breakfast table each morning'?"

Bingley grinned. "No. Tell me, Darcy, you have a good ten thousand acres. Are any of them good for lying beside you in bed at night to warm your cold feet?"

Caroline gasped, and Louisa gaped.

"All these years, my feet have remained as bricks of ice. In fact, I was hoping that the new home I recently purchased in Brighton might be useful as the mother of my children, but it appears rather lifeless, still."

Caroline straightened, pursing her lips. "You both are very amusing. Ha-ha."

"You, however, Caroline, are not," Bingley said, in a voice gone abruptly cold. "Mrs Bingley has done her utmost to overlook your rudeness, but I am sick to death of it. You shall not be welcome in my home, nor in Darcy's, unless we see a rapid, complete change in behaviour. To that end, I have set you up your own household—"

"That is certainly fine with me," Caroline interrupted. "You know I have been wishing to live—"

"—in Scarborough, where we have so many fine family members willing to ensure you are well-looked after. In fact, our great-aunt, Dora Bingley, in obliging my request to find you a respectable companion, has unselfishly offered to fulfil the duty herself."

"Scarborough? But why not London? And you cannot mean *Dora*. Why, she is dreadful!"

"When you are five-and-twenty, or marry, your living arrangements shall no longer be my concern. Until that time, I have been charged with your care and well-being. Did you think I would not notice your snide remarks to my wife, your constant criticism of her and her family these last two weeks since our return? I saw quickly how it would be, and thus have made other arrangements for you."

"Louisa?" Caroline cried, turning to her sister. "Surely I can make a home with you instead?"

"Mr Hurst would not care for that, I am afraid," Louisa whispered, not meeting her sister's eyes.

Caroline bolted from the room.

"Louisa, you have allowed Caroline too much sway over your own opinions. I am not your guardian, but you and your husband often enjoy my hospitality. If you wish it to continue, I demand greater courtesy towards my wife. Am I understood?"

Louisa nodded, curtseying to both her brother and Darcy before following her sister out.

Elizabeth looked at Jane; Jane smothered a giggle.

"I believe our beloved, gossip-less, warm-footed wives might enter the rest of the way into the room," Darcy called.

Elizabeth hurried in, laughing, Jane rather sheepishly following behind her. The gentlemen immediately stood. Jane kissed Mr Bingley on the cheek, while Elizabeth took her new husband's hands in hers.

"I should not laugh," Elizabeth said. "I know what

it is like to have no control over one's own life. Perhaps it led to Miss Bingley's bitterness in the first place."

"Rather, I have given her too much control, I think. I cannot allow her to mistreat my wife, regardless," Bingley replied.

"Of course not, and I appreciate your defence of our happy home," Jane, ever the peacemaker, put in. "I believe my sister only wishes that Caroline could see the truth of her feelings' origin, instead of blaming the Bennets."

"Come, come now, Bingley," Darcy objected in his haughtiest tones. "Your sister was madly in love with me and has today suffered a crushing blow. Give the poor girl a few days to recover."

Elizabeth elbowed him, and he placed his arm about her as if to restrain her—but really, she knew, for the excuse of touching her.

"I have some very fascinating books you might send to Miss Bingley in Scarborough, which might help her pass the time as she, um, ages," she said innocently.

"Very kind of you, very kind of you," Bingley said, smiling. "Caroline is not much for reading, but—"

"But perhaps if you told her that Mr Darcy says the most eligible gentlemen prefer their females to be proficient in these *particular* books, she might take more of an interest," Jane suggested.

Darcy gave the two sisters a suspicious look and a raised brow.

They gazed innocently back at him.

"You have been sharing your latest reading material interests with your sister, have you?"

"All my sisters," Elizabeth agreed. "And my mother.

Discussion at mealtimes—when we do not have company—has become rather extraordinary."

"Your father brought it upon himself," he shrugged.

Bingley appeared confused. "What is this?"

"Worry not, darling," Jane replied. "I will take things slowly. Lizzy, are you ready for the first leg of your wedding journey?"

"I will change into my carriage dress, and then I will be," she replied—a bit quizzically, for obviously she was still in her wedding clothes. They were to spend their first night together as man and wife in London.

"Changing is not necessary," Darcy said.

Dubiously, she glanced down at her white dress—an extravagance that would be difficult to keep clean at the best of times and impossible to protect from road dust.

"Should we inform Colonel Fitzwilliam and Georgiana that we are nearly ready to depart?"

"Just go with your husband, dear," Jane said, in an annoying 'elder sister' voice that proclaimed she knew something which Elizabeth did not. Darcy let go of her and extended his arm formally, which she took.

It was a very nice arm, she thought, tempted to giggle. They had had almost no time together since leaving Brighton, and she longed to be private. But there was the journey to London to undertake; at least they could hold a conversation during it.

"This way," Darcy murmured, escorting her to the servants' stair.

"Oh, we are being secretive, are we?" she asked, keeping pace down the narrower stair, following his broad back and long legs as he easily navigated the old steps while only half minding them, continually looking back at her to ensure her safety. Such a big man, but one did not realise it because he was lean and graceful in every movement.

"Only a bit," he answered. "I have conversed more this morning than I have in weeks. Every person in the valley has wished to ensure I am aware of what a prize I have captured. I would prefer not to talk any more *about* my good fortune and set about *enjoying* it."

She smiled, and was smiling still as he exited the stairwell, took a half-hidden door, and slipped out from one of the smaller chambers. Instead of opening out onto the terrace, as the larger dining parlours did, this one seemed only to connect to another small corridor in the maze of corridors Netherfield possessed, each leading to a warren of parlours and tiny sitting rooms designed for no reason Elizabeth could guess. But Darcy did not pause, and before she knew it, they were out of doors and circling around the terrace. She could hear the sounds of laughter and conversation—but muted, as they side-stepped, apparently, the entire company, where a number of relations and neighbours were still enjoying themselves at heavily loaded tables of food and drink. From there, he escorted her swiftly and silently into the park.

Elizabeth, busy watching that her dress hems and new slippers stayed unspoilt, did not realise where they were going until their destination was suddenly upon them.

She inhaled sharply. The Netherfield summerhouse folly stood before her, perched upon its little escarpment, its diamond-shaped windows sparkling in the sunlight, tall Prussian blue doors standing open and ready to welcome them indoors. She glanced at her new husband, but he only held out his arm with a flourish, the roguish glint in his eye expressing an impishness his features would never otherwise reveal.

The first time she had been here, she had barely noticed it—in her fury with Darcy, it had only been an obstacle in her path, requiring she either climb its stone steps or else admit she had turned the wrong direction in her headlong flight from Jane's wedding breakfast. Then, the interior had been dark and dampish, the furniture enrobed in holland covers, the limestone floors chilly beneath her slippers.

It could not have been more different now. While not at all large, it possessed an octagonal shaped front parlour with tall, pointed Gothic arches encasing Venetian style windows. Pale yellow walls complemented hand-painted wallpapers of country scenes, and a fire burned brightly in the marbled fireplace. Comfortable chairs of velvet and leather surrounded a low inlaid-wood table set out with tea, biscuits, and other dainties.

"This is lovely," she murmured, taking it all in.

"Do you recognise this table? It is the one I rescued you from crashing down upon once."

Elizabeth bit her lip, hiding a smile. "It does not look too soft a landing place. I must apologise for putting you in danger of it."

"Apologise!" he cried, in mock dismay. "It was the most wonderful moment of my life!" He grinned. "At least, in retrospect."

"It was the beginning of wonderful, one might say," she said, looking up at him. But now that she was here, alone with her husband, she wondered how in the world she was to proceed.

As if he had read her mind, he took her hand in his. "Are you anxious?"

"A little, I suppose. I did everything in my power to avoid conversing with Mama on the subject of...um... what happens next."

He nodded wisely. "Heaven forbid you hear the 'blancmange' speech again."

She startled a bit in surprise. "What...how did you—"

"My room at Netherfield was adjoining, if you recall," he explained. "The panel between us was a thin one. I had quite a time resisting an interruption—and of course, every day since then wishing to show you something quite different."

"I know that-that you are not anything like my father. Nothing will be the same between us as it is with my parents."

"I am thankful to hear it," he said, his voice low.

Inexplicably, her cheeks flooded with colour at the sound of something new in his voice, although he had not yet touched her.

He pointed out a small dining parlour, a modern water closet, and bathing room. "Come with me," he said. "I want to show you something."

"I wager you do," she muttered.

He gave her a rather solemn look but commented nothing. A small curving staircase led up to a loft-like room extending the whole length of the folly, which had been converted to a large bedroom, complete with elegant four poster, chinoiserie fabrics, and an exquisite marble mantelpiece.

"I had it redone for us," he said.

Redone? It was exquisite, tasteful...expensive. In a home not even his own. "For one night?"

"We can stay two or three if you would like, but yes.

It is for us, for our stay, however fleeting, at Netherfield. It is a very important fleeting stay, you see."

"I suppose it is." In order to have something to do within her own awkwardness, she went to a massive bureau that held a large mirror atop it and began to unpin her hat. Before she was half-finished, he came up behind her and completed the removal for her.

"There is a dressing room right through this door." He pointed to it.

"I notice your man and my new maid do not join us here."

"There is little room, I am afraid. Luckily, I am happy to act as your lady's maid, unless you do not wish it. If you prefer Nottley, we have only to place a light in one of the house-facing windows, and help will quickly arrive."

Experimentally, she leant back against him. He was solid, warm.

"I wish this part was finished with."

"What part is that?" His voice sounded offhand, casual. Like any good lady's maid, he was unpinning and uncoiling her hair.

"The part where I am awkward, untutored, not knowing what I should do, how to please you, how to ensure that all the money you put into the redoing was not for nothing."

She felt the touch of a hairbrush as he combed it through her thick tresses, in that gentle, too-careful way of the inexperienced. *He has never brushed a woman's hair before*, she thought, and it helped, a little, to realise he did not know *everything* in the world already.

He turned her to face him. "You could smile at me."

Her brow furrowed.

"You wanted to know how to please me. That would do it. I wish only for your happiness, you see."

She raised a brow. "I may not understand much, but I know you wish for a bit more than that."

"No," he disagreed. "That is all. If I touch you, hold you, make love to you and with you, it is with the intent of pleasing you. If I do anything you do not care for, you must tell me."

"I will not know what I feel about it until you try it."

"When you say stop, I will stop. No matter when it is."

"You will not want to."

He smiled at last, kissing her forehead, her nose, her cheeks. "I am a man," he said, "with an only partially functional brain. I am happy to simply look at you. Granted, I would prefer to look at you wearing a good deal less than you are now."

"What if I tell you to stop looking?"

"Then, I stop looking. I promise, however, that I am not looking to find fault. Every part of you is beautiful to me, right down to the hairy mole sprouting on your back."

"I have no hairy moles!" she protested.

"Truly? Perhaps it is on mine. You might check."

She gave him a look, and he held up his hands in surrender, still smiling.

"We have all the time in the world to grow accustomed to each other, darling. I know it will take time." His smile grew wider. "In the meanwhile, you may look at me all you wish."

Tentatively—and somewhat to his surprise, she saw —her hands moved to the complicated knot of his cravat and began working at it. He held utterly still as she freed it and unbuttoned his waistcoat. It gaped open, revealing fine, nearly transparent linen beneath.

He turned her then, working at the row of buttons down her back. "There must be a hundred of these," he said roughly. "You chose it on purpose, I suppose."

She could not answer, feeling the weight of anxiety, the barrier of ignorance. "I asked Jane what would happen. She was worse than Mama."

"I find that difficult to believe."

She felt the dress give, felt it drawn gently down her arms, felt the cool air on her shoulders and back as she stepped out of it. Stays, chemise, and petticoats were beneath, of course, but she still felt very exposed. And nervous.

"'Tis true. She was full of proverbs and 'trust your husband' and 'all will be well' and 'the pain does not last' nothings. I asked her if it would be like the time we saw our stallion breeding with our mare, and she gasped in shock and said absolutely not."

She felt more than heard his soft huff of laughter. "Absolutely not today, anyway," he said.

Elizabeth whirled to face him. "What?"

He pulled her into his arms, kissing her; after a few moments, when he did nothing but kiss her, her tension eased a little. She had done this with him before, not many times, but enough. Slowly, by some means of affectionate ensorcellment, without her quite realising how, she found herself in the big bed with him.

Her fears began to grow, but so did the passion in equal measure. Heat sizzled between them, and she could tell that—despite his efforts to be careful—he was not quite under the strict regulation she was accustomed to with him. And who could blame him? He had been a patient, tender suitor, a man who had been in love with her for a long while. She must simply urge this new experience on, allow it to happen, and—although she hated to even think the words—*get it over with*. Thus, she pressed forward instead of fighting it, encouraging rather than voicing aloud the fears in her brain, vacillating between fierce passion and unwillingness to lose control.

Wholly unnerved and feeling increasingly wild, when a large furry face popped up on the mattress right beside hers, she lost all dignity and gave a loud, startled scream.

"What the devil!" Darcy cried, leaping back and swinging his fist around, ready to annihilate any intruder.

Dubitz, his great tongue lolling, smiled happily at them both.

❦ 29 ❦

Reginald Goulding had watched as the pair slipped beyond the terrace and onto one of the paths leading into the park, his face twisting as the loveliest girl he had ever known took the arm of the tall man beside her, briefly clinging before tripping away, forever out of reach.

"How does it feel to know you could have had her yourself, had you not been such a chucklehead?"

Perfect. Grandmama. Just who one wants to speak with on the worst day of one's life.

"She was not for me," he said, trying to keep his teeth from clenching, while his grandmother plucked an olive from a tray of savouries upon the nearby table.

"But she could have been, if you were not such an imbecilic, ham-fisted lover. She told me, you know, what you did to her."

Alarm coursed through him. He had tried, over the years, not to think of that night. He had been carried away, he knew that. But she ought not to have worn such a dress—emphasising all that he could not have.

His father ought to have made clear that there would be no familial objections had he offered for her.

"It was not my—"

"If you dare say you were not to blame, I will stab you with this fork."

To his dismay, his tiny grandmother's hand hovered near a large serving implement from a nearby tray of meats. He regarded her warily.

"You are naturally aware that I cannot stop you from inheriting. It is not within my power. I can, of course, make your life very uncomfortable while I yet live. I find I have missed Haye-Park."

She could refuse to return to Brighton, and no one could make her, he knew. She was like a black serpent—one never saw her striking, nor felt the pinch of her bite. One only saw the poisonous results, as the servants began answering only to her, the household ruled entirely by her whims and nonsensical ideas. He had been a young boy when she left, but he remembered how even his late mother had yielded easily to her will; his father was putty in her hands.

"What do you want?"

He knew his tone was surly, in a manner unlikely to convince Lady Lavinia to cease her complaints, but he could not help either his dislike of her nor being required by his sense of pride to attend this wedding—a performance at which he must pretend he couldn't care less that the girl of his dreams was marrying another. It ought to be easy by now; he had been pretending for years.

"What I *want* is for you to be a man who a woman can trust and rely upon. I *want* for you to be the kind of man who a pretty, sensible female might want to *keep* instead of *run* from."

He flushed, but his expression remained hard. "Miss Harrington would take me in a heartbeat."

"She and a dozen like her. Do not you want anything more?"

He glanced over to where Pearl was hanging onto Hubert King's every word. They had not spoken since that day in Meryton when they had argued so bitterly over Wickham. She had easily—and obviously—transferred her affections to King, but he knew he could have her back with a few murmured apologies. He was the more handsome of the two, and outward appearances were all that mattered to the wealthy, beautiful Pearl Harrington.

Of course he wanted more! For what other reason would he have woken at an ungodly hour and raced to Brighton to propose to Elizabeth, when he had believed there was a chance?

But he only shrugged.

"You *could* have had Elizabeth. Obviously, it is too late to repair your blunders in that direction. But the fact you wanted her means you are not hopelessly stupid. If you are at all interested in understanding how you managed to ruin things, I can help you learn. She is not the only sensible, lovely girl in the world. Or I can leave you to it, and you can take the Harrington girl or someone exactly like her, who only cares for your looks —which, I assure you, *will* fade—and your money and property."

"What is it to you?"

She stared at him for a long moment, until he grew uncomfortable. Pride alone kept him staring back.

"I married a man because he *appeared* the Ideal, despite my father's opinion that he was not the sharpest arrow in the quiver. For the entirety of our married life, I never had a real conversation with him. He seldom understood a word I said and avoided saying anything at all, for the most part. You look just like him. For the most part, you act like him, too. I am tempted to believe you irredeemable. But there *is* occasionally something about you that seems different. I am unsure—perhaps the ability to learn something? Or perhaps it is only wishful thinking.

"If you are interested in becoming *more* than you are now, perhaps even discovering a woman who might appreciate such improvements, write to me."

Abruptly, she moved away from him, stalking to the other side of the terrace, inserting herself into the group around his father and proceeding to terrorise him for her own amusement.

She is out of earshot, so how do I know that is what she is doing? he asked himself. But he did.

He turned back to where he had last seen the newly wedded couple—but they were out of sight. Gone, forever out of reach. For perhaps the first time in his life, he allowed his shame and guilt to prevail.

"I am so very sorry, dearest, loveliest, Eliz…Mrs Darcy," he whispered to no one.

"Dubitz!"

Elizabeth clapped a hand over her mouth. Somehow, at the sight of her tousled, half-dressed husband cursing inventively at the ridiculous dog, she began to giggle, and the laughter overflowed to real mirth. After a moment, he joined her, shaking his head.

Sighing, he climbed off the bed.

"My guess is that the stableboy charged with exercising him is standing just outside the summerhouse in fear for his life," Elizabeth said, when she could speak at last.

"I must not have closed the front door properly," Darcy admitted. "Or, as excited as I was to be alone with you, I may have left it wide open. Come with me, you blackguard." He grabbed the dog's dragging lead and led him away.

The respite gave her a few minutes to collect herself —which was nearly undone when he returned. He stood in the doorway clad only in his breeches, shirtless, his muscular arms braced against the doorframe in a deceptively casual pose—looking at her, just looking. Waiting. The sight of him, beautiful, masculine, patient, tender, willing to do whatever she needed, even when she did not understand quite what that was...it eased something within herself.

There had been too many voices in her mind before, but now there was only one, and it was her own. It said only one word, born of the pledges they had made to each other before God and man this very morning:

Mine.

"I love you," she said. She held out her arms.

A few hours later, they shared the forgotten meal which had been laid in the small dining parlour. The tea was cold, but shortly after a lamp was placed in the window, renewed refreshment arrived. They sat together *en désha-billé*, sharing small bites between kisses, both feeling languorous and fulfilled.

"Did you really buy a house in Brighton?" she asked, taking the strawberry he offered her.

He pretended to think about it. "Will I be maligned for making such a purchase without discussion, if I did?"

She rolled her eyes. "Tell me truly!"

Darcy smiled. "As your youngest sister, it appears, will be making her home with Lady Lavinia for the fore-seeable future, and as I recently sold the home in Rams-gate, I thought it might behove us to have a home on the coast. One not quite so gilt-encrusted as the house I so recently borrowed from Lord Middleton. Someplace we can all stay when visiting Miss Lydia and Lady Lavinia for now, and a seashore retreat for us, hopefully with our children, in the future," he explained. "It could use some renovation." He pulled her closer.

"That sounds wonderful. We shall plan a trip to arrange for its refurbishment."

He asked her so many questions about her likes and dislikes—from furniture to paint colours—that her mind was awhirl. "I know more about what I dislike than what I like, I think. I like this summerhouse, I know. Do you suppose we can cart it away in our trunks, stone by stone, to Pemberley? Would anyone notice?"

"That would require a considerable number of trunks, I think. I will build a private place of escape of our own at Pemberley," he promised.

"Escape? Escape such a beautiful life as we, the happiest couple in the world, mean to have? Why should we ever want to?"

He laughed, a low sound that shivered down her

spine. "Come with me," he said, standing and holding out his hand. "I wish to show you something."

She allowed him to raise her up, leading her to a window looking out over the escarpment, the late afternoon sun already colouring the horizon with colours of red, pink, and orange.

"It is beautiful here," she said.

"The view is, yes. But I mean to show you the direction of something utterly out of sight of the summerhouse."

"If it is out of sight, how can you show me?"

He tsked. "You have an imagination, I am certain. It is to the west of us, over yonder hillocks. It is a pond—an utterly private pond, where we shall not be disturbed as I teach you how to swim. There is another such pond at Pemberley, and it is near there where we shall construct our own summerhouse."

It touched her that he had remembered that seemingly long-ago conversation and her expressed desire to learn a skill not accorded to most females. She did not simply love him—she loved being with him, loved the sense of adventure the future held, loved how he loved her—and told him so.

"I meant to give you this much sooner," he said, lifting a hitherto unnoticed long box of black velvet from a side table. "But you have been in the habit of indiscriminately disappearing. Consider it a wedding gift, or perhaps an earnest payment on Pemberley's promised summerhouse."

Elizabeth took it, glancing up to measure his expression. It was part amusement, part steadfast intensity.

"Open it," he urged.

Inside, on a bed of cream-coloured velvet, lay a necklace of emeralds and rubies. She gasped as he lifted it, encircling its heavy weight of stones around her neck. Rising, she went to the mirror over the mantelpiece; the jewels had a glow of their own, lending their beauty to the wearer.

Darcy stood behind her, his hands large and tanned as he placed them upon her collarbones, turning her this way and that to catch the sparkle within the candlelight.

"I do not know what to say," she breathed, looking up at his reflection. "I wish I came from great wealth, and I could give you gifts of equivalent value."

He shook his head. "Your 'price is far above rubies and the heart of your husband doth safely trust in you'," he quoted. "What more could the happiest man in the world ask for?"

"Or the happiest woman?" She smiled. "I can think of one thing."

He raised a brow in question.

"The last time we stood alone together in this house, quite near this exact spot, I berated you for your 'sins'," she said. "In retrospect, however, I have come to believe you could engage in one or two more." She stood on tiptoe to whisper in his ear because she was not yet proficient in speaking requests of an intimate nature aloud. His expression did not change, but before she could anticipate his actions, he swept her up in his arms and headed for the stairs; for the second time that day, she gave a startled shriek.

But he only smiled his devil smile, the one that told her she was in for it now.

"I take it the answer is 'yes'," she said, breathless.

"You know, my dear, how I do love a good challenge."

EPILOGUE

THE PROVERBIAL THIRTIETH CHAPTER

Five Years Later

There was to be another race. Oh, they called it a friendly challenge, but there was no doubt in either's mind of the level of competition involved. She had, of course, demanded equalising factors, for there was no getting round the fact that Darcy was far larger and stronger. Still, she knew he would give no quarter. If she won, it would *be* a win.

Elizabeth never won.

He had offered additional handicaps, for he was nothing if not fair. But she had set the original ones and would not concede defeat. She did not wish to win only because he had made it impossible for her to lose.

She wanted to *beat* him.

He smiled at her as he began disrobing, and she took a moment to admire the view. They were utterly private here, would never be disturbed. The windows of the summerhouse sparkled a welcome in the sunlight, and she briefly contemplated how much cosier it would be to watch from its interior.

"It looks freezing."

"Oh, it is," he replied, grinning devilishly in an obvious dare as he lifted his shirt over his head.

Elizabeth watched as it floated to a growing pile of discarded clothing near his feet. When he was clad only in his smallclothes, he jumped into the water in a singularly graceful motion, practically like a sea creature himself. He emerged some distance away, shaking water from his curls and laughing.

She was a fish, caught on the hook of that laughter, that challenge, that exuberance. She began unbuttoning as he shamelessly ogled her, until down to her chemise. Some might believe that, even before her husband of several years, she would go no further.

Some would be wrong. She plucked off the chemise, too. He raised a brow, his laughter fading.

"Devil take it, but you are exquisite," he remarked, as matter-of-factly as if he commented on the unseasonably warm, early June day.

She glanced down at herself. While fit, there were signs that she was no longer the twenty-year-old he had married, marks upon her belly and breasts proofs of the two new lives she had brought into the world. She refused to be ashamed, for either modesty's sake or vanity.

"I am, am I not?" She smiled back and dove into the icy depths of Pemberley's pond.

The cold water was a shock, one that she was prepared for; yet, it still took her back to those first swimming lessons, of discovering that the Derbyshire weather did not accommodate temperate waters even when the sun shone brightly, of learning how to float upon the impossible, freezing liquid mattress, of swallowing more water than she would ever care to admit before finally, finally, achieving something like proficiency.

She had surprised him this time, she knew—she always went into the water slowly to accustom herself to the frigid depths. But no longer. For months, she had been practising, preparing herself, strengthening herself for this 'friendly challenge'. Nevertheless, she knew his surprise would not slow him, and she gave it all she had.

Her hard work was rewarded. She emerged at the boulder on the pond's opposite shore approximately three seconds before he did.

"I did it!" she cried breathlessly, pleased to note that he was panting as well. "I won!"

"That you did," he said, some chagrin upon his face as he flipped his hair, grown a bit overlong, out of his eyes. "So, why do I want you more than ever?" He reached for her, and she floated easily into his arms, triumph and passion fuelling her response. The depth of the water here was well over her head, however, and staying afloat while giving expression to her feelings was somewhat of a trial.

"Perhaps," she said, pausing for air, "even the Darcy mettle might find this pond an unsuitable location for further diversion?"

"Have you noticed the Darcy mettle affected in any way?" he asked, his low laughter adding additional chills to her already chilly flesh.

"I have never seen, er, mettle, for which nature has done more, and natural beauty so little counteracted by frigid temperatures," she said, grinning back. "But I won. It is my choice where I receive my prize. I choose our bed in the summerhouse."

"As my lady commands," he said, tugging her towards the embankment.

"Chivalry is as alive as the Darcy mettle," she said, a reply which only caused further delay.

It was a good two hours before they were ready to eat the ample breakfast supplied by the very discreet team of Pennywithers and Nottley—who jealously guarded the privacy of the master and mistress on this, the one Saturday morning in the last month that they had managed to spend together without stewards, tenants, children, or puppies. Dubitz had fallen in love with a large, elegant poodle a few years prior; his progeny were prolific, beloved, surprisingly sought after, and would likely populate Pemberley for generations. It was the happiest of households, but its affairs did not leave much leisure time for the busiest adults within it.

After finishing the meal, they settled down together to read personal correspondence just received; on this occasion, they had letters from their sisters, and Elizabeth began with Jane's, who was visiting Louisa Hurst in Suffolk after the birth of her son. It was not long before she made a small exclamation of surprise.

Darcy glanced up from his letter from Georgiana, one he could hardly wait to read, as it was the first one received since her wedding to a very amiable, canine-loving young viscount. "What is it?"

"Caroline refused the marquess's proposal."

He set his letter down. "Truly?"

His disbelief was unsurprising. The marquess, a handsome, wealthy man in his early thirties, had once answered Caroline's every ideal. His courtship of her had been the talk of town—a talk she had certainly seemed to enjoy.

"She told Bingley that she was unready to relinquish her freedom so soon. I do not understand—Bingley gave her control of her fortune at least three years ago. Perhaps she has never truly recovered from losing you."

Darcy shook his head. "She never wanted me, only what I represented in her mind. In truth, I, and the marquess, and men like us come with a great number of burdens. Chains of society, of duty, of family, of tenants. Of utter, unmitigated responsibility. I think she has finally realised it." He looked at her gravely. "Sometimes I despise the weight of obligations I place upon your shoulders."

But then he grinned and kissed the bare shoulder nearest him. "Such exquisite, perfect shoulders."

"You and your mettle may admire my shoulders after I finish my letters," she chided, but then ruined her severity by giggling, a sound he still loved. "Your shoulders have not suffered terribly under the strain, either, I notice," and laughed again when he flexed for her.

"Will you trade letters, Jane's for Georgie's?" she asked a few minutes later. "Jane has even included a note from Mama describing La Scala."

"I never dreamt your father would actually take her to Italy."

Elizabeth shrugged. "He is seldom proof against her wishes these days," she said, offering Mrs Bingley's missive.

"Due to your interruptions, I have not finished

Georgie's yet. Read Lydia's whilst I attempt to," he advised.

For the first couple of years after their marriage, Lydia had shunned Elizabeth utterly, making their first visits to Brighton very uncomfortable. Darcy had found it frustrating, but Lady Lavinia had advised them not to worry overmuch, and Elizabeth had not appeared to— there had been far too many other 'weights of obligation' to occupy her time. After Edward was born, however, she had received a very brief, stiff congratulatory note from Lydia, which his warm-hearted wife had answered as though it had been a proper letter and not a communication likely forced by her ladyship. They both had been rather surprised when a newsy letter followed a month or two later. Lydia was a dilatory correspondent, but every few months or so thereafter, they received a letter from her. Their first holiday in Brighton after his birth, she had doted on Edward to an astonishing degree, and when Esme was born, had visited Pemberley for the first time. Still, she had refused—politely, at least —all of his own attempts to dower her. Mary, who had married Pemberley's vicar last year, claimed that Lydia still harboured improper pride but Catherine—happily wed to Mr Lyford, a well-to-do physician who kept her coughs to the merest rasps—believed it was embarrassment, not pride.

"Lady Lavinia has an uncomfortable way of making one see oneself through new eyes," Catherine had said. "*I* would certainly never agree to live with her, however fine her home." Darcy did not know which it was, pride or shame, and did not try to guess. He had sins enough of his own, without taking on judgment of someone else's, and was simply happy if his wife was.

"Listen to this," Elizabeth interrupted his rambling thoughts, beginning to read aloud from Lydia's letter.

I have long supposed I ought to write this letter, yet always believing that it could wait for another day—preferably one far in the future. I do not have what her ladyship calls a 'reflective nature' and generally believe that the past ought to stay there. Still, when I received word from Mary about Wickham's death —she did try to restrain her natural inclination to turn the whole tale into a moral lesson for me; Mr Palmer really is good for her—I felt the most peculiar detachment. The man I once thought myself most desperately in love with was dead, and I could not recall his face. Then, even more curiously, I cried as if my heart would break. 'I could not care less for his death,' I sobbed. 'I have not thought of him in years.' It was beyond confusing, mortifying, even, and so of course Lady L could not leave it alone.

'You do not cry for him, silly girl,' she said. 'You mourn the girl you once were, the girl he hurt, whose trust he exploited, for lost innocence and remembered shame at the hands of an abuser. Why should you not? What I want to know is when will you forgive her, instead of simply bawling over her?'

I do not agree with everything her ladyship says—part of why she loves me so much, she claims—but in this instance, the words struck true. I do forgive myself. And because I have, Lizzy, here are the words you are long overdue hearing.

I am sorry. Sorry for what I put you through, not simply that fateful night when you saved my life, but for so many times before and after that, when I ignored you or worse, laughed at your fears over me. I am ever grateful that you and her ladyship were willing to leave your beds in the middle of the night for a likely futile journey to save a girl who would never thank you for it. She still would not—but I am no longer that girl.

You never bring it up, and I know you never would. But since I have forgiven that stupid young girl, I dare hope someday for your forgiveness as well.

There, I have written it. It was not so hard as I believed it would be, mostly because you are kind, and I am still enough myself to feel proud of the effort, rather than chagrined.

Elizabeth seemed rather tongue-tied. "I never thought she would apologise."

"I have felt her much improved with each visit to Brighton," Darcy said. "I am happy to hear this. Are you?"

"I forgave her long ago, if my forgiveness was ever required. I only want her happiness."

"How very like you," he said, leaning over to place another kiss on her bare shoulder.

They both returned to their letters, but within moments, she gave a little gasp.

"What is it?" Darcy set aside his own letter once more, shaking his head a little ruefully. At least he had read enough to know of Georgiana's continued utter happiness.

Now for my other news: I am returning to Longbourn. Are you as surprised as I am? The fact of the matter is, Reginald Goulding is courting me.

She dropped the letter and looked at him in astonishment. Taken aback himself, Darcy plucked it up and continued aloud.

We hated each other for the longest time. I thought him a dull, pompous numbskull.

Darcy nodded in agreement. "She thought it because that is exactly what he is."

"Give me back the letter," his wife said, trying to snatch it away from him. But Darcy held it out of reach and continued reading aloud.

He thought me simply an obnoxious, empty-headed brat. Truth to tell, I think we were both correct. Of course, Lady Lavinia cannot tolerate empty headedness, whatever her forbearance for more obvious flaws. I hated the way she poked and prodded, but she is patient in her impatient way and refused to abandon hope that there was a brain in my head somewhere. She had less patience with her grandson; the first year I was at Sea Terrace, he visited twice, and both times, he left in a fury after only a few days, unable to endure her assaults upon his character. I do not know why he continued to return—unless it was because he thought of the perfect insult only after departure and could not resist. But return he did, staying longer each time, much to my annoyance.

I am unsure as to when the annoyance faded, but probably at least a year ago. We grew a friendship, and then something more. He says he loves me, but I know he loved you once, and I am not overly trusting. I could love him, I think, if I allowed myself. Lady Lavinia says that he is only half as tedious as he once was and that the other half of the time, I would find amusement in making sport of him. Her age is affecting her, Lizzy, although she does not like to admit it. She has decided to return to Haye-Park, and so when our parents return from Italy, I will return to Longbourn where I might keep a close watch upon her, and who can tell? Do write, and give me your opinion on the matter, else the next letter I send might have news of another wedding.

Darcy returned the letter to Elizabeth with a snort of disgust, making her laugh.

"How shall you like having Reginald Goulding for a brother?"

He shook his head, his expression one of amused disbelief. "I suppose it is rather more supportable than having Wickham as one. But I believe her taste in men could still stand much improvement." He took his wife's hand in his. "What of you? Would it be odd, having the man who was, once, the love of your life become your sister's husband? What will you say to her?"

Elizabeth turned to him, grinning. "I will tell her that I have had only one love in my life, and she ought to do as I have—marry the man who loves her for who she is, whilst challenging her to be the best she can become. Speaking of challenges, I have thought of several new ones I should like you to commence, if my loving husband is brave enough to try."

He looked into her eyes; she claimed he had a devilish side, but in hers, he saw mischief and passion and a deviltry of her own. They were well matched, he and his Elizabeth.

"I cannot wait to hear what is next," he murmured, lifting her to him, sheets of parchment falling heedlessly to the floor. "Letters will have to wait."

The End

ACKNOWLEDGMENTS

Sincere thanks to Lisa Sieck, Sarah Cooper, Jan Ashton, and Paula Lester

ABOUT THE AUTHOR

Julie Cooper lives with her husband of forty-one years in Central California. She spends her time boasting of her four brilliant and beautiful children, doting on her four brilliant and beautiful grandchildren, and cleaning up after her neurotic Bichon, Pogo. Somewhere in between the truly important stuff, she peddles fruit baskets and chocolate-covered strawberries for a living whilst pressing penitent Mr Darcys on an unsuspecting public.

ALSO BY JULIE COOPER

NOVELS

A Stronger Impulse

Nameless

Tempt Me

The Perfect Gentleman

NOVELLAS

A Yuletide Dream

Irresistibly Alone

Lost and Found

Seek Me: Georgiana's Story

A companion novella to Tempt Me

MULTI-AUTHOR PROJECTS

'Tis the Season

A Match Made at Matlock

Made in the USA
Las Vegas, NV
04 January 2025

15800812R10225